# ADELE
# PARKS

*If You Go Away*

headline
review

First published in Great Britain in 2015 by
HEADLINE REVIEW
An imprint of HEADLINE PUBLISHING GROUP

First published in paperback in 2015 by
HEADLINE REVIEW

1

Cataloguing in Publication Data is available from the British Library

ISBN 978 1 4722 0547 6 (paperback)

Typeset in Bembo by Palimpsest Book Production Limited,
Falkirk, Stirlingshire

Printed and bound in Great Britain by Clays Ltd, St Ives plc

Headline's policy is to use papers that are natural, renewable and recyclable products and
made from wood grown in sustainable forests. The logging and manufacturing processes
are expected to conform to the environmental regulations of the country of origin.

HEADLINE PUBLISHING GROUP
An Hachette UK Company
Carmelite House
50 Victoria Embankment
London, EC4Y 0DZ

www.headline.co.uk
www.hachette.co.uk

For Conrad,
my independent thinker

# MARCH 1914

# 1

*27th March 1914*
*Dearest Diary, I have waited for such a long time for today. Eighteen*
*years, nine months and ten days. My entire life. <u>Forever</u>.*

VIVIAN CAREFULLY UNDERLINED the word *forever* and in a somewhat uncharacteristic gesture hugged the diary to her as
though it was a child. Vivian Foster wasn't prone to being especially
giddy – amongst her friends she was considered the most knowing
and realistic – but today was, without doubt, exceptional.

Forever? There must have been a time when she wasn't aware
of how important marrying was, when she was just a child and
concerned with paddling in streams, making perfume from crushed
rose petals or picking brambles. Then all she'd waited for was the
next sunny day. She just couldn't remember that time. Perhaps
she'd written what she had because writing in diaries made her
nervous. Stomach fluttery. She was not sure she wanted to be so
known, and certainly not by her already far too controlling mother,
nosy younger siblings or a cheeky maid, which was the risk. Diaries
were dishonest. When she wrote in hers, she fell into a persona
that was quite close to her best self but far from her true self, an
insurance against prying eyes. She kept her true self buried practically all of the time. Eighteen-year-old girls weren't exactly

encouraged to say what they thought; in fact they weren't encouraged to think at all. Writing that she had waited 'forever' for this day was the sort of thing that could not cause any real trouble; it was the type of comment that people expected young, virginal debutantes to write. Naïve. Forgivably imprecise.

Almost the entire Foster family understood the importance of today. Vivian's two younger sisters Susan and Barbara (the latter known to all as Babe, as Mrs Foster's way of signalling to Mr Foster that there would be no more babies) were obligingly awestruck. They sat on Vivian's bed, mouths slightly ajar, eyes glazed with excitement, as she wafted around her room, opening the wardrobe door, fingering the tin of talcum powder, playing with the ribbons on her dresses, until she sent them back to the nursery with an imperious wave of the arm. Of course they were impressed. Vivian was older than them (by two and six years respectively) and had been attending balls whilst they were tucked up in bed, a fact that was too compelling for them to ever consider contradicting her. Her brother Toby, four years her junior, was nonplussed. His gender gave him a strong sense of superiority that, somewhat annoyingly, overrode the age discrepancy.

It was absolutely true to say that since coming out eight months ago, Vivian had been waiting for this exact day, and there wasn't a huge difference in her imagination between eight months and forever, because before she came out, she was more or less nothing.

She was simply waiting.

A schoolgirl who could be bossed and directed by almost anyone: parents, close and distant relatives, Nanny, the governess, neighbours, the vicar and anyone Mrs Foster had ever been intimate with, who still might be found in the drawing room on Thursday 'at homes'. Providing a person was old and wealthy enough to have opinions, it was accepted that they could foist them upon young girls, who had to receive them (however ridiculous) in silence. That was why Vivian believed today to be so important. Everything changed.

Sometimes it had seemed as though this day would never come around; irrationally she'd feared that longing for it so ardently might lead to a catastrophic, logic-defying interruption to the passage of time, but time had ultimately surrendered and the day had arrived.

Nathaniel Thorpe.

The big, athletic sort, over six feet tall, straight white teeth, blond hair, lashes a woman might envy and a chin a man might lose an eye on. He was always ruddy and muddy from the games he played: football and rugby, cricket in the summer. He was forever shooting or hunting or riding. The things people said of him. Vigorous. Handsome. Dashing. Eminently marriageable. Evidently desirable. He left her feeling tremulous.

She'd known of him for years, although they'd only been able to speak once she came out. He was her aunt's neighbour and the sole reason a month in the country every summer, since she was thirteen years old, had been bearable. His family owned hundreds and hundreds of acres of land, perhaps thousands, all around her aunt's village, as far as the eye could see. She'd often watched from the upstairs windows, longing for that rare occasion when he was home from Eton and she might catch him, his cousins and friends discharging their guns and making their horses sweat as they galloped across the adjacent fields chasing something or other: a fox, a hare, good times. She had wondered how rich he was exactly. There seemed to be no limit as to what he could afford. It was hard to imagine. He'd finished at Oxford. Or maybe it had finished with him; it wasn't clear if he'd been sent down or had even gone up. Even though they were friendly now, it was not the sort of thing she could ask. She didn't want to bother or nag. Her mother no doubt had made enquiries. Discreetly. She'd have wanted to know if there were debts or prospects, scandals or intentions. She couldn't have heard anything too awful or off-putting, as Vivian had been allowed to pursue him. Gently, appropriately, unobtrusively. There was a way to do these things.

She knew that.

Well before her own coming-out ball she'd been instructed as to what she needed to do to draw his attention. She was lucky enough to have been born with what everyone agreed to be the sort of face that – more often than not – pleased. It was the first and last thing people thought about her. She was lovely to look at. They never wondered whether she was kind or reliable, able or resourceful. She wasn't encouraged to give these attributes too much consideration either.

Mrs Foster often began her days with a quiet feeling of superiority. It was hard not to. Her daughter had been such a success this season. As a child her relentless energy and impulsiveness had, frankly, been rather exhausting, but it was a skill that transferred quite nicely now they were husband hunting. Vivian was obsessively attentive to her grooming. Her hems did not dare to hang; the maids in the powder rooms at dances never had to come to her rescue with a quick stitch – she was far too in control to need that sort of service. Other girls were so sluggish and neglectful by comparison. Vivian's younger sisters would linger in bed far later than was polite if permitted. Susan in particular had a slow sort of nature. Her voluptuous figure was testament to that; she was entirely lacking in will power. So many girls, restricted by corsets and convention, only ever moved languidly, as though they were wading through wet sand. Vivian was altogether different, luckily. She was sprightly. Energetic. Every bit of her had a use; there was nothing unnecessary or wasteful.

Of course, as a mother, Mrs Foster had a duty to control and direct that energy, subdue her impulsiveness. It was a good thing her daughter was noticed, but she didn't want her to be set apart. That would be a catastrophe. Vivian was trained and instructed on the importance of utilising her looks, charm and energy to the full but never hinting at wilfulness or independence. She must delight absolutely everyone. She had listened and soon the mothers trusted her, the fathers were charmed by her, the other girls adored her and the men insisted they would fight duels for her, if such a thing still went on. The opinion was that despite her waning family fortune, Vivian Foster was a success. Behind their fans the more honest chaperones often commented that she put other young ladies in the shade. She had something rare.

Mrs Foster's feeling of superiority would have been entirely obliterated if she'd known that occasionally Vivian stood naked in front of the mirror admiring her lean long legs, her tiny waist, her small but pert breasts, whilst thinking it such a pity that no one else ever got to see any of it. She was used to accepting compliments about her face, hair and eyes; she could only imagine the sort of things *he* might say about the rest of her body. And imagine it she did as she gently trailed her fingers down her body. Luckily Mrs Foster's peace of mind was never disturbed, because her involvement with her daughter was formal, superficial, while Vivian, for her part, understood the value of secrecy. She never undressed without wedging a chair under the handle of her bedroom door.

For all Nathaniel Thorpe liked hunting and shooting and fishing and what-have-you, Vivian was relieved to discover that he also spent a lot of time in London. Young men did. Why wouldn't they? This was where the best parties happened. Vivian believed she simply couldn't live anywhere else, although when she said as much to her mother, Mrs Foster simply raised her eyebrows and commented that Vivian would live wherever her husband decided she'd live. Vivian had mumbled 'Poppycock' under her breath.

'What did you say?' asked Mrs Foster, who believed she had a right to her daughter's every thought.

'I said you're probably right, Mother.' Vivian threw out a disingenuous smile.

'I *am* right. I'm always right.'

'Yes, Mother.'

Mrs Foster had endeavoured to tell Vivian the basic facts of life, although she was keen to avoid going into embarrassing or tedious detail. Instead she offered three rules, two of which had subsections. One, Vivian was told never to travel alone in a railway carriage with a man. Two, she was never to contradict or interrupt a potential suitor when he was talking, though she should stop him if he tried to touch her body anywhere higher than her elbow or knee. Three, she was never to discourage any man who asked for a dance, but she should not allow a chap more than two dances in a row.

Vivian was aware that this was inadequate preparation for anything much, most of all a season.

Her friends were a far better source of information. Even before she came out, she'd heard the words adultery (something old marrieds did) and fornication (something maids and sluts did); and, more shocking still, therefore necessitating a Latin word, cunnilingus (something she couldn't imagine anyone really did).

She was curious.

In the past year, Vivian had sent herself to sleep by rubbing her stomach, a slow, circular caress. The tips of her fingers became familiar with every sensation her nightgown could provide: the smooth rise of embroidery, the flat glide of ribbon, the slight friction offered up by cotton. She liked to feel her bumpy ribs, the gentle inward curve of her waist and then the hardness of her hip bones. It wasn't long before she started to send herself to sleep by laying her hand flat on the mound that created a triangle between her hip bones and where her legs joined. It felt warm, safe, to leave it there. Then she wanted to know what it would feel like if there wasn't the barrier of fabric. She told herself there was no harm, it was her body. No one need know. Yet it stirred a sudden muted pang, a quickening of the beating of her heart.

When she slipped off her bed socks and allowed one foot to stroke the other, she could almost imagine someone else touching her bare flesh. She moved the foot up her calf to the back of her knee. No one had ever touched the back of her knee. She had no idea! Soon it was only ever enough if her fingers crept up under the hem of the nightdress and danced across her entire body.

Yes, she was curious.

A few years older than Vivian, Nathaniel had already caused a stir in society. Everyone was mad about him. Vivian was all too well aware that she was not alone in thinking he was the one to catch. Wealth, youth, looks, he had it all. Vivian did not have wealth – at least not nearly enough – so she had to be very clever about the whole business. She'd never been much of a scholar; she had no interest in where countries lay on a map or the elements lay on the periodic table, but she was sharp enough to know that it did matter where men laid their affections. It was all that mattered.

Vivian was dressed beautifully; she was instructed to be careful and quiet, and to befriend Nathaniel's mother. They had been to dances, charity fund-raising lunches and afternoon tea together. Nathaniel and Vivian (and a necessary host of others who lent respectability to the flirtation) went to balls, cocktail bars, the opera and the ballet. She always singled him out for at least the first and last dance on her card. For the first four months she made sure to have a number of other partners and encouraged him to do the same. She didn't want him to feel trapped; she refused to appear desperate. In the past month she had become more focused. If he danced with other girls, she tried to sit with his mother and smiled on, making it clear that it was she who had made the choice. If she was forced to take a turn with someone else, she was sure to roll her eyes behind her partner's back, letting Nathaniel see her exasperation and preference. She made him laugh. He liked the fact that his mother adored her and thought she was an angel; to him alone she revealed a hint of insolence, her ability to have fun, to be a devil.

It worked. He sent flowers and notes. He invited her to take tea at his house, not only with his mother but with an aunt too: obvious vetting. His people were all divinely aristocratic-looking: thin skins, bright eyes, glowing. Then last week he'd called at her house in Hampstead. Unfortunately Mr Foster wasn't in, so he'd walked around the small garden with her mother, faking an interest in the colourful geraniums that knelt in the borders. He appeared distracted, almost irritable. It was clear that he was disappointed not to have been able to ask permission from her father. He was not the sort of man who expected to be thwarted. As he left, he whispered to Vivian, 'I'd hoped to catch you alone.' She didn't have the chance to reply. What was she to say? Weren't boys funny? How could he have imagined she might be alone? Girls were never left alone. How wonderful, though, that he wanted her to himself.

It was the nervous nature of his visit that allowed them all to hope; that made Vivian absolutely *know*. She knew how it would go now. He would propose tonight and they would have a year-long engagement. Anything more was a bore; anything less meant they would not be able to guarantee a wedding at Westminster Abbey, something she longed for and something that was possible, as Nathaniel's father was a Knight Grand Cross. Spring weddings were a delight. They'd honeymoon in Europe. She didn't want to go to Egypt or Africa. The risk of peculiar diseases or bites from awful things was high, and besides, Vivian wouldn't be captured so often by the papers and illustrated weeklies if they travelled too far away. After a year she'd produce an heir. Then, eighteen months later, a spare. She'd decided she'd have up to three children. No more. More had an irretrievable effect on one's figure, no matter how young one was. They'd return to the Continent every August. She'd wear furs and pearls. She'd dance with dukes and earls. It would be heaven.

The preparations for tonight had to be perfect: a long bath

with scented salts, soft towels, and then clouds of lavender talcum powder. Vivian had found a dress that made everything else she owned – everyone owned – look insipid and lacking. She'd wanted a raspberry pink or even a scarlet. Her mother had declared that these colours were out of the question; she had to wear white, cream, silver perhaps. Mint was as far as Mrs Foster would go. Vivian was blond. Mint wouldn't work. Mint would be ruinous. Eventually they agreed on a pearl-coloured silk. Mrs Foster found the most fabulous roll in a darling London store. Vivian was secretly impressed, although she didn't indulge in a silly show of pleasure; she was cultivating a more sophisticated persona, and girlish shows of enthusiasm towards her mother over a roll of fabric were now unheard of (although she was still very willing to show displeasure).

A lot had depended on the cut. She was fed up of the same old pattern that she'd always worn, that every eighteen-year-old girl wore: short sleeves and round neck. Her mother had not suggested the local dressmaker for tonight; Hampstead was choked with women who, whilst undoubtedly competent with a needle, seemed very confused when Vivian tried to suggest they look at pictures in magazines for their inspiration. It was 1914! Queen Victoria was long dead. Her grandson was on the throne. Why couldn't they see how things had moved on? Why were the old so slow? The dress had to be made in Bond Street. Fortunately, Mrs Foster agreed. There had been two fittings. It had cost an obscenity but was worth every penny.

Vivian's underwear for tonight was thin white cambric lingerie from Eaton Lodge, the very place royalty had their trousseaus embroidered; no D. H. Evans mass-produced department store underwear for her. Mrs Foster knew the importance of investing and had not stinted; ever since Vivian had come out, she had been awfully well looked after. She had three or four pretty waltzing dresses, but this new one was her favourite. It had more. Held more. It was a promise.

11

She had enjoyed her preparations for this evening, which had begun at two this afternoon. Scrubbing, plucking, tweezing, brushing, painting and adorning all required time. She laid out her clothes, had the bath filled and steeped in it for simply ages. Nanny thought she'd catch her death bathing for such a long time and circled the room, wondering about lighting fires and muttering about the scanty nature of Vivian's underwear. It was hard not to dismiss Nanny as a silly woman who didn't understand. How she prattled on. Such nonsense. 'Now remember, Miss Vivian, a girl can only be safe if she marries well, or at least carefully, and she's not safe until then.' Vivian did not appreciate Nanny talking about her prospects so openly. It was vulgar. 'Everything has to be weighed up. His family, his wealth, his ambition, his character.'

'I know, Nanny. We all know.'

On Vivian's dressing table, candles in Victorian silver sticks burned. There was a bowl generously proffering apples, grapes and oranges (they were all keen for her to keep trim) and a cluster of family photographs showing relatives at their most stiff and serious. Vivian glanced at the one of her grandpa and let out a secret sigh of exasperation. She hardly remembered him – he'd died when she was seven – but when Nanny was blathering on, she often turned to these photos of her relatives for amusement or escape. Grandpa was a vague mass of hazy impressions. Pipe smoke, a large girth clad in a tartan waistcoat, a tickling beard that briefly brushed her forehead when she stood in front of him to say good night. He'd left his estate more untidy than he ought to have done. Clearly he'd counted on having a few more years to sort things out. Or perhaps he hadn't cared. He was rather a disappointing man. He'd inherited a pile and left less. Poor show. It was his fault Vivian had to make such an effort; if she'd been a little better off . . . well, it would have been easier to be noticed, to count. A decent dowry was so comforting.

'There is no use in falling in love with the first man who fills your dance card and turns your head. None at all. What's the rush? That's what I say. What's the rush? You could enjoy two or three seasons,' declared Nanny. The Fosters couldn't afford two or three seasons, a fact Nanny was oblivious to but Vivian had been made well aware of. 'Marry in haste, repent at leisure. Everyone knows that's the case.'

Nanny knew nothing, of course. Still, one felt sorry for her. Her sort were not gifted a season. There must have been dancing. Must have. Dancing happened everywhere, but most likely for her it had taken place in tea rooms with dusty floors and curling sandwiches, not ballrooms with luminous chandeliers and gilded chairs. It was a pity but not everyone could be wealthy. Could they? No, they couldn't, it was an impossibility. Anyway, Nanny clearly hadn't been successful; if she had been, she wouldn't have wound up looking after someone else's children. She might have had some of her own, which would have been nice for her but not for the Fosters, because she was a good sort after all, good at what she did. Vivian conceded that on the whole she'd been a reliable and sensible nanny, neither too sentimental nor too strict.

'Who said that first, I wonder?'

'Said what?' Vivian snapped. She didn't mean to, but when Nanny talked she became less attentive, and the woman had forced a hair clip right into Vivian's scalp.

'Marry in haste, repent at leisure. Shakespeare, do you think? He said almost everything, didn't he? But then, not a man, surely. What have they to complain of? More likely something a woman would say. Lady Godiva, or Cleopatra.'

Vivian wished Nanny would simply leave her to get on. Concentrate on Susan, Toby and Babe as she was employed to do. There was no denying it: Vivian was beyond her now. Nanny would be no more use until Vivian had children of her own, and then she might hire her in her nursery. Or she might not. She might get a young girl with modern ways.

13

'Help me into my dress.'

The dress was a success. Floating, transparent and delicate, it swathed her body, flattering and clinging to her breasts and waist, then flowing away to leave her bottom half to the imagination. It transformed her from girl to woman. At the fitting her mother had pronounced it too low cut and insisted that a lace trim be added to the neckline. At Vivian's secret instruction the seamstress had tacked it in place so very lightly. A snip or two in the powder room tonight and there would be no sign of the veiling lace.

Then, when she was almost done, having decided between two different headdresses, Mrs Foster joined them. She did not knock. She never knocked. It was infuriating. Vivian comforted herself that after tonight, when it had all passed as it ought and she was no longer simply a girl but a fiancée, almost a married woman, Mother would be compelled to knock at her bedroom door. Surely.

'Have you said good night to your sisters and Toby?'

'I was just about to.' Vivian liked to visit the nursery when she was all done up and looking magnificent. It sparked her sisters' admiration and envy, which she was still young enough to luxuriate in.

'Do. They are saying their prayers.'

Vivian resisted showing any irritation. Of course Susan was going through a religious phase; she was forever kneeling and fasting and she liked to wear plain clothes. It was a terrible affectation, and whilst Vivian had many affectations of her own, she was pleased to say faking religious fervour had never been one of them. Nanny, however, somehow knew that mentally Vivian was sighing in exasperation.

'Your sister will do very well. Far better than you might imagine,' she scolded.

Was that possible? Could Susan, ponderous in action, ever do well? Nanny turned to Mrs Foster. 'I bet *you* know who said it,' she commented as she shook out the hem of Vivian's dress, carefully and somewhat unnecessarily. She was forever fussing, couldn't quite let go.

'Said what?' asked Mrs Foster.

'Marry in haste, repent at leisure.'

Mrs Foster stared coldly. It was as though the words had cast a shadow. 'William Congreve. Now come along, Vivian. We can't be late.'

# 2

HOWARD ENJOYED THE hours before curtain up more than any other of the day. There, in among the warm, golden backstage light, the smell of waxy make-up and the soft murmur of actors doing their voice exercises, was a real sense of trembling anticipation of the performance. The actors belonged to him more at this moment than any other. After the show, when they were showered with roses and accolades, they greedily hogged the limelight, sopped up all the credit and forgot him. And if, oh horror, the performance was badly received, met with apathy or indifference, they loathed and resented him; they plummeted into a dark pit of despair and depression, insisting that he had shoved them there.

Now, in the lazy early evening, when day was slipping into dusk and outside men were lighting the street lamps, women scurrying home ready to prepare their families' teas, he was kingpin, top dog, the man. At this point the words he'd chosen, the characters he'd formed – placed in jeopardy and then either rescued or damned – were all. The actors would invite him into their dressing rooms, ask him exactly what he meant by a particular line, check he agreed with their intonation. They looked to him for nurturing, advice and inspiration. He, the playwright, had them in his possession, the popular faces that appeared on billboards and in the newspapers, the men women screamed for, the women

men bankrupted themselves for. Whilst he was aware that the actors' and actresses' interest in him was largely fuelled by their insecurity and desperate need for attention, combined with the fact that they dared not bother the actor-manager, Mr Warrington, still he wallowed in their notice and respect.

Sometimes he thought it incredible to imagine that people read and believed what he had written, and yet every fibre of every bone knew it was the case and that it was as it should be. He was a writer, a fact as plain and simple as him being a man. He had an instinctive, intrinsic need to write; to express himself, to create, to think, to be heard. He wrote because it helped him make sense of the world he lived in and also allowed him to escape from that world. He'd long since known that he could not do the normal work other people did. He could not paint signs, or work as a clerk, or build ships or mine coal. He knew these jobs were real and honourable; he admired the men who did them, but he knew that all he could do – and live – was write. He didn't often try to explain to people why he wrote. They would misinterpret what he had to say, think him arrogant or distant. He was neither. He loved mankind and felt closest to them when he wrote about them.

Howard was amused by the actors (some womanisers, some queer, all his friends), but he enjoyed sitting in the actresses' dressing room best. Not least because they walked around in their underwear, teasingly sat on his knee, mussed his hair, dropped light kisses on his eyelids, his cheeks, his lips as they chatted to him. The actresses were a brave breed. They laughed in the face of what society thought was respectable. They had their own rules and made their own way. Rigid and rosy at once. There was always a decanter of whisky or sherry for him to help himself to, and cigarettes in pretty lacquered boxes for him to smoke. He loved the colours, the warmth and the sensual creativity that oozed from every object, every nook and cranny; the general sense that all was right with the world.

This latest play, *The Blackest Night*, was doing extremely well. It had enjoyed a run of nine weeks so far and, largely thanks to the stellar reviews, there was no end in sight. Howard was revelling in the attention this brought him, sucking it up while he could, always aware of the ephemeral nature of the career he had chosen. He was a sanguine sort and took the punches and the praise as they came his way, but naturally he enjoyed the times when he was appreciated rather than denigrated.

A pretty young actress sat on his knee. He wasn't absolutely sure of her name. Ethel, or Ettie, or Beryl? She had dark curly hair piled up on her head in precarious, defiant loops; shorter, springy tresses bobbed about her ears and above her eyes with a life of their own. She was wearing only her underwear and a thin Asian-looking robe.

'It's a kimono,' she stated haltingly, betraying the fact that she was unsure of the pronunciation. 'All the way from Japan.' A gift no doubt from an admirer.

Her cotton chemise was scooped low, presumably designed to show off a full swell of cleavage; in this case her collar and breast plate were a xylophone of bones stepping to tiny, tight breasts. He could see the outline of her nipples pointing up to him. Hopefully. She was trying to persuade him to give her a part by writing lines especially for her. Young starlets sometimes came to him in this way, keen to offer him favours in the hope he could move them out of the chorus line. Howard didn't condemn the girls. People got what they could. His friends were generally that sort. The sort who were born with nothing and had to work hard for everything. The occasional easy something was appreciated. They thought he had influence, and so he did, sometimes.

Of course no one ever vulgarly discussed this arrangement; it was all dressed up in the relative respectability of a love affair, but the rules were understood. He always upheld his side of the bargain. If he could press or sway, he would try to do so. The girls who were prepared to make this sort of deal knew the score: sometimes he could help, other times he couldn't. He didn't lead them on or misrepresent his weight. In this case, he'd equitably and carefully explained that as the script had already been approved by Mr Warrington – the man who managed, produced, directed and starred; his boss, her boss, *the* boss – securing her any lines was unlikely.

Mr Thomas Warrington was a respected actor-manager with an ever-widening and formidable reputation. He wasn't a rich man, because instead of putting his profits into a bank, he ploughed any revenue he made back into his theatre. His one and only ambition was to produce a more spectacular, impactful, memorable show than the last. The Warrington was not the grandest of playhouses in the West End but nor was it the smallest. More often than not the cast played to a more-or-less full house. Warrington respected Howard but he would not be persuaded to do anything he did not want to do. Howard's hands were tied on this occasion, but the starlet did not believe him. She wanted to believe his power was infinite because she thought she had some influence over him. It was all about clout, fame and fortune for these women. Howard liked all three things but there was more to it for him.

The little actress had hold of his script, where she'd written suggestions as to how he might, exactly, give her a part. She had fingered the ink-stained pages so often, they were not only crumpled and grubby, but actually wearing thin. He studied her neat bone structure and noted her skinny bottom, which didn't feel especially comfortable on his lap; he understood she was hungry. Hungry for fame. Hungry for food. She might not even know how to tell the two things apart any more. It was the case for most thesps.

He addressed her in French to amuse and distract. '*Ma chère*, if it was up to me, I'd cast you as the principal, but it isn't.' He did not believe in leading them on. He didn't have to. He was gloriously handsome, dark and tall. He found he could have whoever he wanted anyway.

'Would you? Would you really?' She was breathless and hopeful, but then became scornful and sulky when she caught him winking at the leading lady, who sat just three feet away, powdering her nose and scowling. 'Don't play with me, Howard R. Henderson, it's not fair.' She used his full name as it appeared on the script, searching for defence in formality.

'I tell you what, I'll buy you dinner after the show,' he suggested affably. Kissing the top of her head.

'Fine.' It wasn't what she wanted, but it was something. Her eyes dropped longingly once again to the script. She drew her forefinger over the print of his name. 'What does the "R" stand for anyhow?'

'Guess?'

'Ronnie.'

'No.'

'Robert?'

'No.'

'Richard, Raymond?'

'No, no.'

'Reginald?'

'No.' He laughed at that one. 'Do I look like a Reginald?'

'Well I don't know.' Pouting now.

'Rumpelstiltskin,' offered the actress at the mirror, her eyes trained on him through the reflection. He let out a huge belly laugh and thought, that is why she is the one they queue to see.

# 3

Vivian stepped out on to the glassy wet pavement. Spring showers were a curse to the season. The doorman, spruce and energetic in his top hat, opened the door for her, bowing ostentatiously. It was impossible not to let out a little sigh of delight; the hired hall was such a ravishing, glinting place. The pillared entrance was awash with chatter and anticipation. A blast of mingling voices — sweet light ones, gossipy nasty ones, raucous low ones — drenched her like a wave. Cloaks were deposited, dresses smoothed by anxious hands, and then they climbed the stairs.

The ballroom was plush; the red velvet seats and heavy curtains, gold braid and tassels, purple walls and carpets made her feel like royalty. Men were wearing roses in their lapels; women carried small ivory or silver dance cards. There were multiple candelabras with protruding branches; gleaming silver, gleaming flames. The room was full of all the people Vivian had seen a hundred times already this season. A tight group of people she knew well, and the rest no longer strangers, although not quite friends.

There was, as always, the dull set of chaperones; mothers and aunts, stout women with indistinct faces, dresses and hair. It was hard to believe they had ever been young, individual or vibrant. Had they once quivered in anticipation, dreamt, wept? Had they really? They always seemed to have sprays of artificial flowers pinned to their persons. On the waistband or the bosom. Dried flowers were depressing. Vivian didn't like heavy handbags either, the type chosen for their usefulness rather than their beauty; the ruddy-cheeked, thick-featured chaperones all carried useful bags.

There were the inevitable groups of ageing men too, with thinning white hair and broadening waistbands. Their chins sank into their necks, then slid into their chests and bellies. Food seemed to be the only pleasure of the old. Vivian didn't particularly care about food. She found the endless hours she had to spend at dining tables dull. She was often placed next to just this sort of gluttonous man. A lecherous old uncle or friend of the family; men Mrs Foster described as harmless but Vivian considered abominable. Men who she suspected had once flirted with her mother, or perhaps had been her mother's lovers. No, that couldn't be so, could it? One's parents might have had intrigues, people did, but *her* parents? Was it possible? Likely? She didn't want to think of it. These men often had false teeth, and they struggled when eating rolls, teeth slipping and sliding as they masticated. Their hands were forever clammy and banged down on top of Vivian's to pet her unnecessarily when she was trying to slice through the beef wellington. They seemed to find breathing hard. It was all rather vile. The best she could ever hope for was that they'd fall silent.

And now, here in the ballroom, here were the *real* people. The people she had come to see. Her pretty friends. The handsome boys. The rich parents, with their dazzling power.

Vivian liked rich people. Properly rich. She'd been taught to think of them as more complete. They were tall and strong, not bent with bunions or bumpy with chilblains like the poor. They were carefree and frivolous, not oppressed with dull concerns like middle-class families so often had to be. The rich didn't have to struggle with thoughts about whether there might be enough hot water for all, or clean and dry underwear and stockings for the entire week; issues that plagued her. The fabulously rich always had the proper outdoor and sporting gear, carriages or even cars waiting and a box at the theatre. It was delightful.

Of course, Vivian's family were not what anyone would call poor, but they were far from rich. Vivian thought the respectable middle classes had a hard time of it. No one expected much of the dreadfully poor; they were able to drink or gamble themselves into sordid stupors; who could blame them? But being upper middle class was such an effort. There were standards that absolutely must be met; people expected certain things. Money had to be found for governesses and school fees, the maids and the sweep practically demanded Christmas bonuses, and if this meant one had to go without new party shoes (when absolutely everyone else had a pair!) then one simply had to bear it. The properly rich walked with wonderful posture and a sense that they had no clue that someone had to worry about laundry, cooking, bills and so forth. Frankly, Vivian ached to clamber up to their ranks. Ached.

Men were forever making their fortunes. Being born poor did not absolutely necessarily mean a lifetime of poverty for a man. Not nowadays. He could work hard or get lucky. A scholarship to a grammar school was very useful to a certain type of boy, or he might invent something super. It was such a pity women couldn't make their own money. Vivian thought she might be rather good at it, given half a chance. Much better than her lazy younger brother was ever likely to be, and people fell over themselves to give *him* opportunities. Tutors, Eton, and then he'd be off to Oxford. His education gobbling up the family resources. No doubt he would make friends with someone influential there who would carry him through. They could only hope! Men could open factories. Become lawyers. Sail to America. There were options. It was galling. Those suffragette women might smash shop windows, blow up cricket pavilions and fling themselves under horses, but

23

the way things stood, there was only one career path for girls like her, and only one chance to secure a decent place in life. Marrying well was all.

A spider of nerves tickled her stomach. Yet she was exhilarated too. This was it.

The large swathes of candles bathed the room in a murky yellow light that was somehow synonymous with music halls and theatres; it created an atmosphere of intimacy. Promise and excitement lingered on the air like a whisper. Vivian spotted her best friend, Emily, just a few feet in front; if they could exert any influence at all, they always contrived to arrive at around the same time, so as to enter the party together. Besides the confidence such support provided, they were aware that together the impression they made was bigger than the sum of the parts. She linked her arm through her friend's and gently led her away from her mother. 'Emily, I need to remove this lace on the neckline, and then let's go and find the fun.'

Lace unstitched and carefully stowed in her bag, she glided into the ballroom, a wisp of something. Chiffon. Silk. Youth. Inexperience. Heads turned. She felt eyes upon her. She imagined that everyone knew how important tonight was. They must. Vivian scanned the room and immediately spotted Nathaniel's parents, Sir Robert and Lady Thorpe, standing in a cluster with other similarly rich and influential types. She wished she hadn't ditched her mother quite so swiftly. Mrs Foster might be intrusive and interfering, but there was no denying the fact that she knew her way around every social situation. Vivian didn't dare approach Lady Thorpe without her mother to smooth her path. She and Emily must wait until someone came to talk to them. Her empty dance card hung from her wrist, limp on a green cord.

'There's Ava Pondson-Callow,' gasped Emily. They both stared with undisguised curiosity. Vivian adored and admired Ava; the only debutante she considered completely, naturally perfect. Ava was what Vivian longed to be. Effortlessly gorgeous. Carelessly rich.

'Who is she dancing with?' Vivian didn't bother to hide her intense interest from Emily, whom she trusted implicitly; for a year or two when they were younger, they had shared a governess at Vivian's home and all that entailed. They didn't have secrets.

'The Earl of Clarendale's eldest son.'

'She looks bored.' Vivian gasped; she couldn't help it. She was unsure whether she was impressed or shocked that a girl might be bored whilst dancing with the heir to an earldom *and* dare to let it show.

'She always looks bored. It's her thing,' replied Emily flatly.

'Did you hear the rumour that Reggie Fairfax popped?'

'Did he really?'

Vivian loved it that she was always the one to impart the news; she got most of her information from her mother, who believed it was important to keep abreast. 'Yes, with his dead mother's ring. An heirloom. A yellow diamond cluster. Worth a fortune.'

'I imagine she turned him down,' guessed Emily.

'Flat.'

'Do you think she'll ever accept anyone?'

'Two years out and no sign of it yet.' Vivian did wonder who or what Ava Pondson-Callow was waiting for.

'I imagine her parents are livid.'

'Must be.'

They broadened their attention, discussing who was looking well and who had dressed badly. Frustratingly, Vivian couldn't spot Nathaniel anywhere. They each accepted a glass of crisp champagne and men came quickly enough. Vivian turned them away but Emily started to fill up her dance card. She always did well for partners. She wasn't quite beautiful – her eyes were a fraction too far apart and her hair was a flat brown that looked a lot like everyone else's – but she smiled constantly. She had large bosoms, a pleasingly round behind and the tiniest waist; the sort of figure that put ideas into men's heads, if they were not there already, which they probably were. She swiftly melted into the waltzing throng, leaving Vivian alone by the marble column.

Vivian spotted pockets of other girls she knew and could talk to, but her favourites were all dancing and she didn't want to be seen clinging to the walls with the other flowers. The non-dancing dulls. Her mother was talking to Lady Henning; her father was dancing with Lady Cooper. Everyone seemed so delightfully occupied except for her. Usually she would wait, shoulders back, smile broad, hold her nerve until Nathaniel appeared and claimed her; but then usually she was standing with his mother, or at least her own. She didn't dare seek out her mother, because she was sure to notice the altered neckline and Vivian didn't want a row.

For something to do, she took another glass of champagne. She felt strangely cut adrift, not as brave as usual; knowing how much was riding on tonight made it impossible for her to be her usual confident, somewhat aloof self. In the end she accepted invitations from Charles Rushmore, the Honourable Freddie Wittington and Matthew Fulham. Dances five, six and seven were spoken for; this meant Nathaniel wouldn't be able to hold her until the number eight. It was a shame, undoubtedly, but not within her control.

As she twirled around the room, frock swinging out, luminous, she tried to spot him. Where was he? Why so late? Charles Rushmore was a pleasant man; he wore a closed pink rose in his buttonhole and seemed not to notice that she was distracted, trying hard to make conversation. He asked her if she went to the theatre often, and talked about a play he'd seen recently.

'*The Blackest Night*, frightfully good. Reviewers are raving.'

'I must try and catch it,' she mumbled, but in an instant she'd forgotten what it was called and knew she'd never bother to see it unless someone else arranged it. All she could think of was Nathaniel. The absence of him.

They danced for a few more minutes in silence. She was content not to have to speak, but Mr Rushmore looked anxious, frantic.

'I've taken dance lessons, you know. For tonight,' he confessed in a rush.

'I supposed you must have.' She smiled vaguely and tried to bring herself to care about his effort. There was evidence of lessons. 'You're rather good.'

'Oh, do you think so?' He looked delighted. He was accomplished, certainly. So many young men stumbled over their own big feet and seemed confounded by their overgrown limbs. Needless to say, he was not as good as Nathaniel, who danced as he did everything else – extremely well. He spun, stepped, stopped and side-slipped then started the routine all over again with absolute precision, not a step out of place. He didn't reveal whether he was counting or concentrating, his expression declaring that he took it all in his stride. Where was he? Where?

Oh, there!

She spotted him and quivered. 'There he is,' she gasped.

'Who?' Mr Rushmore tried to turn to see who had caught her attention. She shouldn't have cried out. It wasn't polite. She followed Nathaniel's broad back and slim hips as he bobbed through the party. Who was he dancing with? Lady Feversham. Well, that was fine. She was married. Old. Must be at least twenty-six.

'I just noticed Nathaniel Thorpe.' Vivian couldn't resist saying his name aloud, even though she saw that doing so caused Mr Rushmore to look queerly; something between irritated and disappointed. 'He's so nimble,' she gushed.

'Yes. Assured,' replied Rushmore. It didn't sound like praise.

In her opinion, cutting in was the height of bad manners. Dances so carefully secured, so often longed for, could sometimes be ruined just because a chap could say, 'May I?' and your partner had no choice but to agree. Twice, when she'd been dancing with Nathaniel, this awful thing had happened. His friends had cut in.

27

Carried her off. How rude. But now she just wished a woman had the right. She would waltz up to Lady Feversham and say, 'May I?', bow her head a little, drift into his arms. Impossible, though. Women didn't have the right.

Knowing he was in the room was some sort of comfort. Now the party could become everything she needed it to be. It wouldn't be long before he found her. Singled her out. Talked to her. She could enjoy her dances with the other boys, whilst savouring what the night would bring. He would ask her for the eighth, she was sure of it.

So she whirled, twirled and smiled, and when she was not dancing, there was always some man or other keen enough to fawn and flatter. She sat out the number eight. Champagne continued to be generously poured into glasses, carefully at first so everyone could relish the excitement of watching the bubbles rise to the top and then disperse, but as the night wore on the waiters became sloppy, the champagne slipped over the rim and flowed on to gloves and fingers. No one cared. One two three, one two three, the rhythm swept through her body. She looked past the endless sea of swaying dark shoulders, trying to locate him. She caught a glimpse of his strong, straight back on two occasions. Then he vanished again. It was hard to track him amongst the countless identical black suits, shiny lapels and bobbing heads. Everywhere there was laughter, loud, louche men, flirty, flighty girls.

The ninth, tenth and eleventh were suddenly done. Been and gone. Not to be recaptured. Might he be on the balcony? Or playing billiards? The young men did tend to prowl in packs, making the entire place their own. Rather daring. The room was hot; women fanned themselves with gusto. She should probably get some air herself, but who was there to take her outside? That was Nathaniel's special and particular role. He'd taken her for air at the last four dances. They'd managed to snatch a few minutes alone before someone was sent by Mother to subtly supervise.

Precious minutes when he'd smiled and whispered, joked and flattered. His lips so close to her ear. His eyes staring into hers. Her mouth was dry now; she swallowed. Keeping it all down. Keeping it all in.

The room was full of flashing thoughts; messages were sent out in a glance: invitations, rejections, requests, rebuffs. Vivian watched them all, the successful and the hopeless. So many youthful sorts trying to find a place. The music swelled. Was that the fourteenth already? It couldn't be. Why hadn't Nathaniel come to find her? She searched around again. Wet, smiling lips were everywhere. Bright eyes, fluttering lids. Dance steps remembered, forgotten and sometimes ignored. The question *Where is he?* repeatedly drummed inside her skull. Everything was floaty. The air was taut and intense; no one cared that later it would become damp and overused.

'There you are!' She forced her mouth shut before she added 'at last' or 'Where have you been?'

'Here I am!' he replied. Two feet away from her. His mouth was slack and his eyes misty. Gosh, it occurred to her that everyone was a little tight. There was lemonade and ices but still people had gotten tipsy. She didn't want him to be. He wasn't as careful or thoughtful when he was drunk; he made silly jokes and preferred spending time with his friends. That was probably why she hadn't seen him tonight: he'd been flitting away his time with them. But then perhaps he needed Dutch courage before he popped. The thought excited and cheered her. She started to giggle. Perhaps she was squiffy too; she'd danced far less than usual and as a consequence had drunk more than ever before. She didn't want that either. It was harder to be perfect. Actually impossible. And yet she was a little bit fuzzy-headed. The evening was not going to plan, which was frustrating and devastating by turn. Her brief optimism vanished. Her mood wouldn't stay constant. A wave of sadness drenched her. She felt it as completely as if she was standing on the beach and a breaker had crashed in from the sea. She was heavy and indisposed. She had to get back on track. He ought to ask her to dance now.

'The orchestra are rather good, aren't they?' She enunciated carefully, not wanting to slur her words.

He glanced about him as though noticing for the very first time that there was music, which wasn't the case: she'd seen him dancing with Lady Feversham and others. 'Yes, I suppose. Good enough.'

'I do feel so very energetic tonight.' Hint, hint. Just ask, why don't you?

'Do you?' He didn't smile. Where was his dear smile?

'Yes.' He didn't catch on. She couldn't ask him! It wasn't done. She opened her dance card as though checking to see who she was committed to next. 'Matthew Fulham has begged me for the number sixteen. It's a two-step.' He nodded absent-mindedly, his eyes scanning the dance floor. Was he looking for someone? Who? Desperately, 'Do you know, I still have number seventeen free. It's a waltz.' It was too, too shaming. Her face was aflame. Number seventeen before he asked her to dance? There were only twenty-four in total. Would that be enough time?

Something had slipped. They weren't as they had been when he'd visited her home last week. That afternoon had passed so nicely. Simple smiles had fallen readily from his lips; he'd been charming and attentive. Now he seemed distant, distracted, a different man. Officially, of course, he needed her father's permission, but enough couples reached understandings and then fulfilled the formalities later.

They hadn't reached an understanding.

Not quite.

He had not made any clear speeches emphatically stating his intentions, although he often whispered with her in the quiet corners of rooms, littering his conversation with insinuation and intimation. He wanted her, he admired her, he couldn't sleep because of thinking about her. Often he'd wormed his finger inside her glove, caressed her wrist; once he had secretly brushed his lips on her neck. If others knew of his behaviour they would condemn it as too much. It was not enough. Never enough. She wanted so much more. Naturally, she was curious. Actually, she was burning.

How much time did these things take? If he was not going to ask her to dance, then perhaps they could go and get something to eat. Not that she was in the least bit hungry, but they could find somewhere away from the eyes that were boring into her – inquisitive, insensitive, amused.

'Should we dance?' She spat out the words, despite her better judgement.

He shrugged. 'If you like.'

Confident, he took hold of her hand, not her arm as formality ought to decree, and led her on to the dance floor, right in the middle of the number fifteen. She liked the fact that he'd clasped her hand and laced his fingers between hers. It was perfectly wrong of him but it made her feel endorsed, approved of, among and belonging and yet distinct, apart. It was difficult to explain. He gave her a sense that the world was vast and there was so much she didn't know or understand. It was daunting and exciting. Like boarding a train but not knowing where it was heading. Smoke and noise, a feeling of churned excitement. They forced other couples to make way. Some smiled, others glowered; she didn't care. His hand was on her waist now and the other one still clasped in hers. At last! Even through gloves her skin scorched.

'Have you had a beastly day?' she asked. She always felt the onus of conversation. Mother had instilled in her a necessity to be amusing.

'Why would you ask that?'

'You don't seem your usual self.'

'I'm bored,' he sighed.

His words came down like a governess's ruler. A stinging thwack. No! His emotions were so far from her own, it was a shock. She was nervous and desperate, then light-headed and excitable by turn, or at least she had been until he had declared that he was bored. Bored? Being bored was the worst. It was so close to indifference. Did *she* bore him? It was not possible to ask. She mustn't. She really mustn't. 'Do I bore you?' She looked him in the face, aware that her eyes must be glinting with hurt.

'All girls are bores. To some extent,' he replied with another sigh.

Betraying, stupid tears immediately crawled on to her eyelashes. She turned away from him and forced herself not to dip her head. No one must notice. The worst thing was, what he said was true. Sometimes she felt it herself. Girls, virgins, were all kittens, still ambiguous and folded like tiny green shoots in allotments. Closed, tight. Then, with a loose, relaxed smile, he added, 'Women are wonderful.' Blooming flowers were more desirable. Even fat, overblown roses had something interesting about them. The smile was some sort of a balm, but she was still unsure. Where did she fall in his estimation? Girl or woman? She was eighteen. Not a girl, and yet she'd never been kissed.

A girl.

Then he seemed to lose interest in the thought and asked, 'I can't remember, do you play bridge?' Vivian considered bridge an old woman's game. She thought about the endless afternoons her mother and her friends whiled away, cards slipping from their hands to the table, brows furrowed with concentration or arching with glee. Clock ticking. Vivian, Susan and Babe, all dressed in velveteen day dresses with mid-length sleeves, sat by and looked on. Hers was green, Susan and Babe in pink. They were too young for bridge but too old for children's board games; even if Susan might still have liked a game of snakes and ladders with Babe,

Vivian's presence somehow wouldn't allow it. It was most fun when the weather was right for croquet. Did he want her to play bridge? Lady Feversham was a demon at the game, known for it throughout London. Vivian was not sure why this thought unsettled her, but it did. An older, married woman. She ought not to be in the picture but Vivian held a vague, indefinable sense that she was. Oh, she wished she'd paid closer attention to the rules.

'No, I don't know how, but I could learn. You could teach me.'

He didn't look keen. 'You're more of an outdoors sort of girl,' he asserted confidently.

'Yes.' It seemed easier to agree. It was true that she liked being out of the house. She liked striding down Bond Street or Piccadilly, dipping into shops and coffee houses. Did that count as outdoorsy?

'Do you hunt?'

'I have.' Whenever Vivian thought of hunting, she thought of whisky. Tangy, leathery, spicy. Male. The first and only time she'd joined a hunt was when she was fourteen. The men in their pink coats had looked terrific; she'd enjoyed it enormously at first. Not so much when the hounds started to tear at the fox, throwing it yelping into the air, catching it again in their slobbering mouths, tugging it between them. She was the youngest on the hunt so they'd daubed her forehead with its blood. The smell of the iron was too much, left her queasy, light-headed. She'd been given a nip of whisky. Her father thought the incident amusing and often recalled it at the dinner table when they had guests.

Nathaniel sensed her lack of interest and asked in a tone that was distinctly challenging, 'Golf?'

'It's rather a man's thing, isn't it?'

'It doesn't have to be.' He looked peevish. His vitality was in danger of flagging when confronted with her lack. Why suddenly was he so interested in her hobbies? What did it matter? He was wondering what she did with her time. She danced and dreamt. She shopped. She sat by her mother's side and waited. 'Then what *is* your sport?' Truthfully, she didn't have one but saying so made her seem small, inadequate. For all her energy, she hadn't been encouraged to play an actual sport to any sort of level. It was not considered feminine. Her parents didn't believe a girl needed to be channelled or challenged the way a son did. She had little to offer except her good looks and her embroidery (actually, she wasn't too wonderful at that, but she was forced to persevere). She could play the piano (a little heavily, but hardly anyone ever complained) and she could sing. Yes, her singing voice was really quite lovely. It had never crossed her mind that this collection of attributes might not be enough.

Until now.

Nathaniel was big and bold, almost brutish. She adored that about him. He was a conduit to life. That was what a husband was. She had been to his house and seen the silver trophies on the mantelpiece in their second drawing room, the guns, bats and rackets on the shelves in the back rooms. He was vigorous, which made him promising in a way she didn't quite understand. In a way that made her nervous and breathless when she was with him.

'You're a slacker,' he muttered. She was stung, as he no doubt had intended.

He continued to dance in a deliberate silence, haughty and sulky; he couldn't be bothered to speak to her. It was awful. She wanted him to like her so much. She'd thought he did. She'd been so sure. They continued drifting between the other couples but she began to lose the sense of him. She knew he was holding her but she couldn't register it. What could she do? Her head was swimming; it was too hot in here. Intermittent smells hit, as couples danced past: lavender toilet water, male sweat. It was overwhelming. She needed air and a drink. No more champagne. She'd had enough. She ought to find a cordial but she didn't want lime juice. It reminded her of childhood picnics. Immature. She didn't want that at all.

'Oh, say something,' she spluttered.

'Like what?'

'Something nice,' she pleaded. It was undignified, but she didn't care. She just wanted him to be kind to her again.

'I like your dress. You are a wonderful adornment.' His voice dripped with sarcasm. It wasn't a compliment; wasn't intended as one.

'An adornment? Like a cherry on a cake but not an ingredient to life, you mean.' Not essential like bridge, hunting, golf.

'Quite so,' he said dismissively. Decisively.

She preferred the silence. She must not let him see her pain and confusion. How was this happening? Why were they falling apart so suddenly? He seemed to hate her. She had to do something. Had to. But what? What could she do or say to keep him interested. He was right: all she was was an ornament. She tried to think very hard through the pain and champagne. What did that mean?

It meant she was desirable.

That was no trifling matter.

'I'll show you what I am.' She grabbed his hand and pulled him away from the dance floor; they weaved through the crowds, jostling people's elbows rudely. Temporarily amused, he didn't object, but followed her swinging skirt out of the room, down a dimly lit, narrow passage. She led him to the powder room where earlier she'd discarded her lace. The little one, on the second floor. It didn't have a maid handing out towels or a seamstress poised with a needle ready to help a girl in trouble. She and Emily had commented that that was a poor show, rather cutting corners; now she was glad. She put her head around the door.

'Hello?' No one replied. Deserted. She tugged at his cuff.

'I can't go in there.' He followed anyway.

'Lock the door,' she instructed.

He did. It felt wonderful to have him do as he was told in that way. Follow her instructions. Without thinking about anything. Best not to think. Not about where they were or what she was doing. What was she doing? She was clawing furiously and desperately at his attention. She knew it. That was all that mattered to her. Gaining his attention once more. All.

She turned to him and took hold of his hands, then deliberately placed them on her breasts. She couldn't feel his touch through the layers of cotton and silk, but his mercurial face dissolved in an instant; anger, confusion finally became delight. 'Are you drunk? Are you *that* sort of drunk?' he asked. She wasn't any sort of drunk. Didn't one have to be frequently drunk to develop some sort of pattern? She smiled. 'I see.' He thought he was seeing her properly for the first time. He thought she was game. *That* sort of girl. It wasn't true. She'd never done anything like this before. If there had been a horse nearby, she would have just as likely jumped on that and galloped through the ballroom to hold his attention, to prove her bravery, her audacity, her *difference*. Bringing him here to forge this intimacy was the first thing that had come into her head. She was not even sure how it had. The long bath, the smell of male sweat in the ballroom, Nathaniel's bulk; all of that combined had somehow brought her here. She had to mark them out. Make them firm. She just had to. And what they were doing wasn't too bad. They were practically engaged, which was almost married.

He started to knead at her breasts, quite roughly. His face became pink; his expression was a strange, almost sneering excitement that she didn't understand or recognise; it shimmered and vanished. At least the bored lethargy had completely disappeared now. His other hand grabbed her behind and pulled her tightly to him. Her hips hit his. Then he kissed her. Not in the slightest bit the way she'd been kissed before. Kisses from her parents and siblings had fallen smooth and gentle, brief and neat on her cheeks and forehead, never her mouth. His kisses were hard. Insistent. Exhilarating. His lips seemed to want to be inside her mouth. His tongue was! She tried to copy what he was doing. He murmured and groaned. He called her wonderful. Ah, now she was wonderful! She watched their reflections in the mirror. He was stooped, melting into her. His head bent in that way looked so sweet! She put her fingers in his hair and started to comb his locks as she might if one of her sisters or her brother felt miserable and needed cheering up.

'Oh, you minx.'

He seemed pleased. He put his hands on her neck, clasping her hard to him. She liked the feel of his warm hand actually on her skin; it was a bit closer to how she felt in bed when she ran her fingers over her thighs or waist. She really didn't understand what all the fuss regarding breasts was, not exactly. She honestly couldn't feel much except a sense that she was making him happy. Suddenly he moved his hand inside the low neckline of her dress; his fingers wiggled. Oh God, he was touching her actual nipple. Her stomach turned to water.

This, *this* was what the fuss was about!

She should stop him. She must, but it felt so lovely, and the way he was moaning, repeating her name as though he was almost praying to her, well, it was wonderful! She felt powerful, charged. He picked her up – oh, how easy it was for him to do that – and sat her flat on the unit that held the washbasin. His hand slipped along her leg. Down to her ankle, back up to her knee. He seemed to have so many hands. Naturally, instinctively, she opened her legs and like a bee to a flower his hand shot to the top of her thighs. His fingers worked quite roughly. It wasn't exactly pleasant, but he seemed to be having such fun that she hardly minded the brusque force. When should she stop him? Soon. Now? She'd proven her point. It was wise to leave him wanting more. Although it was so very, very exciting. His face was so close to hers. It slipped from handsome to grotesque and back again. Spittle and urgency were all she noticed.

She was glowing. A woman. It was, quite frankly, rather awkward, not all *that*. She wondered why on earth the entire human race was quite so obsessed with it. Still, she'd done it with her brilliant Nathaniel and now she was a woman. A girl no longer. He'd clearly loved it. Grunted, cried out. The way he'd looked at her! So urgent and intent. It felt marvellous to know she could move him so.

'Just think, when we are married, we can do that every day. Two or three times, if we like.' She threw out a wide, eager beam; she was keen to give the impression that she'd enjoyed it as much as he had, because no one liked a moaning Minnie.

'You funny thing.' He buttoned up his trousers, adjusted his braces. Then kissed her nose. 'Come on, we have to get you back before anyone notices you are missing.' He led her by the elbow.

They met her mother on the stairs; the three of them stood in shock. Distrust and disgust seemed to ooze from Mrs Foster. 'Where have you been?' she asked. A bloodhound, sniffing the air.

'Looking at the portraits in the hall.' The lie slipped out glibly. Vivian felt rather proud of herself, her ability to protect Nathaniel. To conceal. It felt adult.

'You should be dancing.'

'I was tired.'

Mrs Foster stared coolly at Nathaniel. He'd dropped Vivian's elbow. They were apart again. He wouldn't meet her mother's gaze. He looked at his feet. Vivian wished he'd stare back. She wished he'd tell Mother to leave them alone; that they were an adult couple now, that they were going to get married, that Vivian would be a bigger society success than her mother and that she didn't need to breathe down her daughter's neck all the time. He didn't say any of this; he said, 'If you will excuse me, I had better return to my party. We've spent far too long looking at the portraits. I think I'm engaged for the last waltz.'

Mrs Foster stepped aside and he dashed off.

'Who?' Vivian called after him. She meant with whom was he engaged to dance the twenty-fourth? He couldn't dance with anyone else. Not after that. 'No,' she added, but he didn't hear her; he was halfway down the stairs. Her mother shot her a look that made it clear she ought not to say another word.

'Who are *you* dancing with next?' she demanded.

'I am not engaged for any more dances.' An unheard-of occurrence.

'Why not?'

'I didn't agree to any.'

'You've managed the evening very badly, Vivian.' Mrs Foster tutted and slid her gaze over her daughter.

'You don't know,' Vivian spat back. Mrs Foster gave her the queerest look, as though perhaps she did.

It surprised her how quickly everything collapsed. The urgent expectation, once quenched, seemed to have immediately ceased to exist, and nothing replaced it. She felt irked and rebellious. She felt as though everything inside her had shifted, but not in an emotional sense as she'd expected. Hoped. Simply a physical shift. She felt stretched. She needed her bag; there was a handkerchief in there. Where had she put her bag? She was sticky. Sore.

'It is time to go home,' snapped her mother.

As they hailed a carriage, Vivian could hear the strains of the band playing 'God Save the King'. The evening was over.

# 4

THE CARRIAGES CAME at eleven and took the audience away, a buoyant, satisfied mass of humanity who had enjoyed the passion and deceit of the evening as it had been confined to the stage. To speak of carriages was a euphemism; nowadays the tinkle of the hansom was often drowned out by an electric brougham or the engine of a car, but the theatre respected tradition. At the top of the programme ladies in the pit and gallery were requested to remove their bonnets, and at the bottom there was an instruction that carriages ought to be called for eleven. It was archaic, quaint, but so what? Howard allowed that the theatre could be what it liked. It did not have to be modern or move with the times like so many other industries; it was a magical place above and beyond the demands of reality or progress.

Beryl hurriedly scrubbed off her make-up and he waited for her at the stage door, smoking a cigarette, blue plumes drifting on the night air. Neither of them minded the late hour at which they were venturing forth; thesps were nocturnal. He knew he did not have to try hard to impress her. He could take her to a pub and spend just coppers on jellied eels and stout, but he liked her well enough and so he took her to the Grill Room at the Cumberland Hotel and spent three times what he had to on lamb cutlets and red wine. He watched as the greyness left her skin, her cheeks turned pink; it was money well spent.

She was a pleasant enough dinner companion. She told him she'd been working in the theatre since she was a baby; her mother was an actress too, 'Although she struggles for work now. She's thirty-seven.' The information was whispered, and Beryl looked about her as she made the revelation, aware that it was a betrayal to admit as much; she had fewer scruples about admitting that no one really knew who her father was. She declared she couldn't imagine doing anything other, certainly not factory or domestic service, which were, after all, her only genuine alternatives.

He thought they might be friends if only she didn't keep leaning so desperately across the table, trying to manoeuvre her small breasts into a cleavage by folding her arms. Not that he thought there was anything wrong with her breasts; he'd always believed more than a handful was a waste. He could sleep with her. Tangle his limbs up with hers for the night, get some brief warmth and luxury from her body, but was it fair? It was obvious he didn't care about her as much as she cared about him. Women had to care more; they had more to lose. It would end in tears. It always did. He should probably try to avoid that sort of hassle and mess at work.

They came outside and drew in deep breaths. It was just before two in the morning but the blue-black night wasn't too chilly or inhospitable. They lingered; he had one foot in the gutter, one on the pavement.

'Shall we go back to your place?' she asked as he'd expected her to. The warm tug of companionship, the raw promise of passion had threaded its way through her mind and body. He knew what she imagined, something rather more plush than the reality. In the dressing rooms, before the performance, he often wore a plum-coloured velvet smoking jacket; therefore those who didn't know any better thought he was a toff. His face was chiselled and his skin luminous in a way that suggested something other than his working-class origins. It was misleading. His face was his own, true enough, but he'd been given the smoking jacket by their Mr Warrington, on loan. The savvy and ambitious actor-manager liked to cultivate a particular image with regard to his writers. He wanted people to assume that they smoked expensive cigars, slept on crisp linen, washed using the best Selfridge soap. They did not. Warrington's wages couldn't stretch to any of that.

If Howard took Beryl back to his lodgings, she'd be disappointed. The place was spartan. His landlady was alarmingly respectable; it stopped her from being fun or even kind. Dry and widowed, she had strong views on what a young man in London should do with his time. She did not think he ought to sit in his room reading books and burning coal unnecessarily; she thought he ought to take long constitutional walks to keep warm. She did not think a real man needed to bathe more than once a week (although he should wear a clean collar every day). She did not think he ought to have another young man visit in the evenings if he was on his own (because that was suspicious), but she certainly did not allow more than two men visiting at once (because that was a party) and *never* could a woman call (because that was simply wrong). His room was clean, though bare and austere (the landlady did not allow posters and such to be pinned to the walls). In the final analysis it was scrubbed and, crucially, it was cheap. As his aesthetic influence on the room and the number of guests he was permitted was so severely limited, Howard hardly spent any time there and instead hung round coffee shops and bars with other writers.

He did enjoy walking the streets of London, not strictly for the constitutional benefit but to drink it all up, the life, the vibrancy. Adventure. London was the centre of the whole world. Wealth, power, creativity, decency, indecency; it all poured from here, from England, like the Thames itself. He found it inspiring. It was a city of smiles, peace, security, self-satisfaction. He could walk the streets now, left to his own devices, even at this late hour. He was too big to fall into any trouble. He'd take in the nippy air; let it go deep down into his lungs. But Beryl was wearing heels; she'd never keep up. He should put her in a cab.

He liked striding, feeling his long legs cover many feet of pavement in just one step, his arms swinging by his sides. He frequently wanted to break into a run, a strange impulse for a man – most people quashed that urge as they left behind childhood – but Howard often thought he was in a hurry. He wanted to cover as much ground as possible, as quickly as he could, both literally and metaphorically. He ran for miles when he lived in the country, every morning, every night. People used to ask him where he was going and found it hilarious when his only answer was, 'Nowhere special.' He didn't think it was hilarious; he thought it was tragic. A waste. So he ran to London. However, he soon discovered that if you ran in the streets here, you wouldn't get away with just a few raised eyebrows and mocking comments; a bobby would quickly be feeling your collar. The assumption being that a running man must have stolen something. Still, he could run in the parks until sweat poured into his eyes and made his shirt damp. It was one of the many ways he showed the world that he simply did not accept limits, that he would not be hemmed in or slowed down. That he would explore and conquer if only with his boots and his mind. Space was all.

He'd been brought up in a small village in the Midlands, in a small cottage, in a small family. Just him and his younger brother and his mother. There were five, six, seven children in other families in the village, but he always thought his mother made up for the lack of other people. She was a neat, bony woman who looked like a girl from the back, but in her heart, her energy, her vision, she was enormous. His father had vanished when he was a boy, just a month after his brother had been born. If he was dead, no one ever said. He was just gone. His mother didn't latch on to anyone else, although she could have, he supposed; she was attractive enough, striking some might say, and hard-working, clever. She chose to bring them both up alone; she enjoyed the freedom and managed her financial concerns with minimum fuss, never asking for handouts, never selling them short by limiting their lives. She told them it was all theirs if they wanted it, the world and what it had to offer; if they were brave enough to reach for it.

His mother was perhaps the only truly independent woman he knew; she did not depend on a husband or father for her financial or emotional security. Ahead of her time, she didn't believe the world started and ended between her parlour and the front gate. She didn't believe that the poverty you were born into had to brand you all your days. She made a living painting portraits of children from well-to-do families. She was able to see and capture innocence in a rare way. Bravely, she also found room to express the less adorable side of children's natures; she did not shy away from boisterousness, temper, anguish or arrogance, and the parents were compelled by the honesty of the portraits, could not deny or resist them. Walking away from the portrait would be like walking away from the child itself. When she needed to, she took in washing and mending. She approached those tasks with the same dignity and honesty as she did her painting, although with considerably less pleasure. Scrubbing someone else's sheets and underwear on a wooden washboard, removing their yellow and brown stains, could not be as satisfying as working on a canvas, loading it with emerald, scarlet and violet. Yet she never complained.

There was always food on the table, boots on their feet, and as a treat, once a year she took them into London, something special. The annual trips were a bigger excitement than Christmas. He remembered all of them with complete precision. The tangle of trains, tubes and buses that got them to their destination. The clouds of smoke and fumes mingled with the treacly wonderfulness of the boiled sweets they were allowed to suck on the journey. Crystal Palace, the Natural History Museum, the theatre to see a play. *Caesar and Cleopatra* by George Bernard Shaw changed everything for Howard. He loved every moment. They'd queued outside the door for hours. It was a vigil made entertaining by street performers who sang and recited Shakespearean sonnets with more gusto than talent, holding out greasy hats to those who could barely afford to spare coppers but would not refuse. Then, when the doors finally eased open, the queue fell apart and the glorious, eager rough-and-tumble crowds pushed, shoved, shouted and scrambled as they made their way inside. Half-crowns and shillings were slammed down with violent excitement on to the counter of the tiny kiosk, checks were given in exchange and people dashed to their seats.

Howard had never known anything like it.

It was breathtaking. Right there before his eyes, ordinary men became soldiers and kings, lovers and warriors. He knew immediately that theatre was limitless. Possibilities endless.

When he turned fourteen and told his mother he was going to London to find work in the theatre, ultimately to write plays, she did not laugh or discourage or yell with exasperation the way so many parents might have. She insisted it was a grand idea and it was best that she shared him with the world because he was the sort that couldn't be contained by one woman. If she resented the fact that he wasn't planning on earning a regular wage and contributing to the household, or staying close by her side to offer her company, she never for a moment let it show.

'I'm cold. Are we going back to yours or not?' Beryl tapped her feet on the ground to bring some feeling back to them; she'd wrapped her skinny arms around her body. Her skin was covered with goose bumps. Howard thought of the chickens that ran around his mother's yard, eventually ending up on the table.

'Don't you have a coat?'

'Of course I do.' She wasn't going to admit that she only had a hand-me-down brown overcoat that was just about acceptable in the daytime but not at all glamorous enough for a night out. He took off his own coat and wrapped it around her shoulders.

'My landlady doesn't allow guests.'

'You can sneak me in. I can be very quiet.' Her nose was pink, her eyes glistened. He wondered what her lodgings were like. Grim, he imagined. Foul. Worse than his. And she wanted more lines. She was as keen as mustard. He could probably take her to the park and have her up against a tree, she was that eager, but he wouldn't. Not tonight. There was something about the anxious fluttering of her hands that warned him off. This starlet was the sort that needed saving from herself. Besides, thinking about his mother had quelled his desire; she'd gifted him good looks, freedom, confidence but also (somewhat inconveniently) a conscience. Subliminally as he'd observed his mother deftly move away from the chubby, pawing hands of various widowers and would-be adulterers who dropped off their washing with her, he'd come to understand that as the world was currently constructed, men had a choice. They could exploit women, use and abuse them, or they might protect them. He knew he had to treat them fairly and honourably, because the law didn't, and history hadn't. Might the future?

'I'm tired, Beryl. I have to be up in the morning at six. Warrington wants me to run through his lines with him.'

'Why? He knows his lines. He's very good. You saw the crowd tonight – they are wild for him. Always are. Always will be.' She was suspicious; she didn't trust his excuse.

'Warrington is the sort of man who knows that always is a very long time indeed. He doesn't want to be good; he wants to be the best.' Howard kissed her on the forehead and gave her some cash for a cab. 'I'll ask him if we can find you a line.'

She lit up, sunshine emerging from behind a cloud. 'Will you, will you really?'

'I'll ask. No promises.'

# 5

VIVIAN'S MOTHER BARELY slept. She'd guessed it all. She couldn't believe it but she knew it. The girl was stupid. Impatient and rash. Mrs Foster feared the worst. The very worst. They had left the ball immediately after meeting on the stairway. Vivian could not have been allowed to return to the throng. Not in that state. It was all so obvious to anyone who wanted to look. She was flushed, her eyes were bright and unfocused, the lace had gone from her neckline.

He looked as guilty as hell. Wet-lipped. Swaggering.

His mother must not see it. That was their only hope. Lady Thorpe was fond of Vivian, but was fond enough? The boy's interest would wane now, that was certain. Might he be propped up by a combination of a belief in doing the right thing and his mother's endorsement of Vivian? Not that Lady Thorpe would endorse her if she ever suspected . . . How far? How far had the girl gone? Not too far, surely. Mrs Foster shivered, felt sick and exhausted. Her eyelids scratched. Had Vivian whetted his appetite or doused the fire? Stupid, stupid girl. Women were given so little to play with, and now she had not just shown her hand by clearly admitting to her affection; she had thrown in the cards by indulging with him physically. How far had it gone? That was the only pertinent question. She could not ask her daughter directly. If she did, there was no going back. No pretending it wasn't the case. Tight lips were required today.

And for ever.

Last night the ball had been rife with rumours. None of them good. For weeks the talk had been how adorable Miss Vivian Foster looked when dancing with Mr Nathaniel Thorpe. No one had seemed unduly concerned that the daughter of a banker was shooting for the eldest son of Sir Robert Thorpe with his thousands of acres of land. People had simply concentrated on how exquisite she was to look at, how charming and demure. Mrs Foster had been seduced into believing it was a possibility; other less cautious types spoke openly of it being a probability; one or two used the word 'certainty'. Last night everything had shifted. It was like standing on the shore whilst the tide dragged at the wet sand, the ground slipping away from under one's feet, causing one to stumble. They had all talked about Lady Cynthia Winters and Nathaniel Thorpe. Besides the fact that Cynthia was the daughter of Lord and Lady Winters – a highly respectable, influential and wealthy couple – she was also Lady Feversham's god-daughter. Mrs Foster's oldest and most loyal friends had pointed out that this meant she came with a fortune and the fringe benefit that her godmother was an incorrigible flirt, by which of course they meant the most outrageous seducer, currently rumoured to be looking for a new young lover. Nathaniel was a young man who might be able to have his cake and eat it. The question was whether he was worldly-wise enough to realise as much and cynical enough to accept such an arrangement. Mrs Foster thought of his wet lips. His swagger. She feared he was.

Vivian slept until late, or at least she lolled in her bed insisting that she was exhausted and couldn't get up. Nanny sympathised. 'Too much dancing, that's your trouble.' Mrs Foster knew there hadn't been much dancing. 'You just don't know when enough is enough. When to say no.' *That* Mrs Foster could agree with.

She allowed the indolence. She didn't want to see her daughter's stupid face. A slack mix of expectancy, hope, shame and glee. If she was at all ashamed. She hadn't seemed it last night. Quite drunk, anaesthetised.

Mrs Foster found her husband in the drawing room waiting for the newspapers to be brought to him. In big houses the papers were ironed; the butler brought them to the master on a silver tray. The Fosters had three members of staff and none of them had time to iron newspapers, although some standards were to be maintained so Mrs Foster insisted that the housekeeper bring in the newspapers on a tray; she tried to ignore the fact that it was wicker. Mr Foster always grinned at this affectation and Mrs Foster always grimaced at the compromise.

Theirs was a sincere and reasonably candid relationship. It had not been without its strains and bleakness, but they had settled into a comforting, not overly demanding familiarity. Twenty-two years of intimacy and concessions, combined with ever-reducing financial circumstances, meant that they chose to talk to one another quite openly about most things. Mrs Foster admired her husband's integrity; he admired her foresight; together they were a strong team. She explained it all to him.

'Well, what's the harm of a bit of kissing? They are practically engaged, aren't they?'

'Practically, in this case, is synonymous with not at all. You have to remember, Cecil, we have three daughters and Vivian's position as the eldest is key.' Mrs Foster had spent years intervening between the girls. Delicately, trying not to show that the first-born, careless one was after all her pet, that the next, slightly chubbier one (who tried so hard) in fact rather irritated (her very gusto grated), and that she barely noticed the smallest one, who came after a boy and had been neither expected nor celebrated. Two girls were more than enough for any mother to settle. Still, she did her duty for them. She quelled giggling fits, reminded them of their deportment, brought governesses and dressmakers to the nursery, introduced the girls to the right people. She knew they must whirl and flush; she also knew when they must sit tight and wait. Each was intrinsically linked to the next whether they liked it or not. If Vivian married well, it would help the younger two enormously. She had a duty; she must follow instructions. 'If she messes it up, then their chances are scuppered. There is so much at stake.'

'So you've said, my darling. Often.'

'Susan is such a dear, she deserves to do well, and Barbara is shaping up nicely too, don't you think?' Mrs Foster didn't sound convinced. They both knew Vivian was by far the prettiest of the three. Mrs Foster now despaired of the fact. It was horrifying to think that no good would come of it, only trouble.

'You can't expect to have more than one satisfactory daughter, not nowadays,' he commented. 'We're all losing our grip. There's not so much obligation or fear knocking about; at least one is bound to fall off the rails.' He chuckled, resolutely light-hearted about the matter. Mrs Foster bit down on her lip. Her husband didn't seem to accept that the marrying business might be at all grave; he made a big joke of it. But then he was a man; his career and his marital choice were able to remain quite distinct. 'I'm sure it will all turn out well. He'll no doubt call today or send flowers, you'll see.'

Everything was now in the hands of Nathaniel Thorpe. It all might turn out to be rapturous or disastrous depending on him: his actions, his words, his intentions.

The conversation was cut short by the maid delivering the papers. Mr Foster opened his *Times*, shook it and then held it like a wall between them, clearly indicating that he didn't believe the subject required any more discussion. Mrs Foster's *Daily Mail* lay neat and undisturbed on the chaise longue. She had not shared her thoughts that the interlude might very well have gone further than a bit of kissing (although that would be damning enough);

no one would ever hear her articulate her worst fears. She would not admit to such catastrophic failure. Besides, Mr Foster was not the sort to reach for a shotgun and demand that Nathaniel Thorpe do the proper thing. He was too bookish for that. Happiest sitting by the fire with a difficult, weighty tome and his pipe. He lacked ambition and fury. It was what made him the most delightful husband in the world, and the most useless. She had to manage it all.

They sat in comparative silence for twenty minutes, the only sounds being the regular ticking of the clock and the slow turning of the pages. Mr Foster occasionally made some comment connected to whatever he was reading. 'My God, the Irish'; it wasn't clear if it was an oath or a prayer. 'The House will have to look at that. Can't ignore it any longer.' Recently when reading the papers he tended to become agitated, distressed. He often huffed and puffed impotently at the issues that were being reported. It saddened Mrs Foster to know that whilst he was clearly still very aware of the political landscape, he didn't consider himself young enough to be part of a solution or an outcome; he had consigned himself to the role of outraged observer.

'Oh, I think you need to see this.'

She was not too concerned by his tone; she imagined it was some article about the latest desperate atrocity the suffragettes had committed. But when he lowered the paper and caught her gaze, she saw the grief and compassion in his eyes.

*Lord and Lady Winters of Belgravia announce the engagement of their eldest daughter, Cynthia Mary Elizabeth, to Nathaniel William Henry Thorpe, son of Sir Robert and Lady Thorpe. The marriage will take place at Westminster Abbey in April 1915.*

The announcement was perfect. Worded exactly as it ought to be. Mrs Foster despised announcements that included adjectives like 'delighted' when referring to the parents' response, or 'beautiful' when referring to the Abbey. It was absolutely correct and spot on. Except, of course, for the name of the bride-to-be.

# 6

WARRINGTON WAS PLEASED with Howard, although the entire company was aware that his approval was fitful; often swiftly bestowed and hastily retracted. The man had an obsessive need to feel he was forever sharpening his game. His ambition sustained him, fed him and would quite likely ruin him, but not just yet. Competition was fierce; new theatres popped up all the time like mushrooms in a boggy field. Warrington tried to take comfort in the fact that other, newer actor-managers might not be classically trained, they might take short cuts, be lazy or unoriginal, but it was impossible to deny that – even if the actors needed prompts, the scenery was rickety or the costumes lacked authenticity – the new companies were novel. Novelty went a long way with audiences, who were not always as discerning as Warrington desired. It took daily effort to push the doubt from his head, to ignore the fact that other theatres were discounting seats or serving several flavours of ice cream in the interval, and to stay focused on the important matter of the acting.

Howard was an ace up Warrington's sleeve. His writing was perceptive and witty; in tune with the spirit of the age but challenging too. He was so very young and yet already causing a stir; Warrington could only imagine how far his young prodigy might go, under the correct guidance. The early-morning rehearsal had been extremely productive. Howard alone was prepared to drill Warrington, correct him, coach him, offer unflinchingly honest feedback. He understood nuance and character like no other writer. Today he was the favourite.

As a reward, Warrington had invited him for drinks at his club, an undoubted honour that was occasionally bestowed and always gratefully received. Howard enjoyed visiting the mahogany and leather rooms in St James's that smelt of cigars and stored masculine secrets. When he arrived, he found Warrington sitting with an assorted group of men, none of whom Howard knew personally, most of whom he knew by reputation. There was an eminent barrister who often visited the playhouse, a renowned novelist, two popular artists and several journalists. A gifted and influential bunch. He felt a shard of pleasant pride shoot through his belly at the thought of being counted amongst their number. He sat on a worn green velvet armchair and drank whisky without ice. The fire and laughter roared simultaneously.

One of the journalists was a fellow called Basil Clarke. He worked for the *Daily Mail* and was considered quite the bright young thing, even though Howard guessed he must be in his mid thirties, more than a decade older than Howard himself and therefore hardly young in Howard's opinion. Clarke was prematurely bald and wore glasses; the two factors conspired to give him the appearance of a middle-aged man. However, alert intelligence oozed out of every pore and somehow countered the physicality, made the man young again. If he happened to glance your way, you felt interrogated and invigorated; he was the sort of man that made other men up their game. He was witty, caustic, it was known that he didn't suffer fools gladly, and however good anyone considered him to be, he believed he was better still.

So ferociously intellectual and testing by reputation, Howard was startled by the subject matter Clarke introduced. Surely he could only have stumbled upon it because large quantities of alcohol had been consumed.

'I'm writing an article about which city is the home to the fairest women in the land,' Clarke announced. The company erupted into laughter and catcalls. None of them could believe he was serious, and then, once they had established he was, every man had an opinion on the matter; a strong one. The Irish writer insisted it was his home town, Dublin, that bred the most beauties; others called for *their* home towns, Manchester, London, Sheffield; others still would argue equally vociferously against the same spot.

Liverpool seemed to be edging ahead in the dubious poll. A number of the men commented that there was something of note in the clearness and texture of the skin of the women there.

'Yes, walk along Bold Street or Lord Street or Church Street, you'll be struck, I promise you. Far higher average beauty than in any other city, not even equalled in London itself,' Clarke stated authoritatively. 'The problem with London,' he continued, 'is that the beauties are suspiciously sensitive to prevailing fashions. Let copper-red be the fashionable hue and suddenly the streets are awash with the colour. The unanimity dulls.'

'I agree,' commented the barrister with a sigh.

'Besides, Londoners often look careworn, tired,' Clarke added.

'Aberdeen girls are bright-cheeked,' piped up another journalist.

'Yes, but they dress so badly,' murmured a third.

Howard thought the perpetrator of this comment was probably not all that interested in females. Personally Howard didn't care how a woman dressed; it was all about the undressing. He smiled benignly but did not argue too passionately for any town or city in particular. Experience had shown him that there were pretty women everywhere.

Howard was a pleasant drunk; he became mellow and dreamy rather than annoyingly didactic or opinionated. He simply smiled and smiled and grew quieter and quieter. Clarke noticed his reticence and with the challenging authority of a more abrasive drunk demanded, 'You are very quiet. Do you have an opinion on the matter?'

'Yes, I do.'

'Well, what is it then?'

'My opinion is that you ought to be writing about something more important.' His thoughts had tumbled from his head to his lips and into the room before he could consider the effect of confronting such an influential newspaperman. He caught Warrington's scowl, pitched accurately across the table of full and empty glasses.

Three or four of the other men burst out laughing and agreed, 'Yes. Yes, no doubt he ought.' Clarke said nothing, but held eye contact with Howard long enough to make Warrington squirm with fear and fury.

Later, as they were leaving the club, Warrington demanded of Howard, 'Why did you have to make an enemy of that fellow Basil Clarke?'

'I wasn't aware I had.' Howard shrugged his way into his coat that was being held wide by a manservant.

'Couldn't you simply have gone along with the chatter? Wasn't it convivial enough for you?'

'It was convivial, but I was asked my opinion.'

'Must you always give it?'

'Yes. That is what it is for.'

'He's an influential man at the *Daily Mail*. We need to keep him on side.'

'I didn't mean to offend. I'm quite certain I didn't. He struck me as the sort that could take it as well as he dished it.'

Warrington's bonhomie, which Howard had carefully galvanised through the exhaustive morning rehearsals, disappeared under a dark cloak of unreasonable panic. 'I hope you are right,' he snapped.

Bullish and bullying, he added, 'Because young playwrights are easier to come across than sympathetic reviewers, you know.'

Howard nodded, understanding completely. His job was eternally precarious; he always had to be grateful, careful. He put on his hat and stepped out into the street. The first glow of dawn showered the city with a hint of silver light. He took a deep breath and walked away.

# APRIL 1914

# 7

THE DAYS DRAGGED into weeks and she heard nothing from him. He did not call by, or send anyone in his stead; he did not write. Not a line to explain or apologise. Her mother laughed when she expressed her dismay and surprise that this was the case. It was a bitter, sharp and knowing bark of laughter. She muttered under her breath about Vivian's stupidity. Furious, she asked how she could have hoped differently.

'You were incredibly foolish to trust him in the first place; you are a complete imbecile to continue to do so. You are nothing to him, Vivian. He probably looks blank when your name is mentioned.'

Her mother's irritation and his indifference were formidable enemies. Mrs Foster thought she was destroying him for Vivian; she thought she had to. She didn't have to. Vivian saw it as it was.

He did not want her.

She was not to be his wife.

She was just a delicious diversion to him.

These thoughts were so bleak that they cut, but Vivian repeated them to herself over and over so that no one else had to. She wondered exactly when they had become engaged. Was it before his visit to her house? Was that what he had come to tell her? That the flirtation must stop. Or was it that very evening, and if so, when: before or after they had . . .? It didn't matter anyway. Whenever it had happened, it was a betrayal, a crime. There was no point in hashing over the timings. Already Vivian was not the fool she'd been just a few weeks ago. She was, at least, a fast learner. Or was she? She felt a century older. Maybe it had taken a hundred years to accept his betrayal. She would never be young again. It was all gone.

The last she remembered of him was that airy smile, a slight shrug, not even a wave of the hand as he sauntered down the stairs towards the ballroom. She had been very casually dismissed, she saw that now. She became conscious of the fundamental difference between the sexes. They were so apart. He simply didn't care. An impossible, impassable gulf had opened up between them. He had moved on.

Vivian was instructed to write a letter to Cynthia Winters passing on good wishes at the news of her engagement, as she had with all the other debutantes of the season. Mrs Foster sent a silver carriage clock from the family. She stood over Vivian's shoulder and dictated every word. She was not leaving anything to chance. Not any more.

Vivian thought perhaps her mother knew what she was now, although she hadn't said anything vulgar and direct (or comforting and honest, come to that). Mrs Foster had previously admired her daughter and was proud of her, as Cook was proud of a well-risen cake, a product of her making rather than an individual. She had seen Vivian's value. Now she was ashamed of her and wondered if she was worthless. Vivian caught her mother looking at her, no doubt trying to work out if she was intrinsically evil or imbecilic, or whether she herself had done something wrong, missed a trick in nurturing and preparation. Vivian had lived a perfectly lovely and proper sort of life. She had played hopscotch and skipping rope, worn a hat when she was told, practised the piano, eaten her broccoli, retired to bed when instructed without argument.

She had come out to glorious reviews; indeed, she had behaved beautifully and appeared to have great respect for the wisdom of elders, authority and tradition. No one had anticipated any trouble. Now her future was ill defined, hazy. She'd brought the instability upon herself. It was pitiable.

The pen scratched on the thick creamy parchment. *Wishing you a lifetime of felicity.* Vivian felt it, as though the words were being tattooed on to her chest. She must be more like him. More like a man. It was her only chance at surviving this. Indifference.

Initially, she was too terrified to process the anguish and vicious disappointment. For ten days she existed in a numb state of desolation. All she feared was that there would be a baby; a dear, sweet hybrid of her and Nathaniel (his lashes, his vigour, her colouring, her curls!). She imagined this, longing and despairing of it simultaneously. She stayed dry-eyed and silent, hardly eating or sleeping, certainly not writing in her diary – not that, never again – just waiting. Waiting. When it became clear that there wouldn't be a baby, she was overwhelmed with relief and grief. Her legs literally gave way beneath her; as she collapsed to her knees, she banged her head on the wall in the water closet and howled. Nanny found her, pulled up her drawers and put her to bed for the afternoon. 'Good pet. Lucky pet,' mumbled Nanny, who after all understood more than she was given credit for. She knew of girls who had caught and were sent away. Sometimes for a year. Sometimes for ever.

Vivian was stunned to discover how short-lived desire could be. She'd been so full of need and want for him, but now there was nothing left. Nothing. Almost overnight. That sense of needing him, craving him, wanting him above all others, above anything, had disappeared. After all the longing and planning and edging ever closer, it had stopped. Abrupt. Final. She found that she was humiliated, insulted, irritated, but not in love. She'd been shocked or shoved out of it. When she scanned the weekly publications for an engagement picture of Cynthia Winters and Nathaniel, it was not so that she could place her finger on his face and trace his features with yearning or desire; she simply wanted to know what *she* looked like. What was it about her? How had she succeeded where Vivian had failed? She couldn't imagine Cynthia was as tall as she herself was, or as slim, or as . . . The thoughts didn't bother to stay in her head, but vanished, dissolving like fireworks into blackness. It didn't matter. It didn't change anything. Cynthia would make a home and babies with him. She would honeymoon on the Riviera, dine at the Savoy, dance the quadrille, the waltz and two-step in every stately home in Britain. Not Vivian. She resented the thought that she'd somehow been tricked. By herself.

Susan came home, breathless and excited, Vivian's crisis making even her slothful sister act out of character. 'I saw the girl he is to marry,' she gabbled, once their mother was out of earshot.

'What is she like?'

'The plump, appealing sort.'

'Blond?'

'No, dark. A mop of soft curls.' Vivian could hear admiration in her sister's voice. 'Nothing like you.' She skipped away down the passage towards the kitchen. Vivian wanted to bite her cheek.

Inexplicably, once she was sure there wasn't going to be a baby, Vivian became more hysterical and tearful than when she had feared there might be. Nanny mumbled that she was grieving for what might have been. Mrs Foster looked as though she wanted to fire Nanny on the spot, and possibly would have, but Nanny knew too much.

'It's purely a physical reaction, nothing we should concern ourselves with. Nothing we should speak of,' snapped Mrs Foster.

Vivian thought that maybe she was right. After all, she didn't feel the hysteria and tears in her heart. That was numb. She felt a fraud and a fool. She almost wished she did feel more. She wanted it to be so important that it might be for ever. If not this, then what was? But largely she felt blank. Bleak. Any pain she did feel came from her knowledge that whilst she was not yet nineteen years old, it was all finished for her. Specifically, what she had hoped for, planned, expected would *never* be. She must let that go.

The house was in mourning. It seemed as though the very walls, chimney, roof and floors grieved. The servants had caught the gossip, or at least the mood, and talked in whispers, moving quietly and carefully as they lugged coal, chopped vegetables and scrubbed the steps. Her younger siblings knew she was disappointed but not that she was disgraced. Sweetly, they tried to comfort her. Babe brought a bunch of white waxflowers, picked from the garden, and Toby offered an ounce of his sugared almonds, an enormous self-sacrifice. Vivian tried to smile, to show her appreciation, but Mrs Foster scolded the little children for daring to venture down from the nursery and sent them packing. She didn't want them tainted with all this. Best keep them away as much as possible at the moment. Such a delicate time. She was scared that Vivian's insolence and irresponsibility might be catching; that she might infect the girls. Vivian pitied Susan and Babe; she had brought her mother's wrath down on them. They would never enjoy the freedom she'd briefly had. They'd be locked up, Rapunzels. Regrettably, rather than open doors for them, she had walled them in. As much as she pitied them, however, she pitied herself oh so much more.

They were searching for a husband for her. A make-do husband. Her mother was frantic, all too aware that time was of the essence, but it was paramount that no one sniffed panic, as they would guess at scandal. Rumour spread so quickly. Like a gas it crept everywhere, under closed doors, over high fences. Vivian had to be seen to be indifferent towards Nathaniel; somehow they had to convince the world that she had never had any particular affection for him, and certainly no affection that she'd acted upon. It was a big task unpicking what they'd worked so hard to achieve. Vivian had wanted him to feel particular. She'd wanted the world to know.

'I could remain single,' she offered. Now that there was no baby, she wondered whether she really had to be married.

'What a ludicrous thought. Impossible. Failing to marry is not an option.'

Vivian supposed her mother was right. It was ludicrous because what else would she do? Other women in her position might teach, but she had no education, vocation or inclinations to direct her into a career of any sort. 'You cannot become one of those women who doggedly tells anyone who will listen that she had her chances but was fussy,' snapped her mother.

'No, I could not.'

'For a start, they always seem so wild and unkempt.'

'Unloved.'

'Exactly.'

Colour throbbed first in her cheeks and then down her neck and chest. In fact, embarrassment seeped through the entire room.

'Or you'll become one of those other types of women,' piped up Susan. Mother looked shocked to hear her voice. Frozen. When did she sneak into the room? What had she heard? What did she know? Mother scowled.

'Which other types?' Vivian asked warily.

'The ones that are all a little bit *too much*,' sighed Susan, suggesting she understood more than was ideal. 'You know, the sort with sherry-coloured hair, white powdered faces, lipstick.' Susan looked alert and excitable, which was a rare and – under the circumstances – loathsome thing. 'You'll be forever smoking, childless, wear your hats too wide, shoes too high, *that* sort of woman.'

'I shan't care if I am,' Vivian muttered defiantly and untruthfully.

'Why won't you contrive to be respectable?'

'Enough, Susan.' Mother no doubt knew it was a question that was probably already being asked in various drawing rooms throughout London; she didn't need it to be asked in her own.

'No one visits any more,' groaned Susan. She threw Vivian a look. She knew who was to blame. It was true: their 'at home' days had been dismal of late. No one called. It wasn't clear whether people were embarrassed. Pitying? Disgusted? Vivian longed for company. They all did. It had become apparent that they needed other people to make each other bearable. Vivian had heard that Emily was visiting an aunt in Newcastle. She'd heard this not from Emily herself but through their maid, who was friendly with Emily's maid. Vivian hadn't been aware that Emily had an aunt in Newcastle. She hadn't written. Vivian felt the loss of her keenly. With each moment of seclusion that ticked by, she wondered whether if it lasted just one more, she might fall to her knees, as they were all so clearly hoping, and beg forgiveness. She didn't, because it would change nothing. She gazed out of the window despondently. The very neatness of the manicured lawns trapped her.

'Look, an Oldsmobile, it's pulling up outside the house. It's stopping,' she cried excitedly.

'Is someone getting out?' Mother asked. She sounded shrill, agitated.

'Yes.'

'Who?'

'I don't know.'

'Susan, come away from the window at once. Pick up your embroidery. Vivian, keep your eyes to the floor,' she hissed.

They listened attentively as the maid opened the door. A voice Vivian couldn't immediately place skittered through the walls. The maid entered with a card.

'Where's the tray?' Mrs Foster asked, despairing. She read the card. 'Miss Ava Pondson-Callow.' A reprieve? Aid?

'Are you at home, ma'am?'

'Of course we are. Show her in immediately.'

Their house wasn't enormous, so no sooner were the words out of her mouth than Ava was standing in the drawing room. And what an entrance. She was wearing a huge flat hat at least twice as wide as her shoulders, and a marvellous ecru floor-length raw silk dress. It had heavy soutache lacing along the seams and intricate knotted crochet button trims and yoke collar insert. It was tightly corseted, and belted with velvet (naturally, to show her minute waist), but over the top there was a layered pinafore that swept down to a fringed trim bottom, suggesting a fluidity and modernity that Vivian hadn't seen in a dress before. In fact it was a statement rather than a dress. The sort of statement an older woman might have been expected to make. It was an outfit that declared that she was taking herself, and this visit, seriously. She looked like a work of art. She was always exquisite, and she'd dressed up for them. Vivian appreciated it.

'Good morning, Mrs Foster, Miss Foster, Miss Susan Foster.' Ava's voice was cut glass. 'How wonderful of you to be in. I'd have been so disappointed to miss you.' She was towering yet graceful, her limbs extended and lifted purposefully. Her teeth were milk white, eyes light and bright, lips full and fluid, ready to beam or scowl in an instant. She looked like someone enchanted from a fairy tale, out of this world.

Mrs Foster offered a limited smile, accepting Ava (who was close to her daughter's age) as her social equal. In that single line, Ava had conveyed warmth, by implying that the Fosters might have had somewhere else that they could be, somewhere where they might still be welcome; it was generous.

'Is Lady Pondson-Callow with you?' Mrs Foster asked hopefully.

Ava did not seem disconcerted, but replied, 'My mother doesn't make many calls, but she did instruct me to invite you to come to us.'

'How thoughtful.' Mrs Foster was no doubt wondering whether she was being palmed off or welcomed in. How it must have cost her to add, 'When exactly?'

'May the fifteenth. For dinner. Do keep the date free. She will send a proper invitation, but we'd all be so disappointed if you couldn't make it, so we thought it important to give you notice.' Three weeks. How clever of the Pondson-Callows. In three weeks' time, Mrs Foster would have either found someone to marry Vivian and she'd be respectable again, or else her notoriety would have peaked – either way she'd be an interesting guest. Still, it was the only invitation they'd received since Nathaniel had announced his engagement; Vivian knew she ought to be grateful.

'You are looking lovely, Vivian. I heard that you have been unwell.' Miss Pondson-Callow had heard no such thing, but it was rather sweet of her to offer up an excuse for Vivian's sudden absence from the social scene.

Vivian grabbed the lie. 'Just a cold.'

'But you are fully recovered now, I trust.'

'Almost,' piped up Mrs Foster. 'Would you take some tea?'

'How thoughtful, no, but a glass of water perhaps. Iced with a slice of lime, if you have it, lemon if needs be.' She let out a little breath that clearly communicated that a lemon slice would be a profound setback.

The Fosters drank their tea, Ava drank her iced water. Vivian was relieved to note that it arrived with a slice of lime; she felt incredibly grateful to the kitchen maid. Mrs Foster and Ava made small talk about the weather and the theatre. The visit was progressing exactly as it ought.

'I went to a variety show last night at the London Opera House. Too amusing for all the wrong reasons. The audience and actors were ghastly. Quite fascinating.'

'Which one?' Mrs Foster had no interest in variety revues, but she understood how important it was to make polite enquiries.

'Do you care? Really?' Ava showed her surprise. It seemed she refused to play the game. 'You'd hate it, Mrs Foster, I assure you. It's called *Come Over Here*. A case of sadly misspent energy. There were some tolerable numbers that almost compensated the patient spectator for sitting through the duller moments of the evening, but.' She stopped emphatically, so sure she had Mrs Foster's understanding and concurrence that she didn't need to continue. 'It was their two hundredth performance. Hard to believe.' She groaned. 'No. I wouldn't bother if I were you.'

Mrs Foster was so astonished by the honesty and confidence of Ava's damning review that the room fell silent. Vivian wondered whether anyone expected her to speak. She could ask if Ava had been to see . . . oh, what was the name of that show Charles Rushmore had recommended? *The Blackest Hour*? *The Darkest Night*? Before she could bring it to mind, Ava took up the mantle again.

'You know they gave each member of the audience this rather strange little jar to commemorate the anniversary. I think I still have it.' She opened her bag and fished for a moment, retrieving a small, delicate, rather pretty glass jar with a silver lid. Vivian was on the verge of admiring it when she noticed Ava's bewildered, slightly mocking expression. Her excitement was ironic. 'I hate this sort of nonsense, don't you, Mrs Foster? Well, you must. Although you have a very young daughter, don't you? Perhaps she might like this. To put her buttons in or what have you.'

'How thoughtful.'

'Nothing.' Ava's expression confirmed she really did think it was nothing.

'Babe will be enchanted,' Vivian ventured.

Mrs Foster shot a glare that was meant to silence her. She wanted Vivian to behave like a Victorian child, seen but not heard; by contrast, Ava looked genuinely delighted.

'Will she? Will she really? I'm glad.'

After twenty minutes, Ava stood up and Vivian's heart sank, certain she was about to leave. She felt abandoned, lost. She wanted to cling to Ava's skirt like a life raft. This last twenty minutes had reminded her how life had been before, and she didn't want to lose it again. However, Ava didn't make her excuses and exit. 'Miss Foster, your garden looks charming; you must have the most frightfully clever man to manage it. Do you? Would you be so kind as to show it to me?'

The Fosters' garden was a modest one, prim and trim, and besides, Ava hadn't so much as glanced out of the window so she couldn't possibly have known if it was charming or not. Still, Vivian jumped up and practically ran to the door, ignoring her mother's calls that she probably needed a shawl and would she like Susan to accompany them.

The air was colourless, ghostly. A flat April day, not one of those boastful ones that offered a cobalt sky and vivid-leaved trees, bursting with bud and promise. There was a disconcerting hint of the bittersweet scent of decaying vegetation. Summer seemed a long way off. It was as though winter would never leave. Ava made an expected comment about the extraordinary selection of perennials in the borders and then immediately lost interest in the garden. Vivian's eyes stayed trained on the long fingers of ivy clasping the wall around the perimeter, clambering and pouring over the top. Momentarily she imagined doing the same – clawing at the wall until she could get a grip and then vaulting right over, escaping. But to where?

'I'm so sorry for your recent disappointment.' Ava's voice was clear and sincere. It was not dripping in pity, or urgent with nosiness. Vivian knew she ought to pretend not to know what was being referred to, but her head ached and she was too weary to feign.

'Thank you.'

'I admit I was surprised by his late U-turn. I thought you had him bagged.'

Vivian was taken aback that Ava had taken any interest what-soever in her romantic life, and simultaneously gratified that she was not alone in feeling astonished. The beautiful and worldly Ava Pondson-Callow thought he had – well – *cared*. She felt a little bit less of a fool.

'Men.' Ava exhaled, and the way she blew out her breath was very articulate. She found them discouraging. Second-rate. The idea that it might be Nathaniel's behaviour that was below par, rather than Vivian's, was refreshing. Although Ava didn't know everything, of course; what would she say if she did? Would she admire Vivian, a minuscule amount, or would she be shocked?

Vivian walked slowly because it took just a matter of minutes to cover the garden but she didn't want to go back inside. They lingered by the bench but neither girl sat; the creeping moss would ruin their clothes.

'Your mother seems disproportionately irritated that your liaison with Mr Thorpe came to nothing. I never guessed she'd be so worried that your heart might be broken.'

'She isn't worried about that.'

Ava glanced at Vivian. Read her in an instant. 'Oh, my good Lord, Vivi. It's your heart *and* hymen, isn't it?'

Vivian loved the way Ava had shortened her name – no one had ever done that before – but she could hardly believe the word she had just used. One that Vivian was only aware of because as a child she used to read her father's encyclopedic books on dull, rainy afternoons, hovering with particular interest over the sections about the human body. 'Do you have to be so biological about the matter?' she gasped.

'Did you have to be so romantic? I suppose you think you're in love with him.'

'At the time I did.'

'But not now?'

'No.'

'Well, that's something.'

'Is it? I'd have thought it was far, far worse.'

'No, much worse to be in love, I should imagine. Much harder.' Ava grinned, then reached into her bag and pulled out a silver cigarette case. She offered Vivian one but Vivian knew her mother would be watching from the window so didn't dare accept. Ava lit her own using a slim, engraved silver lighter. 'You're not pregnant, are you?' she asked as she breathed out the blue smoke into the air.

Vivian blushed. She could not believe Ava had actually said the word! Everyone she knew coyly referred to the state as 'with child' or 'expecting', even when the mother was a respectably married woman. 'No.'

'Well, that's all right then.'

'It's anything but. They are treating me like damaged goods. Practically chaining me to the house whilst they are all running around like headless chickens trying to find me a husband before anyone finds out I'm not a virgin.' Vivian couldn't hide the outrage in her voice.

'Gosh, how boring for you.'

The outrage instantly evaporated; Vivian wanted to laugh for the first time in weeks. Ava had such a perfect way of looking at everything. She seemed to think that perhaps this didn't have to be a tragedy after all. Or even a drama.

'They are trying to guess how much everyone knows. Are people avoiding me because I made a show by pursuing him so ardently, or has . . .' Vivian paused, not sure how to say what she wanted to. 'Or has word of my indiscretion leaked?'

'I haven't heard of it, and I hear absolutely everything.'

'Oh, thank you, Ava.'

'Chin up, darling. I'm sure they'll find you someone top-drawer. You have such a lovely face. Some faces are so hopeless, aren't they? Tight with correctness most of the time and then shockingly they break up into cunning or hatred in an instant. Yours doesn't do that. You are lovely, Vivi.' Ava gazed at Vivian with sincere appreciation and approval, and Vivian began to get a vague whisper of a sense that things could be decent again. She was not always going to be loathed and disappointing.

Flushed with the success of their intimacy, she dared to ask, 'And what about you, Ava? Who shall you have?'

'Not one of them. Not if I can help it.'

After Ava's visit two things occurred to Vivian. The first being that Ava had not asked what *it* was like. She couldn't imagine any virgin passing up the opportunity to glean some information on the mystery of intercourse. She could only surmise that Ava Pondson-Callow had had a lover. Possibly still had. Possibly more than one. The thought was breathtaking. How had she managed it? There was not a hint of scandal or shame about her. Secondly, despite her assurances to the contrary, Ava must have heard rumours about her indiscretion with Nathaniel, because what else, other than a show of solidarity, had motivated her visit? The same thought must have occurred to Mrs Foster too, as she redoubled her efforts to marry off Vivian as swiftly as possible.

MAY 1914

# 8

It was a long and bumpy train ride north, although what third class lacked in the way of comfort was somewhat alleviated by the rowdy, entertaining company. The carriage was packed full of people determined to make the most of their bank holiday. They swore, sang, swapped sandwiches and shared boiled sweets; some of the young men surreptitiously drank bottles of beer, hidden in brown paper bags that fooled no one, especially as the journey progressed and they became more voluble and argumentative.

Howard and some of the lads from the theatre – Jack, Will and Ted – had made a plan to travel to Howard's home village, which was almost as far up the country as Derby, and much further north than any of them had ever travelled before. He'd often talked to them about Blackwell village fair, his mother's baking and the local ale, which he swore every man should try once in his lifetime. Not many of the thesps had any experience of a warm home life and no one had a better idea for a day out, so the suggestion was quickly adopted. Beryl hadn't been invited but she hadn't let that subdue her fervour. She galvanised the chorus girls and in the end a party of nine set off to Blackwell. Beryl had carefully thought through the numbers: the extra girl not only lent respectability to the trip, but she might do for Howard's brother, Michael.

His mother and brother met them at the station. She'd brought a picnic big enough for everyone. It weighed a ton; she'd been baking for four days solid. Howard's brother joked that his arms had stretched two inches carrying the wicker basket as far as the station. The brothers shook hands and beamed. Howard couldn't stop himself: he pulled Michael close and slapped his back.

'You've grown, little brother.'

'Not so little now.'

'No, I think you are nearly as tall as I am.'

'Taller.'

'Oh well, if that's the case, I won't offer you any help with this massive bleedin' picnic basket.'

Michael made as if to jump on his brother, or shove him. Howard deftly dodged. Choreography they'd been practising for years. They grinned at one another. Close. His mother held back until he turned to her. Her arms were rigid at her sides. He knew she'd have wanted to fling them wide and fold him into them, but she was made shy, or at least cautious, by the presence of his London friends. She wouldn't want to make a show of him. He pulled her tight into an embrace. Little Mother. A foot smaller than him now, yet his rock still. She squeezed him tight. Five months since she'd seen him last.

The introductions were hasty, and so many new names were difficult to remember. Mrs Henderson insisted they all dispense with formality. They were to call her Enid. Suddenly she made the decision to reassert her authority and tucked her arm through that of one of the girls. The girl seemed chuffed.

The chatter bounced effervescently between the women, and the men strode ahead, unsettling the dust on the road. Sentences were started but not finished, jokes were cracked and laughter was thrown out almost before the punchlines were delivered, such was everyone's desire to have fun. Howard felt his mother's eyes on him the entire time. He knew she missed him and was drinking him in. He missed her too, but he was young, a man; he knew his place in the world. It was out there. Not back here. Back here was for holidays only. He'd make the most of it. She would too, because it was the only thing to be done.

Flags fluttered. Boom, a drum in the brass band was hit with gusto. Cabs, barouches and chaises brought the middle classes to watch. The working classes got there on their feet; flies on meat couldn't keep them away. A sea of flat caps, bowler hats and wide-brimmed straw hats trimmed with feathers surged towards the jumble of tents and scattered deckchairs. The girls peeled off; it was hot and they wanted ices. Howard stood still and breathed it all in. Deeply. Laughter harmonised with the brass band and the jingle of the carousel. The grass was sweet-smelling, recently cut. It was just like it had always been when he was a boy. Donkey rides, a helter-skelter. Too much choice turned children pale and stupid when faced with the decision of how to spend their penny coins. A tent displaying flower arrangements; another with cakes. Women stood by tense and agitated, desperate to win the silk rosettes. They laughed at their grotesque shapes in the hall of mirrors, the London girls using the opportunity to fish for compliments.

'Don't I look a sight!' cried Beryl. 'Who'd want me?'

'Nothing could make you look ugly, Beryl. Not even a mirror that stretches your neck and shrinks your legs,' replied Jack obligingly. He slid his eyes along the floor and crossed his fingers that Howard hadn't heard him. Howard had, but decided to pretend otherwise. He didn't feel jealous, or even indignant. He didn't want a quarrel. It was too hot for anything other than pleasure. Michael, ever the diplomat, suggested they make a start on the picnic.

Howard's friends lavished compliments on his mam and she, not usually a vain woman, beamed, basking in it. He knew that half her pleasure came from making him happy. The other half from making Michael happy.

ADELE PARKS

After they'd had their fill of tongue sandwiches, pickled eggs and pork pie, they queued to hook-a-duck and then to test their strength by hitting a target with a hammer and hoping to shoot a weight up to the bell. Howard made the bell ring and attracted a crowd of appreciative girls. Both his mother and Beryl noticed the admiring glances and giggles; his mother was proud, his lover peeved. She made a big show of huffing and flouncing off to buy candy floss or a toffee apple; it wasn't a display that revealed any of the skill and subtlety of a trained actress. Her gaggle of girl-friends loyally followed her.

One of the lads had brought a ball and started to kick it around; soon there were over a dozen chasing the leather. Howard decided that would be more fun than trying to turn Beryl's mood. He played for half an hour, worked up a sweat and a thirst, then chose to join his mother, who sat alone on the picnic rug watching the young people play and quarrel. Laugh and lose.

He lay on his back and pulled his cap down over his eyes. It was hot enough. He wanted to take off his shirt but he knew his mother wouldn't like it. She believed that only those who didn't know better did so.

'Is it serious between you and Beryl, Howie? Ought I to be trimming my hat?'

'No, Mam, I'd have come here without her, but she made it difficult to do so.' She clung like a leech. She was so thin, he had this irrational fear that if he left her alone she might blow over, snap. He'd brought her along because she'd have been hurt if he'd not allowed it. He didn't want to hurt her; he pitied her even when she tried to act tough or indifferent, or when she tried to provoke him. Especially then. Women's attempts to capture him slipped off him; men's attempts to buddy up or imitate seemed absurd. He rarely had to try.

'If you are not interested in her then you shouldn't lead her on.' His mother was never one for mincing her words.

He blushed, despite his age and height. He wished his mother wouldn't talk about such things with him. He was always left feeling like a cad, even when he was behaving with the utmost sincerity. It was as though she knew about the bony, uncomfortable sex he and Beryl had started to have. He wanted it, of course – what man didn't want sex? – and Beryl almost insisted on it, but he did feel bad. He knew that she thought of it as some sort of bond, tie. He thought of it as a hobby. He told himself she was doing all right out of the deal. He bought extra coal for her digs (which were as squalid as he'd imagined). He took her out for dinners; had even bought her a new coat. He wanted to be kind. He wanted sex. He didn't love her.

'She's falling in love with you.'

'I think she's tougher than that.'

'You don't understand women.'

'I understand women like her, Mam. It's you who doesn't. You judge her fairly densely protected heart against your own very tender one. Beryl is the sort that does all right.'

'If you say so.'

'I do.'

He could hear that a group of morris dancers had started their performance. He sat up and looked around, spotting them near the carousel.

'I can't take them seriously.'

'I'd have thought you'd have appreciated them more than most. What with your mind that's been made wide and tolerant by your experience in theatre.' His mother threw out a playful grin. He raised an eyebrow at her. 'It's an art form,' she insisted, but her good-natured grin betrayed the fact that she was pulling his leg.

'No, it's not. It's a bunch of men with bells tied to their legs poncing about with handkerchiefs.'

'I blame your father.'

'For morris dancers?'

'No. For your inability to commit.'

'Do you?'

'Yes, well the lack of him, I suppose. You see, if I'd put my mind to it, I could have got myself another husband, but for you and your brother it was different. You couldn't get yourself a replacement. You especially seem to have found it hard, since you had some memories of your dad.'

'Oh, Mam.'

'You've grown up rather wary. Sensitive, you know.'

'It's too nice a day for this sort of talk.'

'You expect the worst of people, Howie. Wait for them to leave.'

'I'm just young. Haven't met the right girl. You worry too much.'

'You'll never fall in love properly, because the moment you're shaking their hand to say hello, you're calculating and predicting a retreat. It's a self-fulfilling prophecy. Very sad.'

He would not have this conversation. 'Do you want candy floss?'

'Go on then, I will.'

He stood up and brushed down his trousers. 'And I'd stay off the cider if I were you.'

'Cheeky beggar.' She beamed at her boy. A man towering over her, a silhouette against the bright afternoon sun. 'I love you, son. I just want you to be happy. That's all any right-thinking mother wants for her children.'

'I am happy. Family, friends, football, fame . . . well, a tiny bit of it. What else could I want? It's all fine, Mam. Honestly. *I'm* fine. You should worry about Michael.'

'Why's that?' His mother's face immediately contracted with concern.

'He's the ugly one,' laughed Howard over his shoulder as he headed off to buy candy floss.

# 9

AFTER ALL, VIVIAN managed to see *The Blackest Night*, the play
that Charles Rushmore had recommended. She thought it
rather good; a tale about treachery, infidelity and disappointment.
Mrs Foster regretted her choice and decided that in future she'd
pay more attention to the reviews before she suggested a jaunt.
She kept Vivian close to her side, not that she was straining at
her chains of ribbon because, as they'd dreaded, society wasn't
particularly abundant; there were no invitations to visit anyone's
box. Vivian spotted two or three of her friends but they didn't
come over to talk. They squeezed out taut smiles and waved their
fans in small, barely detectable movements. By contrast, the young
men of her acquaintance – friends of Nathaniel's – suddenly
seemed audaciously attentive. They raised their brows as she passed
them in the stalls; an invitation? An exclamation? They bowed,
but a little too low, when they approached for conversation. Their
flourishes seemed to have a hint of insolence or expectation.
Vivian was used to men being in awe of her; courteous, beleaguered or distant. Now they seemed familiar, carefree, presumptuous.
It was impossible to ignore the fact that she now carried with
her an air that allowed men to expect something. She wanted to
believe that they were simply thrilled that the object of her
affection had been removed from the game, and they were now

able to court her, but it was hard to believe that was the case when twice someone winked at her, leered almost. Colour flooded through her body; an explosive ball in the pit of her stomach blasted through her entire being. She felt her scalp blush and crawl.

She knew who they would pick out for her. Well, if not who *exactly*, then certainly the sort. He'd be polite, clean fingernails, a neat moustache the length of a toothbrush, possibly stooped, the only son of a vicar or the eldest son of a doctor perhaps. A safe pair of hands. To pick her up and guide her.

She was correct. He was pointed out to her at the interval, the man they thought she ought to marry now. He was at the other end of the foyer, a long, low-ceilinged, poorly ventilated room; the inconvenient red and orange lighting, the heat from the crowds and the cigarette and cigar smoke all conspired to blur her vision as she peered across. He looked isolated. He was standing by a giddy group of young men that, in his lighter moments, her father might call bucks. They were laughing, drinking, slapping one another on the back. It wasn't clear whether he was with them or not. He had oil-sleeked hair; Vivian couldn't help but think of otters, which had never been her sort of animal. His shirt collar was stiff; it wore him rather than him wearing it. He had quite square shoulders and he wasn't small, but was he tall? She supposed he was tallish. Darkish. The ishness was the abounding impression. That was the best she could say.

'What do you think?' Susan asked in a whisper. She was still young and naïve enough to imagine that what Vivian thought might count.

'I'm trying hard not to hate him even before I am introduced,' Vivian mumbled.

'You have met him before, at least twice,' Mrs Foster informed her, ignoring the surly rudeness. Vivian knew this was quite possible; she saw no reason to argue. 'You danced with him last year.'

Something that had obviously left a more enduring impression on him than it had on Vivian.

'He has a tailcoat so you think I ought to marry him,' she wailed.

Mrs Foster took hold of her arm with a grip that was firm enough to be called a pinch. 'He has rather more than that to offer.'

'Has he?' Resentment sharpened her voice. She knew she needed to stay calm and be accommodating, but she resented the fact that her mother might be right. Might have a point. He was to save her even if she didn't wish to be saved. He was her access to adult life; without him, or some man or other, she would be tied to her parents for all her days. There wasn't an independent route. There wasn't an alternative. A poor, beautiful man would have her, but she did not want to be poor. She would not like to be one of those women who had to manage and make do. Their windows were always smutty; they began to dread the sunlight because it showed up their slovenliness and difficult circumstances. She had visited such homes that were not at all quite all. Scuffed wallpaper. The smell of staling cheese drifting from the pantry, through the kitchen, sometimes as far as the dining room. She didn't want to become one of those women whose hands smelt of the washing-up bowl, with weak nails that were forever snapping.

They had told her he was affluent enough. Wealthier than she expected; not the son of a vicar or a doctor. She would never be as rich as she'd hoped, but nor would she struggle. She'd heard all the details about his family. Just two or three generations ago they were simple farmers in the middle of England somewhere. The sort of family Mrs Foster took charity gifts to at Christmas. Not the sort of family she would consider for one of her daughters, no matter how slutty the said daughter had proved to be. However, one of the great-great-uncles had been ambitious and gutsy. He'd emigrated to America to become a pioneer farmer. He'd invested in developing farming equipment and apparently invented a plough with a shiny steel blade that cut far into the dense black sod. This uncle patented the design, then earned a fortune selling his equipment to other farmers; bought more land, sold more ploughs, bought more land. All this activity meant that he never found time to marry and had no one to leave the profits to. When he died, the extensive farm cutting across most of an entire state was split up and sold on (Vivian couldn't quite remember which state, although she was sure they had told her). The money, a sizeable amount, came back to England to be inherited by the grandfather of the man they wanted her to marry. He reinvested in more land, this time English soil, and the subsequent generations concentrated on being respectable.

They'd done a good job. It had been a vertiginous social rise. There was even a title now: Sir Charles and Lady Owens were unquestionably upwardly mobile. Vivian's was an old family on the opposite trajectory; she realised that was limiting. How bad might it be to be married to the man with a head like an otter? Aubrey Owens. She muttered his name. Let her tongue play with it. Being married was a safe place to be. What else could she do? There wasn't a choice. No, there wasn't. If she married, heritage and the rules would shield her. The laws and habits provided a protective shell. Over time she'd be able to tough it out.

'Look sharp, his mother is approaching.'

Thoughts crashed into Vivian's head. Would she like spending time with this woman? Would this woman like her? She couldn't imagine it one way or another, but the mothers made the marriages, the fathers gave their blessing, the young men and women just did as they were told, so she must try.

Astonishing! Lady Owens was wearing a large navy hat with ribbons and ostrich feathers flowing around and over the brim. Her gown was a mass of pleats, frills and pearls. Vivian was not

really able to concentrate on the introductions, she was so fascinated by the intricate, incongruous layers. A hat at the theatre?
How awful. She knew that she really ought to try to impress;
instead she trailed her eyes along the white kid gloves, the small,
practical heel on the shoe, the large, cumbersome bag, taking it
all in. Lady Owens had clearly come straight to the theatre from
afternoon tea; what a mistake. Vivian wondered how her mother
could think this was the family for her. Mrs Foster was normally
so pedantic about etiquette and correctness. This woman was at
best eccentric, at worst boorish. Vivian saw it for what it was. In
an instant she understood how low her mother had had to sink
to find anyone interested in her. Eventually she lifted her eyes
and met Lady Owens' empty, small brown ones, so dense and flat
they looked like burnt currants in a pudding. They flicked over
Vivian for a moment and then away again damningly.

'Good evening, Mrs Foster.'

'Lady Owens.'

'So this is your daughter whom I've heard so much about.'

Mrs Foster swallowed. 'Quite. This is Vivian.'

Lady Owens stared at her for what seemed like a lifetime. 'How
delightful to meet you,' she stated politely, not entirely convin-
cingly. Vivian couldn't help but glance in the direction of the son;
she was wondering whether he'd join them. Lady Owens shook
her head, barely perceptibly, but Vivian understood. Their private
business mustn't be played out here in public. 'I am sure we'll see
one another again soon,' she added. 'I shall look forward to it,'
although her face did not reflect the sentiment in the slightest.

Vivian nodded. 'Good evening.' Lady Owens walked away, quite
hurriedly.

'We must go and call on him tomorrow,' declared Mrs Foster.

'Shouldn't he call on us?'

'Yes, but what should and should not happen is no longer a
matter of pertinence to you, Vivian.'

'I'm not sure I want to marry him, Mother.'

Her mother scowled. 'What is marriage except attaching a secret and exciting someone to one's self in a way that breeds familiarity and domesticity? It buries the very thing that attracted in the first place. It's ruinous whether you love the man or not; best you don't spoil anything you really care about.'

Vivian stared at her mother, surprised. She had never realised she'd suffered so.

The weather was shocking. The sky was grey as a morning coat. The rain plummeted from the heavens, ran along the gutters and cobbles, washing the manure and rats underground. It was difficult to believe it was May.

'It's not a day for visiting,' Vivian commented to her mother.

'No, it's not. Get your coat.'

Vivian was relieved to hear that Sir Charles and Lady Owens did at least have a London house. The address was smart enough; the house was Georgian, built from large white stone blocks. It was ample, dignified and had an impressive pillared porch that she admired. Disappointingly, once inside, Vivian discovered that they were (ill-advisedly) determined to boast their countryside creden-tials. Various parts of animals were attached to the walls or laid on the floors: skins, heads, antlers, foxes' brushes. Entire animals were stuffed and displayed in glass cases and domes: cats, birds, rabbits, a combination of the above. Vivian had seen this sort of thing in plenty of homes, but it never impressed her. She didn't understand it. Nature, by its very definition, ought to be outside, oughtn't it?

Their arrival had to seem a little odd considering the inclement weather, but Mrs Foster made some comment about how tedious it was to stay indoors on such a drab day and her reasoning was greeted with polite acceptance. They were shown into the drawing room. A fire blazed in the hearth, but the place might have benefited from more subtle lighting. As it was, three electric lights glared. Lady Owens saw Vivian glance at the ceiling.

'The gas ones used to give off such a pleasant luminous glow, but Sir Charles is so proud of our early adoption of electricity, he will insist on them being on whenever there is company, despite the women's grumbles about unflattering light.'

They had carpets, too, with a pattern of full-blown pink roses favoured by the nouveau. As someone who had rushed to prove just how modern she was Vivian felt a surprising flush of sympathy for the Owens. She wanted to tell them it was a disastrous thing, being too new.

Instead all she said was, 'It's a very pleasant room, so many interesting things to look at.'

The place was rather packed. The grand piano wore a shawl; it looked like something someone had picked up in an Eastern bazaar. Gilt frames cluttered the walls, drawing attention to average-looking non-descript family portraits. Little tables were covered with ornaments and photographs of men holding awards, medals or fish, as well as some school groups. Not Westminster, Eton or Harrow; a provincial public school. Vivian nodded towards the mantelpiece, which displayed a number of silver sporting trophies. 'How marvellous,' she gushed.

'Aubrey has always been a source of great pride and pleasure.' She heard the warning in Lady Owen's voice and understood the part that wasn't articulated. A pretty girl without a title and from a family of diminishing fortune: was it all they had hoped for? Had they imagined he might have done better? Did they regret that she'd caught his eye and that he was determined to fix upon her?

Aubrey Owens was alerted to their arrival and entered the drawing room with a display of assurance and eagerness. He addressed all his attention towards Mrs Foster, which showed manners but not style. After just fifteen minutes and a bitter coffee, the mothers made excuses to leave; there was a book in the library Lady Owens assured Mrs Foster was worth a look. The door was left ajar. Vivian imagined them hovering in the next room, desperate to put a glass to the wall but not quite daring to.

They were alone together.

It was not the proposal she had imagined. He offered it tentatively. Almost shamefaced. He probably thought it was a no go. How was she to accept when even he didn't think she ought? She supposed he was the sort who expected to hang around long enough to wear one down; if she agreed straight away, as she must, he wouldn't know what to do with himself, what to do with her. He did not expect magnificence and therefore could not be expected to value it when he'd stumbled upon it. Vivian felt a bit sorry for him.

'Yes.'

'You will?'

'I said so, didn't I.'

# AUGUST 1914

# 10

'I THINK IT all went off rather splendidly,' commented Mrs Foster as she lowered herself delicately into the chair. She unpinned her hat and took her heels out of her shoes, although she did not discard them altogether; it would not do if the maid came in to be found in stockinged feet.

'Oh yes,' mumbled Mr Foster. 'Very pleasant.' He sighed and fell into his chair with considerably more heaviness than his wife. 'I can't help thinking this Aubrey fellow isn't especially keen on her.'

'What can you mean? Of course he's keen on her. He's just married her, hasn't he.'

'Evidently.' Mr Foster tapped out his pipe on the heavy glass ashtray. 'But I get the impression he'd be happy enough with whichever pretty girl he married.'

'Well, I think that is splendid of him,' replied Mrs Foster firmly. 'Vivian will have to make do with temperate esteem. Habitual amicability and good manners will see them through.'

'Do you think so?' She knew so but could hardly say as much to the man who'd always believed her affection was particular. 'There were occasions today when I was sure I caught Vivian looking . . .'

'Looking what? I thought she looked incredibly fetching,

particularly as we pulled the entire wedding together – trousseau and gown, et cetera – in just three months. Such a short time frame. Say what you will about Vivian, but she always looks beautiful.'

'Quite, I wasn't implying otherwise.'

'Then what?'

'I thought I caught her looking despairing, even resentful.'

'How careless of her,' snapped Mrs Foster. 'I am the one that is despairing. I sometimes think she hasn't got a clue. Do you know what she asked me last night?'

'What?'

'Whether she ought to tell him.'

'Tell whom what?'

'Tell Aubrey about her . . . infatuation with Nathaniel Thorpe.'

'Good God, did she really?' Mr Foster was surprised by Vivian's impulse to be frank with her husband. Briefly, he rather admired it and felt tender towards her. 'What did you say?'

'Naturally, I told her she's a fool to think of it. That it would undo everything we've achieved. She said that it seems dishonest.'

'Well.'

'I reminded her that she is dishonest.' Mrs Foster looked disgusted for a moment, then her face adjusted. The anger dissipated slightly. 'What he doesn't know can't harm him. Onwards and upwards, I say.'

'I do wonder whether we ought to have tried for that Charlie Rushmore fellow. He seemed quite sweet on her throughout the season. Seems rather a decent chap.'

'I don't doubt he was at one point, but he didn't come forward at the crucial moment.' Mrs Foster stood up and poured herself a glass of sherry; she'd desisted throughout the wedding, but now she felt she needed one, deserved it. She held the decanter up to her husband.

'I'd rather whisky.'

She handed over a large glass of single malt. 'Ava Pondson-Callow volunteering to be bridesmaid was a stroke of luck. She gave the wedding a level of respectability and polish that was notably lacking until then.' The acceptances had rolled in after it was announced that Ava would be the chief of six bridesmaids. 'Very decent of her.'

Mrs Foster had always assumed Ava to be an untethered minx. She seemed to elude parental control; despite a veritable cornucopia of chances, she refused to marry. She was confident, knowing, yet not even a wisp of gossip clung to her, so she was at least careful. Mrs Foster's admiration was grudging but definite. Ava had been surprisingly modest about her own needs as bridesmaid, genuinely quite helpful when it came to picking Vivian's gown. She'd understood that a bridal gown must be designed to set off a bride's beauty and to give her individuality and personality, although not too much of either in this case. It would not do to expose Vivian to a fashion error that might draw ridicule. When Vivian had asked what Ava would wear, Ava had replied, 'Darling, it couldn't matter less. The bridesmaid is merely a lay figure and her gown is created for the sole purpose of providing a satisfactory background. If I chance to look marvellous in the mode you pick, well and good, but it is inconsequential.' Of course she was going to look fabulous in anything they alighted on. 'You will make sure the bridesmaids are clad all alike, though, won't you, Vivi. It's just the proper thing. There is concord and impact in repetition. No one wants a motley array.' Mrs Foster felt for Susan, who looked like a sack of potatoes by comparison to Ava, but Ava had a point: the bridesmaids had to match.

'I suppose Vivian's state of mind might have had something to do with this trouble in Europe,' suggested Mr Foster. He shook his head and his jowls wobbled. 'A bad business.'

'Yes, I expect so. Awful timing, rather stole her thunder. I can't imagine that we're going to get much coverage in the newspapers, not with Germany declaring war on Russia and France.' Mrs Foster heaved a sigh. 'Such a shame when we've pulled it off so well in the end.'

'Yes, most unfortunate timing. It's left me wondering whether her marrying was so essential after all.' Mrs Foster couldn't tell if her husband was being sardonic.

'Oh yes, more so now than ever.'

'How do you make that out?'

'Well, if we do become embroiled in this war, men will be yet thinner on the ground.'

'You astound me, my dear.'

'Do I? That's nice. After all these years.'

# 11

'HOWIE DARLING, HAVE you seen the papers?' Beryl had taken to calling Howard Howie ever since she discovered it was his mother's pet name for him. It rather irritated him. She skipped towards him the moment he entered the theatre. Her richly coloured scarves trailed after her, saffron, scarlet and ochre; it looked as though she was alight. Certainly her eyes sparkled and glittered.

Howard yawned. He'd been kept awake all night by a party in the public house across the street. Several of the customers had taken the King's shilling and then quickly passed it on to the landlord; singing and the sound of breaking glass had kept him from sleep.

'I don't tend to care about anything much before eleven a.m.,' he replied with a studied indifference. It wasn't true: he did care, but he didn't need to read the papers. They had been the same for a week now. The very day after war was announced, Burberry outfitters started advertising the sale of 'complete uniforms', as if the war was nothing more than a fashion statement. There were urgent cries for civilian men to join the army, to show the Germans what they were made of, to show the King devotion; the swell of national pride was enormous. The papers yelled that if the worst came to the worst, they could depend on every last British man.

Nobody had any real idea as to what the worst might be, or if they did, they were quite sensibly keeping their voices low.

Warrington strode on to the stage, his very presence calling for quiet amongst the company. The boards creaked, familiar and reassuring, but he looked unusually sweaty and agitated. Like so many in the streets at the moment, he oozed a potent and peculiar cocktail of exhilaration and anxiety. 'We'll have to start without Jack and Will,' he announced. He didn't sound irritated as he usually was if an actor was tardy.

'Where are they?' asked Beryl. She had been awarded a line at long last and was itching to let it loose.

'Attesting.'

'Attesting?'

'Taking the pledge,' Warrington clarified with an undeniable touch of pride and wild excitement. Beryl still looked a little confused. 'They are volunteering.'

'For the war?' Howard asked.

'Well not the Girl Guides. Of course for the war. They're at the town hall right now.'

'Keen.'

'Why wouldn't they be? We need to teach the Hun a lesson. A short, sharp shock is what's required.'

Howard couldn't help but think that if a short shock was all that was required, it seemed unnecessary for them to be recruiting civilians; didn't the King already have an army? Yet they *were* recruiting. Enthusiastically. It didn't add up.

The rehearsal was not a particularly successful one; no one was thinking about the job in hand. The sound of brass bands could be heard drifting in from the streets; they'd been playing ever since war was declared. Crowds were still cheering and people were prone to burst into song. The strains of 'It's A Long Way To Tipperary' lingered around every street corner, and the air seemed to spark. Everyone was straddled between indignation and excitement, fear and exhilaration. They twitched, putting Howard in mind of the packs of bloodhounds that he had seen tear through the country-side when he was a boy, frenzied and tumultuous.

Warrington understood and dismissed the cast early, telling them that they could go and watch the soldiers march through the streets but they should not get drunk in the public houses. 'Curtain up at seven, war or no war,' he reminded them. Giddy at the thought of time off, the cast scampered out of the theatre without having to be told twice.

'Are you coming?' Beryl asked Howard. She already had her arm linked through those of two other chorus girls, and she threw the request back over her shoulder.

'You go ahead. I have some things to do.' He waved his hand vaguely towards the stage. She shrugged and dashed off, giggling. Howard had the feeling his relationship with Beryl might fizzle out soon, now she had her line. And there was a war. He didn't know exactly how or why a war should affect them, but it was affecting everything and everyone so he was sure their insig-nificant romance, little more than a flirtation of convenience, would not be immune. He imagined something new would attract Beryl's attention – or, more accurately, someone new: a man in a uniform. As he'd expected, he found he did not mind too much.

Howard listened to the girls' chatter and giggles fade. The festive mood hadn't licked him. As he began to pack up his script into his leather satchel, Warrington sat down on the edge of the stage and then eased himself to ground level. He looked older than Howard generally thought him.

'So, what will you do with yourself this afternoon?'

'I'm not sure,' replied Howard.

'Will you go down to the recruiting station?'

'Sorry?'

'Will you be taking the pledge in the town hall?' The question was challenging, almost insolent, as though Warrington already knew the answer, even before Howard did himself.

'Why would I want to do that?' Howard asked slowly. Shafts of sunlight exposed dust dancing in the air between them. It seemed to Howard that the dust was disrespectfully jolly; he'd thought the same about just about everyone and everything since the news broke. Birds still sang, dogs continued to bark, children laughed. Shouldn't it all be significantly different now they were at war?

Warrington stared hard and then commented, 'Well, everyone is.' It didn't seem much of a reason to join an army. Howard realised he must look sceptical because Warrington felt compelled to add, 'War will do you the world of good.'

'And how do you figure that?'

'Every girl loves a soldier.' Warrington winked; he was a little flushed, but it wasn't the red of excitement or even stress. 'I'm too old, they won't take me.'

'You've tried?'

'I have.' Warrington hung his head, and Howard understood the rose in his cheek for what it was: he was shamefaced, not an expression Howard had ever expected his jubilant, resilient actor-manager to wear. 'I envy you.' Warrington was speaking to his shoes. 'I envy you your youth and all the opportunities it's going to bring.'

'You don't have to. I shan't be going.'

Warrington's head snapped up. He held Howard's eye. 'Of course you will. You must.'

'Oh, I don't think it's my sort of thing at all.'

'What isn't?'

'War.'

'But you have to do your bit.'

'Do I?'

'Yes. You can't be seen to be slacking.'

Howard shrugged; surely Warrington knew that he didn't much care for appearances, that he tended to do as he pleased. As he felt right. He lived for his art. He enjoyed his life. Loving women, drinking whisky, exercising his body. He never did anyone any harm, and although he was in what could frequently be a bitchy, ambitious industry, he didn't cheat, lie or discourage his fellow men. He could not understand why someone might want him to pick up a gun and kill someone else. He simply couldn't digest the call. It was out of this world. It was not for him.

'The theatre-going public won't like it,' Warrington pointed out. Howard heard something: a thought, a threat. If he didn't go, he'd never work again. The raging patriotism wouldn't allow for conscience or feeble artisan viewpoints.

He sighed. 'I suppose not, but I really don't fancy killing a man.'

Warrington's eyes fell to Howard's soft white hands – as ever, ink was smeared around his fingernails; he never could shift it – a look that Howard was sure was contempt slipped across his face but was swallowed.

Howard put the strap of his satchel over his shoulder, then turned and walked slowly out of the dark theatre. 'I'll see you later.'

# 12

IT WAS IMPOSSIBLE not to see the outbreak of war on one's wedding day as anything other than an inauspicious omen. It could never be the wedding she'd dreamed of but Vivian had gone out of her way to imbue the occasion with as much good fortune as she could. Her actions were motivated by a mix of superstition and desperation. If only she'd married a week sooner, before the affair of war gathered such incredible momentum, but no, Mrs Foster would have the Monday bank holiday; she'd been determined not to give people the excuse of business for non-attendance. They'd chosen a Monday of course, because of the rhyme: Monday for wealth, Tuesday for health, Wednesday the best day of all, Thursday for crosses, Friday for losses and Saturday no luck at all. Vivian had argued for Wednesday but Mrs Foster had been aghast. 'Who marries midweek?' Vivian thought about the state of the marriages of her mother's friends and had been tempted to comment, 'Far too few,' but she'd bitten down on her tongue.

It had been exhausting trying to load up on the jolly luck and avoid bringing more doom. Vivian had had no idea how many superstitions there were connected with weddings. Everything was accountable: her clothes, the ceremony, the bouquet, even the cake! Of course there was no question that she would bake her own cake or sew her own gown – she had neither the skills nor the interest – but discovering that doing either was considered unlucky was an honourable excuse to avoid all labour. Cook took particular care that no accident befell the cake (which was considered particularly unlucky) and Vivian was sure to cut the first slice herself (lucky!). A blue ribbon was sewn into her hem (lucky!), and a sixpence placed in her shoe (uncomfortable!). She carried azaleas (representing moderation, forbearance and temperance) and white carnations (devotion, pure and ardent love), even though she thought lilies were so much more beautiful and made a bigger statement in a bouquet. Mrs Foster vetoed them on the grounds that they represented youthful innocence, purity and modesty; they couldn't take the risk that anyone might see the irony. Vivian tried not to glance right or left as she was going up the aisle of the church, because apparently to do so meant one of them would shortly go elsewhere for love. She insisted that, immediately after the ceremony, she and Aubrey run out of the church hand in hand; she ignored Mrs Foster's comment that the effect was giddy and ludicrous. Vivian wanted to rush towards happiness. She'd thought August would be providential, as the rhyme promised, 'Married in August's heat and drowse/Lover and friend in your chosen spouse.' She thought that sounded lovely.

In her own, rather immature and illogical way, Vivian had tried. She was not marrying through affection or choice but from necessity; all the more reason for her to work hard at it being a success. However, she rather suspected that all the luck galvanised was cancelled if war was declared on one's wedding day.

It was clear that half the guests had struggled to look up from their newspapers as she'd glided down the aisle. It was a great pity because, despite the scarcity of time she'd had to work with the dressmaker, her gown and veil were show-stopping, although not as show-stopping as the outbreak of war, admittedly. The most fashionable brides of the season had drifted to the altar unhampered by a train. In fact, even skirts had been lifted at least two inches off the ground, and veils, whilst voluminous, were decidedly abbreviated. No bride wanted the stale stately wedding array worn a few years ago. This ellipsis in skirt and veil was the newest note.

A subdued chatter among the guests was usual until the strains of the wedding march began, and upon entering the church vestibule Vivian had waited for the guests to fall silent. She'd expected them to gasp at the sight of her swathed in tulle and promise. They had not obliged. There was a low level of urgent murmuring and it did not cease. The vicar had had to ask for quiet. Twice.

The day had passed in a flash. Vivian couldn't quite catch her breath. The ceremony seemed brisk; soon they were in their carriage, next at the hotel, where wraps were removed and deposited in a dressing room, guests filed past the wedding party shaking hands, shaking heads, murmuring about the war rather than expressing simple wishes for a happy future, as they ought. Vivian had tried to catch Aubrey's eye, tried to talk to him about something other. She'd wanted to be fun and flirtatious with him that day of all days; they hadn't had a chance to develop any level of intimacy or playfulness. When she'd smiled at him, he'd summoned up a grimace that seemed to fall somewhere between an apology and a rebuke. At the wedding breakfast, just before the toasts, he'd sent a boy dashing out for the final edition of the *Standard*.

At least Vivian's wedding would be forever memorable. Coming towards the end of the nuptial season, there had been the fear that it would blur in people's memories, smudge as it amalgamated into a vague collective memory of all the weddings of 1914. Now it was distinct. Vivian's was the one at which people excitedly took bets and talked about how long our plucky pals in Belgium might hold up.

'It's nonsense. Isn't it? Such a fuss?' Vivian had asked her father. He hadn't replied or looked her in the eye, just patted her hand.

Whilst she was changing into her going-away outfit, Aubrey

had knocked at the door and asked permission to enter. The maids giggled and blushed, which caused Aubrey to be awkward too.

'Are you decent?' He kept his eyes on the floor as though fascinated by the grooves carved into the boards by years of tread.

'Absolutely. I'm almost done, just fastening the buttons on my gloves. I can't shock you.' She'd wanted to sound light and humorous but feared she came across irritated and knowing. It had been her turn to blush. Despite having assured him that she was quite proper, despite the fact that she'd shooed away the maids and despite the fact they were legally married, Aubrey did not enter the bedroom and close the door behind him; instead he stood on the threshold, holding the door wide open. Vivian didn't understand why he didn't take the opportunity to sweep her into his arms and kiss her at last. This was her lot so it was not unreasonable that she was a little curious as to how his kisses would be. Their three-month engagement had not afforded a single occasion for them to so much as hold hands. She told herself that it was natural that being alone together, after constant and intense observation, was bound to feel a little uncomfortable. They'd get past that awkwardness; things would get better.

He coughed. 'I'm terribly sorry about the honeymoon. You must be awfully disappointed.'

'Why? What's wrong with the honeymoon?' she asked.

'Well, obviously now that the Germans have invaded Belgium and declared war on the French and Russians, we can't go to Nice.'

'But *we're* not at war. You said yourself, it's all those others.'

'Nice is in France, Vivian.'

'I know that.' That's why she'd wanted to go so badly. 'But the Peterson-Smythes went there just last week. Lots of my friends are there right now.' Everyone who was anyone was on the Riviera, dripping in sunshine and diamonds. She couldn't wait to join them.

'Well, I can only hope they have managed to secure swift passages home. Do let me know if you hear from any of them, if there is anything I can do to help.' What could he do? She'd stared at him blankly. 'I thought we might go to Northumbria for a few days. I have an aunt there who has a marvellous house. Or we could consider going up to Scotland, I suppose, since it's almost the hunting season. I expect I'll get most of my money back from the boat trip, although I don't know about the hotel. Can't imagine holiday refunds are going to be top of the agenda for the French right now. Still, hang the expense.'

'Northumbria?'

'Vivian, we may declare any hour now. You understand that, don't you?'

Declare? War? Britain? How awful. She'd had no idea.

But Northumbria for her honeymoon?

Tears had threatened to show her inanity. Going to Northumbria would be deadly, but she instinctively knew that saying so outright to her new husband would be unpopular. They didn't, as yet, think as one. She'd have to get by as best she could. 'Oughtn't we to stay close by, then? In case there's news. Our families would appreciate that, I think, and besides, I don't believe we ought to inconvenience your aunt, not at a time like this.'

'Well, if you don't mind.' Aubrey had looked pleased with her; noticing as much caused Vivian to admit that it was the first occasion she'd ever felt he was especially so. 'Shall we stay here?'

Here, the place they'd had their wedding breakfast, was a very lovely but modest hotel in Highgate. Mrs Foster had chosen it because of its convenient location to the church and their home. The thought of her mother being a stone's throw away from her on her wedding night sent shudders. 'Let's stay at the Savoy; that way we'll be able to walk to Downing Street and Buckingham Palace if there is news.'

London was usually quiet in August, but on their journey from

Highgate to the Strand the streets had been busier than usual, jam-packed with a definite sense of expectation and animation. Children ran alongside the carriage waving flags that had been hastily bought or dug out of the cupboard, last used at the Coronation. Landlords had draped bunting outside their public houses from one street to the next. It was like New Year's Eve but it wasn't a new year that was coming, it was war.

'How marvellous to be here at this historic moment, something to tell our grandchildren.' She'd linked her arm in his and he'd tentatively patted her finger ends.

'Quite. Quite.'

The bridal suite had been occupied but they'd managed to secure a lavishly furnished room with an en suite that provided constant hot and cold running water. It was not abroad but Vivian was somewhat mollified. They were shown to their room; she noted the twin beds immediately. 'There must be some mistake.' The bellboy looked panicked and confused. He checked the key number and shook his head. Vivian stared pointedly at the twins but he still didn't understand. *She* could hardly request a double bed. She waited for Aubrey to say something discreet and effective. Aubrey coughed. Tipped the bellboy heavily. 'That will be all.'

They'd dined in the River Restaurant. Neither of them had wanted anything heavy, so they chose omelettes, then Vivian had *baisers de Vierge* but Aubrey said he didn't have a sweet tooth; that she should go ahead, if she liked that sort of thing. It was hard to enjoy the meringue with vanilla cream and crystallised white rose and violet petals because eating alone made her feel like a child being treated to an ice at the beach. After just four mouthfuls she put down the spoon. Aubrey signed for the food.

As they walked through the foyer towards their room, he hesitated by the piano. 'You play, don't you?'

'Not well.'

'Oh come, I think all young ladies say as much so that when we hear them we are all the more impressed.'

'Maybe, but I actually am rather hopeless.' Vivian glanced nervously around the foyer. A middle-aged couple had slowed down to eavesdrop on their conversation; they smiled encouragingly.

'Do play,' urged the woman. No doubt she thought she was doing Vivian a favour, allowing her to showcase her talents whilst remaining modest.

Vivian smiled but whispered with insistence, 'Oughtn't we to be getting on? It's been a big day.'

'There's no rush,' replied Aubrey. Vivian felt stung; she believed there should have been. For months she'd tried to block out thoughts of Nathaniel Thorpe. Comparisons were useless and odious, but at that moment it was impossible not to remember his desire, his urgency.

Or then again, his transiency.

Aubrey, she supposed, did not have to hurry. They were married. They had forever. He opened the piano lid and pulled out the small velvet stool. He tapped it with the flat of his palm, indicating that she should sit. By now a small crowd had gathered, expecting to be entertained. What choice did she have? She sat and started to play.

She struggled through 'Persian Garden Tango'. She tried her very best but her fingers didn't cooperate. They were stiff and slow. The polite, unenthusiastic applause condemned her more clearly than even booing could.

'Perhaps I should have gone for "By The Beautiful Sea". It's a catchy little ditty,' she whispered to Aubrey. 'Not too demanding.'

He didn't reply. The tips of his ears were scarlet. The middle-aged lady who had initially encouraged Vivian to perform avoided her eye. Aubrey silently offered his arm and led her away to the lift. She stared at him, willing him to laugh off the embarrassment or to say something charming and comforting. Eventually, as the lift doors closed on the unenthused crowd, he muttered, 'You ought to practise more.'

He walked her to their bedroom door, unlocked it. 'I think I'll smoke my pipe. I'll be back in fifteen minutes. Does that suit?' Vivian nodded, grateful for his discretion; somehow his disappointment in her musical ability had made it intolerable for her to undress in front of him. Even if she'd undressed in the bathroom she wasn't sure how she'd make it from there to her bed.

Alone, she changed into her nightgown and pulled her dressing gown tight around her. Both were white silk and embroidered with small flowers and bees, very pretty. She unpinned her hair and arranged it around her shoulders. She sat on the dressing table stool and wondered where was best for him to find her? Should she stay there, brushing her hair, an artfully arranged tableau? The light was flattering. Or should she sit on the chair near the window? Or perhaps the bed? Which bed, and was it better to be in or on? She sat on the edge of the bed nearest the door, but her shoulders drooped involuntarily and a wave of depression soaked her; it seemed an unnatural place to wait for someone. She slipped between the sheets, but the heat was suffocating. She got out and opened the heavy drapes, then the window, just a fraction. The warm London night and noise fell into the room; she was glad of the company. The nets billowed. She decided to take off the dressing gown and return to bed in just her nightgown.

After thirty-two minutes, Aubrey came into the room.

'Good grief, why aren't the curtains drawn? You have the light on. People will see in.'

'No, they won't, we're the third floor up.' Regardless, he slammed closed the window, shutting out the noise and the air. He drew the curtains, turned out all the lights, except for the one on her bedside, and then went into the bathroom. She listened to him running a basin of water and washing himself. When she'd been alone she'd fingered his toiletries: his toothbrush, the sturdy, almost frightening safety razor and hair oil. They seemed alien on her washstand. They made her nervous. She hadn't gained any warm sense of intimacy from touching his possessions; she'd felt that she was intruding. When he came into the room, she caught a faint whiff of carbolic soap and something spicier, too: gin on his breath.

Shockingly, he was wearing a nightshirt, not pyjamas; she had to suppress her giggles. Then he stunned her by falling to his knees next to the bed near the window and praying. She wondered what she ought to do. Should she get out of her bed and pray too? Would he think it poor form if she didn't? She supposed he might assume she'd already said hers. Which in a sense she had; that morning she'd thanked God for a sunny day.

Eventually he got to his feet, neatly folded his dressing gown and placed it carefully on the chair seat. He then pushed his bed next to hers, managing this without too much effort, and climbed in beside her. She felt him tug at the tightly tucked sheets on his bed and at the ones on hers. It was all horribly fumbling and embarrassing. Why hadn't he simply asked for another room? The mattress dipped slightly under his weight as he rolled closer to her; she tensed her muscles so that she didn't fall on to him and look too forward. He edged towards her and she felt his fingers on the trim of her nightdress. Clumsily he started to drag the material up her legs, the fabric rucking around her knees. She wiggled obligingly; she didn't want it to rip as he tugged it up to her thighs. His fingers brushed against her skin and he pulled away sharply.

'Don't you wear anything under your nightgown?' he asked. She could hear the shock in his voice.

'Well, yes, ordinarily. But tonight . . . I thought . . .' It was too awful to have to explain. She'd wanted to make things easier. He laughed with embarrassment and disapproval; she hadn't known that a laugh could sound so ugly. 'I just thought—' She broke off. She didn't bother to explain, couldn't possibly.

He grunted and put his hand back under the sheet. He was on

his side now, oh, on top of her. She put her lips on his. Gently. His eyes were closed; she wrapped her arms around him. He wiggled, poking around a bit, until he was inside of her. She was relieved. It was so much easier than the last time. He opened his eyes now and stared at her. He was pink; there was a thin line of spittle stretching from his top lip to the bottom. His eyes went dark.

It didn't last long. Three, four, five short thrusts. Could that be all? He disengaged swiftly and rolled back to his own bed, sat on the edge, swiftly placing his feet on the floor. He pulled his nightshirt back down over his legs. With his back still to her he offered, 'You can have the bathroom.'

'I'm fine.'

'You don't need it?'

'No.'

'Then I will use it.'

'Right.'

The moment they'd shared wasn't tremulous or tender; it was awkward and embarrassing. As with Nathaniel, Vivian wasn't sure what it meant at all. No doubt she'd get the hang of it. She would, she supposed. She must.

When he re-emerged, he pulled the beds apart again, then walked around to her side to switch out her bedside light. She lifted her head, but he didn't turn to catch her kiss; it landed on his lobe.

'Good night, Mr Owens.' She waited for him to reply, 'Good night, Mrs Owens,' as tradition commanded.

'Good night, Vivian.' He was asleep almost as soon as the words were out of his mouth. He hadn't caught the joke. Could he have believed she might be so formal as to call him Mr Owens? How mortifying.

Spectacular parties had been held at this hotel. In 1905 an American millionaire, a Mr Kessler if her memory served her correctly, had hosted a gondola party. They'd flooded the central courtyard to a depth of four feet and scenery had been erected around the walls. She remembered her mother cutting out photos from the newspapers and pasting them into her scrapbook; the event was so stupendous, so surprising. The staff as well as the guests had worn costumes and Venice was created there on the Strand. The two dozen guests had dined in an enormous gondola. After dinner, Enrico Caruso had sung, and a baby elephant brought in a five-foot birthday cake. Whenever Vivian had had nightmares as a child, Nanny had always instructed her to think about something nice. She'd always thought about that party, which had earned such prominence in Mother's scrapbook. She'd imagined the frivolity, the glitter, the daring, the laughter. So now that she was sleeping on the actual site, it should have been easy to drift into a pretty fantasy, but honestly, she found it hard to believe there had ever been a moment's merriment in the place.

As she thought back through the day, she realised that for all the lavish clothes and ceremony, she'd felt ignored. She scrabbled about, trying to recall a light moment between the two of them. She'd had good intentions. She was not in love with her husband but she was not in love with anyone else; she'd thought it might work. It was odd, cruel, that she could actually feel her good intentions break down. Shatter. Splinter into nasty shards that flew through her body and lodged painfully. As bitterness. She was on her own. It was too mordant to understand as much on her wedding day, but the fact was she'd never been more alone. A hot tear slipped down the side of her face.

I'm just tired, she told herself. Just tired.

She kept her hands above the sheets. She'd wanted to rub her stomach and lull herself to sleep, but she didn't dare. She didn't think that was an option any more now that she shared a room. It was a girlish thing and she'd have to cast it off.

She felt old.

Alone.

# OCTOBER 1914

# 13

W HILST ALL ACTORS and actresses know the truth and sanctity of the old adage 'the show must go on', the concept had never before been put to such a rigorous test as it was in the late summer and autumn of 1914.

It transpired that Warrington was more enthusiastic about a man's duty than many of London's other actor-managers. In an act of generosity he offered his troupe a pound for joining the army and gave a five-shilling bonus to any of his other employees who took the pledge; he also promised to keep their jobs open for when they returned. Combined with staunch loyalty to King and country, the offer became irresistible. Besides Will and Jack, the Warrington Playhouse gave up two men from the ensemble, four from the orchestra, three stage hands and the boy who sold ices in the interval. The audience cheered enthusiastically when, at the beginning of each performance, as much was communicated. They were politely asked to 'bear with' and think of the boys at Sandhurst going through their paces before they were sent 'over there'. People were patient, forgiving, but no one could pretend standards were being maintained. The company managed with simple piano accompaniment rather than an orchestra but Warrington could not take on *all* the male parts (although he tried), and whilst Howard was adept enough at lighting the set, he could not manage it as well as the scene changes because it was simply not possible to be in two places at once. The actresses pitched in. They wore trousers and drew on moustaches so that they could play male roles; they moved furniture and hoisted the heavy, hot lamps. They all made do.

'Perhaps I ought to write something different,' Howard suggested one evening after a particularly excruciating performance in which Beryl had had to play a lothario, the adversary who was supposed to come between Warrington and the leading lady. It had been impossible to ignore the accidental erotic charge that resulted from the two women kissing on stage.

Warrington sighed. 'Like what?'

'I don't know yet, I'd have to think about it. Something with fewer male roles, obviously.'

'And that's your solution?'

'Or I could set about recruiting some old fellows to help with the scene changes and what have you.'

Warrington flashed Howard a glare that could not be misinterpreted; it was one of loathing and disgust. 'That's you doing your bit for the war effort, is it?'

Howard flushed. It wasn't embarrassment, it was irritation. This wasn't the first time he'd been asked what his contribution was to be. The question had been asked in a hopeful tone back in August and early September; now it was hateful and hounding. Shopkeepers, landlords, women on the bus all felt it was their business. His own brother had just signed up and asked when, not if, Howard planned to attest.

The playwright was not a coward. He believed himself to be as brave and as afraid as the next man. He simply had not been hit by the wave of buoyant patriotism that was sweeping the land; he thought the lads who were signing up were doing so without due thought or understanding. Over and over again he wrestled with the illogical call to arms. If the war was to be over by

116

Christmas as they said, then why was such an enormous disruption thought to be necessary? If it wasn't to be over by Christmas, then what were they all heading into? Did people really want war? Of course he could see the attraction of travelling to the Continent, seeing a bit of the world, but what about when they got there? What then? They'd have to kill, put bullets in men they didn't know and didn't hate. He couldn't imagine it. He wasn't a soldier; his pen was his weapon. He could not say all or any of this to the shopkeepers, landlords or women on the bus. He had started to develop some resilience, an outward show of a thick skin, or at least poor hearing.

'Maybe we could do a stage adaptation of *Little Women*.' Howard didn't much care for the book himself – he found it preachy and obvious – but he thought the mood of the people might mean a stage version would be a big success. It was about devotion, endurance and sacrifice; perhaps people would find it comforting. It would also be easy to cast. He thought Warrington would be enamoured by the idea.

'I don't pay you to rehash. I pay you to create and inspire,' snapped Warrington. 'It's not good enough. *You're* not good enough.' The thought was spat out in heat and frustration but Howard knew it was all the more genuine for that. Warrington wasn't referring to Howard's work; it was more personal than even that. The manager bit down on his lip and let out air through his nose. 'I just don't understand your position.' Howard didn't insult his boss by pretending to mistake what he was talking about. They were no longer discussing his writing. 'The French are picking up arms in their thousands, and the Belgians.' Howard thought this was inevitable; it was their countries that were being threatened. Fear, quite probably, made it easier to hurt. Warrington added, 'We have to do our bit.'

'Those continental chaps have become used to being bossed about. They've been doing national service and what have you for ever.'

'And a good thing too,' Warrington insisted.

'For the army and governments, no doubt, but for the men we're talking about I'm sure it's ghastly. Discipline and training are very contradictory to creativity.'

'You sound soft,' Warrington hissed. This from an actor, a manager of a theatre. If there was no understanding of Howard's viewpoint backstage of a playhouse in the West End of London, how could he expect anyone else to comprehend? He had to tread carefully.

'I do believe that most men have gone to war through a sense of altruism, morality and chivalry. All those motives are commendable. I just wonder how well guided we're being?'

'It's you who is misguided. In just nine weeks nearly half a million men have volunteered.'

'Oh, well, they won't get through all of those; they don't need me.' Howard didn't want to sound sarcastic but he felt backed into a corner.

'How can you think that you are right and they, half a million, are wrong?' Warrington sounded sad. He wanted to continue to like Howard; he doubted he could.

'I just do.' Howard sounded equally regretful. He wished this conversation had never had to happen, though for weeks now he'd known it must.

'Your friends are ready to fight.'

'I see that.'

'I hear your brother has joined up too.'

'More's the pity.'

'Even the clergy are urging us on.'

'Don't you find that odd?'

'You're the odd one.' Warrington's eyes shone with bitter conviction; it looked as though he wanted to cry or hit out. Howard was a disappointment to him. The actor-manager was the closest thing Howard had to a father; he wished he could please him. He couldn't.

'Let's not get worked up. The fact is there seem to be plenty of fellows itching to get over there. They don't *need* me.' Warrington glared; a murderous expression. 'There's a rush of young men who seem all too keen to get their heads blown off.'

'Don't be disrespectful.'

'I'm not trying to be.'

'But your reaction just seems sarcastic.'

'It isn't, it's sincere, although likely to be proven pathetic.' Howard breathed out slowly. 'Do you want to talk about it over a drink?'

Warrington shook his head. 'I have plans tonight.'

Howard was used to being a popular man, the sort people courted and fawned over; he felt the distinct chill of a shunning shoulder.

'I see. Suit yourself.'

Howard didn't much feel like drinking alone, but he most definitely did require a drink. It was late and the pubs were full of those already inebriated; there had been a lot of drinking since the fourth of August across the nation. He could not face heaving pubs, hot bodies and heads. He was not a member of a club but he headed towards St James's, hoping that he might somehow blag his way into Warrington's club; the man on the door might recognise him from the times he'd visited with the famous actor-manager. He yearned for the comfort, calm and indulgence of the Gentlemen's Club. He was steeped in an all-pervasive sense of being uncomfortable and out of step – with his boss, with the mood of the actors, with that of the world. He wanted to sip whisky, let the liquid burn in his gut, numb some of the reasoning in his head.

He strode through the door with an air of authority. 'Evening, Roberts.' He was glad to have remembered the doorman's name; he was good with names, a trick that was part of his extensive charm.

'Good evening, sir.' Roberts was clearly disconcerted that he couldn't repay the compliment and so compensated by making conversation as Howard signed in; an illegible squiggle that couldn't be traced. 'It's quiet tonight, sir.'

'I imagine it is.'

'Many of the gentlemen have already left town to start their training.'

'Indeed.'

Howard picked up a newspaper from the table by the door to signal that the conversation was over and headed to the lounge; he ordered double malt, no water, and sat by the fire. The doorman was correct: the club was noticeably quieter than on any of the previous occasions he'd visited. Some fellow was playing a piano in another room, the tinkling notes drifting through with the soft murmur of the voices of two or three of the older chaps and the clink of ice against glass; there was an absence of raucous laughter or bandying of obnoxious or exciting opinions. The place felt deserted.

'Howard Henderson, isn't it?'

The voice, authoritative with a slight northern twang that made it friendly, was immediately recognisable. He nodded. 'Mr Clarke.'

'Basil, please.' The newspaperman held out his hand for Howard to shake. His grip was firm and brief. Without waiting for an invitation, he sat down opposite Howard. Howard felt uncertain about this intrusion; he couldn't decide if he wanted company or to be left alone. On their last encounter he'd found Clarke a disappointment; he'd been trivial, frivolous and not worthy of his exciting reputation. His conversation starter tonight was predictable too. 'Damned quiet in here.'

'Isn't it.'

'All gone to war.'

'It appears so.'

They fell silent. On their last encounter Howard had been invited here as Warrington's esteemed guest; he'd felt valued, important, admired, although it was awkward to recall that he had cocked up the opportunity somewhat by refusing to go with the flow. Warrington was sure Howard had offended Clarke. Howard thought of the manager's mounting irritation. Was it building towards an outright rejection of him? He had to consider the possibility that his position at the theatre was unsteady. Things were changing fast. He decided he had better make amends with the newspaperman; it was what Warrington would want.

'My manager, Mr Warrington, felt that I'd offended you when we met last.'

'Did he now?'

'You know, because I implied you should be writing something more important than an article about pretty girls.'

'You didn't imply it.'

'Quite, I said it.' Howard sighed, wondering why he had been fool enough to remind Clarke of the incident. 'Offence wasn't my intention.'

'It wasn't the result. You made a valid point. I like a man who knows his mind.' Before Howard could revel in this compliment, Clarke added, 'It was in truth the reality check I needed. I'm off myself tomorrow.'

Howard felt something inside him harden, tense up. He could imagine how this conversation would play out: the man would be overbearing and imperious because he was off to war, or he'd be scared sick but desperate not to show as much. Either way he wouldn't make good company. Yet Warrington wanted him on side. Howard dredged up an expression of interest, forced himself to ask, 'You've joined up?'

'Don't be a damn fool. I have a glass eye.'

'Have you really?'

'Yes. Since I was a child.' Clarke stared at Howard, challenging.

'It's very good.'

'Thank you.' Clarke nodded curtly as though Howard had passed some sort of test. 'So you see, they won't be wanting me.'

'Lucky you.'

'For having a glass eye?'

'Well, yes.' Howard felt a fool but believed it was a piece of luck.

'I've never thought it was so.'

'No, I don't suppose you have.' Howard sipped his whisky, imagining Basil Clarke as a small boy enduring the agony of having a glass eye fitted, dealing with the inevitable teasing and taunting of tactless kids. He knew it would be bad form to pass any comment that hinted at sympathy or understanding; instead he returned to the original line. 'So if not to fight, what are you going to do?'

'I'm going out to report. Got my orders today. I've to try and reach Ostend in Belgium before . . . well, you know.'

'Before it falls.'

'Quite.'

Howard felt an overwhelming sense of relief; he hadn't wanted to hear another man's story of bravery and sacrifice. However, reporting? Well, that was interesting.

Basil opened a packet of cigarettes and offered one to Howard. 'Have to set off at the crack of dawn to try to catch a boat from Dover. Probably should stop drinking since I have such an early start.'

'Oh yes, probably,' Howard agreed, then waved his empty glass at the barman, securing refills for them both. Basil grinned.

'One for the road can't hurt, I suppose.'

Furnished with drinks, the men sat back and prepared to enjoy each other's company. 'What do you expect to see?' Howard asked.

'All there is.'

'We're not being told much. The papers are full of flag-waving and rallying calls, not much else.'

'That's Kitchener's clench. He's strangling reporters. Doesn't like them. We exposed too many of the army's errors in the Boer campaigns.'

'I see.'

'He certainly doesn't want our lads to know what they are rushing at.' It was the first time anyone had expressed a viewpoint that was vaguely in line with Howard's; it was a respite from the endless enthusiastic march towards war.

'Have you met Kitchener?' Howard probed.

'Yes. I have had that dubious pleasure.'

'What did you make of him?'

'Inane and fatuous. I thought him rather stupid.' This view of the Secretary of War distinctly opposed that held by every soul in the street. Howard almost spat out his drink in shock. He appreciated the intimacy and trust implied in the controversial disclosure. Clarke continued, 'As soon as war broke out, I was sent to work at the Press Bureau, met him on my first day.'

'You write for the *Daily Mail*?'

'Quite so. Spend most of my day negotiating with censors rather than writing the news at the moment, though. Amongst ourselves we call it the Suppress Bureau. Terrible place.' He shook his head with impatience. 'Chaos reigns. There can be up to thirty reporters crammed inside its tiny offices at any one time. The entrance is perpetually crowded with messengers waiting to take news back to Fleet Street. I promise you the quality of the news rarely justifies the disagreeable working conditions. But do you know what Kitchener said when he saw the place?'

'No.'

'He pronounced it "very nice indeed". Damned silly comment. Freddie Smith . . . you know?'

'F. E. Smith, the MP?'

'Yes, that's the one. He introduced us.' Howard couldn't help but be a little impressed that Clarke referred to the politician by his first name, suggesting they were intimate; trusted peers. 'Damned strangest thing. Kitchener held his hand out for me to shake, and then, before I could clasp it, he withdrew.'

'Were you going to clasp it?'

'I think that was the question he was asking himself.' Basil grinned and wouldn't say either way. 'In my opinion the amount of news issued to the press about this war is the smallest, its value the poorest.'

'I too have had the sense that reading the papers amounts to little more than reading a government press release,' admitted Howard.

'Quite so!' Clarke smiled broadly. 'I can't wait to find out what is really going on.'

'I envy you.'

'Want to see a bit of action, do you, like the rest of them?'

'It's not that.'

'Medical grounds, is it? Have you been turned down and you're feeling the sting?' Clarke took a drag on his cigarette and his eyes flicked around the room. He thought he had Howard pegged.

'I haven't volunteered.'

'Really?' Clarke's eyes returned to Howard's face and searched him, but the comment was made without censure or shock.

'I'm not sure of the value of this war. Of any war,' Howard explained, then let an exasperated sigh fall. 'But I don't know. Maybe they are all right and I'm wrong.' Was it the drink that was causing him to waver? Or the thought of Warrington's hurt and disgust? The threat of possible unemployment? He stubbed out his cigarette, irritated with himself. 'Of course I can't know for sure what it's all about unless I'm out there, and that seems quite a risk. I could go to war and find that I've been right all along, that it is a travesty. However, I would love to know one way or the other. That's why I say I envy you. You'll get to find out all about it.' Of course he was curious; more than that, he was fascinated.

'Come with me.'

Howard did not comprehend the invitation for a moment; the offer made little sense. 'To Ostend?'

'Yes.'

'That's impossible.'

'Why?'

'Well, I'm not a soldier. I told you I haven't attested. I have no intention of joining up.'

'You are a writer, aren't you?'

'Yes, of course.'

'Well, come and write, as I am.'

'I'm not a newspaperman.'

Clarke shrugged as if this fact was neither here nor there. 'Don't you see? This war is *it*. This is our generation's moment. You can't sit on your backside, at home by the fire. You can't miss it. You could write a play about it all.' Howard accepted that that much was true. Clarke added, 'I'd like the company.' This confession sounded singularly honest. 'I think you are the very man to join me.'

'You do?'

'Yes.' Howard couldn't think how Clarke had come to this conclusion but felt flattered. He seemed determined to persuade. 'Do you know how I became a journalist?'

'No.'

'After a chance encounter in a hotel where I joined in singing with some strangers as the fourth voice in a Gilbert and Sullivan quartet. We got along and so on, the way sometimes it happens. One of them invited me to write an article on musical appreciation for the *Evening Gazette* in Manchester. I didn't have a career to speak of but I had a wife and a family. I took the opportunity. Grasped it with both hands.'

'You think our meeting is such an opportunity for me. You are drawing a parallel.'

'Damn right I am, boy. You'd be mad to miss it.'

'I have no money.'

'I have.' Clarke reached into his briefcase and pulled out a bag of coins as though he was a character from a fairy tale producing a magic spinning wheel or a poisoned apple. The coins jingled against one another. 'They gave me one hundred gold sovereigns for expenses – you know, bribes and such.' He chuckled at the absurdity. 'There isn't time to get home to Manchester to kiss the wife but they handed me this. I'll be going to war in a bowler hat. It's all rather odd, don't you think?'

'I do. Seems a little seat-of-the-pants,' commented Howard.

'Isn't the whole damn war?'

'Yes, I fear it is.'

'Shall we go and find out together?' Clarke beamed, a glint of mischievous goading flickering across his face. Howard was tempted to answer the challenge.

Clarke's expression was intelligent and yet accepting, a rare combination and certainly not one Howard had been on the receiving end of since the war broke out and he'd refused to join up. He thought again of Warrington's fury. If this war continued, his popularity as a writer would wane; people wouldn't come to see a show written by a man who refused to fight. He'd lose his job for sure. It was only a matter of time. He and Beryl, whatever they'd had, had petered out. She was writing to Jack, who was already in France. He had heard that she'd sent her worn stockings, a photo and cigarettes. If he went out there then he would know, know for sure, what it was about. What was right and wrong. He was an artist and should know humanity at its best and worst, if he was to write with any truth and conviction. There was nothing to keep him here.

He would go. 'All right.'

'That's the ticket.'

# 14

'WILL YOU JOIN up?' Vivian had asked as soon as Britain declared war.

'Of course, no question. I feel I ought, that I might as well.' He had not reflected for a moment how such a declaration sounded to his wife of a single day. He'd shrugged and added, 'Everyone is.'

'Absolutely, you must do your duty.' She'd smiled, patriotism first.

A few days later he'd commented, 'Some women are extremely angry with their husbands for signing up, I hear.'

'Are they? How selfish.'

'You'd be proud if I went?'

'Of course.' And she would be no less alone with him gone. Thoughtlessly she'd asked, 'Do you think you'll pass the medical?'

He'd looked shocked. 'Absolutely, why wouldn't I?'

'You read such a lot. Your eyesight . . .' She'd trailed off, not sure how to express herself delicately. She somehow intrinsically associated Aubrey with disappointment. It would be dreadfully shaming if he didn't get in.

'I was in the Officers' Training Corps at school, you know.' She had not known that. She knew very little about him. She did know of the Officers' Training Corps, though, because her younger brother Toby was desperate to join as soon as he was old enough. All boys wanted to play at being soldiers, naturally. 'The headmaster told us on Speech Day that "If a man can't serve his country, he's better dead",' added Aubrey firmly.

'The matter is unequivocal, then.' Men held much store by what they were told as boys at school. Women didn't have an equivalent guiding force.

'Yes.' Aubrey had glanced at her, and for a moment she'd almost thought there was something in his face that was willing her to contradict him, ask him to stay by her side, but she must have been mistaken; why would he want her to contradict him? Could he want to hear that she needed him? Or that she'd miss him? It was impossible. She turned the conversation. 'I bought a new bag. It's navy moiré with a velvet drawstring and is decorated with orange roses. It's quite divine. I'm not sure when I'll use it.'

Their life, the house, was exactly as her mother had hoped it would be, as society thought it ought to be and she'd feared it might be. It turned out she'd married without the least idea about anything. Of course no one ever realised they were clueless – by the very nature of being so – until it was too late. She thought perhaps all the time invested in her deportment lessons and art classes might have been better spent; retrospectively she didn't believe it was any sort of preparation for married life.

They'd moved in with Aubrey's parents. He stated it was just a temporary arrangement, until after Christmas, when all this war business was behind them. His father was a shadowy figure who spent most of his time at his club; left alone together, his mother and Vivian performed a wary, polite dance around one another. There was no natural affection or common ground between them as there had been between her and Lady Thorpe; they were each grateful when the other was occupied. It was rather a shame. Vivian wished her mother-in-law would take her under her wing, tutor her, fill in the yawning gaps. The position of mother figure was eternally open in her life. She had no idea what things cost, or how to behave with the servants or neighbours; her sewing was basic, her ability to balance accounts questionable. Where did one buy curtains? She had no idea how to *be*, either alone or with him. She was a wife, but what did that mean?

People expected things from her. Well, they would: invitations, dinners, visiting cards and such. Her mother visited once a week; she always brought a friend and never stayed longer than thirty minutes. She usually timed her visits to coincide with when Lady Owens was out, insisting she didn't want to intrude. Vivian suspected she also found Aubrey's mother distant and dull. If probed, Mrs Foster would tell Vivian which invitations she should accept and which she should issue. She wouldn't suggest menus but she did glance over seating plans. She never repeated herself and her visits often felt like extremely efficient church meetings. Mr Foster and Vivian nodded at one another over coiffured heads at the theatre and opera.

A lot of the time Vivian felt overwhelmed and lost. Her world was insincere. She rarely said what she thought or felt, and as the practice had dwindled, she found that the ability to even know what she was thinking and feeling was dwindling too.

They'd cast her adrift without giving her a lifebuoy or even a whistle. It was clear: she'd made her bed and must lie on it. She could not expect them to be running to her every five minutes. Susan needed supervision. Toby and Babe still required care. Mrs Foster assured her that she would manage. She'd have to. 'Remember, the marriage is a success. After all, you are invited to suppers and dinners, to the theatre and balls.' Mr and Mrs Owens, son and daughter-in-law to Sir Charles and Lady Owens, were welcome in society in a way that a disgraced Miss Foster could never have been.

Timidly, Vivian explored the house. The clutter and enthusiasm for taxidermy was off-putting but on the whole the rooms were comfortably proportioned, the furniture good quality, although heavy and too dark for her tastes. Besides the drawing room, there was a morning room, a dining room, a library, a study and six bedrooms (Aubrey's parents occupied two, and another was kept for his older sister; when she, her husband and children visited, the nursery was dusted off as well). There was an en suite to their bedroom as well as another bathroom and two indoor lavatories. Vivian twice visited the kitchen and the rooms off the kitchen to introduce herself to the servants.

She wandered around the house trying to find somewhere of her own. Certainly that room was not the drawing room. Even if she could get used to the plethora of beady dead eyes staring at her from all directions, it unequivocally belonged to her mother-in-law. The study was out of the question, its masculinity unmistakable and explicit; it oozed the smell of dusty files, pipe smoke and alcohol. She supposed it ought to be the morning room – that was where she entertained – but the chimneypiece was of mean proportions and she found the dark green walls cold and unwelcoming; she pitied her visitors. The hearth in the library was enormous and she sat in there most often, although she couldn't imagine anyone would think that a library could be called her natural home. Books gleamed on the shelves; fine stripes of leafing held between leather. The firelight leapt at them and flashed around the room. It was pretty enough, although on her first visit she'd ascertained that there was nothing to entertain her. She found dusty French, German and Latin books that made her think how close the word tome was to tomb, and skipped past those; her schoolgirl French was adequate enough to allow her to swap pleasantries in a drawing room if called upon (she never was), but not much else. 'Where are the novels?' she'd asked Aubrey.

'There are none.' She wished he hadn't sounded quite so satisfied.

'Why not?'

'There are memoirs, essays and reference books.'

'But . . .' The word came out like the *phut* of a kiss. She didn't finish the sentence. *But what am I to read?* He understood anyway.

'I find studying an atlas can be edifying.'

How? She considered the fact that she should have been pleased that he understood her so well − wasn't that what every new bride wanted from her husband, total comprehension? − but she wasn't. She was embarrassed and frustrated. Moreover, she'd spent the last three months squashed between the two emotions. Despite the smart postcode she did not feel well off; the comfortable rooms did not put her at ease. She doubted she'd ever feel cosy in her marriage. Restful or secure with her husband. The number, bulk and value of the lavish pieces of wooden furniture seemed to bloat around them, locking them in. Overpowering them. Any potential affection between the young couple was subdued by the constant parental surveillance, suffocated by the thick smell of furniture polish that saturated the rooms. The dark walls moved closer every night; soon they would squeeze the life out of her.

As a wedding gift Aubrey had bought her a pianoforte. Every evening, with irritating regularity, he said the same thing to her: 'Play something for me.' She resented his request; she saw it as an order. Her mother used to instruct her to play the piano too; she was not a child any longer who needed to practise her scales.

Once, she'd dared reply, 'I'm not in the mood.'

'Oh, but I am,' Aubrey had replied cheerfully, assuming that his will would dominate, his will *mattered*. She'd sighed; he was right. How was it that she had swapped one form of incarceration for another? She must now do his bidding as she had done her mother's. She'd stood up and moved towards the piano, started to play. The instrument trembled as she'd drummed the keyboard. Too robust to be thought of as skilful by even the most generous of critics, which she already knew Aubrey was not. Vigorous, vulgar sounds filled the room. Banged from one side to the next. The

Rex Begonias and ferns quivered in their china pots, the beads on the overmantel juddered; she imagined even the miniature portraits clapped against the walls. She'd thought if she played badly enough, too awfully, he'd stop asking. She'd been wrong about that. Her appalling performance somehow only strengthened his conviction that she needed to practise.

On Saturday evenings, after the parties or dinners or theatre, he claimed his marital right. It was conventional, organised, repet-itive, commonplace intercourse. She thought it had an air of smugness.

It was oppressive.

It sickened her.

She wondered when he would be called up.

Aubrey's experience with the OTC had stood him in good stead, and it was a huge relief when he obtained a commission with the 10th Sherwood Foresters, a regiment that had some connection to his old school. She joked that it sounded awfully good fun and called him Robin Hood.

'I shan't be robbing from the rich to give to the poor, though,' he said, trying and failing not to betray his irritation.

'No, but you'll be taking back Belgium and France and returning the lands to their rightful owners.'

'Quite so.'

She had to admit that she found Aubrey in uniform infinitely more pleasing than simply Aubrey. The smart stiffness of his costume negated some of the 'ishness' that she believed he perpetually carried around with him. He looked a little firmer, and less like an outsider. However, whilst they had issued him with a uniform, they had not issued orders. She found this odd. She had started to follow the progress of the war in the newspaper (everyone did; it was *de rigueur*, much more exciting than the latest opera or restaurant). There had already been some terrible battles. Marne and Ypres or somewhere (she was not certain how to pronounce such a foreign word). Absolutely everyone was involved. Naturally the outposts of the Empire had proudly stood up; Australia, Canada, New Zealand, India and South Africa were all doing the right thing, doing their bit. She had look at the damned atlases and actually it was quite cheering. Those countries were enormous. Even the Japanese had declared war on Germany, which was awfully good of them because Vivian didn't think the British had ever owned Japan or even settled there. Then the Turks threw their lot in with the Germans. She couldn't understand why they'd chosen to join the losing side but she tried not to be agitated by the fact; who cared about them anyway? The war was spreading at a rate of knots. Recruitment drives were urging the brave young men to join up immediately, which they were, in their thousands. Vivian would have thought they'd need to be training the officers as a matter of urgency, because who was going to lead these men? Who was in charge? It seemed silly, Aubrey sitting around the house all day in his smart uniform; it was rather embarrassing. It would be awful if he missed it. However, she had to be careful, because saying so seemed to offend him. He was easily offended, which in turn irritated her. She didn't think being overly sensitive was an attractive quality in a man.

'When will you go?' she asked, exasperated.

'It sounds like you can't wait to be rid of me.' He pulled his face into something that approximated a jokey smile. Neither of them was convinced.

'Don't be silly.' She wished she sounded more sincere, but she did want rid of him. She wanted his pipe smoke out of the drawing room, she wanted his peculiar odours out of the bathroom, she wanted his body out of her bed. She supposed she wanted his maleness out of the way. Most of all, she wanted his quiet disappointment to be gone. She was so lonely, she thought it could only be made better if she was alone.

'I'll go as soon as I can.' He went back to puffing at his pipe, clenched between his teeth, occasionally yawning or stretching his mouth, creating a sighing sound.

Finally he received orders to start training; after a slow start, they were all rushing. He had been told he must leave the day after tomorrow. He couldn't tell her where he was going. She didn't really mind that he couldn't. It didn't feel like any of her business, and she didn't know how to make it so; war was for men. The servants thought she was brave and stoic, the very model of an officer's wife. His mother glared at her, perhaps reading her cool, calm heart. Vivian thought her mother-in-law would prefer it if she was more overwrought and girlish. It would either show that she loved her son deeply or it would prove the point that Vivian was, after all, rather hysterical. Irrationally, Vivian behaving well seemed to annoy Lady Owens, although Aubrey approved. He was most comfortable when she spoke little and acted with proper care, when she made herself as small as possible. Still, she felt guilty that she didn't feel more distress about his imminent departure.

Her husband had no war experience, of course; his superior rank came from the fact that he could afford to keep a horse. How else could they arrange the war? No one could expect that all sorts of men muddle in together. She was glad he was to take his horse. She'd always been a bit afraid of the animal, so powerful and sleek, but Aubrey suited him; he looked most complete when he was riding. That was certainly when he was at his most likeable. When she'd watched him as he galloped through Hyde Park, she'd thought he was almost attractive; at least from a distance.

Men were already dying, and although it was unlikely that Aubrey would actually see any action – by the time he finished his training the war would probably be over – she still saw her way to indicating that marital relations were not out of the question, even though it was a Wednesday not a Saturday. She did this by putting on a silk trousseau nightdress, rather than a cotton weekday one. If he noticed, he did not act on the invitation.

'Busy day for all tomorrow,' he commented as they lay side by side but separate in bed.

'For you especially.'

'I can only pack the regulation. You have much more to do.' She looked at him quizzically. 'Of course I'm not suggesting you'll need to get it all done tomorrow. No one can expect you to pack up completely in a day. You might need a week.'

'Pack up? What are you talking about?'

'My parents are giving up the house.'

'Sorry?'

'Our London house. It's all my idea. I told them I shouldn't wonder if the War Office couldn't use it.' He continued to puff on his pipe. She did wish he wouldn't bring that damned thing to bed. 'I thought Mother might have mentioned it to you.' It dawned on her exactly what he was suggesting. She had to suppress her panic, remembering that Aubrey didn't like a scene.

'I can't imagine that's necessary. Has anyone asked?'

'Not yet.'

'Where will I live?'

'There are options. Our country house?' Aubrey's family had a home in a village called Blackwell. She'd once located it on a map. It was rather far up the country and she'd never had a desire to visit, let alone live there. The suggestion was barbaric. She stared at him, stunned. 'Or you could go with my parents. They are moving to Wales to be near my sister.' Hilarious.

'No. I want to stay here in London. I could keep the house open.'

Calmly he asserted, 'I can't leave you alone here in London. It's not seemly or economic. It's too big a house to run for one. I suppose you could move back in with your parents.'

She scowled. It was insufferable. As impersonal and impregnable as she'd found this place over the last few months, she had accepted it as her home. It had given her some sort of status. Her friends had been able to call. The married girls were envious of the small garden and the telephone; the single girls were green that she sometimes got to choose when and what to take for lunch. She would not move back to her parents. She could not.

This flamboyant gesture to volunteer their home undoubtedly sprang from extreme devotion to the Crown, but she could not think it was necessary. She scrambled around for a compromise that might save her. 'Couldn't we give up the country house for the war effort?'

'Who would want it?' Who indeed. 'No, the government need buildings in London, if anything.'

'What for?'

'Secret meetings, housing important Allied refugees, all sorts of things you wouldn't understand.' Then, as though to make it easier for her small mind, he added, 'Hospitals. Orphanages.'

'It won't come to that,' she snapped. 'It will all be over before we know it, and imagine the upheaval, the expense.'

'I think it will last rather longer than we initially thought. Anyway, that's beside the point. Whether or not the War Office wants the place, if you go to Blackwell you could grow food on the estate. Turn up the flower beds. Our land could be useful to the war effort.'

He was so damned enthusiastic. So unequivocally partisan. She felt he was behaving like an eager Boy Scout, far too keen to shoot and skin a rabbit even though there were sandwiches to eat.

'What's it like? Your country house?'

'Modest.' What a glum word. 'My grandfather had it built. He never liked London. Always preferred the simpler things in life, even after the money came through thick and fast.' Vivian blushed for Aubrey for mentioning the newness of his wealth. A grandfather inheriting was not something one wanted to shout about. 'There's lots of land to farm. I haven't ever done much with it, but I always knew I would go back there one day. There are tenants and groundsmen and so on managing things. Mostly flowers, fruit. I think there are sheep. We used to visit as children. I do remember enjoying a game of rugger on the green, a swim in the lake. I'm sure you'll find it comfortable. Charming.'

Vivian imagined his long-dead grandfather clad in a lavender-grey frock coat and a top hat, the very epitome of the confident patriarch (that much could be gathered simply by the way his waistcoat stretched across his big belly, chased by his watch and chain). His white beard would have always been neatly trimmed, the long sideburns offering adequate compensation for his bald head. She hated him. Just hated him for ever thinking of a country retreat.

# 15

HOWARD AND CLARKE set off for Dover on the earliest train. It was still dark – even the birds were silent – but when they arrived they were told that no more boats were setting sail for Belgium. They were both momentarily taken aback; the dangers and inconvenience of war suddenly seemed significantly closer than they had done backstage at Warrington's or in the crowded Press Bureau, when everything was theoretical. Determined, they took a cab to Folkestone to see if they'd have more luck from there. As they waited, boatloads of Belgian refugees docked and descended. Frightened, tired bodies that needed a good bath and were embarrassed by the fact flooded into the country. Basil spoke to some of them and soon learnt that they had come from Ostend and that the Germans had already taken the city. They were too late. A blanket of frustration and depression visibly cloaked Clarke.

'What shall we do?' Howard asked. They sat in a tea shop, cigarette smoke and the steam from the huge metal urns drifting around the room like ghosts.

'Well, my news editor's instructions are now impossible to complete,' Clarke stated flatly. This was a disaster.

'I suppose the obvious course of action is to return to the office.'

'Yes.'

Neither of them could accept that they might do so. Howard fingered his note book; he'd been jotting down his thoughts and observations all morning. Impetuous and reckless, Howard added, 'I want to see the war.'

'Yes, me too.' Clarke smiled at his co-conspirator.

They took a steamer to Calais. Clarke thought that he might be able to retrospectively justify his decision if he could send news back from the Front; the sort of stories that got to the heat and heart. The sort that the British public needed and were being denied. Neither man had the correct paperwork, and whilst they didn't articulate the possibility, they were both aware that they might arrive in France and be put straight back on a boat. The bag of sovereigns would come in useful in persuading the door-keepers to look the other way, but it was a risk.

Once they docked at Calais, they visited the British Consulate even before they took a hotel. It was a large grey building that once might have looked authoritative and austere; in the midst of war it was impossible to ignore the ambience of alarm and dread that had invaded it. The place seemed to quiver uncertainly. Howard and Clarke were categorically refused the necessary permit that would give them access to the Front; they were instructed not to leave the town unless it was to return to England. Howard was impressed that Clarke barely broke his stride; he had expected to draw a blank at the consulate and seemed undaunted. He tipped his hat politely and headed across the road to approach the French officials. They also refused to provide a 'laissez-passer'; again Howard wondered if his adventure was to be abruptly brought to a halt. He considered how slim his chances of returning to Warrington's Playhouse were exactly. Less than a sliver. His boss would have found his note of resignation by now. Clarke tutted at him for mooting the thought.

'Damned inconvenient, obviously. I'm rather more used to being helped to do my job than hindered – that's the privilege of the press – but I've no intention of giving up now at the very outset of what will no doubt be the greatest journalistic adventure of my life.' He sniffed the air. He seemed not to notice the tang of the sea, or even the odour of the manure left by the horse-drawn carts frantically moving soldiers, civilians and weaponry; it was the story he could smell. Determined to evade what he saw as the unyielding obstinacy of officialdom, he adjusted his bowler hat, straightened his shoulders and declared, 'Let's go to the station.'

'It's guarded by soldiers with bayonets. I've already checked.'

'Then we'll walk.'

'Where to?'

'To Dunkirk. That will make a decent base. Very close to the action and easy enough to get copy back to England from there, I should imagine.'

'Dunkirk is almost thirty miles away.'

'I thought you liked a walk.' Howard had mentioned as much, the night before in the club. He laughed, unable to be anything other than impressed by Clarke's tenacity. Once again they picked up their small, hastily packed suitcases and set off.

After a mile or so, Howard's shoes began to rub painfully but he didn't mention it, and nor did Clarke say whether he felt the pace Howard set was too demanding. Both men maintained a breezy manner. Clarke talked more; he had recently returned from extensive travels in Canada and had endless entertaining tales to share, but ever the journalist, he took the opportunity to quiz Howard about his life.

At times they were quiet, just one foot in front of the other. Plodding on.

Luckily, just three miles into their journey they were able to cadge a lift for fourteen miles, then they walked another seven. Still some miles before they reached Dunkirk they came to a checkpoint. The soldier refused to let them pass. For the first time

Howard saw dejection and exhaustion creep into Clarke's face. He dug out his handkerchief and mopped his brow.

Howard realised it was his turn to offer fire and motivation. 'I saw a roadside café not more than a few hundred yards back. Let's go and get a cuppa.'

In the hot and heaving café, Howard queued for refreshments whilst Clarke searched for a seat. The place was throbbing with soldiers, some British, some French, all young. By the time Howard was served with two cups of strong black coffee (there was no tea), Clarke seemed somewhat recovered. He had found a seat and struck up a conversation with a French soldier who, before war had been declared, had worked as a printer on a French newspaper. The soldier evidently remembered reading Clarke's work and treated him as though he were a celebrity. Clarke wasted no time in explaining what he was hoping to achieve. 'We have to get to Dunkirk. Can you help?'

The soldier looked excited at the opportunity, challenged rather than daunted. 'I am shortly leaving on a train that will stop at Dunkirk. I can help you get on that train.' Howard was impressed by his English and his willingness to defy the rules. He was cocky and credible all at once. Howard hoped he would survive the war. 'Go to the station,' the soldier instructed.

'The station is guarded,' Howard pointed out, confused as to what his plan was exactly, although willing enough to go along with it. He knew they were placing themselves in physical danger, but neither of them was overly concerned. The people back in England thought he was a coward because he wouldn't join up; it wasn't that at all. He simply didn't see the point of war, but he did see the point in investigating exactly what was going on out here in France; that goal was worth taking a risk for.

'Just go there.'

When Clarke and Howard arrived at the station, they found the restaurant door unguarded and were able to walk straight through the restaurant on to the platform, where they found the young soldier waiting for them.

They squeezed on to the train, which was packed with French soldiers, chattering, laughing and quarrelling loudly. The soldiers all smoked, and if they could carve out even a foot of space, they played cards for centimes. No one asked Howard or Clarke for their papers.

The two men stood with their noses pushed against the window and observed as trains crammed with refugees from Belgium sped past them, heading in the opposite direction. Some of the trains were so overcrowded that men lay clinging on the roofs; at one station an unconscious woman was offloaded and left on the platform. Howard caught Clarke's eye but said nothing.

Clarke nodded understanding. It was, to say the very least, disconcerting. 'It seems that all of Belgium is pouring into France. I feel like a salmon swimming upstream.'

When the train ground to a halt just outside Dunkirk station, they decided to disembark in the hope of avoiding the guards at the turnstiles. They bid a grateful goodbye to the soldier who had helped them, then, holding their suitcases above their heads, they inched their way through the tight throng to the door. It was dark when they jumped down on to the track. In silence, as there was no need for discussion, they scrambled up the bank. As they rubbed the mud from the knees of their trousers, they noticed that they had been spotted; an armed soldier was watching them, though he did not call out to them. They took their chance and dashed towards the main hall but could not get out of the station; again it was guarded. The two men exchanged a glance that confirmed they each thought arrest or deportation was imminent.

'There's a refreshment buffet,' pointed out Howard.

'Is food all you ever think about?' asked Clarke, but not with any sharpness. He too saw the sense in delaying facing the officials, and if they were doomed to spend the night in jail before they were deported, then it made far more sense to do so on a full stomach.

As they tucked in to a passable beef bourguignon, a train full of Belgian refugees arrived. They were made to disembark suddenly, and confusion rained down on the station. Men shouted, babies cried, women scolded their children as exhaustion and fear ate away any residual patience they might once have had. 'This could be a stroke of luck,' Clarke commented, a born opportunist. He dabbed his mouth and then threw the napkin on the table, eyes alert for their chance. Howard mopped up the gravy that remained on his plate with the crusty bread roll and pushed the last morsel of food down his throat before he turned to monitor the scene. They stared as hundreds of people, who all seemed desperate to get a train to Calais, filled the platform and then spilt into the station and even the buffet room. Like the refugees they had seen clinging to the train roofs or pouring on to the dock at Folkestone, these people were frantic, wide-eyed with pain and panic. It made them argumentative and selfish. They were distraught, disgusted to hear the station official announce, 'There are no more trains tonight. Tomorrow perhaps.'

The crowd began to groan, their reaction gathering momentum and becoming a low grumble that somehow threatened unpredictable, possibly dangerous behaviour. Then someone heard someone else say that they had heard there were no vacant rooms left in all of Dunkirk for that night. The rumour swept like fire catching dry grass. Hungry, homeless, hopeless, the news of the accommodation shortage caused a violent rush towards the station door. Howard and Clarke were on their feet in an instant, seeing the possibility of surging through the doors with the mass. People pushed and shoved, careless of who they stood upon. Howard felt irritated at their selfishness but not shocked; he had seen crowds trample one another for a decent seat in the stalls, he knew there would be no scruples among desperate refugees. He was a tall man and had an advantage over most. He saw a woman with two small children lose her footing; luckily she could not fall completely because the crowd was so densely packed, but she lost her grip on her daughter's hand.

'I've got her,' he told her. He lifted the small girl up on to his shoulders to protect her from the crush, leaving the woman free to concentrate on the other child, who was not much more than a baby.

'Stay close,' yelled Clarke.

At that moment the half-open station door suddenly burst wide under the pressure of the rolling and swelling mass. They were all carried past the officials and out on to the street like flotsam and jetsam.

No one could demand paperwork.

When Howard collected himself, he realised he still had the small girl on his shoulders but he could not see the mother with her other child in the crowd. Clarke looked amused. 'What are you going to do with her?'

'I suppose there's nothing for it but to wait and see if her mother reappears.' Howard shrugged. It was a risk hanging around the station, near the guards and officials, but there was no choice. With a weary, resigned air, they sat down on their suitcases among the refugees. Howard did his best to comfort the small girl, who was crying. She smelt of urine. 'I wish I'd saved my bread roll,' he commented to Clarke.

'Here.' Clarke pulled a chocolate bar from his inside pocket. Howard was surprised he hadn't eaten it earlier, on the long walk to Dunkirk. 'Emergencies only,' explained Clarke. A distraught five year old was an emergency.

It was a long half-hour before Howard spotted the headscarfed face of the Belgian mother racing towards him. She fell to her knees and hugged the girl to her breast, squashing the baby between them. Her face was streaked with dirt and tears; she closed her eyes so that she wouldn't cry in front of her daughter. In French she told Clarke that she had been trapped inside the station when staff shut the doors. She feared that Howard had run off with the girl. When she admitted this, she cast Howard a look that was caught between fearful and grateful. She felt guilty for not trusting him, but he had the sort of extremely handsome face that made certain women suspicious. She explained that she had lost her luggage in the crush. She owned nothing now except what they stood up in. Clarke translated.

'Oughtn't we to go back into the station and help her look for her things?' Howard asked. 'She won't be able to manage with both children.' The girl could barely stand with fatigue. He and Clarke had been on the move for twenty hours; he wondered how long this family had been journeying.

'We can't. We might be arrested.'

'But—'

'There are going to be some hard decisions ahead; this is just the first.'

Howard hung his head, accepting Clarke's point but hating it. All they could do for the woman was to buy some warm milk for the children and a coffee for her. They drank sitting on the cobblestones of the square just outside the station. Afterwards, they found a nearby furniture store whose owner let the family sleep on the floor for the night.

'It's not the Ritz,' joked Howard as he looked around the chilly, dark shop. The only comfort was one blanket and one pillow between the three of them. The woman kissed the men on both cheeks. It was a graceful, careful thing to do in amongst the chaos and turmoil; she could just as easily have turned away from them, forgotten them in her exhaustion.

'I am very happy. Grateful.' Her English was heavily accented. 'Goodbye.'

The men returned to the station square because they had no

clue as to where else they might go. Both were wondering whether they might be able to find a bed for the night. Howard felt dizzy, surreal. He was a fit man, used to walking and late nights, but even so, his legs felt like lead weights. The foreign air, the constant travel and the mass and mix of new people made him feel light-headed, disconnected. This expedition was impetuous.

Irresponsible?

Irresistible.

The curtain at Warrington's would have been up and down by now. Howard tried to bring to mind the smell of the costume rail, sweaty and spicy, oddly delightful, and he imagined the smell of lilies that would no doubt be in the leading lady's dressing room, intense, heady. What had Warrington thought when he discovered his resignation letter? Was he angry? Impressed? Relieved? After all, Howard's presence was becoming an increasing embarrassment to the theatre. There was no value in being nervous or regretful at this point; he had to press on. His thoughts were interrupted when a police officer approached demanding to know where they were from. 'I need to see your papers, please.' He was polite but firm.

Clarke did not answer the question; instead he asked, as though rather irritated, 'When will the next train for Calais be?'

The officer spoke in a mix of French and broken English but Howard could understand. 'Oh, it is impossible to get a train to Calais tonight. *Impossible.*'

'But we must!' Clarke insisted, the very picture of indignation.

'You cannot.'

'We must.'

'Not possible at all.' There followed a long explanation about the difficulties station officials, local government and police were facing keeping any sort of public transport running (all accom-panied by hearty gesticulation). The armies had commissioned many vehicles. The situation was dire. Clarke and Howard nodded;

they did not interrupt. 'All you can do is find an 'otel and then set off with 'ope tomorrow.'

'You think so?'

'I know so.'

'But where will we find a hotel? There isn't one to be had,' added Howard. He had understood that Clarke was purposely distracting the police officer from his initial line of questioning regarding their origin and paperwork.

The tactic worked. The policeman, whether puffed up with self-importance or through a genuine wish to help, took them to a local café, where they negotiated a rate for a bed for the night. The rate was inflated but Clarke nodded, accepting that war and profiteering were always bedfellows.

They slept head to toe on a thin mattress under a scratchy blanket. The room was dark, lit only by the moonlight flooding through a gap in the curtains. 'Tomorrow we'll see about getting to the action.' Clarke was irrepressible, determined.

'Do you know, in all of the history of mankind, I doubt there have ever been two men who worked so hard to get to the front line of a war,' murmured Howard sleepily.

'No, I don't imagine there have.'

# 16

THE SKY WAS a white veil; the autumnal sun glowed patheti-
cally, its luminosity rendered ineffective behind the sheet of
nothingness. They were at the top of the hill when the driver
paused, waved and made a sound that amounted to little more
than a grunt. Vivian understood he was gesturing towards the
place where she was to live. From this viewpoint she could look
down on the farms, the village, the green. Well-trodden footpaths
left brown snails' trails. The smoke from the chimneys rose straight
up like arrows aimed at God's feet. Women had hung out their
washing; patches of creams, greys, off-whites were everywhere.
She wondered where the crimson, saffron and turquoise clothes
were hung out to dry. She sighed, accepting that it was perfectly
possible that the village didn't know such colours.

How would she bear it? It sat in front of her, offering itself up
like an unappetising dot. Its smallness instantly made her feel pity
and boredom. Self-pity. She already missed London. The broad
streets full of carriages, Oldsmobiles and automobiles dashing
notable people to exhilarating places; the shops with their infinite
variety of delightful and pleasing goods; the theatres, the cinema
and the opera. The houses here looked poky and unhygienic; they
huddled and sagged. She accepted that some might say the village
was picturesque, even idyllic. If villages were one's thing, then

Blackwell was quite adequate, but they were not her thing. She saw no charm in the lines of washing and the fences that criss-crossed, dividing small lives into still smaller segments. The roofs, whether tiled or thatched, could not matter less to her; she did not care about the tight houses or the people who inhabited them.

As she approached, she noticed that the gardens were full of ferns and hardy shrubs, and whilst some of the shrubs were still in flower, the buds looked commonplace and didn't make her feel cheerful; they just somehow reinforced the provincial nature of her existence now, reminding her that she'd attended balls where Calla lilies were shipped in from Holland. There was a pump on the green. Please God the house had running water. Of course, she'd never have to fetch water herself, but even the thought of the servants doing so made her want to shrivel up and die; it was humiliating and bound to cause inconvenience.

The driver appeared to read her mind. 'There's plumbing in the house, ma'am,' he intoned, his comment somehow seeming to rebuke, as though he knew she was thinking about her own ease. She shivered and stupidly thought of witches being ducked and peasants held in the stocks. Of course, primitive medieval punishments, torture and such, had been carried out with horrible regularity in London, but somehow being in the countryside seemed so much more primal; she felt closer to history and she didn't like it. She'd always been a modern girl.

The house was screened from the road by tall trees, and even as they got closer a laurel hedge contrived to taunt her by blocking her view. The wheels turned on the gravel; the place was not as impressive as she'd hoped nor as disappointing as she'd feared. Glimpses of a high slate roof and spacious windows suggested it was at least tall, a reasonable size. The coloured panes of glass in the porch suggested an element of taste. She did not want to leave the car. In here she felt she was somehow still a part of the London scene, but if she stepped out she was a landowner's wife. Nothing more. Unequivocally. Not even a terribly affluent landowner at that, because Aubrey's family did not own the thousands of acres Nathaniel's family did. Their farmstead was humble by comparison.

The heavy wooden door had warped with rainfall and the driver had to shove it with his shoulder to get it to open. She stepped over the threshold. Ghosts greeted her, the furniture covered with dust sheets. The house smelt earthy, damp. They needed to open windows. She feared the servants must be slackers.

# 17

HOWARD AND CLARKE were effectively outlaws and fear of arrest weighed heavily upon them at first. However, it became clear that the French officials had far more to worry about than a couple of rogue journalists. As the days went by, many an officer, soldier and citizen went out of their way to befriend them. It seemed people had a need to tell their stories, knowing that Clarke might tell the world. Howard was passed off as a junior journo; no one enquired too closely, and when they did, Clarke always implied that he too was filing copy for the *Daily Mail*. Howard didn't know what to say. He was here for the truth, but after only days in France, the word became meaningless. Truth? Did anyone want it? Really? In the back of his mind he'd thought that he might be inspired to write a new play, something significant and important. He was sure that he'd go home with some fresh material. What had Warrington insisted he wanted? He wanted Howard to create and inspire. But it was not possible. The things he saw. It was too much to contain in the space of three acts.

Even before they'd reached the front line, Howard's understanding of truth had been obliterated. That first day they'd woken to the crunch of boots thumping on the gravel roads, left, right, left, right. Some of the regiments sang or whistled. The Scots went out to the distinctive sound of bagpipes and wearing kilts, which the other regiments liked to call skirts. The Scots didn't care; comfortable, assured in their manhood and courage, they countered that the English were soft for needing trousers to fight in. It was banter; brave, almost joyful. They kissed the pretty French girls and accepted a swift cognac from friendly landlords as they marched. These men were trained soldiers, not wet-behind-the-ears volunteers. These were the men who had decided to make a career out of war. They knew their duty. They were fearless, doubtless, sure. They knew what to expect.

Except they didn't.

By early afternoon, the town was awash with the returning wounded. Not the exact same men, obviously. The ones who had left in the morning were being sent to replace these casualties; they'd crossed en route. Howard couldn't expect to find the soldier who had given him a letter to post, the pretty French girls wouldn't see the men they'd kissed, but to all intents and purposes they were the same men because in just the space of a day Howard had lost sight of individuality and personality. All he saw was vast numbers, a sea of khaki. Lines of ambulances brought in the endless tide of wounded. They were laid out, stretcher by stretcher, in station yards, four, five, six hundred at a time. It was impossible to keep count, although someone must. Some of them had lost legs or arms. Bloody stumps were tied up with bandages that had already turned brown and putrid. Howard wanted to call out to a nurse, 'Come, come quickly. Give this man back his arm.' But it was impossible. They couldn't sew limbs back on to these young bodies. It was already too late. The nurses couldn't even get round all the wounded to administer morphine and drinking water. These men had lain this way for days in one holding place or another. That was why they stank so high.

Howard did what he could. He ran to a café and begged a carafe of water. Backwards and forwards he ran between the filthy lines and the café. He fetched water for thirty, forty maybe. Some he couldn't offer even that to. Their faces were grotesque masks of clotted blood, like a mask an actor might put on to play the devil. Some of their faces were hardly there at all. Bone and gore only. They couldn't breathe properly or speak. Some didn't even bother to moan. Their bodies were hideously ruined. Torn.

He was dripping water into one chap's mouth when the soldier died. Howard didn't know what to do. Should he tell someone? The dead man lay amongst the wounded. Panicked, Howard felt responsible. He hadn't shot him, but walking away was just as heartless, wasn't it? Of course not. But yes, certainly. He stayed put, frozen.

'Come on, young fellow, we have to get a move on.' Clarke's hand was on his shoulder. Howard was speechless. Dumb. Clarke reached across and gently closed the dead soldier's eyes. 'Nothing to be done here,' he commented, but it wasn't callousness, it was fact. Howard looked about him and noticed that they were swilling down the station hall with disinfectant fluid. Over half of the wounded had been cleared. Clarke sighed. 'I hear the French doctor in charge received a telegram from the director of medical services.'

'What did it say?'

'It said, "Make ready for forty thousand wounded." So I'm told.'

'Some mistake, surely. An extra zero inadvertently tapped.'

Clarke shrugged.

They walked to the Front. It took them close to four hours. Military cars, trucks and wagons drawn by horses and mules, all heavily laden, rattled past but did not stop. Why should they? They had a battle to fight, a war to win. The air was sharp, urgent. Howard and Clarke did not talk much to one another as they trudged through the ever-blackening evening, both lost in their thoughts. When they got close, talking was an impossibility. Nothing could be heard above the eternal shelling and batteries firing barrage after barrage.

There was death everywhere. Howard could taste it on his tongue and feel it in his nostrils and lungs. Death stung his eyes. Here there was just more. More ambulances roaring and crashing over the thrown-up mud, more stretchers carrying the wounded, more bodies lying prone. Finished. An unforgivable, unreasonable thought struck Howard. The dead were the lucky ones; this was hell. He wanted to vomit with shame at the thought; he wasn't a defeatist. He looked around helplessly, wondering what he could do to aid; to ease someone, anyone. Those on the stretchers who were being carried away cried out; each furrow in the ground that forced a bearer to slip or slide caused the wounded to yell in pain. This lot were in a worse way than those Howard had tended to in Dunkirk. These men were still shocked and furious; they hadn't moved on to acceptance or denial. They were writhing in agony and screaming with dismay or horror. Nurses dashed from one to another, doing their best to ease and comfort. The worst were those who were too delirious to cry out. It was their eyes that screamed. Howard wondered how they bore it. Did they know that the foul smell came from them?

In the opposite direction, young men teemed towards the enemy's guns like ants on a picnic rug swarming towards cake crumbs. Horses laboured to pull carriages carrying artillery. They neighed, straining with the weight, but stumbled through. Several thoroughbreds lay freshly dead. Enormous and powerful still, they oozed blood, entrails smoking pitifully. The deluge stretched out in front of him, yard after yard, mile after mile. As far as he could see. On and on it went, oceans of bloody, muddy men, crowds of dejected, humiliated prisoners, endless dead bodies lying in the filth, blood still weeping from their wounds, the plummeting shells plunging ceaselessly into the earth, blasting up streams of soil and flesh.

Clarke pulled out a notebook.

Howard was stunned, almost sickened by the man's presence

of mind; he himself could no more have put pen to paper in that moment than he could fly to the moon. 'What will you tell them?' he yelled.

'Who?'

'The men and women who still think of war in terms of heroic pageantry. The mothers at home who are giving up sons, the women who are sacrificing husbands, lovers, brothers.'

Clarke shook his head. 'Not this. We don't tell them this.'

Howard knew that it wasn't that Clarke suddenly agreed with Kitchener's policy of throttling the press; it was simply that he didn't have the words. How could he begin to draw the picture of civilisations collapsing, men tearing one another to shreds like cannibals? He would have to find something but not give them everything. Everything was far, far too much.

*Severe fighting is taking place today near Nieuwpoort, south of Ostend. Very heavy firing has been heard at Dunkirk since eight in the morning. It is suggested that torpedo boats or gun boats are being used in the canals.*

*Daily Mail*, 18th October 1914

# 18

I T WAS NEARLY always wet in the countryside; she simply could
not remember it raining this much in London. There was no
noise either. No distraction. If anyone spoke or sang or read, it
was her, which meant there was no real entertainment; ticking
clocks filled her days. She remembered, not so long ago (although
it felt like forever), when she used to erupt into involuntary gusts
of giggles. Now she was all about sighs. The silence stretched
through the house, out on to the lawn and beyond through the
fields and up the ancient sleeping hills. The silence was in the
root of plants and trees. The wet garden, the petals of the dead
roses.

Vivian introduced herself to the staff, such as it was. Mrs
Rosebend, the housekeeper, and a housemaid. She quickly
employed a plump woman from the village to cook. Cook came
with references and an understanding that she was looking
forward to feeding Mrs Owens up, as long as Mrs Owens respected
the fact that the kitchen was her domain, Mrs Owens was
not expected to visit, ought not to. It was an arrangement that
suited Vivian. She'd brought her own maid from London, but
unfortunately the girl only lasted a week before she announced
she was going back; she was confident she'd easily find work
in a shop or factory, even an office, now that so many of the

men had gone to war. Vivian didn't have the heart to stop her. Why would anyone stay here if they didn't have to? The place was meagre and uncomfortable. Isolated.

She walked through the muddy, sodden streets and found little to divert her: a church, a village hall and a small store. There she asked if they knew of a girl looking for work; someone was sent to her by the afternoon. The girl had no experience as a lady's maid, but she was neat and quiet and Vivian wanted to believe she'd be adequate. Any port in a storm. She did at least acquire a certain amount of esteem by employing four of the village women. Nevertheless, when she went to church or walked around abouts people whispered behind their hands and raised their eyebrows in her direction. Some remained frosty because she was a Londoner, and townies were never trusted by country folk; others were more sympathetic, even awed by her glamour. They all agreed she was not the right type of girl for this sort of thing: farming, visiting the poor and such. War.

Vivian knew what they were saying. What they were thinking. One couldn't expect too much from such as her. It wasn't fair to do so. They thought a hefty girl or a plain girl was likely to do a better job as mistress, and dismissed her as inadequate. Vivian agreed. She'd always been so proud of her looks, her trim figure, her delicate frame. Now her skinny arms seemed useless.

She spent a morning unpacking her clothes and another arranging the paintings and photographs around the house, then devoted a third to placing the small knick-knacks. She wondered what Aubrey expected her to do with her days here in the middle of nowhere. It dawned on her that he had probably given the matter no thought whatsoever. He was not in the habit of looking out for her; he was no more used to being a husband than she was to being a wife.

She had a work basket, of course. They were asking for socks for the soldiers. She could knit as well as the next girl (providing the next girl was also a careless amateur). She pointed out rugs that needed beating and floors that needed scrubbing, but soon found that her interest irritated the maids. They could see the grime as well as she could, and since they were the ones charged with removing it, her notice only appeared rude. The garden needed tending to. In fact everything needed attention. Not least Vivian.

On the fifth day she was sent a surprise. The maids skittered about excitedly as a pianoforte was unloaded from the back of a horse-drawn cart. Mrs Rosebend fussed that the rain had ruined the instrument; Vivian doubted she was that lucky. So this was how Aubrey thought she could use her time. Practising. Why was he so insistent that his wife become musical? She hoped to God he was still training, because she wouldn't want to wish ill on a man in battle.

Vivian considered another walk to the grocer's to enquire about a man for the garden, and she supposed she must ask about a piano tuner too. Although the streets were patched with puddles, there was a gap in the clouds, and a shop was a shop was a shop, no matter how utilitarian or cramped. She found her hat and purple kid gloves, although she feared her fashion statements were a fruitless declaration here in the land of aprons and mob caps.

She was greeted with a level of excitement. 'Good morning, Mrs Owens. Are you well?'

'Quite well, thank you. Are you?'

'Can't complain.' And yet he did. For a full ten minutes she listened to a list of Mr Walker's aches and pains, his woes. He had a touch of arthritis, possibly gout too, he had an ingrowing toenail that was bothering him, he couldn't digest tomatoes easily. She smiled politely and kept her eyes trained on the lips of the rotund grocer as though she'd never heard anything more fascinating in her life, managing not to hint at her exasperation at having listened to the same inventory of ailments several times already in their very short acquaintance. A thin line of saliva tapered from his top teeth to his bottom; she scrutinised it, fascinated, wondering when it would snap. One or two other customers came into the shop but it didn't slow down Mr Walker. He was on a roll.

Vivian risked slipping her eyes away and studying the other patrons. One was a child, who took the opportunity of Mr Walker's extreme obsession with his own health to slip an apple into her pinafore pocket; the second was a woman about Vivian's mother's age. Normally Vivian was deeply distrustful of women in their forties and fifties. She found them snobbish, judgemental, sanctimonious and damning. They seemed to find her careless, irresponsible, giddy and improper. Their age terrified her; her youth threatened them. She prepared herself for a cool, meaningless exchange peppered with barbed criticisms and vainly proffered unsolicited advice. She had been faced with so many grudging and pessimistic women of a certain age that she thought all she could do was hold her chin up and wait for the onslaught of negativity. She wished she'd kept her eyes on Mr Walker's saliva.

However, this woman was a surprise. She did not wear her greying, wiry hair in a neat, constrained bun; instead it was caught into a loose, tumbling ponytail that sprouted from high on her head, like a girl's. Her free curls showed that her hair had once been a joyful mix of auburn, copper and gold. She had a small, symmetrical face with deep-set, intelligent dark eyes beaming out, a narrow, long but elegant nose and the sort of mouth that danced, always ready to burst into a smile. She offered one up to Vivian. It was quietly complicit; she'd heard Mr Walker's list of ailments on countless occasions too, no doubt, but she was not mocking him, she was asking Vivian, the stranger, to bear with. Her smile was gentle, reassuring. It was like climbing into a warm bath. Vivian smiled back. It was hopeless to try not to. The woman had a petite, lean figure; she was dressed in misshapen, ill-fitting clothes, but not in a way that suggested she was poor and wearing cast-offs (although that must be considered). She was wearing them in a way that suggested she had no idea that she had clothes on at all; they were an irrelevance, she had greater things to think about.

The idea of someone having greater things to think about than clothes came to Vivian from nowhere and it took a moment for her own mind to accept the very thing it had suggested. She shrugged contritely at the woman, apologising for ever enquiring about Mr Walker's health.

'It's quite all right, I'm not in a hurry,' the woman whispered in a low voice. Irony? A criticism? A condemnation? Everyone was in a hurry nowadays, surely. The woman smiled and Vivian saw that no, it was just a comment, the truth.

Eventually Mr Walker ran out of ailments or breath and got to the matter in hand. 'What can I do for you today, Mrs Owens?' He knew she didn't do the shopping – Cook managed that – but he afforded her the respect of a customer because ultimately she paid the bill. Or rather Mr Owens did, but she approved it. Still, Vivian never liked to visit without choosing some small thing; it seemed wrong that all she was picking was the grocer's brains. She asked for a quarter of boiled sweets and another of toffee. As he was pouring the treats into thin brown paper bags, she asked whether he knew a young man who might like to tidy the garden.

'No, ma'am. No man. Not young or old.'

'None?'

'Every spare lad has gone off now. The older men are picking up the slack on the farms.'

'Really?'

'They came recruiting and our lads were not lacking. Twenty-five our village has sent. My two boys among them.'

'Oh, bravo.'

'Thank you, Mrs Owens. Six more volunteered but weren't found fit. Timmy Durham isn't right in the head; they couldn't take him. A couple had problems with their eyes and a few were too short, scrawny you know. That said, it's no wonder young Jonny Joyce was thought too small – he's not yet sixteen. Still, as keen as mustard he is. Swore blind he was nineteen. So did his da. Not his mammy, though. She told the recruiting officer what was what.' Mr Walker chuckled at the memory. 'But even those exempt from attesting . . .' He paused, aware that he was using new words that sounded rather grand; he wanted to make sure they were sufficiently impressive and impactful. Vivian widened her eyes appreciatively. 'Them boys, left behind, are up to their eyes in it doing the work of four men each.'

'Well, you must be a very proud village.'

'That we are. Recruiting officer told me that farm boys are proving to be just the sort of soldiers they want.'

'Are they really?'

'Muscles. Hardy. Had good food, you see. Great British milk, barley and pigs have fed up our boys, good and strong. Now they are off to fight for that very greatness.'

Vivian smiled; it was difficult not to, faced with Mr Walker's animation and pride, although she did wonder whether he wasn't being a little bit romantic in his assessment of Blackwell village. She had noticed plenty of neglected cottages; she could imagine the scenes of deprivation inside them: unswept, untidy, unwashed, signs of mice and threadbare linen, that sort of thing. Not that she was being judgemental. Since moving here she had had to wonder how the really poor managed to keep themselves clean; it was such an effort lugging and heating water and such. One had to rather admire them for bothering at all, she supposed. She hoped they'd be fed well by the army.

'You should have seen them go. Such laughing and fooling there was, and a brass band.'

'Surely some of them must have been scared,' she blurted.

'No, not one of them,' he assured her firmly. He grinned,

161

forgiving her girlish squeamishness, actually enjoying it. Vivian heard a slight sigh from the woman in the shop, the one with the lovely smile. She was about to turn around to her and draw her into the conversation, but Mr Walker pushed on. He was a force to be reckoned with. Vivian thought that if they could talk the Germans into submission, he would be the man to send. 'Have you heard from Mr Owens? Am I right in thinking he is with the Tenth Sherwood Foresters?'

'Captain Owens now.'

'Begging your pardon, ma'am.' Mr Walker's grin widened; he clearly loved her husband's title. 'I won't be surprised if they put him in charge of our boys. His boys. They'll all be going over together.'

'I'm not sure how it works.'

'He must want to lead the local lads.' Mr Walker's confidence and certainty were enchanting; she couldn't help but agree.

'I'm sure he must. I read that they want them to stay with their pals, don't they?' she offered.

'Not that I'd presume my lads to be pals of Captain Owens, but they have grown up with one another, after a fashion. When he visited here in the summers, as a lad, like.' Mr Walker puffed out his chest. She knew he was delighted to be associated with Aubrey. It gave her a queer, unrecognisable thrill to see his reaction. She hadn't had any occasion to be proud of her husband during their short marriage. It was rather pleasant to find she was, somewhat.

'Absolutely,' she beamed. 'How old are your sons, Mr Walker?'

'One's twenty-three, the other is nineteen.'

'Your eldest is the exact age of my husband.' The younger son was her age, but she was somehow shy about admitting as much.

'Is that a fact?'

'It is.' They stood in silence for a moment, rather pleased with themselves for some intangible reason. There was a connection.

It was slight, but it was the first Vivian had felt since she'd moved to Blackwell. Who knew the war could be so bonding?

'Big, my boys. We'll whip the Huns' miserable thieving backsides right back over the border.' Vivian looked a little startled, which caused Mr Walker to add apologetically, 'Sorry to be vulgar, Mrs Owens.'

'Oh, that's quite all right. It's nothing. I agree with the sentiment.' There was another sigh behind her, and Vivian was reminded how rude she was being in monopolising Mr Walker. His other customers had waited patiently throughout the conversation.

Mr Walker turned. 'What about you, Mrs Henderson, are your sons gone?'

'Michael, my younger boy, went with your lads, Mr Walker, as I'm sure you know.'

'And the older?' There was a moment of something in the air. A blade.

'He's already out there, as a matter of fact.'

'Is he now? Already? Well, you do surprise me. Didn't think he was the sort. Theatre types make good soldiers, do they?'

'I wouldn't know, Mr Walker.'

'What regiment is he in?'

'Not a regiment. He's there with a newspaperman.'

'A what?'

'A journalist. A Mr Basil Clarke from the *Daily Mail*.'

Mr Walker looked nonplussed. He took Vivian's money for the sweets and then folded his arms across his barrel chest. 'So do these newspapermen just stand by whilst it's all going on around them?' he demanded. His tone was obviously confrontational.

Vivian wished to smooth things for Mrs Henderson. 'Well, we need to know what's going on, don't we? My cousin has poor eyesight and so can't fight. He's volunteered as an ambulance driver.'

'Luckily my son is the picture of health.' It was impossible not to be shocked. Was she saying he'd refused to volunteer?

'Well, everyone is doing their bit. Newspapermen, ambulance drivers,' Vivian mumbled, embarrassed. The older woman reached out and patted her arm. Vivian was startled by the touch.

Mr Walker shook his head. 'Aye, *ambulance drivers* are vital.' He placed meaningful emphasis on the words.

Mrs Henderson seemed to deliberately misunderstand him and commented, 'Sadly, they are, Mr Walker.' She waved a small tube of chlorophyll toothpaste. 'I'll take the price of this off what you owe me for the washing.'

'Right you are.'

Then, turning to Vivian, she added, 'You could perhaps tackle the garden yourself.' It wasn't said as a criticism, or with any hint of interference or censure; somehow her suggestion was affirming, as though she believed Vivian was indeed capable of such a thing. That she might do a fine job.

'I'm not awfully good at that sort of thing,' Vivian confessed.

'Aren't you?' Mrs Henderson's smile was teasing, gently challenging. She was an odd woman. She didn't fit into any of the types Vivian had come across before. She seemed to have very peculiar views on the war, almost unsupportive, and yet she was all smiles and humour, which Vivian couldn't help but think of as anything other than lovely. Vivian didn't know what to make of her. All she did know was that Mrs Henderson's spontaneously illuminated face was a great relief. She instantly felt less alone. Before she got the chance to confirm that she was absolutely not capable of sorting out the garden, the bell on the shop door rang, signalling Mrs Henderson's exit.

'Be careful with that one, Mrs Owens, you don't want to get too involved.' Vivian couldn't think what to say to that, so chose to say nothing at all. She gave the sweets and toffee to the light-fingered girl who was still skulking, instructing her to share them with her siblings, and then she headed home too.

# 19

THE WEATHER WAS wet, dull and gusty. The wind flung brown and yellow leaves this way and that. It was the worst sort of day. She stared out of the window at the oaks that divided the once coiffured, now neglected garden from the wild and rough fields. Further still were the grassy hills, dotted with sheep, and ploughed land, churned and brown. 'I'm stuffed with discontent,' she blurted. She hadn't meant to say it aloud.

Mrs Rosebend calmly put down the breakfast tray and looked at her mistress uncomprehendingly. 'What a funny way you have of phrasing things. It's jolly good to be discontent. It leads to improvement. You should find a hobby or go to the talks that the vicar organises. Last week's was all about bandaging wounds.' The housekeeper left the room evidently irritated.

Bandaging wounds? How was that likely to come in useful for the women of Blackwell? Mrs Rosebend didn't understand. Vivian didn't understand herself. She knew she wanted more. But more what? More comfort? More clothes? More freedom? More fun? More knowledge? That was it. Most of all she wanted to know more. She felt locked out. Life was going on all around her, but she felt she was being kept out. People thought she was easy-going, perhaps lazy, but she was not idle. She was underutilised.

She didn't understand the fields and all that went on there. The land manager had paid her a courtesy visit, but it soon became apparent that she would not be interfering with his work. Sewing, growing, chopping, gathering: it was a mystery to her. The rain lashed down on the pane; was there ever a more depressing sound? It was only nine in the morning, but the room had the gloom of a late afternoon after a wasted day. The fire was going out; it needed a new log and a poke. She was about to ring for the maid when she decided she might as well just throw on a log herself. She knelt near the hearth and gave it a prod too. It was satisfying to see the flames leap. Vivian had become almost grateful that the rooms were so poky; at least she could stay warm. With the flames licking confidently, she returned to the window and stared out again. The lawn was soaked, waterlogged; the autumn leaves were strewn like jewel-coloured confetti.

She supposed she could rake them up, as she had seen the gardener at home do.

The trees were yellow now and gold, red berries had sprung from nowhere, although a few last fat, loose roses still gripped the pergola, and there was the odd clump of bedraggled drumstick allium. The tight purple umbrellas clung to the border, soaked, despondent. Their season had gone.

Vivian could relate to that.

Yet. There was still something attractive about them. There was something interesting about anything that could endure. Gardens always had an indefinable sense of the unexpected. One never knew what was next, what might suddenly appear, shoot up out of the earth or blossom from the most unpromising seed. It was an encouraging thought. Red, green, yellow leaves at the end of branches sat in front of the colourless sky, indomitable, undefeated, despite the persistent autumn gloom. Those dropped leaves really did need sweeping into a barrow.

Oh my goodness, what was that? At the far end of the garden a deer burst out from the hedgerow; it shuddered into the air. So frail yet strong, elegant but panicked. In a flash it was gone. Vivian laughed out loud with the surprise of it. She'd never been so close to a deer. What a wonderful creature. She ran into the kitchen to find someone to tell about the experience.

'Oh yes, we get all sorts of wildlife, ma'am.' The housemaid bobbed a curtsey, trying not to be flustered at the sight of her mistress in the kitchen. Cook wouldn't like it, though luckily she was paying a visit to the water closet. 'Hares, badgers, foxes. Things are forever darting and scampering all around.'

Vivian returned to her spot by the window in the drawing room. Once again she looked out to the horizon, half hoping she'd spot the deer for a second time. She didn't, but the vista seemed to morph and mutate in front of her. Perhaps after all it wasn't *deadly* boring.

She would garden.

She had nothing to wear. That was a frequent cry of Vivian's, but in this case it happened to be literally true. She was grateful that she'd grown up in a time when barbaric cinched-waist corsets had been abandoned. How had her mother ever moved, let alone breathed, when she was young? The new straight-line corsets were far more comfortable and elegant; she could at least freely drift around the house and village in her flattering, form-fitting gowns. She wore her waistline high, and her skirts stopped at the ankle, which meant there was a lot less laundry for her maid to worry about; hems used to get caked. Still, everything she owned was far too fussy and restrictive for outdoor activities. She needed a shirtwaist; that was the uniform of working women.

She asked the maids if they had anything suitable that she could borrow. They both looked horrified and each confirmed that they only owned two dresses. 'The one I'm standing up in and my Sunday best,' admitted her lady's maid. As an afterthought she added, 'I suppose I could run home for my Sunday best, Mrs Owens, if you really need it to garden in.'

'No, no, that won't be necessary.' Sweet girl, but silly. Vivian made a note to herself that she ought to sort out some of her own dresses for the maids. She had things she hadn't worn for an age, and the girls were both slim like she was, although a little shorter. She couldn't imagine that would be a problem; they were both bound to be good with a needle.

Vivian opened the wardrobes and drawers in the three bedrooms, hoping to unearth something useful. She was just beginning to think she'd have no alternative but to pin up her skirts when she came across some men's clothes, hung neatly on the back of a door in the smallest spare room. They were Victorian and large, likely to have belonged to Aubrey's father or even grandfather, but they were clean. She considered her options. The garden was waterlogged, swollen. As the rain hit the ground, mud splashed up the fences. Nearly everything she owned was white, cream, lavender or pale blue. Even her most basic dress would have to be written off if she tried to garden in it. And then there were these men's trousers. Men's trousers? What use were they to anyone else? They were too out of date to ever be worn by any chap. There was a shirt, a jumper, an overcoat. So practical for the rain. Did she dare? Who would spot her if she stayed in the back garden?

The maids giggled when they saw her, and Cook gasped, but no one insisted that she abandon the masculine garb. No one told Vivian what to do here in Blackwell. That, she supposed, was the beauty of it. She might very well be starved of company and without occupation, but she was in charge.

Later, as she stood staring through the window once again, her arms, back, thighs, hands were all sore and raw, but somehow she felt well. She felt purposeful, fresh, for the first time in longer than she could remember. The small drawing room no longer felt as glum; it was edging towards cosy. The fire was roaring, throwing light and warmth over the chairs and tables, the embroidered headrests and crocheted coasters. There was a tray with tea, buttered crumpets and jam waiting for her. Importantly, the garden looked tidier. Raking had turned out to be considerably harder work than it looked, as had weeding and moving the wheelbarrow, but the smell of the violet smoke from the smouldering rubbish heap tickled her nostrils. Look what she had achieved! She had worked for six hours, only stopping briefly when Cook insisted she have some soup, bread and cheese at two in the afternoon.

'You'll faint, ma'am. I ain't having Mr Owens coming here and saying I neglected you.'

'I have work to do, Cook.'

'Aye, well that's as maybe, but I do too, so come in and eat.' Her chins were wobbling with anxiety and determination. The sleeves of her dress were pushed up above her raw and hard elbows as was her habit, her pink, fleshy hands firmly on her waist. 'Please,' she added.

Vivian left the shears and rake for a spell and did as she was asked because she knew she was causing Cook to worry. It had been tougher going back to it in the afternoon; her muscles were already beginning to feel the unusual strain of exercise and a blue chill had set into the air. The damp clung, although she wasn't cold, as the labour kept her warm. The rain had stopped. The exercise had brought colour to her cheeks, which she felt anyone would have to agree suited her rather well, if there was anyone to see her, that was. She had left her wellington boots at the kitchen door but hadn't yet summoned the energy to change out of her strange costume. She drank her tea and ate the crumpets standing up because she didn't want to get mud on the furniture. She was starving.

Upstairs, she slowly undressed. The trousers were thick and stiff with mud. Vivian thought she must tell her maid to brush them rather than wash them, because she might need them again in the morning and they would never be dry in time if they were washed.

She didn't light a candle but looked out of the bedroom window over the village and fields. Rare specks of light from cottage windows interrupted the calm darkness of dusk like fireflies. Such a contrast with London, a city of bright and glaring lights; streets, carriages, houses, theatres, restaurants, cars all lit up, bright, brilliant and blatant. She did miss it, but she missed it a little less today. Which way was London? she wondered. Which way was France?

She drew the dark green curtains against the night. The material was dusty and heavy, even faded in streaks, but they made the room seem comfortable. Perhaps it was the gold tassels, which brought to mind theatres, restaurants and other places of fun. Here in her bedroom it was hard to believe that London and all its activity, gossip, creativity, discussion and fashion even existed, and it was incredible to imagine war at all. The whispers of battles waned and faltered. She couldn't hear the men's boots marching to the ports or the explosions and ambulance engines across the Channel. The papers were full of it, but all that din and disarray dwindled into unreality beyond the edge of the herbaceous bush.

Kindly, the housemaid filled the bath right up to the top. Vivian lay in among the scent of lavender, scrubbing at the mud under her fingernails and thinking about what else she should do with the garden, what might she do with the land. She could try to learn something or other about those fields. She should know what they were growing. Who was farming them now that the men were away? Old men? Boys? Women? She should find out.

# 20

*There were over 2,500 German bodies in the Yser Canal this morning after the fighting in the night. Many of them had drowned, others bayoneted. The very water itself was bloody. Dixmude's streets were strewn thick with dead.*

*Daily Mail*, 27th October 1914

'THAT WILL SEND up a cheer at home,' commented Clarke, without hiding his satisfaction.

The German dead were being gathered into heaps like autumn leaves and drenched in petrol; oily smoke was rising from them. Howard turned away. 'Do you think anyone will wonder how many of our men are lying in heaps?' he asked.

'I don't know.' Clarke sighed, then admitted, 'I don't know if I want them to.' Howard raised an eyebrow in question. 'Not knowing seems some sort of merciful anaesthetic right now. I'm a man who has always admired curiosity in my readers and I seek to bring the news to people, to tell them how it is. But now . . .' The sentence was left hanging in the air; it was unthinkable, unrepeatable.

Clarke handed Howard a sheet of paper to read. They had got into the habit of him reading Clarke's copy before it was sent to London. He wasn't sure why Clarke valued his opinion, but he was flattered. Maybe the journalist needed to know that what he wrote was in some way real, accurate. Howard understood his uncertainty. It was increasingly difficult to understand the reality of what they saw. Howard was only managing to jot down the odd sentence each night; he'd thought he'd be prolific here where there was so much being felt and done but, in fact, he was frozen. His thoughts were tangled. He was at once disgusted and in awe. Whilst flattered to be included in Clarke's process, he did not know what to make of his new friend's approach to reporting. He admired Clarke's ability to highlight decisive and potent details in amongst the colossal carnage. His copy was undoubtedly effective, raw and gripping, and yet Clarke did not rely on extreme use of adjectives; he refused to be sensationalist or alarmist. Howard read how the journalist described the previous night's battle. *Men even wrestled and died by drowning each other in the canal's waters.* He told the story of *a huge Belgian who used his rifle like an axe and felled man after man until a bullet took him through the thigh and fetched him down.* He made it sound gallant, almost clean. Of course he must. The people back home needed it to be so, but it wasn't like that. Men wrestling each other to their deaths was filthy. Did Clarke see it? Howard saw nothing but.

The two men headed to the bar. They needed a drink. They, and everyone else, often did.

The first few weeks of Howard's time on the Western Front had been dominated by the Battle of the Yser, a frantic, violent struggle in which the Belgian and French armies desperately tried to prevent the Germans advancing across the Yser Canal. There had been plenty for Clarke to report, but they were still operating without the correct paperwork, so he had to find ingenious ways to send his reports back to the *Daily Mail* without betraying his whereabouts to the authorities; overuse of the telegraph office would do just that. Usually he gave his stories to a French courier; sometimes he depended on a friendly soldier who was going on leave to England. Howard had noticed that people were inclined to do one another favours: they'd hand over a cigarette, stand another man a drink, pass on a message or post a letter. He was always struck how affable people could be. It seemed bizarre that such a stream of small considerations and kindnesses could be happening in the same time and place as men were ceaselessly blowing each other to bits.

The bar was heaving. This was where men came to sink into patchy conversation and slightly manic laughter. They got drunk, sang songs, lost money at cards and then noisily fought over it; anything to camouflage the fear. Howard ordered a carafe of red wine while Clarke busied himself finding a man to take the copy home. A private promised he'd deliver it; he was shipping out that evening for three days' leave, 'Thank Christ.'

'You're on the five o'clock boat? You're sure?' Clarke demanded gruffly. Time was always of the essence.

The soldier looked jubilant. 'Yes, sir, and not a minute too soon.'

Howard knew his friend thrived on the excitement of delivering something ahead of the other newspapermen. He himself wasn't the competitive type. Even back in the theatre he'd had a different approach to most. He loved a full house (more than anything!), but he didn't resent the other playwrights the same. Was there any real need in rushing this news home to Britain? Did it make any genuine difference to know more men were dead? It couldn't be a surprise to anyone, not any more. It seemed futile. So much about the war did. He knew that the boat would be laden with letters from men who might already be dead. Was there any point in delivering the letter of a dead man?

Any point in killing a man?

Since he found that he could not write he wondered, with increasing frequency, what he was doing out here. What were any of them doing, come to that? Clarke was not offering the full picture; beyond the concern for the families of those fighting, the government's censoring of his work meant it often failed to reflect the truth as to how the battle was progressing. God only knew what was really going on in the war. Who was winning and who was losing seemed an incalculable thing to report.

Howard sat down on the small wooden chair and gulped back half a glass of wine. He noticed a little vein pulsing in Clarke's forehead, blue like a new bruise. He was pressing his lips tightly together so that they almost vanished. He pushed his gold-rimmed spectacles up his nose, two or three times over.

'You don't look like a man who believes his own reports,' commented Howard. Clarke had described the German army as 'despairing'. He'd even gone so far as to claim that there were old men and sixteen-year-old boys in the German ranks and that this was a sign of desperation, the implication being that they were running out of troops. Howard knew his friend well enough to bet that the account was not fictionalised; Clarke must have spotted the occasional old German patriot, a boy soldier or two, but Howard had only seen tall, strong, virile men in the enemy ranks. They looked a lot like the Allied men. Both in life and death. There was no shortage of them; they kept on coming. Line after line. Clarke had written about Germany approaching the end of its tether in northern Belgium, but that wasn't the belief in Dunkirk. The streets were strewn with spiky barbed wire and smashed bottles. A neglected, hopeless air had descended on the cobbles; people breathed it in, and spewed it out. True, the Germans had met with gutsy doggedness, but what was doggedness in the face of superior military power, greater reserves in ammunition and endless waterproof boots?

'I saw more locals packing up today,' Howard added. 'Who can blame them?'

'Not me.' Clarke reached for his cigarettes and offered Howard one.

'They're scrambling to safety whilst disbelieving in the concept.'

'Yes. The poor buggers. I wonder how they've managed this far. To live for days on tenterhooks in this nightmare of anxiety and foreboding, the threat of invasion ever present. That's what it is to live here.'

Both men felt it. The tension, palpable. Choking. 'Do you think the Germans will break through?' Howard glanced around the bar as he asked this and then bit the nail of his thumb. He felt disloyal and defeatist just giving the question life. He was surprised to notice his hand quivering. It wasn't that he was afraid for himself – he didn't feel that in his core, he really didn't – but he was afraid for the people of Dunkirk, for the Allied soldiers, and although he could never say this aloud, for the Germans too. Truthfully, he'd begun to fear for mankind. He couldn't tell anyone, not even Clarke, but when he was alone at night and doing the thing most people would call praying but he didn't know how to name, what he wished and longed for was peace. Not victory. Just peace. He wanted it to stop.

'I don't know.' Clarke's glass eye was very convincing and Howard generally forgot about it except when something brilliant or painful slipped into Clarke's mind and flooded across his one good eye, leaving the other dead by contrast. 'It's a silken slimness of a margin by which we're avoiding disaster. So who knows.'

Howard and Clarke had struck up a sort of ritual. In the evenings, after they'd eaten and retired to their own rooms, they would each lean out of their hotel window to observe the battles on the front line. They would nod to one another across the darkness but then behave almost as though the other man wasn't there. They did not speak; there wasn't anything to say. They listened intently to the sound of guns as though they were listening to an orchestra in the Albert Hall, and they surveyed the flares in the sky and the fires blazing in the distance as closely as if they were watching rare wildlife. As he looked on, Howard speculated whether he was watching the Germans breaking through the

Allied lines. Were they advancing? He imagined Clarke must have been wondering the same. After twenty, thirty, sometimes forty minutes, Clarke would say good night and pull his window closed on the horror. Often Howard stayed awake all night, until the apology for dawn – the murk of the autumn morning – signalled that a new day had blundered through. He'd sleep for a couple of hours, and then after breakfast they'd visit the Yser Canal and count the bodies of those who had been killed while they'd looked on.

As they made their way to the canal, there were wounded everywhere, some walking, others being carried on stretchers, some lying on the ground having given up or been given up on. Howard now expected to see maimed soldiers at every junction; he knew the hospitals were packed with blind or otherwise injured men who moaned and wept in confusion and agony as they inched towards their deaths. They'd started to live in a way that made the state of crisis the usual.

The two men stood back and watched as the wild war raged and wrecked.

'Are you writing?' Clarke asked Howard. Howard fought a blush. He hated it when this no-nonsense northerner fixed upon him and asked this particular question, which he did regularly.

'No,' he admitted. He'd thought as an artist he might salvage something, some understanding or insight, but he remained blocked. The horror of it was too immense.

'Yesterday I heard of a jeweller who buried his stock in the sand dunes.'

'Did he really? To prevent it being looted by the Germans if they take the city, I presume.'

'Quite so.' Clarke paused, measuring how closely Howard was following. 'You know, I talked to an officer friend of mine today. He sought me out.'

'And said?'

'He offered me a place on a boat that is to leave if the Germans break through. You and me both. He made it clear that it would be unpleasant for us if we were caught here.' Clarke paused, gulped back the red wine and then leaned in close to Howard. 'He said if Fritz arrives tonight, we should slip down to the dock and get aboard pronto.'

'He's never mentioned this boat before?'

'No.'

'Things must be getting tight.'

'They are.' Clarke gave a grim nod, whispering in his ear now. 'Just this morning, a friend in the Belgian Flying Corps told me that the Germans had got through the line at one, maybe even two points.'

Howard swallowed hard. 'So then it's a question of whether the Allies can cut them off or whether we will be overrun.'

'Yes.' Clarke nodded over to where the young soldier who had been charged with delivering the copy was standing. He was laughing a little too loudly at some joke or other. The men were often shrill and giddy; it was camouflage for fear. 'You could catch the five o'clock boat with our soldier friend. I'm sure we could hitch you a ride.' He slipped the suggestion on to the table casually; it seemed to seep into the wood along with the rings of red wine. Howard felt momentarily untethered, almost dizzy. Did he want to leave? Yes, yes, more than anything. Could he?

'I don't imagine you are planning on going?'

'No. I'll stay until they tell me I have to leave, while there are stories to tell.'

'Ever the newspaperman.'

'Quite so.'

'I don't feel in any personal danger,' commented Howard truthfully.

'Don't be fooled, you are.'

'Then maybe I don't mind it if I am.'

Clarke winced. 'War can do that to a man. I saw the same in the Boer Wars.'

'What do you mean?'

'It blinds one to the value of one's own life.'

Howard wondered whether that was what had happened to him. He wasn't sure. It was true that he didn't feel quite himself. His role as a constant observer had rendered him not just an outsider, but almost invisible. His inability to write had left him feeling futile.

'You're not taking care of yourself, son,' added Clarke. He didn't usually refer to Howard in that way. There was an age gap, but both of them had been careful not to refer to it. Clarke didn't want to feel old, Howard didn't want to feel young. 'To tell the truth, I'm a bit worried about you.'

Howard had found that it had become more difficult to enjoy food of late. Here in Dunkirk it was still possible to sit in a restaurant with a tablecloth and shining cutlery, to be served a juicy pork chop with green beans, even a butter sauce, but the food had lost its taste. It was a chore to chew; each mouthful was bitter with guilt. He didn't sleep well because he observed and listened to the battles. Purple sacks had bloomed under his previously much-commented-upon clear blue eyes; eyes that were now hooded with heavy, tired lids. Perhaps he wasn't paying as much attention to personal grooming as he used to. He hadn't shaved for a week or so; he didn't have time to bathe but made do with quick wash-downs with a sponge. He saw it as a waste of time, preferring to be out on the streets giving wounded men cups of water.

The men at the Front weren't eating well or sleeping on beds. If they wanted to bathe, they had to fill a tub with cold water and then heat bricks in a fire. The hot bricks were dropped into the tub until the water became at least tepid, then they queued for a turn. Naked and exposed but delighted at the opportunity to douse their lice-ridden bodies for ten minutes or so. Howard's heart stretched between pathos and admiration. He wasn't deliberately neglecting himself; it was just the basics had become unseemly luxuries in his mind.

'How old are you, Howard?'

'I'm twenty-one.'

'You've seen a lot for one so young.'

He shrugged. 'There are men out there dying who are younger than I am.'

'That's my point. This can't be easy. You know, the peculiar thing is, when I met you in London, I pegged you at twenty-five or six.' He'd been assured in London. Popular and following a career that amounted to a calling, his certainty had made him carefree; he'd had the confidence of an older man. Now, nothing was certain. He was stripped and out of his depth. He looked like a boy.

'I feel older than ever.' Older than anyone who had ever lived.

'Yes, we all do.' Clarke didn't mean it as a challenge, far from it. He wanted to see the boy far away and safe, but Howard felt spiked.

'I'm staying,' he declared defiantly. 'I don't want to hear about the boat.'

Clarke nodded, lifted his glass and made a toast. 'A bold decision.'

Another bold decision finally turned the Battle of the Yser in favour of the Allies. The Belgians daringly decided to open the canal locks at Nieuwpoort and flood the German trenches. Large areas of Belgian countryside were deluged, fields of precious corn, standing proud against the blue-black outline of a church, sunk under a blanket of water. The German soldiers slipped and sloshed in the mud. They had no choice: they would either drown or they must launch an all-out assault on the Belgian trenches, trenches that were on higher ground.

Both sides shot and bombed, blazed and raged. Equally distraught.

Equally vicious. Reserves were moved forward. Allied men and boys, soldiers all, marched past fields where wild flowers grew and sheep grazed. The flowers trembled and the sheep raised their heads in humble amazement when shells dropped with a harsh, shrill growl and threw up the earth about them. The soldiers were equally startled at first but became accustomed horrifyingly swiftly. This time the Belgians and French were luckiest, if luck came into it, which Howard doubted it did any more. As far as he could make out, every one of them was luckless to have been born at this time, and damned no matter which side they were on. Even if they lived through this show, it seemed to him they'd be caught at the next. However, the men who had long since called the land their own had an edge; they were the most desperate, reckless and fraught. They did not have as much to gain but they had so much more to lose. Their houses could be burnt, their women raped, their babies murdered or, if left to live, forced to speak a foreign tongue and to be a subjugated race. It was motivation enough. The Germans were eventually pushed back and were forced to abandon the idea of crossing the Yser.

Howard read Clarke's article about the German retreat and could not fail to notice that it betrayed a profound sense of relief. He described the Germans as having been *smashed like a fallen wine glass*.

'Do you think those *Daily Mail* readers you have worked so hard to protect from the reality of the threat of disaster, and who might not have realised we were so close to an end here, might now be surprised by the utter relief and joy of your report?'

*The Germans in northern Belgium are on the run and Dunkirk feels safe at last, Calais too and all the little towns and hamlets round about. You need to have lived in the midst of alarms such as the Dunkirk region has known this past month to realise the relief that is felt, the intolerable load that is lifted.*

'Do you think it's too much?' asked Clarke.

'God, no. Leave it be. They need it.'

The two men were in the bar again. It seemed the entire town was. Tonight the landlord had dug out bottles of champagne and was selling them to the soldiers at a fair price rather than an inflated one. The men were ruddy with delight at their success. They had lived! Lived to see another day. They would drink too much and kiss the pretty French women – more than kiss if they were allowed. Why wouldn't they want to get drunk and get laid? Feel life in their veins? They were gods for the night. Immortals.

The bar rang with the sound of laughter, bottle knocking against glasses, singing and seducing. Howard wondered if tonight he'd find a woman for himself. It had been a long time. There had been no one since he arrived in France. He was picking up the language and spoke enough to persuade a girl to be good to him; his looks alone could do that, even if he never uttered a word. They called him 'the brooder' and 'the artist', and looked at him with curiosity and longing, but somehow he had never felt inclined to pursue the opportunities that presented themselves. Perhaps because he saw the cruelty of the soldiers being immortal for a day. Somehow he thought he was last in the queue.

'Have you heard what they are saying?'

'What are they saying?' Clarke looked immediately alert. He enjoyed the titbits Howard fed him. Howard had a helpful way of eliciting stories from troops and civilians alike. He had the sort of overpowering good looks that made people want him to like them; they wanted to be his friend and found him easy to confide in.

'Today the "barbarians" carried the Belgian wounded back to the Belgian trenches and handed them over to safe keeping.' Howard emphasised the word barbarians in a way that clearly indicated he was using it with heavy irony.

'Did they really?'

181

'Yes, they did.'

'I must write about it.' Clarke pulled out his notebook and scribbled something down.

'Will you?'

'Of course.' Both men glanced around at the celebrating crowds. Men who had killed and slaughtered now kissed and slow-danced. 'Strange thing, war.'

'Isn't it.'

# NOVEMBER 1914

# 21

*5th November 1914*

Dear Vivian,

I hope this letter finds you well and settled in at Blackwell. I'm certain you are finding it charming. I'm pleased to hear the pianoforte arrived safely. Have you found a man to tune it? You never said in your letter. I hope you are practising.

I am quite well here. The chaps are all decent sorts, as you'd expect. I am comfortable. We each sleep on a narrow camp bed and we've been given a sleeping bag, which takes one back to when one was a boy and camping with the Scouts, especially as the bag is a bit thin, but there are plenty of blankets so nothing to complain about. I share the tent with a terribly talented chap who goes under the incredible name Ace Cuthbert. He can play the viola and the lute, which he does to entertain us all as he brought both of them with him and says he's looking forward to taking them to the Front.

We each have been allotted a manservant to make the bed and keep the tent tidy and what have you. My man seems honest and reliable, I'm pleased to say. The officers' mess is enormous, utilitarian rather than luxurious, of course. I'd be horrified if it was anything other. There's a war on. It's not a building but a tent, with boarded sides, quite robust even when it's inclement.

*I'm relieved to inform you that the food is excellent. The men are always commenting that they are well fed. Some say they've never eaten better in their lives. Sausage, eggs. They think they've died and gone to heaven. Fish and chips are served on a Friday. There's also an anteroom where we can go to read a book or write letters. Yes, all very pleasant.*

*Please will you post this letter on to Mother and Father so they get my news too. I shall write to you and them alternately, and arrange for their letters to be forwarded to you. This way I will not have to repeat myself.*

*Fond wishes,*

*Your husband,*

*Aubrey*

*PS There's every chance that I shall be home for Christmas because the 10th Sherwood Foresters will not have completed training until the New Year and so we won't be posted until after then. Invite my parents and yours too, of course.*

There were things that Vivian accepted about her new life and things she couldn't help but resent.

It had soon become apparent that the village felt the lack of twenty-five men. Her lady's maid only came to her one day a week now; the housemaid managed two. The rest of the time the girls helped their fathers with farm work, taking the place of their brothers. Initially this was another vile shock for Vivian, but she knew she had to muddle through. They all did. Soon she began to realise that rather than a horrible inconvenience, the lack of maid was actually quite liberating. It did mean she was required to do rather more for herself – she had to pick out her own clothes, draw her bath, take washing to the kitchen (although things weren't yet so bad that she had to do her own washing!) – but frankly, what else would she be doing? There were no shops, theatres or balls; there were no friends to talk and giggle with. At least these small chores passed the time.

To this same end she requested another meeting with the land manager, Mr Pickering. As a thirty-four-year-old married man with four children, he luckily had not been lost to the army. Of course he'd wanted to volunteer, but he'd been persuaded by his wife and father-in-law to stay put, at least for now. On his return visit, Vivian concentrated very closely. He told her that there were no men to be recruited from neighbouring villages or even the town to help on the farm. Everyone was in the same boat. Labour was terribly scarce.

'The village women have rolled up their sleeves,' he declared with a cheerful beam.

'No doubt they are glad to be picking up the wages of their husbands and brothers.'

'That, and they are proud to be doing their bit.'

The phrase was beginning to irritate Vivian. One of the delights she had anticipated in being married and independent of her mother was that she would be able to buy any number of wonderful items of clothes. However, since the war broke out, she'd been doomed to serviceable dark brown and navy. The most she could hope for was a selection of becoming cream Viyella blouses paired with plain, neat skirts. Before she had married, her wardrobe had at least boasted a splash of colour. She hadn't been allowed turquoise or ruby; mostly she'd worn white (oh, the irony), but the ribbons had been little slivers of delight that weaved their way in and out of her consciousness, in and out of her very core. She'd dearly hoped for more, but the war had put a stop to that.

Not buying pretty clothes was a way of doing one's bit. Where would she wear pretty clothes to anyway? Stuck up here on a farm. The most exciting thing she did was take the car in to Stafford once a week. There was a tea shop there she loved to visit. The china was floral, the tablecloths were embroidered, and whilst it was a far cry from anything she'd frequented in London, the little waitress was sensitive to the fact that she visited on her own and always found her a copy of *The Lady* to hide behind. Oh, how she loved to read the comforting tips about handsome coats being a good investment ('especially if it lasts a second winter for smart wear'). The place seemed to exist without men and was impervious to their war, and she was glad of it.

'I notice you've been gardening, Mrs Owens.'

'Yes, that's right.' She straightened her shoulders, waiting for Mr Henshaw Pickering to chastise her, perhaps for wearing men's trousers, or maybe because she wasn't doing something as well as it ought to be done. She lowered her eyes to the plate of scones, as she used to when her mother began a barrage of criticism.

'Tackled it pretty successfully, from what I can see.'

'Oh, do you think so? Thank you.' She flashed him a full, heartfelt smile. She knew he was paid by her husband, and strictly speaking she really shouldn't care what the staff thought of her, or anything at all but she swelled under his compliment.

'We'll have to turn the gardens over, though.' He threw out an apologetic shrug.

'How do you mean?'

'Flowers are no use to anyone. We need potatoes.'

'Oh. I see.' She found it bizarre that growing flowers had become unpatriotic, but understood that food was needed. Food for themselves, for their horses and others.

'Would you be willing to do that?'

'If it helps, of course. I want to do my bit.' She bit down on her tongue, desperate not to laugh at herself for using the pat phrase.

'I wondered whether you could do a little more on the farm.'

'Do you think I could?'

'Yes, ma'am.' Pickering was enthusiastic. 'I do. I could run through some basic jobs that you could manage, and it might lighten the load for everyone else. If you're willing, like.'

It was no longer enough to be adorable. There wasn't anyone to adore her. Besides, she feared the whole worshipping thing – which she doubted had ever been substantial enough to mean much – had ceased to exist now, because of the war. How could anyone simply love a thing any more? Other women used to envy her, want to be her. Now she frustrated them. 'I find I am willing, Mr Pickering.' It was extraordinary what boredom could drive a girl to do.

Basic jobs! Hard labour, more like. Vivian found she was thrown in with the village women and old men, who were all obviously mindful of her superior social position but also quite aware of their own superior skill set. They settled into a relationship where she tried to ignore the girls' giggles and they tried to ignore her inexperience. The young boys touched their caps, some in a manner that expressed dejection, others with flirty enthusiasm. They didn't quite know where to peg her. Pretty enough to be somebody, but her house was the size of the doctor's. They were unsure. Still, everyone agreed she was *doing her bit*.

No one could say otherwise. She was forever scrubbing, lugging, chopping, weeding or feeding. The animals' mouths seemed eternally open, their rears incessantly depositing. There was nothing adorable about these animals. Pickering didn't start her on sweet lambs or cute calves (apparently it was not the season; she hadn't appreciated there was a particular time when animals had their young). The animals she helped to tend were huge beasts, cows or pigs (yes, pigs were actually enormous!), or scratchy hens (which she found quite terrifying, with their beady eyes and nasty sharp beaks). It was smelly, dirty work but it was not actually difficult, if one followed instructions. No one had suggested she milk anything yet (which did seem to require a knack), and the benefit of winter, as she understood it, was that nothing needed reaping, which she imagined would be quite a task. Thank goodness the men would be back in time for that.

She accepted that she had been thrown into a war herself, the unrelenting war on domesticity. She now darned stockings to wear the next day; she scrubbed, shovelled, brushed and polished alongside her maids. In her weaker, bleaker moments she sometimes wondered how she'd become trapped in this life, and then she would remember. Such a small slip. Now it was always going to be this way. Married to a man she didn't love, who didn't love her, who might not be able to love at all.

Yet slowly, over the weeks, she found that the animals' neediness and the relentless, repetitive nature of the chores required to run a farm was a blessing. On the whole, it was good to be busy. She had purpose for the first time. A purpose that was not related to her looks and attractiveness. She'd spent her life measuring her worth by an invisible standard of achievement: could she get some particular man to dance with her, to hold her hand, to send her flowers? She always could. She hadn't had to exert herself. Until that last occasion, when everything fell apart. Now she was often exhausted. Every night she fell into bed aching and found sleep quickly, no longer perturbed by the hooting owls or other country sounds. The reality of food, sweat, faeces, earth exhausted her. Her knuckles were red raw, as was her face, as often as not. She felt the muscles in her arms, legs and belly tighten. She liked her strength and leanness. She learnt not to mind the lack of a lady's maid, the paucity of pretty clothes, friends or entertainment. She didn't resent the extra work.

But her husband's letter? That made her quiver with fury.

# 22

I T WAS A battle, not the war.

The end to the imminent threat to Dunkirk made life for all the inhabitants much more tolerable, although it immediately became apparent that the Germans' retreat from Yser did not mean an end to danger. Attention quickly focused on the strategically important city of Ypres. About twenty-five miles from Dunkirk, its position as the last city before the coast meant it was vitally important to the Allied supply route and must be protected at all costs. No one had calculated what all costs might be. The Germans were regarding the area as equally essential, as it was the last defence before their railway network that allowed them to dominate Belgium and freely transport troops. They would fight tooth and nail. Howard thought hard about that expression until he understood it for the first time. The men would bomb and shoot, and when that didn't work, they would claw, scrabble and tear at one another like animals.

He found it breathtakingly disappointing that no sooner was one victory secured than another had to be sought. Of course it must. There were miles and miles of front to defend. Hundreds of battles still to fight. He could not imagine how many more lives had to be sacrificed before they would be able to say it was over. People had stopped talking about being home for Christmas. That previous optimism simply seemed foolish now, laughable.

So the battle for Ypres began; it roared, ravaged, then it lurked. Howard had been beginning to think he knew war. He thought he had seen everything dreadful that there was to see. He was wrong. Nothing had prepared him. No one could have imagined it. The Germans came: boots, boots, boots, bang bang bang.

'They are children!' the British officers cried. It was true that two out of three of the German troops were pimply youths, surely no older than nineteen, but the Allies could not afford to be sentimental.

Howard watched as the battle was relentlessly slogged out every day for over a month. The casualties piled ever skyward. Men were shot, burnt, blown to pieces, drowned and stabbed. He saw it all. Despite the vicious intensity of the fighting on the front line, Ypres itself, by some miracle, remained relatively unscathed. At least it did until the Germans began to periodically shell the city, and then, two weeks later, as they became more desperate and vicious, to send a heavy stream of shells directly into the centre. Howard considered the possibility that the bombardment was designed to conceal a repositioning of German forces, because surely the destruction of the city itself could have no strategic value. Clarke disagreed. 'The attacks are motivated by malevolence.'

'It seems there are no limits to man's anger and spite.'

'Quite so. Finding that with all their men, and all those guns, and all their struggles, and their sacrifice of lives they could not take Ypres, they've set out to break it. Peevish children are sometimes like that.'

The city was razed. Everything. Houses, farms, schools, shops, the Cloth Hall and the ancient cathedral that other men had built in 1230. All reduced to ruin and rubble. The two men watched as fires blazed, then smoke lingered; finally there was nothing other than grey wreckage.

'It sickens me!' Howard cried.

'This sickens you more than the things you've seen on the Front?'

'I can't measure one against the other. War sickens me. Must men destroy everything they have created?' Howard was white with horror. How clever and inventive we have been, he thought. So many ways to kill a man. For thousands of years we've been honing the art of warfare, and now it seems we've really become efficient. Snipers, machine guns, shells, torpedoes; bayonets if all else fails. What a creative breed we are.

For all that, on 22nd November Clarke was able to tell the world that the Allies had secured an essential victory. With excitement and new vigour he drafted the copy and then gave it to Howard for comment. Howard held the paper in his hand, his wrist limp, his fingers slack, almost letting the sheet blow away in the wind. Clarke snatched it from him. 'Don't you like it?' he demanded.

'You always write well.'

'So?' He wanted to know why his friend wasn't jubilant.

'It's this phrase here: "bloody battle".'

'What's wrong with it?'

'I've heard it before.'

'Of course, and you will again. It's what it is.' Howard was unimpressed. Clarke pushed on. 'Would you prefer gory? Grotesque? Gruesome?'

'Of course not, they're all gratuitous.' The men glared at each other. They'd been living on top of one another for some weeks now, under circumstances that were more than testing.

'Well, you give me some fresh words to pin this hell. You're a writer too.'

'I can't. I'm not.' Howard looked as though he was in pain, actual physical pain, like some of the men who lay about waiting for the attention of a nurse. He thought about it. He was a playwright, or at least he had been once. It was not something he believed in now. Not something he could hold on to after France. Creativity and ambition had been blown to bits along with everything else. He returned to the copy and shook his head. Finally he muttered, 'You call it a victory.'

'We held the line.'

'It was no sort of victory for mankind.'

'We've dug in, our trenches are secure.'

'Yes, I fear the men are already in graves. They've dug their own.'

'You can't talk like that, man.' Clarke was impatient. Howard knew that his attitude wasn't acceptable. It didn't do to grumble. There was a tacit agreement: everyone had to keep their pecker up. Even whilst killing or being killed.

'What are they estimating? Twenty-six thousand British men dead, the British Expeditionary Force broken?'

'Where are you getting these numbers from? Only eight thousand are confirmed dead, eighteen thousand missing.'

'Oh, and you think they are just going to turn up, do you? Maybe they will.' Howard shrugged, his body oozing sarcasm. 'They might stagger through the mud any minute now, only they'd have to get past the twenty thousand Belgians and the seventy thousand French bodies first.' An accidental spray of spittle leapt from his mouth and landed on Clarke's cheek. Clarke calmly took out a handkerchief and dabbed it away.

'The Germans have had losses too.'

'That doesn't comfort me.' Howard dropped his head into his hands. He half expected it to roll off; he'd been having nightmares about that recently, about decapitated bodies and detached limbs. In his nightmares he'd be walking along a French street when suddenly his leg would fall off, or he'd trip on someone else's arm; one time he dreamt he found an ear in his soup. Lots of the men were having similar disturbances, but when they woke up, the nightmare carried on. 'They were kids, just boys. They were massacred.' He let out a low groan. It was animalistic. Guttural.

'We're at war, Howard.'

'As if I could be in any doubt.'

Clarke thought he ought to change the subject, but looking around him, he struggled for a diversion. They were billeted behind the lines, near the casualty clearing station. Getting between Dunkirk and the Front every day had become untenable; during this heavy period of shelling there were no vehicles that could give them a lift. If vehicles were taking that route, they were laden with ammunition on the way out, and carrying wounded when they returned; there was no room for newspapermen. It was safer to stay put, but Clarke was beginning to worry that Howard had chosen the wrong place to base himself. Maybe he should be in Dunkirk, or better yet, England. Yesterday they had come across an incineration device where the amputated limbs were disposed of. Howard had observed the nurses do their hellish work and then he'd vomited and wept.

Clarke pointed to a soldier sitting on the floor outside the doors of the clearing station. There were almost a hundred men awaiting treatment, their wounds distinct and obvious. Heads were bandaged; they lay on stretchers or wore slings. 'Look at that man. What's wrong with him?' Clarke enquired. Howard tended to know more about anything medical because he spent as much of his time as he could helping the nurses and stretcher-bearers. The man in question was shaking, a quivering wreck. Every inch of his body trembled, including his eyes, which seemed to dash around his skull as though they were trying to escape. His mouth hung open.

'They are calling it shell shock.'

'But the generals are saying there's no such thing.'

'Of course they are. They think this war is a good idea,' spat Howard.

'I see your point. He's certainly not sensible.'

'No.'

'Completely out of his wits.'

'It looks that way, and who can blame him.'

'It seems genuine enough to me. Should we go and talk to him?'

'It won't help. He can't speak.'

'I can't see any facial injury.'

'He has a tongue; it's his nerves that have been blown to smithereens. He can't make sense. I talked to the men who brought him in.'

'And?'

'He lay in a caved-in shell hole for six days, trapped, with nothing to eat. The hole was filled with water, and in that water lay the decaying body of his best friend. He had to drink the water to stay alive. Pleasant, isn't it?'

'Good God.'

There was something more important that Howard needed Clarke to know. 'But that's not the story.'

'It isn't?'

'The generals are calling for these lads to be court-martialled and shot for faking injury. Fucking animals.'

'Steady there, son. Steady.' Clarke glanced around.

Howard glowered. He didn't understand Clarke's calm; they'd seen the same things. The older man placed his hand on Howard's arm, a conciliatory gesture. Human contact was rare and therefore disproportionately appreciated. Howard tried to breathe in and out, remain calm. He had begun to hate the generals, who to his mind at least were indistinguishable and interchangeable, physically and mentally. They were all in their fifties; they had heavy square jaws and ruddy faces, small, stern, searching eyes and closely cropped white hair. They all had neat moustaches that made him think of toothbrushes; they oozed self-belief and stupidity.

'What's your view?' Clarke probed gently.

'They are calling them cowards, saying it affects the smaller, nervous types the most. Making the sufferers feel emasculated and ashamed on top of everything else. After all this.' He threw his arms in the air and gestured around. 'After all they've been through. But look at him. He's an ox. Illness doesn't segregate, and shell shock *is* an illness. Last week I saw a case where a man clawed at his own mouth so severely he made himself bleed. His eyes were livid with horror. No one could fake that. I've worked with professional actors. These men are not cowards; they are wrecks. They've seen too much and something in them has snapped. No doctor will ever be able to mend such a man. You should write about it.'

Clarke sighed. 'Maybe I will.'

'If they let you,' Howard snapped bitterly.

'Yes, if they let me,' Clarke agreed.

# MARCH 1915

# 23

Vivian had a visitor. The novelty was breathtaking. Mrs Henderson, the smiley lady she'd met in Mr Walker's shop right back in October, had taken it upon herself to come and call. Vivian had seen her at church every week since they'd first met, and Mrs Henderson had always thrown a friendly nod or wave in her direction, but after the service she never lingered to chat. Vivian had thought of inviting her for a drink on Christmas Eve, but Aubrey had coughed at the suggestion and pointed out that Mrs Henderson wasn't the proper sort of society. Instead he invited the vicar, the doctor and their wives. Both women were absolutely rigidly polite; Vivian thought her mother would have found them tolerable – if her mother had accepted the invitation to visit for Christmas, but she hadn't. Vivian found them boring.

Mrs Henderson lived in a cottage at the end of the village; Vivian had had Mrs Rosebend point it out. It was a very overly decorated cottage. The slate roof slipped into carved gables, hung tiles and a dense stucco facade. It was one of three tied cottages that had been built by Aubrey's grandfather in Victoria's reign. The grandfather had no doubt been a generous employer, ahead of his time; however, the congested decor advertised not only his benevolence but also his lack of taste. There was a little iron gate, which was stiff and creaky. Vivian knew that because she'd twice very nearly called in on Mrs Henderson, but the slight resistance the gate gave was enough to put her off, bring her to her senses. How would she explain the nature of the call? 'Oh, hello, I'm a little bored and lonely. Some months ago you encouraged me to garden, which turned out rather nicely, and because of that I thought you might want to be my friend.' Pathetic! Ridiculous.

Mrs Henderson had left a card yesterday. It was hand-painted with a border of intertwining forget-me-nots; her calligraphy was exquisite. The card stated her intention of calling at 3 p.m., if convenient. Lovely manners. Without the warning she might have found Vivian dressed in trousers and digging in the back, which wouldn't have been the thing. As it was, Vivian had time to instruct Cook to bake a sponge.

Mrs Henderson arrived at three on the dot. Vivian was relieved she hadn't plumped for being fashionably late, as she'd been ready for an hour. As her guest entered the room, she stood, with her hand already extended to shake. Mrs Henderson ignored it and pulled her into a brief but heartfelt embrace. She had the smell of a woman of a certain age. Vivian didn't quite understand the smell, but she was familiar with it. It sat amongst the clothes in her mother's dressing room. It snapped bitterly at her nose and yet was comforting and welcome as she knew it was her future one day and she could not despise it.

'Mrs Henderson, how lovely of you to call.'

'Do call me Enid. I'm not one for formalities, Vivian.' She paused for a moment to see how Vivian would react to being called by her Christian name even before she'd given permission to do so. Vivian didn't know what to do. She supposed she would have offered it. She smiled.

'Tea?'

'Love some.'

They sat opposite one another, holding their saucers and smiling. Despite clear willingness on both sides to be friendly, they stumbled around the obvious subjects. They agreed that the sponge was light, delicious, and that it had been a wet winter – dreadful. They also agreed that they mustn't complain because the brave boys must be having far worse a time of it. The minute Vivian threw out the comment she regretted it. Enid's face clouded. Vivian remembered.

'Your boys are out there, aren't they, Mrs—' She corrected herself. 'Enid.'

'My younger son, Michael, is leaving for France today, actually. All the boys in the village are. Their training is complete.' Vivian thought that maybe that was why Mrs Henderson had called on her today in particular; perhaps she needed a distraction. She smiled weakly.

'Oh yes, Mrs Rosebend mentioned it.'

'Your husband too?' Was she here because she thought Vivian was the one who might need company and consolation? How lovely. Unnecessary but lovely.

'No.' Vivian blushed. She'd just received a letter from Aubrey (via his parents!) saying that he had not been sent abroad with the men from the village. They'd all expected he would lead the Pals regiment. It made sense. He was bitterly disappointed that another officer had been sent instead. He must stay behind. He'd been put in charge of some home defence or training or something. He couldn't give details. Security risk and all. It was humiliating. Why hadn't they sent him to France? Vivian knew she ought to be delighted that he was safe in England. She imagined that women up and down the country were desperate to hear that their men had been detained. The fact that she didn't feel the same depressed her. It was all rather embarrassing.

'Well, that's good,' stated Enid firmly. Vivian couldn't lie to her by agreeing, but contradicting her was unthinkable. 'My husband fought in the Boer War.'

'Did he . . .' Vivian stuttered, suddenly aware she was being vulgar and leading.

'Die? Oh no. He left, my dear.'

Vivian gasped. 'I'm so sorry.' In an instant she felt ashamed. She should not have made Mrs Henderson confess as much.

'He left before Michael was a year old. Howie was just four. Quite a shock. To me at least. Everyone else seemed to be expecting it. Told me they'd never liked him. It's not comforting.' She smiled, her lips buoyant, her eyes still regretful.

'No,' Vivian confirmed. 'It's not.' Although she was stunned and saddened by Mrs Henderson's confession, she couldn't drown out the overwhelming sense of relief and deep empathy. It was selfish, but there was something cathartic about meeting another dissatisfied and disappointed woman.

'Because I did, you see. Like him.' Hopelessly intrigued, Vivian was gratified when Enid added, 'He never struck me as a woman-iser, yet he did leave for another woman. I think men tend to, don't you?' Vivian thought it astounding that Mrs Henderson believed she might have an opinion. It was liberating to find she did.

'Yes.'

'Not secure enough to simply walk away, they have to have someone to walk towards.' Enid sighed, pitying and regretful at the same time, as a mother might sigh if her son had chopped the heads off a neighbour's roses with a stick. Vivian's experience, for the first time, did not seem a disgrace to be worn like a scarlet letter, but something a little more commonplace. Women made mistakes in love. It was as simple as that. 'I was so shocked and hurt. I had to get on with it, of course. There was no point in making a fuss. Chin up.'

Mrs Henderson could have pretended he was dead if she'd wanted to appear to be respectable. If she'd gone down that route, Vivian would have accepted it, perhaps even admired her all the more for her discretion, but she was prepared to share secrets, to be forthright. Vivian was grateful for her confidence. Friendship, a demonstration of trust, was more important than even the most heartfelt admiration for discretion. However, she didn't know how to reciprocate.

'Is it chilly in here?' She stood up, noticed the scuttle was empty so rang the bell.

It was all very slow and awkward. Mrs Rosebend came into the room and Vivian explained there was no coal; the housekeeper left and eventually waddled back hauling a full scuttle, reminding Vivian that the housemaid had been given the day off because she had gone to try to see her brother off at Portsmouth.

'A wild idea. She'll never find him in the crowds,' muttered Mrs Rosebend with exasperation. She glanced at Enid and threw out a brief, tight smile. 'Your Michael going?'

'Yes. And you have a nephew leaving today too,' replied Enid.

'That's right. My brother-in-law tried to sign up, but flat feet and too old, so you know.' A shrug.

There were posters everywhere urging men to join up and insisting that if a chap couldn't join himself he must try to get a recruit to fill his place, so zealous men were sending their green sons. The adverts promised, 'There's still a place in the line for you!' They made it sound so irresistibly cosy and chummy. The stations and ports were always crowded with soldiers. War involved a lot of movement and confusion. It was all about taking people away. Enid and Mrs Rosebend were too mature to dash to Portsmouth on the off chance they'd spot their boys in the crowds of khaki, but it was clear where their thoughts were. The men of the village had left for training camp in a blaze of brass bands and bunting; now the mood was considerably more sombre. Vivian understood. The papers were full of casualty lists.

Enid rallied first. 'Leave the fire, Mrs Rosebend. I'll see to it. You must be busy.'

'If you don't mind.' Mrs Rosebend looked at Vivian for guidance but didn't find any. Vivian was pretty certain she shouldn't allow her guest to build a fire but Mrs Henderson had practically swept Mrs Rosebend out of the door and was on her knees in front of the grate before she knew how to stop her.

'Allow me,' she offered weakly, standing up from her chair.

'Oh no, you mustn't. You need your rest. You know, it won't be long before fires are unnecessary during the day. Won't that be nice?'

'Do you think so?' Vivian could hardly imagine it. Blackwell was such a cold place. The winter had seemed eternal here. It was almost April, but there was no hint of spring warmth in the air. 'I can't believe summer will ever arrive,' she confessed with a sigh.

Mrs Henderson smiled, refusing to take her gloom seriously. 'We do get warm spells, like the rest of Britain. Just maybe a little later than in the south. The fact is, time does drag so in your condition.' Vivian cocked her head to one side. Her condition? 'So, my dear, I hope it's not too cheeky to ask, but when are you due?'

'I'm sorry?'

'The baby.' Vivian was stunned. Mrs Henderson carefully finished building the fire and then sat down again. She poured them both a second cup of tea. Softly, 'You do realise there is a baby?'

Thoughts scrambled into Vivian's head, a monstrous jumble that she quickly sorted. When had she last had a monthly? She racked her brains. Just before Christmas. Before Aubrey came home on leave. She put her hands on her belly. She had been feeling exhausted and sick. She'd joked it was the country air.

A baby. She was growing a baby. It was incredible. 'I had no idea,' she spluttered.

'Am I right?' Enid was beaming now, jubilant and delighted as women always were when they heard of a married woman's pregnancy. Vivian nodded.

'I think you are.' A baby! What a shock. She'd had no idea that it would happen. Of course she knew what led to what and she had been doing her duty, especially at Christmas time when he came home on leave in uniform, but there was such a lack of affection between them that she had never thought a baby might spring from it. That all his grunting and all her enduring might lead to a gurgling, smiling actual baby.

'I have thought so for a few weeks now. I've seen you in church. First the green and exhausted stage, then recently the bloom in your cheeks. I'd say you are over three months gone. Do you agree?' Again Vivian nodded, wondering how this woman could possibly know more about her than she did herself. Suddenly Mrs Henderson's face fell from its exuberant confidence to concern. 'I hope you don't think it's disconcerting that I've noticed.'

'No, no, not at all,' Vivian assured her, genuinely surprised that she didn't find it intrusive that an interest had been taken. In fact she found it was a relief.

'It's just I've been aware that since you moved here you don't seem to have had many visitors,' Mrs Henderson commented carefully. 'I haven't seen your mother.'

It was awkward. Vivian didn't like people noticing her mother's neglect. 'No, she likes London.'

'Or friends.'

'I don't really have any close friends here,' she admitted.

'But back in London, surely. Couldn't they visit?'

Ava had visited in January. This was the ultimate compliment because, really, who came to the countryside in January. There was nothing to shoot. 'Filthy month, diabolical,' Ava had declared. 'Promise me you won't suggest a walk.' She wrote regularly, pithy one-liners on fabulously funny postcards, and had promised another visit in the summer. Vivian thought of Emily and how she had only agreed to be her bridesmaid after Ava had. Emily had just got engaged to Charles Rushmore. She hadn't written to Vivian to say so; Charles's sister had. Vivian hadn't received an invitation to the wedding. She imagined they'd have a very small do. Most were nowadays; no one wanted to be seen to be profligate, no one wanted to tempt fate by appearing too happy. Even so, it would have been lovely to get a letter from Emily saying as much.

It stung, actually.

There were other girls too, but Vivian hadn't kept up with them. Blackwell seemed so far away from, well, anywhere. 'There used to be so many friends, at the dances and theatres and such,' she murmured. In truth, they had been friendly but they were not friends. It had been difficult to cultivate intimacy, as their mothers kept the girls close by their sides until they could be safely handed over to some man or other. It was accepted that only as a married woman would one have the opportunity to develop friendships, but the chances of doing so were severely reduced if banished to Blackwell. 'I loved my season,' Vivian confessed to Enid in a rush. Enid smiled encouragingly. The thought of it bubbled up inside, effervescent and delightful. The perfume and possibility, the dresses, the dances, the daring. 'I was happy and enthusiastic the whole time. I enjoyed everything like mad. In retrospect, I suppose I should have played it a little calmer, a little safer.'

Oh Lord, what had made her say that? It was far too revealing, but somehow Enid's gentle face and wild hair invited confession. To counter her words, Vivian broadened her smile, possibly too wide. Silly tears pricked her eyes like tiny sewing pins caught on flesh during a fitting. She turned to look out of the window, stare out across the field, until she calmed down. Its expanse struck her as brazen, defiant, cocksure. Despite her efforts to regain composure, she muttered, 'Look where it has landed me, all that enthusiasm.'

Enid Henderson nodded slowly and gave a sympathetic, soothing smile. She seemed to understand it all and more. Enid was standing by the fire; she hitched up her skirt to let the heat reach the back of her legs. It wasn't ladylike. She stared off into the middle distance. Was she thinking how Aubrey Owens' marriage had been a speedy, shy affair, and wondering whether there had been some sort of scandal. Full blown? Near miss? There had to have been something.

'Maybe it wasn't your enthusiasm that landed you here, but society's lack of it,' she offered after a moment or two. It was a lovely thought. Vivian allowed it to flutter and settle. 'I do believe that one only earns the right to strong and cherished friendships once one has learnt to stand alone. You have to like yourself very much, Vivian, before you can expect others to.' She held Vivian's gaze. Vivian was at a loss as to how to respond to such frankness.

'Oh.'

'So I should imagine you'll very soon find yourself inundated with new friends, because haven't you done well?'

'Have I?'

'Managing the house and the staff. The garden. Mr Pickering says you've done a marvellous job, pitching in. There's something rather wonderful about work, don't you think?'

Vivian was not sure she did agree in entirety; being idle was nice. She was often cold, dirty and sore. 'What do you mean?'

'Well, having your days filled from start to finish. Purpose followed by bone-aching exhaustion. I like being so weary I can't worry.' About Michael, of course. Mothers, wives and sweethearts everywhere wanted to be too busy to think. Vivian didn't really worry about Aubrey, though she knew she was supposed to. She stayed silent. Enid no doubt assumed she was being stoic. 'You must be very proud of yourself. Very proud indeed. You are doing extremely well, Vivian.'

'Do you think so?' Vivian wasn't sure she could remember anyone praising her about anything since she first came out in society, when everyone agreed she was brilliant at filling her dance card. Since the Nathaniel incident – which was the only way she could refer to the horror – she'd been nothing but a dumping ground for irritation and disappointment. She'd been out in the cold for so long, it seemed bizarre to be welcomed unconditionally.

Vivian liked Enid so very much in that moment that it took all her nineteen years of training and repression to stop her from saying so. All she did was smile and offer another slice of sponge cake.

# MAY 1916

# 24

HOWARD WAS BRUTALISED. Scar tissue had no feeling and his heart and mind were entirely scarred. He'd seen enough. Too much. The military world, where humanity was crushed under the weight of duty and honour, was not for him. He accepted that most of them, the boys and men who dashed out to kill with such surety and zeal, thought they were doing the right thing, if they thought about it at all, but he was sure they were mistaken. A war would not end a war. Love, peace, a refusal to pick up arms: those were the only things that could make a difference in the end. His experiences with Clarke at the Front had convinced him of the futility of war. No one could win. Wars were for losers. Besides, it was pretty clear that responsibility and dignity were too bloodstained to survive. What a world. What a world.

In January 1916, the government made it law that single men between the age of eighteen and forty-one had to be conscripted into the war effort. Howard was back in England when the news broke. He'd left France in October 1915, shortly after he had come to understand the full horror and ineptitude that had led to the deaths of fifty thousand Allied men at the Battle of Loos. His brother Michael being one of them. Howard understood there was a need for conscription. The country was haemorrhaging men; youth was being massacred at a diabolical, unimaginable rate. He understood it but could not condone.

'I've seen enough. I just want to go home,' he told Basil Clarke.

'You think we will lose?'

'No.'

'You think we will win?'

'No. We've all lost already.'

Leaving France did not mean he had left behind the horror; he found it came with him. Everywhere. His nostrils could never be rinsed of the smell of blood, he was sure that mud sat under his nails, and sickness – a deep, deep sickness at humankind – lay in his heart. He did not approach Warrington to ask for work, he was clueless as to what he might write now; an adaptation of *Little Women* was a ludicrous thought. He struggled to find anyone who wanted to hire him to do anything at all, a healthy man who ought to have been at the front. Eventually he found work washing up at a big hotel in Mayfair. He was prepared to do the night shift and he cleaned the lavatories without complaint; he was paid cash in hand and below the going rate. When he received his papers calling him to arms, he walked to the police station and told them to arrest him.

He would not kill. He could not add to it. Really, he could not.

He swiftly became something of a celebrity conscientious objector, though he didn't look for it. A dashing playwright who had been to the Front – taken serious risks to get there, gained a level of notoriety whilst doing so – was extremely interesting to the British public. The press pounced on him, persecuted and vilified him, whilst liberal groups held him up as a lone voice of reason.

It seemed most people enjoyed being swept up in the mass. They felt as though they belonged and had purpose in a crowd, in a mob, in an army. It was only the very secure who could suggest that following the masses might not be all there was. Those intelligent enough to understand as much, who recognised Howard's peculiar and particular strength, were the most afraid, and hatred flowed through their veins. His handsome face was effectively used for and against him.

Why would such a healthy, tall, strong man refuse to fight for his country? *Coward!*

How could anyone let this model man march to certain death? *Madness!*

He did not have the option to quietly sit through a local conscription tribunal, to try to privately explain his position and conscience in the town hall. He was to be publicly and relentlessly baited like a bear. The tribunals were set up to look into men's hearts, but man is a tricksy beast. Very few are pure. How could the local doctor and mayor tell if a man was battling with his conscience or his nerve? The entire tribunal process quickly disintegrated into a farce. Local bigwigs, stuffed with prejudice and wielding axes they wished to grind, could hardly be expected to judge the market gardener who insisted his work was vital or the Cambridge student who asked for a closer inspection of the New Testament. Certainly not the playwright who had simply seen too much. The process was perhaps well intentioned, maybe even worthy, but not very effective, and certainly not just. Clerics, choirmasters, councillors and such – men who sat with their heads in their hands and looked for all the world as though they wished they were somewhere else – did not have the answers. No one did. Two and a half million men had volunteered to take up arms for King and country. A few thousand refused. Why? It was vile, despicable, unfathomable.

Objectors were ordered to work at munitions factories or to load ships, or were sent to the Front as part of the Non-Combatant Corps – soon to be dubbed the No-Courage Corps – where they laid barbed-wire fences and could be easily picked off by German snipers. Some absolutists refused to cooperate with any aspect of warfare. They wanted nothing to do with it, largely on religious grounds, sometimes political. They would not load ammunitions on to ships or even peel potatoes in the officers' mess. What could be done with these slackers, these deviants?

They were sent to prison.

Howard seemed to particularly frustrate and disgust those who settled this sort of matter. His height and physical magnificence taunted, aggravated them. They needed men like him the most and they disliked needing him almost as much as they disliked his refusal to help. Of course they must make an example out of him. It was what the mob demanded.

'Do you believe in God, Mr Henderson?' asked the elderly local dentist who was the designated chairman in charge of Howard's tribunal. He was neither elected nor a military man, but these things were settled by whoever would take them on, because trials were work-intensive and manpower was scarce; that was the irony.

'I believe in humanity.'

'I'm trying to understand. Are you a religious man?'

It wasn't that Howard was a holier-than-thou sort. He'd done things that some might question morally. When he'd been a playwright (was he ever? It didn't seem real or possible. Was that another man?), there had been fringe benefits and he'd taken advantage. He was flesh and blood, after all. He drank, swore, lied if necessary. Not over big things; he only lied about trains delaying his journey to work when really he'd stolen an extra half-hour of sleep or sex and had been reluctant to leave the warmth of his bed. He was decent enough and that had been adequate then, before the war. Not especially godly or moral in the way that the tribunal might understand the word, but he was a thinker. Always a thinker. The thing people said to him most often (besides complimenting him on his big blue eyes) was that he thought too much. There was no such thing; for a writer it was impossible to overthink. That was his oxygen: to foresee, to second-guess, to imagine.

He wasn't any more or less moral than any of the men out there fighting, but he knew it was wrong. This war. It couldn't fix anything.

'No. I'm not a religious man.' If he ever had been, his belief lay bloody and stomped upon on the dirt tracks between Dunkirk and the Front.

'Then your objection to taking up arms is not because you adhere to the sixth commandment. Thou shalt not kill.' The Quakers and other extreme religious groups weren't liked for their refusal to go to war but they did at least have arguments that might be excused as valid, respectable. This playwright, this artisan, what were they to do with him? What was the meaning or point of him, this man who threatened national unity?

'I do not want to kill,' Howard confirmed carefully. Was the sanctity of life something only a religious man could appreciate? Was the futility of war something solely a Quaker could see?

The dentist shook with outrage. 'But it's your duty,' he insisted forcefully. He was the sort of man who had never had a moment's doubt about anything in his life. Howard envied him.

'I disagree. I would rather be killed than kill.'

'That can be arranged!' yelled a woman from the gallery. 'My brother died out there. His mates in his regiment would know what to do with you.' The crowd cheered, indicating that they supported her. Poor grief-stricken woman, thought Howard. He hoped her brother had had a swift death.

This interruption seemed to inspire a new line of enquiry for the dentist. 'Would you fight a man who violated your sister or wife?'

'I don't have a sister or wife so this question is hypothetical.' Howard regretted sounding glib, but he knew where this was heading. The chairman glanced again at Howard's papers, shuffled them in annoyance. Were these notes another man's? Another coward's?

'Your mother, then, everyone has a mother.'

'Yes, probably. I would.'

'So you are not a pacifist.'

'Not as you might know one, sir.'

'You are simply a coward.' Again an assertion. Not a moment's doubt. There was another general murmur of agreement. It seemed this matter was unequivocal, clear-cut.

'I just think war is wrong.' Howard realised he sounded childish and ludicrous even to his own ears, but there were no other words. His argument was no more or less complicated than that.

'Germany violated Belgium's neutrality and started on a meticulously planned journey of destruction, sweeping through France.'

'I know.' Howard met the chairman's eye. It wasn't defiance, it was respect, but his gaze caused the dentist to splutter with indignation, jowls quivering with irritation. Dread.

'What were we supposed to do? Stand back whilst they bullied?' Howard wondered whether he was the only man who was taught as a boy that two wrongs didn't make a right. 'There was the treaty that said we were guarantors of Belgium's neutrality. We couldn't allow the Germans to bully us or poor, brave little Belgium.'

Howard had heard this phrase a number of times over the past couple of years, and he found it ludicrous and patronising. He'd seen the Belgian soldiers. They *were* brave. Lean, dedicated, fearless, fearful. He couldn't imagine the paunchy dentist defending any one of them. It seemed ridiculous. Belittling. It showed the arrogance and ignorance of these elderly men who told young men to go to war. To die.

The bloody bodies of Belgian, French and British men flooded into Howard's head. Limbs loose then lost, bone floating in weeping pus and poison; the agony, the waste; boys walking, left right, left right towards the machine guns. Obedience and lunacy inseparable.

Duty and doom indivisible. Outrage soared through his body. He spat out his thoughts. 'We signed that treaty in 1839.' Forever ago. 'I say *we*, although in fact I never signed it. Nor anyone I've ever met. It was some old men, long dead, who did that.'

The assembled men who sat as judge and jury muttered resentfully amongst themselves. 'But still it means something. Keeping one's word has to mean something,' insisted the dentist.

'Yes, it meant Asquith had no choice. But I do.' Howard stayed firm and calm. He didn't raise his voice. He knew there was no point. Sometimes the quieter you were, the easier it was to be heard, and he must have been heard because the crowds in the gallery booed and spat at him.

'You do *not* have a choice! We're all agreed, we'll fight on to the last man.'

'Do you include yourself in that, sir?' He knew he was being inflammatory, but his patience was wearing thin.

'War is a young man's game,' asserted the dentist.

'It isn't a game at all.'

'It's heroic.'

'It's barbaric.'

'You don't think our boys are brave?'

'I do. And damned.'

There was a surge of outrage from everyone in the room. Of course it was uncomfortable, all those people yelling at him. It crossed Howard's mind that they might be the same people who used to cheer for him from the stalls. It took a good few minutes and repeated calls for calm before the questioning could continue.

'What time do you get up in the morning?' This question came from the retired officer who was the obligatory military representative at the tribunal. He was a stocky, soldierly fellow who stood with his legs wide; he had a square block of a head and a weighty jaw. His brief from his superiors was clear: he was to protect the nation by obtaining as many men as possible for the army. He'd never seen actual military service personally and always deeply regretted the fact. He did not understand this deluded and awkward young man who could not see what fun there was to be had from a war.

'I try for eight.' Nine, sometimes ten. Getting up had become less compelling since his time on the Front, but even under oath Howard knew that was not something he should confess.

'Do you drink?'

'Sometimes.'

'What time do you go to bed?'

'I try for ten.' He didn't sleep. Often he was still pacing the floorboards at two or three in the morning.

'Do you go to church?'

'Not as frequently as some.' Christmas was the last time. Midnight mass because his mother had wanted it. She'd come to London to be with him; it was the least he could do.

'Do you bathe?'

'Regularly.'

'This man has no conscience,' the retired officer stated confidently and definitively. 'He's a sly shirker and must be sent to war as soon as possible. The army will do him good. We are doing him a favour.' It was clear that he would have liked to slam down a hammer.

The women in furs clapped and cheered; the old men groaned and waved their umbrellas jubilantly. Howard knew they needed to carry on with their shrill cheerfulness, talking about heroes and duty. He was a nuisance. Defeated, infuriated and insulted, he yelled, 'It is callous slaughter. Butchery. Don't pretend it's anything other, not for a minute. Those men – good, bad and indifferent – are being cheated out of their lives. Tricked. I'm not giving mine up so easily.'

'So this is about self-preservation?' sneered the dentist.

Exhausted. 'I'm making a stand. Interpret it as you will, but

I'm not killing a single man. Not for you, my King or country. Not for bloody anybody.'

Howard was dragged from the court into a military van. His body was a lead weight. It wasn't that he was refusing to walk as such; his legs just wouldn't work. He was thinking about the corpses they'd dragged into mass and shallow graves. Sometimes he'd helped dig the graves, then stood with his cap clasped to his chest and mumbled a prayer. A ritual as much as anything. The soldiers in the van didn't know he'd buried their comrades. They stamped on him, broke his ribs and nose through fear and frustration.

He was patched up but wasn't sent to a military hospital; no doubt it was deemed a waste of a bed. Howard agreed and felt lucky enough that he was allowed to rest up in the barracks. Once able, he participated in the drills, shaved, kept his kit tidy, saluted, even picked up a gun and learnt to shoot it. They thought they had him, but when it was time to go to France, he would not get on the ship.

'Not unless you can guarantee non-combatant duty, sir,' he said to his major. Straight-backed, loud voice, meeting his eye. This request was within the major's power, but he was an angry, rigid man.

'You don't get to make fucking demands.'

Howard was sent to Richmond Castle, held in a cell that was little more than a dungeon: a filthy, damp, light-deprived room with deep, bleak walls and chilly flagstone floors. He tried very hard to think about his mother and home. The green fields and trees, the cottages with thin lines of smoke towering from their chimneys; he wanted to remember that there were Sunday lunches, bank holiday fairs and bookshelves. He doubted that his place of incarceration was arbitrary; Richmond Castle housed some of the absolutist conscientious objectors, the ones who were most feared and loathed. They would not accept non-combatant war work so were starved, beaten and isolated on occasion; a rule of silence was strictly enforced because everyone was petrified of what they might whisper.

The soldiers who guarded Howard looked at him with naked resentment sometimes; ferocious hope at others.

# JUNE 1916

# 25

SUMMER DRAGGED ITS feet, but eventually the weather softened. Doors and windows could be flung wide open for the entire day. Vivian and Enid's friendship intensified daily, and now, over a year after they first had tea together Vivian wondered how she'd ever managed without her. Enid's judgement always seemed so sound; not sour, but not too trusting. She oozed confidence and serenity, and somehow her abundance of both attributes covered Vivian's paucity. Indeed, fixed it.

Their visits to one another's houses were now regular and impulsive rather than starchy pre-planned appointments. The piano-forte finally had a use, as Enid played beautifully, in a way that made one glad one could stop and listen. The music seemed to flow through her body. Visiting Enid's home was one of Vivian's greatest pleasures. She'd thought she'd known what to expect, but she had been wrong. Enid's was not a melancholy, solitary cottage, nor was it a twee, poor yet cherished sort of place, one with far too many embroidered tray cloths and wooden stools with woven seats. Everything in her home was hard-wearing, shabby and mismatched but somehow wonderful and enduring. Rather like the woman herself.

Instead of the predictable patchwork quilt, there was a good-quality peacock-blue Paisley shawl draped across the rocker. Her tea tray was set with tiny cups and saucers from Russia; there were three shelves packed full of books, and throughout the house there were any number of receptacles (jam jars, milk bottles, vases) holding cowslips and paintbrushes, all splashed with indigo, emerald and scarlet, having been used and loved. It seemed that her things had been acquired almost accidentally, certainly whimsically, Vivian included, but they were all treasured. Vivian included. It was a colourful muddle, a scene of delight and domesticity. Whenever Vivian visited, the place invariably smelt of hot buttered scones with an undertone of turpentine. She was always made to feel welcome.

That was the utter bliss of it. Enid Henderson liked her. It was the most liberating feeling ever. Her approval gave Vivian chances and confidence even though her endorsement highlighted the fact that throughout Vivian's life no one in a position of authority had ever truly felt that way about her before. Vivian decided, through a great show of determination and will, not to take this personally. Girls were often overlooked. Her governess had been dour and sour. Her father was forever busy at the office or idle at his club. Her mother was too concerned with world approbation to ever consider looking for happiness domestically. Enid and Vivian laughed and talked together. The older woman valued her, listened to her, answered her questions truthfully, even when it was uncomfortable to do so. Not the done thing. Such a wonderful thing!

Enid had delivered Vivian's baby. Actually brought her into the world. Unbelievable. Unsurpassable. Dr Nicholson had been twenty miles out of the village when Mabel decided it was time to make an appearance. Mrs Rosebend didn't hesitate in calling for Enid.

Giving birth had been hell. The pain, the blood, the fear for and of the baby. It was all so awful. Almost intolerable to bear, and she couldn't have borne it if Enid hadn't been there.

'Breathe. Slowly. Slowly. Good girl. Well done. Not long now.'
The tangy iron smell of her own blood lingered everywhere

in the room. On her nightdress, on the mattress. She became morbid and afraid. It made her wonder about the war. Could pain be compared? Were the soldiers in any more pain? Scientifically she doubted it was possible. There had to be a limit. She'd yelled and screamed at the horror of it all, but when her daughter arrived, the pain was forgotten.

Darling baby Mabel.

Literally her everything.

The men didn't have life at the end of their pain. Only death. There had been two Christmases now and the soldiers hadn't returned home. No one muttered the hope that they'd get back by the third. It seemed ridiculous and naïve to do so. It was going on and on. They all stood back and quietly watched as the leaves on the trees began to seep from one colour to the next; the green leached out and they turned the brown of toffee, marking the passage of time. Time slipping. Time marching.

It was not fashionable to be quite so besotted with one's own child, but how was it possible to be anything else? Not that being a mother was easy. It wasn't; it was fraught with worry and responsibility. Babies were a hideous encumbrance to one's liberty; and the terror one felt when they shrieked and turned red, or worse still, blue. On very bad days, the terror morphed into fury. Why wouldn't she just settle? What was wrong with her? What was wrong with Vivian? Then the crying stopped: such jubilance, such a feeling of triumph and purpose. This little being loved Vivian so much, and she loved the little being. It was glorious when you thought about it, how much they needed each other.

It was the day after Mabel's birth that Enid received the form from the War Office to say that Michael had died of his wounds. It had taken him four days of suffering. It was hard for Vivian to believe or imagine; it was intolerable for Enid. Four days. They hadn't even known he was injured. Why had no one sent word? Enid could have gone to him. Sat with him. Had anyone sat with him? Instead Enid had knitted a matinee jacket in lemon, the click-clack of her needles only stopping when she stood up to make ginger tea for Vivian, who had moaned about being fat and uncomfortable, constantly wished the days away, longing for the baby to arrive. Vivian felt such guilt.

Enid carried on. She washed the baby, taught Vivian how to latch her on properly and then stayed by her side. For hours, for days, for weeks. Vivian thought Mabel saved them both at that time. Her chubby clasping hands, her small, irresistible mewing sounds, her needs – feeds, nappies, sleep – gave them both something to focus on. Enid settled quietly on a chair in Vivian's bedroom, holding Mabel close to her heart. Sometimes her tears splashed down on to the baby's cheeks. Vivian was glad that Enid turned to her then, in that time of vile and black misery. She wished her confidence in their friendship could have been asserted in any other way. She confided as much.

'There might be another opportunity,' Enid replied with a slow sigh. She'd lived enough to know that tragedy wasn't dolloped out in fair measures. She had another son.

For all their intimacy, Enid did not often talk about her elder son, Howie. Of course she told stories about both men when they were boys: grubby, noisy, cheeky, forever apple-scrumping, fishing for tadpoles, playing knock-and-run. Stories that were the staples of a mother's repertoire, especially a grieving mother. Vivian knew that Howie had not volunteered; perhaps that was the reason they did not often talk of him. For nearly two years now it seemed that the only conversations women ever had were about whether a welcome letter had been delivered, a comforting parcel sent, a devastating telegram received. Such conversations did not pertain to Howie. As conscription had been introduced some months ago now, Vivian assumed that he had finally gone to training camp to do his duty alongside all the other men. It wasn't a matter of choice any more. It was law. Vivian did feel it was harder, in some ways, to be one of these late conscripts. The early volunteers had had no clue as to what they were signing up to; now everyone knew. The casualty lists were printed in the newspapers, the wounded men hopped in the streets. It wasn't easy, what was being asked of them.

Due to her previous reticence, Vivian was surprised when one fine early June morning, as they were sitting with Mabel on a rug, enjoying the sound of birds singing in the blossoming trees and the first lick of warm air promising sun, Enid murmured, 'I haven't told you much about what Howie is up to at the moment, have I?'

'No.' Vivian hadn't even seen a photo. She was familiar with the one of Michael in his uniform. Stiff, proud, fine-looking, doomed. The picture on the mantelpiece of every mother and sweetheart.

'Howie is such an exceptional boy.' Asserted with a mother's pride.

As he hadn't volunteered, Vivian couldn't help but imagine a pale, slight, effete boy with the sort of face only a mother could love, but she allowed her friend the courtesy of describing him.

'He's very handsome. Beautiful, actually. Bright. Emotional. Thoughtful. Did very well at school. Eventually, when he put his mind to it.' Enid was not boastful, so Vivian was a little taken aback. 'Drew far too much attention to himself. Others were jealous, naturally. I think they rather liked reminding him that his father had left, although it was no fault of his. I think they wanted to feel he was less. You know how children are.' The words caught in her throat. 'He learnt not to care what other people thought. He made up his own mind about things. Everything. I encouraged his autonomy. I never told him there was any value in being one of the crowd.'

Vivian feared that Enid was about to announce that Howie was to be shipped to the front, or worse that he had been shipped and some woe had already fallen on him. Injury? Death? Why must they live like this? It was a beautiful day, but the mist of grief and despair lingered above them, ready to descend and saturate everything. Always.

'Is he going to France?'

'No. But he's been packed off.'

'Where to?'

'He's at Richmond.'

It took Vivian a moment. She did try to stay informed; she forced herself to read the papers, even though all the news was the same. Endless battles, endless losses. It made her feel so heavy. It was difficult to stay bright for the baby if she read too much. But *Richmond*? It rang a bell. It wasn't a training camp. Those were at Sandhurst, Staffordshire, Tring and such. Those names came to her quickly enough.

Richmond was a camp for conscientious objectors.

The shirkers. The men who wouldn't do their duty.

Vivian forced her gaze to meet Enid's watery blue eyes. The older woman waited patiently and allowed the younger one to join the dots, make the correct leap. 'He's a conscientious objector?'

'Yes.' Enid was firm. She didn't sound ashamed, or even apologetic.

'Is he a Quaker?' If there was a belief, Vivian might be able to understand. It might be forgivable. She wanted there to be a valid excuse for her friend's son's cowardice.

'No.' Enid chuckled as though the idea was somehow amusing. 'You know we're not Quakers. I'm not even sure if he believes in God. You'd have to ask him.' Vivian would never do any such thing. Why would she ever have cause to talk to a man like that? One who wasn't prepared to do his duty. Even if he was Enid's son. 'He's a playwright.'

'Is he really?' Vivian thought she probably should not be so openly impressed in case she came across as shallow, but everything had been so dull since the war. It was irresistible fun to think of happier times. The theatre in all its glamour seemed an incredible concept now, but she had once liked playwrights, actors and such. Dream-makers. Thinking about it, she had been quite the actress herself throughout her season. She'd presented herself as though she was in a play, or maybe one of those Hollywood films. The beautiful daughter from the respectable family with a declining fortune, drifting about like a fairy-tale princess, making it clear she was waiting for a knight in shining armour; not with any vulgar word of encouragement but by flashing her eyes here, lowering her gaze there, laughing heartily at mediocre jokes, appearing very impressed by run-of-the-mill sporting achievements. Eyes, teeth, chest. Yes, she'd played the role to perfection; well, until the final scene of the final act. Then, after Nathaniel, she supposed she became more like one of the audience. Infinitely detached.

'Has he written anything I might have heard of?' she asked.

'*Mrs Cooper's Boy, All This Time, The Blackest Night.*' Enid raised her voice at the end of the name of each play, asking Vivian to recognise them.

'Really! It was at a performance of *The Blackest Night* that I first met Aubrey. I still have the programme somewhere, I think.' It lay in a dusty toffee tin in the bottom of her wardrobe, in amongst other keepsakes: dance cards, wedding invitations and so on. She rarely looked through them.

Howard R. Henderson! Of course. It was a big case, all over the papers, attracting attention, but Enid called her son Howie, and Vivian had had no reason to link her friend to the infamous playwright. She'd read all about it. First he'd dashed out to France with a famous newspaperman. Apparently he'd made himself useful, quite the hero; he certainly had a heart. There were countless reports of him doing what he could to help the wounded. Some had said he saved lives; he at least made deaths more comfortable. It seemed he was willing to do his bit, but then he'd slunk home, tail between his legs. He'd started telling everyone that no one could win this war and that they ought to just *stop*. As if that was possible. Stood on a box in Hyde Park yelling about it. Disgraceful. He was now refusing conscription, which was a crime. Leading at the very least to internment. Some were saying it should be punishable by death.

'You said he's in Richmond? You mean . . .'

'Yes, in prison.'

Enid must be torn: ashamed and fearful at once. Vivian wondered which of them her friend felt most. She pitied her either way. Her eyes dropped to where Mabel sat, propped up by a number of cushions, pulling at the grass, trying to cram it into her mouth. Vivian carefully put her finger in and eased out the earth before she swallowed.

Fearful. Of course. Enid was more afraid than ashamed. Her child, locked up.

She floundered about for something reasonable to say. Something polite but true. 'That must be very hard for you.'

'Harder for him, I think,' Enid replied with an unaccustomed touch of irritation. 'I blame myself.'

'Yourself?'

'Sometimes I think I shouldn't have had children at all.'

'What an odd thing to say. Why do you say that?'

'To lose one to war. The other in prison. Why couldn't I look after them better?' Enid closed her eyes, pushed her lips together, a thin line.

Vivian reached out and rested her hand on her friend's arm. Was it any comfort? Was anything? 'No one has any choice at the moment.'

'But that's just it. Howard thinks he has. What have I taught him?' Enid clenched her fist and pounded it pointlessly on the grass. 'I'm not the right sort to make a mother. I'm too challenging of the world. Too disappointed in it. I want so much from it.'

Vivian's gaze inadvertently drifted back to the open door of Enid's cottage. It was not what anyone might describe as ostentatious or lavish. It did not look like the home of someone who wanted a lot from the world.

'I don't mean in monetary terms. I've always found money falls my way when I need it. Just enough, never too much. I mean in terms of equality and decency. I brought him up to question too much, to accept nothing. I demand far more than I should. I never imagined it would land him in this mess. My son makes me feel at once proud and dismayed.'

'Would you rather he joined up?'

'Never.'

'Is that because you've already lost Michael?'

'Of course, and yet not that alone.'

Enid never shied away from honesty but threw herself into its epicentre, risking pain and bruising, so Vivian knew she could ask: 'Which of them do you think right?'

'Both of them. Michael fought for what he believed in; now Howie must too.' Vivian didn't know what to say. She wasn't sure how that could be. 'I want him safe. Safe from bullets and safe from the brutality of people not understanding independent thinking. I'd wrap him in my skirts if I could. I don't care about the name-calling.' How oddly and magnificently self-sufficient. Enid paused. 'There's talk of taking him to France. To be shot.'

'Good Lord.'

'It's hard to believe.'

'Can you persuade him to fight?'

'I won't try.' This was said with staunch determination. Enid allowed Vivian a moment to think it through, then with less certainty she added sadly, 'Besides, it would be a waste of time. Howie simply does not care what is going on around him. He's always been the same. He's not the puppet of ambition or acceptance, as other men and boys are. If he does not want to fight, he will not fight. No amount of cajoling will change his mind. He always judges for himself what matters, what doesn't.'

'But the war matters.'

'Yes.'

'But not to him, is that what you are saying?'

'I think it matters more to him than to some of the men who are out there fighting.'

'I can't believe that.'

'I can't believe anything other.' Enid turned. 'Vivian, will you help?'

'Help? Help how?'

'Bring him here to work on the farm. Vouch that you need him as an essential worker. Farm manager can be classified as a reserved occupation.'

Vivian hesitated. It wasn't an entirely impossible idea. The general consensus was always that women would benefit from the presence of a man; for this reason many a bow-legged, snaggle-toothed, bent-backed man had found employment during the war. She didn't want to dither, but, 'Aubrey won't like it.'

Enid shrugged and looked towards Mabel. She didn't have to say anything more. Vivian was a mother. Having a child sharpened everything complicated about being human. Mabel made Vivian want to run and skip, sing and dance. Jump, laugh. Take huge gulps of air, actually breathe in sunlight and even brisk winds. With her Vivian felt untied. Free, yet settled. Part of the world in an intrinsic and vital way. Life with her daughter was exciting and easy. Yet she also represented everything that terrified Vivian about humanity. The responsibility she had towards her child made her ache. The world's shadows cast themselves long and heavy. What if Mabel was to become ill, or someone was to snatch her; what if the Germans invaded and did eat babies as they'd been told, something Vivian had believed to be preposterous until she'd had one of her own, something she couldn't quite dismiss now because fear lingered. It clung. Whether they ate them or not, children were killed in war. Even if her baby did grow up safely and happily, what if she had sex with a worthless man and then was forced into a loveless marriage with . . .Vivian couldn't finish the thought. It was too horrible, too much of a betrayal. Aubrey was Mabel's father. How could she be disrespectful towards him when he'd given her everything that was wonderful? Fear and love were side by side.

'Yes, yes, all right. I shall see about it. Of course I'll help your son.'

# 26

THEY HAD MADE it hopeless. It was difficult to follow, difficult to understand, what the military wanted from him. He did not fit in anywhere. The army loathed him. The conchies irritated him. He was friendless. Hopeless.

The absolutist conscientious objectors were an embarrassment to the government. They would cheerfully dig deep holes in heavy clay land and fill them back up again, keen to show they weren't afraid of hard labour, but they would not accept the work of carrying a stretcher or even bandaging a wounded man; they thought that patching up a soldier to send him back out to fight was as bad as pulling a trigger. The conchies were dismissed as misguided and self-righteous, but everyone from the most ordinary shop girl to the Prime Minister himself was ready to forgive them; they were more than keen to get them involved in the war somehow. They had to be defused; no one wanted their ideas to detonate. Every conchie who picked up a box of shells and placed it on a lorry heading to France was considered a victory. A conscience overruled was cause for celebration.

However, Howard was on a different track. As the powers-that-be at his tribunal had ruled that he did not have a conscience, let alone a right to objection, he was conscripted into the army. No one acknowledged the illegal press-ganging. He'd drilled and picked up a weapon; that was acceptance enough of the status they'd foisted upon him. He was a soldier, and now he was a soldier who had refused orders. Maintenance of discipline was a serious matter in the military. Crucial. Following Howard's third bout of solitary confinement (the safest way to avoid ideas spreading, which was especially necessary if those ideas undermined morale or questioned authority) and a diet restricted to bread and water (hungry men were generally more cooperative), the prison's commanding officer came to his cell to explain just how essential and serious the matter of preserving discipline was.

Howard had to stand for the CO. Despite the bitter cold of the underground cell, he did not want to shiver; it was important to him that he didn't appear afraid. The CO looked directly at him. Intense brown eyes that suggested intelligence and impatience.

'Do you know what punishment befalls a soldier who shamefully delivers up a garrison to the enemy?' the CO asked, his enunciation clear, his tone crisp and efficient; suggesting he had an agenda.

Howard knew very little about military law. He was having trouble focusing; his head felt like a knot of cobwebs, his belly an empty barrel. His throat scratched, his tongue felt fat and useless. 'No.'

'Death. And what of a soldier who shamefully casts away arms in the presence of the enemy?' Howard raised his hands an inch or two from his sides, then regretted the gesture. He'd been in the army long enough to know that shrugging at an officer was foolish. 'Death. What do you think we do with a soldier who leaves his CO to go in search of plunder?'

Howard felt he could hazard a guess. 'Death?'

The CO nodded and began to slowly pace the cell. His boots snapping down on the concrete floor beat out a rhythm. 'Doing violence to a person bringing provisions to the forces?'

'Death,' Howard mumbled.

'Committing an offence against the person of a resident in the country in which he is serving?'

'Death.'

'Breaking into a house in search of plunder? Discharging fire-arms intentionally occasioning false alarms? Causing a mutiny? Striking a superior officer?'

'Death, death, death, death.' Howard got it. War meant death. The military meant death. What had this to do with him?

The CO stopped pacing, the snapping heels silent. He turned, leaned towards Howard's ear and whispered menacingly, 'Wilful defiance of authority, disobeying a lawful command given personally by his superior officer?'

Now Howard understood.

Death.

They meant to kill him. He moved his head from left to right. Left to right. Slowly. But he couldn't clear it. Couldn't make sense of anything. 'It's just stupid. I don't agree and I won't be that man,' he muttered.

'What man?' The CO sounded genuinely curious.

'The man who just does as he's told. Unquestioning.'

'You are in the army, Private Henderson. Of course you will be that man. You *are* that man. You'll be any man we decide. You must.' The CO exhaled. Suddenly moved away from Howard as though he'd got too close. He pulled out a clean white handker-chief and blew his nose. 'You've got a visitor. You'd better get shaved. Clean up. You stink.'

He wished they hadn't let his mother come. He longed to see her but he didn't want her to see him. Not like this. Prison life – scant food, regular roughing-ups, little sleep, hard labour – had taken its toll. His trousers slipped down, his ribs popped out of his blue-white skin and his chest rasped. It was impossible to smarten up sufficiently to disguise the effects of the prison walls, turned glassy with damp.

# 27

VIVIAN HAD WRITTEN to Aubrey to ask for permission to visit Enid's son and to invite him to work on the farm. She'd slipped the request in towards the end of the letter, after she'd told him about Mabel eating stewed apple for the first time (messy, exciting), that she'd had the two farm horses reshod (expensive), and given him a full review of the recital in the village hall (dull, tinny, inexpert but at least a diversion). She hadn't wanted to draw too much attention to the matter. Aubrey wrote back and stated that if she could, in any way, help persuade the man to do his duty then that would be a good thing. He'd offered to throw in his influence with the army if necessary but questioned whether she needed to travel to Richmond personally. He thought that Mr Pickering could go on her behalf, that it would be more seemly. She'd replied that Mr Pickering had been called up and was now in Flanders, so otherwise engaged. Aubrey eventually gave his permission but cautioned that she must try to avoid becoming 'too involved' in Mrs Henderson's business.

Having secured Aubrey's permission, she expected that they'd visit Enid's son immediately, but Enid's applications were turned down. Twice. Point blank. No discussion. Then suddenly she received a letter informing her that a date had been set for her son's court martial. The day after tomorrow.

'What does it mean?'

'They are letting me say goodbye.' Enid didn't look at Vivian; she couldn't. She looked out on to the corn fields, the bold summer that had emerged from the brown crumpled earth; the letter trembled in her hand.

'No. We're not going to let that happen, Enid,' stated Vivian. When Enid did turn to her young friend, Vivian almost wished she hadn't. She looked at her pityingly, Vivian's youth and naïvety misguiding and embarrassing them both.

The journey to Richmond was profoundly uncomfortable. Vivian paid for first-class tickets and they sat in the ladies-only carriage – although this was an ever more redundant form of segregation, there were so few men with loud and vulgar laughs or dirty pipe smoke to disturb their travel – but even so, the journey was unbearable. There was nothing Vivian could say to reassure or comfort. They stared out of the window; towns, sheep, chimneys whipped past. Occasionally, one or the other would find it in themselves to raise a small responsive wave to the groups of children scattered on the bank sides, splitting the light into sharp shafts of bright and shadow as they ran, excited by a train passing, clueless as to where the passengers might be heading.

The prison was as horrifying as Vivian had feared. The guards looked irritable and severe. The prisoners looked dejected or ferocious. They stood around in disconsolate, ashamed huddles. They were grey. The entire place was. The walls, the floors, ceilings, wires and fences. Vivian had thought mud was brown, but it was not here, it was grey.

They were led through a series or corridors, doors locked behind them. Loud clanks holding back freedom. Eventually they opened one on to a room where a man sat hunched over a square table; another wooden chair, empty, faced him. He had the blackest hair, almost blue, and even though he was sitting down, he gave the impression of being tall and elegant; his shoulder blades, elbows, jawbone all jutted with just the correct angle and confidence to suggest grace and athleticism. His sleeves were rolled up to the elbow. His forearms were muscular; she was close enough to see the wide blue veins running like streams beneath his pale skin. He obviously hadn't seen enough sunshine of late.

He jumped up to greet Enid, his movements fluid, very much part of the world. Enid lunged towards him, desperate to wrap him in her maternal love. 'No touching,' barked the guard.

Enid froze; she looked as though someone had assaulted her. Desperate to do as instructed, not to annoy in any way, she instantly clamped her arms to her sides and threw a brief apologetic look at her son. She'd been promised thirty minutes; she didn't want to lose one. 'You're so thin,' she whispered. The words scratched in her throat.

'Don't look glum, Mam. I hear we're having tripe and onions in milk for supper tonight.' Enid's son sat down again and indicated she take the seat opposite him. Vivian hovered near the door. There was something decent, tender in the use of the word *Mam*. He'd acknowledged her, given her warmth and authority. Affection flowed between them, undeterred by his age, ideas and size, or even the thick, wet concrete walls.

'I know they keep you on bread and water for days,' pronounced Enid, refusing to be comforted.

'Do they?' Vivian didn't mean to let the question escape but it did. Enid's son seemed to notice her for the first time.

He smiled. His lip was cut and swollen and the thin skin underneath his eyes was purple: lack of sleep or fading bruises? Despite this, he had an air of serenity and magnanimity about him. He remained untouched. Not at all what she'd anticipated. She'd expected arrogance, a know-it-all, fire. Or a pale, effete weakling, a wet blanket, a limp handshake, sloppy. He was neither thing.

'Only if we misbehave.'

'By which he means if they talk or sing. Then they are starved,' stated Enid, casting a wary glance at the guard.

It didn't sound right. It didn't sound very British. But then Vivian had to remember that what this man was doing *wasn't* very British. For all he looked harmless, he was an oddball. A trouble-maker. However, he jumped up and indicated that Vivian must take his seat, a gesture that seemed superior, polished. At the very least courteous, considerate. She shook her head. 'I'm happy to stand. We've been sitting on the train for ever such a long time.'

'This is Mrs Owens. I've written to you about her. She's here to help.'

His face did not flicker with any recognition. It occurred to Vivian that he might not have received his mother's letters; she knew that he'd never sent any in return and they'd often wondered why.

'Are you a lawyer, Mrs Owens?'

He knew that was not possible. 'No.'

'A doctor? A magistrate?'

'I'm a woman.' So of course she couldn't be any of the things he mentioned. Defensively she added, 'A friend.'

'I see.' He smirked, and it seemed to Vivian that he was dismissing her as no possible earthly help. He'd looked at her cream dress, her gloves, her parasol and made an assumption. He thought she was a sightseer, a ghoul. Someone who had latched on to his mother to get a better look at him. For Enid's sake, she smiled politely and didn't allow him to rile her. She had a job to do, yet the sense that he thought she was intruding was palpable.

'Would it be better if I waited outside?'

'If you didn't mind,' he replied.

Enid was emphatic. 'No, stay with us.'

Vivian hesitated, torn, embarrassed. The room smelt dank. There was no window to throw in any natural light, and they relied on just one electric bulb that hung on a cord over the middle of the table. The place was shrouded in an atmosphere of hostility and violence; Vivian had to remind herself that they were on military property, this place was run by the good men in khaki uniforms who were fighting for her.

She wished she was anywhere else.

Neither mother nor son said a word; they stared at one another until it became too much for him to stand, and then he looked at the wall just above her left ear. Enid didn't have any small talk to retreat into either. She couldn't ask how he was keeping, or how they were treating him. It was all too bleak and obvious.

'Your court martial is this Friday.'

'I see.'

'Haven't they told you?'

'No.'

'Do you understand what this means?' He finally met his mother's eyes. Vivian noticed that his were blue, like Enid's, but a shade more intense, youthful and vivid. Enid's were watery and full of pain. Concern.

'Yes.'

For the avoidance of all doubt, to shock him or because she was traumatised, Enid added, 'They will execute you.' Her voice sounded unnaturally high and more officious than usual. It was an impossible thing for a mother to have to say to a son.

'Possibly.' She glared at him and he conceded, 'Probably.'

'Don't pretend it is anything other than horrifying,' she snapped, the concern in her eyes instantly drowned by fear and frustration. 'They will take you into that courtyard out there . . .' She pointed randomly to her right. None of them really knew where the courtyard was, but they didn't doubt its existence. Her hand was trembling. 'They will blindfold you and shoot you. You might be dead by Saturday.'

'If they shoot me for my beliefs, I haven't lost much. If I go to war, I'll be shot for *their* beliefs. I know which I prefer.'

Enid gasped and pushed her fist into her mouth. 'I can't talk to you.' She stood up with such haste that the chair fell backwards; Vivian caught it and righted it before it clattered to the floor. Enid turned to the guard. 'I need some air.' She must have noticed at the same time as Vivian did that the guard looked even younger than her son; despite the chill, there was sweat on his upper lip, no hair. As an afterthought she added, 'Please.'

Enid glanced at Vivian as she left the room. No one had ever looked at her that way: desperate terror, her only hope. Pity surged through Vivian's veins. She knew what Enid wanted her to deliver, but now that she was in front of this strangely composed, fearsomely determined man, she wondered whether she could. He seemed so sure. Set on a path that was hurtling him towards self-destruction. The door banged.

Vivian took Enid's seat and smiled politely. As she wondered how to open the necessary conversation, he demanded briskly, 'Can I ask why you are here, Mrs Owens?'

'To keep your mother company. I didn't think she should have to make the journey on her own and we didn't know what to expect.' She glanced around the wretched room. He knew they could not have expected this. This sort of bleak purgatory was put beyond women's imagination. Men built prisons, fought wars.

'Thank you. That was very thoughtful. Why has she left us alone?'

'I . . .'

'Does she want you to persuade me to fight? Has she sent in a pretty face to do the job that heavy boots couldn't?' He smiled. It was an easy, unaffected smile. The smile of someone who was always a step ahead.

'No.' Vivian felt colour rise in her cheeks. She was furious with herself for responding, but she couldn't help it. It was not just that compliments were as scarce as silk stockings, and had been for years, but he was notably handsome. Quite disturbingly so.

Such an odd thing for her to see in this bleak place and time, but she couldn't fail to. She'd always been quite useless when resisting accomplished flirts. She tried to recover some dignity.

'I think you should know, Mr Henderson, that I find you and your way of thinking rather cowardly.'

'Do you?'

'Yes.' His smile didn't falter, which made her feel more awkward. Embarrassment quickly dissolved into something else. Irritation. She was incensed by his certainty.

'And that's what you've come here to tell me, is it?'

'Quite repulsive,' she appended meanly, and then to be sure she clarified, '*You* are quite repulsive.' She felt ridiculous saying this, but believed she must. He didn't look shocked or angry. Hurt. He looked disappointed. *He* was disappointed in *her*. It was unbelievable. It was insulting. Heat flamed through her body. 'Why won't you fight, Mr Henderson?'

'I simply do not believe that the boys on the other side of the barbed wire are so different from the boys on our side. How are they different? The ones we are shooting at?'

'They are the enemy.'

'But they are not *my* enemy. I am for Europe, not just England. It seems so parochial to me to limit oneself to one's country. Or even continent. I'm a man of this world, a global citizen if you like, and they are all my brothers: the French, the Germans, the Egyptians, even the chaps in Papua New Guinea, wherever that might be. I don't think the men out there are wrong to be fighting if that's what they believe; it's simply not what *I* believe.' His tone was assured, confident but not impassioned. She realised he must have repeated this particular argument dozens of times. He was somewhere close to listless. Dangerously close. She wondered whether he'd already given up. She couldn't bear the thought. For Enid. For him.

'They started it!' She regretted that the last time she'd used this justification was to Nanny when she'd been scrapping with her brother and sisters following some minor wrongdoing: a stolen pencil, a shove or pinch. She also regretted that Mr Henderson seemed to know that the nursery was the best place for that particular line of argument. He grinned, playfully. Not acting anything like a man who might soon be facing the death penalty. He seemed unconcerned. Untouchable. She looked closely. At the centre of his oh-too-blue eyes was a dull, dead coal-black pupil. What had this man seen? What had snuffed out the light? 'Don't you feel at all compelled to do your duty?' He looked at her as though she'd said something amusing. 'Can't you find your courage for your King and country?' This time he let a laugh explode from his beautiful mouth. Not a heartfelt one, but a bitter bark.

'They want us to live a life of clichés, Mrs Owens. They don't want us to think or feel anything deeply or thoroughly, but it is dreadful not to. I've heard it all. It's all been thrown at me. "Courage of a lion", "Glory of God", "Responsibility to the Crown", "Fall in, Your Country Needs You". What does it mean? What does any of it mean? Nothing. That's what.'

'It all sounds very admirable to me.'

'I think you'd find it less so if you were knee deep in blood and guts.'

The boy guard coughed. Vivian supposed he'd be going to the Front soon. 'Pardon me. Frog in me throat,' he mumbled. She dug around in her handbag and unearthed a packet of butterscotch sweets; the butter had left greasy smudges on the thin white paper bag. It was not a pristine gift but she offered one to the guard all the same. He hesitated.

'To suck on. Ease your throat,' she urged.

'Better not, ma'am. On duty.'

'I won't tell.'

'Nor will I,' added Mr Henderson laconically.

Unable to resist the small treat, the soldier reached for a sweet.

246

'Take the lot. Put them in your pocket. Share them with the others.' He did, compliant, like a child. She turned back to Enid's son. Howard R. Henderson. The playwright. A man with big, difficult ideas. There was something about the young soldier's grateful demeanour that made her feel more intensely infuriated by Mr Henderson, and yet abnormally absorbed by him. 'Millions have volunteered. Why must you be different?'

'Yes, millions, yet they still need more. They are powering through our brave young men, aren't they?'

'Is that what you are worried about, dying out there? Mr Henderson, I have to ask, what makes you think you are so special that you don't have to go?' She paused, glanced over her shoulder at the young man sucking his sweet, then lowered her voice in an inept attempt to shelter the soldier from what he must already know. 'Go, and yes possibly die out there, like the good men who—'

'I'm not drawing comparisons. I'm just saying it doesn't seem to be very effective, this strategy of ours.'

'Strategy?'

'You know, simply throwing men at the problem. Cannon fodder.'

'It's a sacrifice. No one is arguing that, but this will be the end of it. The war to end all wars.'

'I seriously doubt it. That's never been the case. Why would the biggest and bloodiest war turn out to be the one that stops it all? Why isn't anyone in the least bit logical when it comes to this?' He sighed. It seemed they were equally dissatisfied with one another.

'I do realise it must be dreadful.' Aubrey had twice been back to England since he was sent to France; she could see he was affected, although he never spoke of it. Still, best foot forward. He went back. Of course he did. 'Other people learn to bear it, you know. Piano tuners and schoolteachers.'

'They should not have to be soldiers.'

'But *you* could be. You're big and strong.' He stared at her with something close to contempt. Did he believe she was trying to flatter him. She was not. She was stating what was patent.

'I'm a playwright, or at least I was, Mrs Owens. I don't want to *bear it*. I don't want to become a brute.'

'They are not brutes, they are brave.'

'I don't doubt that.'

'Wouldn't you rather die than end up speaking German?'

'That's just it, I wouldn't. I won't be told what to do.' He was emphatic and she knew she was losing.

'You are very introspective.'

'It's not a weakness or a sin.'

'Are you sure about that? I'm certain it means you will be damned.'

He laughed. 'You are clever, Mrs Owens. You really are.'

She hadn't meant to make a joke and therefore couldn't respond to his compliment. 'And you are very stubborn, Mr Henderson. As well as rather vain. Who is to say that you know best?'

'Who is to say *they* do? There's so much squandering of life. I won't be a part of it. I demand the right to my life.' Glancing around the room, he added, 'Or at least the chance to choose how I die.' He banged his hand down on the table, causing it to shudder and her to recoil.

'Steady on, keep it civil.' The interruption came from the guard. Vivian realised they were both shouting.

'I don't know why you insist on treating the war like an intellectual debate,' she snapped.

'Anything but. It's more real and visceral than that. Don't for a moment doubt it.' They glared at one another, combative. The silence that ensued was unpleasant, tricky. Was there anything more to say? If she let his arguments into her head, she might lose her grip on all that seemed secure and all she'd thought to be true. She was made most uncomfortable by the realisation that knowing Enid's son might demand exactly that of her.

He looked weary. Quietly, not meeting her eyes but staring at his hands in his lap, 'Did you know that in September 1915, the Germans were so horrified about how many of our men they had slaughtered, they held their fire so we could retreat.'

'I don't believe you.'

'No, I don't expect you to.' Disappointment again. It was so galling. 'It is true. I knew someone who was there in the battle. He was injured. I visited him in the hospital and he told me.'

'Who is this friend? I should like to meet him and hear it from his lips.'

'It was my brother, and he's dead. Gangrene.'

'Oh.' Vivian wondered whether Enid knew that her boys had managed their goodbyes. She'd never mentioned it so Vivian didn't think she could. Why hadn't he told her? It would be some comfort. What *couldn't* he tell her? 'They are saying you are a coward, a traitor even. Don't you care what they are saying about you?'

'I know I'm not. Taunts and humiliation, misconception and anger: it's the price I have to pay for saying what I believe. Moral fervour must have its compensations. A life lived with beliefs must mean more than a life lived belonging to someone else.' His full, strong voice trailed away. She was left feeling empty. She needed more from him. She needed something to hang on to. She wanted to learn his intonation, his mannerisms and tics. She wanted to learn him. Suddenly he seemed to feel a duty to be chirpy for her. 'Anyway, what do I care what they call me? A little derision isn't going to hurt me. I'm a playwright. I've endured scathing reviews,' he joked. Then, more seriously, 'What people say about me has never been as important as what I do. The posters once read, "Your Country Needs You"; now the pointing finger isn't welcoming, it's rather more accusatory. "Is Your Conscience Clear?" Well, mine is, Mrs Owens. I've seen war and I can't be a part of it. I won't.'

Vivian had just one more card to play. 'Don't you care that your mother has to bear it?'

'I am sorry for that, but she understands I suppose that there's a balance to be struck, conscience against duty.' His head stored a separate world, one steeped in art and bohemia, intellectual strength and moral certainty. He was different. He believed in the individual. Particularly in himself. She found it confusing. All that said, he was not made of stone; he had a heart. He shook his head and muttered, 'Poor Mam. Things have changed from the days when she could brag that I had a show on in the West End. Not that I've written anything lately. I've given her absolutely nothing to brag about, come to that. Given her nothing but grief.'

'She's very proud of you.'

'I know she is.' The thought seemed to make him even more distressed.

'Your mother doesn't want you to be shot.'

'No, I don't imagine she does.'

Deep breath. 'I wondered whether you'd like to come and work on my farm. I need someone.'

'I see.'

'It is essential work.'

'Yes.' He didn't look convinced. No doubt he knew that she could hire more conveniently to do this essential work.

'She's lost your brother. Isn't that enough?'

'More than. I'm not arguing with that.' Like his mother, he had warmth, but his heat seemed less benign. It wasn't that he was threatening or evil in any way; he was simply . . . unsettling. His words and the soft, easy, assured way he delivered them burrowed into her head and colonised there. There was something about him that was insinuating, pervasive.

'Then say you'll come.' She was unsure how she'd fallen into the position of begging him to allow her to save his neck.

He said nothing. The hands on the wall clock slipped round.

She imagined Enid anxious outside the door, gambling that this thirty-minute visit might best be used by Vivian talking to her son; trusting Vivian to deliver her more time. But Vivian was failing. She was wasting Enid's visit; Enid would have been better off being with him, saying goodbye.

'I once fought the system and you can't win,' she whispered to him. This cost her. Revisiting the time before Aubrey. When she'd thought she loved Nathaniel and could have him. 'I thought I'd never find peace or happiness in the world as it was, but I was wrong. I have a daughter.' She hurriedly reached for her bag for a second time and pulled out a picture from her purse. She placed it on the table between them, waiting for the approbation that always followed when people saw her baby's image. He barely glanced at it. She'd laid it all out. Her story, her girl, her soul, and he had ignored her. Horrible, horrible man. 'I am sorry for you. You are going to drown in self-righteousness,' she snapped.

'Not I.'

'Well, then, in your stubbornness.'

'I'll come.'

'You will!' Wonderful, wonderful man! She was so surprised she stood up and moved to hug him in her exuberance.

Luckily the guard checked her. 'No touching.'

'What makes you think the army will go for it? Won't they want to pursue my court martial? I offered to do non-combative work before and they turned me down.'

'They've dug themselves into a hole with your case. This gives everyone an honourable exit. I think they'll be relieved. They don't want any more controversy around conscientious objectors. Besides, my husband will intervene if needs be. He's a decorated officer, very well respected. I am married, you see.'

It was a non-sequential comment and the emphasis was all wrong. All she meant was that Aubrey could offer some insurance, security. That was all. She blushed again. He was beautiful.

Compelling. She'd called him repulsive but she didn't mean it. She thought she would but she didn't.

She was apologising for being married.

'Yes, you are wearing a ring. I'm not blind. You mentioned a daughter.'

'I . . . I just mean he's still alive.'

'Good for him.' He seemed amused at her confusion.

'Many women are widows. I only say it to be patent.'

'Loud and clear, Captain.' He looked at her and his glance was provocative, playful, but his interest had to be trivial and fleeting. Of course it was. She knew that much now. Men's attention was rarely fixed or sincere. She had done as Enid needed. That was all that mattered here. Nothing more.

# 28

OH GOD, HOW he'd missed it. It was almost painful to look at,
in all its glorious perfection. How could he have ever found
the village dull? The land flat? This life boring? Now he worshipped
every inch. Clean, good land that sprouted crops, not corpses.
Children playing, running and squabbling in the streets. Bootless
and grubby but smiling and natural, not twisted, haunted. He
noticed everything as though for the first time. Sparkling drops
of dew like necklaces on young, smooth skin. Lettuces were
strangely beautiful: greens and yellows, blossoming and swelling
at the same time; they put him in mind of the rosettes given out at
the country fair. He breathed in deeply. No stench of burning
skin, blood or bombs. No hint of the acidic tang of decay. The
air was beyond fresh, it was raw, as was his head. Noise unsettled
him. Crowds and shouting made him wary. Birds singing, cows
mooing, sheep bleating, however, there was nothing to cause alarm
there.

Largely he was alone, and he liked it. He wasn't sure if Vivian
Owens had assigned him to the furthest fields from the village
out of spite or consideration. He often had to walk five or six
miles before he could begin work, but at least then he was left
to it. It was true that whilst he was buoyant about being back in
Blackwell, not many of the villagers were pleased to see him.

Besides his brother, six of their boys were dead already, and two left with no legs. Of course they hated him, with his principles, limbs and life. He inadvertently taunted the grieving mothers and fathers, the wives and children. His strength and vitality were torture to many, so he didn't assume people would want to pass the time of day with him in the street or the store, he didn't expect to get served in the pub and he got used to the children interrupting their games to throw stones or dried manure at him.

Today she'd sent word via his mother that she'd like him to walk around the boundaries, patching up the fences where he could, identifying the gaping gaps that really demanded the highly coveted wood and expensive wire. Some might think it humiliating that he received his orders from a woman and via his mother, like a schoolboy earning a penny or two for doing odd jobs, but Howard had no debilitating hubris about this matter. Yes, he was a proud and ethical man, but he picked his battles. He didn't know if agreeing to come back to Blackwell was wrong or right. He didn't know if it mattered either way. The thing was done. There was no point in making it more awkward than it had to be by finding fault in how it was here. After all, the army had been relieved to get him out of sight; ultimately the Powers That Be thought that this war couldn't afford objectors to be either shot or tolerated; they were in an impossible, tenuous position. They were sick with the whole business and ready for someone to offer a quiet solution.

It turned out that Vivian Owens really was his mother's friend, perhaps the closest friend his mother had ever had in Blackwell, a village she and his father had adopted after they married but not one that either had been born to. In all his life he'd never known his mother visit another woman every day. He supposed that when he and Michael were young she simply hadn't had the time for such intimacy, even if it was ever offered, and he wasn't sure it had been.

His mother, an abandoned woman and artist, had always operated on the fringes of Blackwell village. She wasn't ostracised as
such, but she wasn't welcomed either. She was always asked to
donate cakes to fund-raisers, but hers were the last to be purchased
and then usually by the vicar. The women were polite enough
and nodded to her in the street and church, but he couldn't
remember her being invited in for a brew or anyone saving a
space for her in a pew. It was only now, when he saw how enthusiastically she took up her friendship, that he wondered whether
she had ever hankered after female company, or had her boys, her
painting and her washing been enough to keep her from feeling
lonely? He wasn't sure. He felt protective of her, and wary; this
Vivian Owens seemed too good to be true. She was young, elevated
in society. Beautiful. Surely she could befriend anyone she chose.
Then again, maybe she didn't want just anyone. His mother was
special. Someone different and valuable. He knew that; it wasn't
unreasonable to assume that Vivian Owens might have worked
out the same. Nonetheless, it niggled him that whilst his mother
visited Vivian Owens nearly every day, notably she didn't come
to them.

'Doesn't Mrs Owens ever fancy the stroll to ours?' he asked
one evening with a studied disinterest as he dealt the cards. They
liked to play a hand or two of whist after supper.

'It's trickier for her. She has to uproot the bairn, work around
nap times and such. Easier if I visit them.'

'But wouldn't pushing the baby out in the pram make sense?
Fresh air is good for children, isn't it?' His mother wouldn't
comment; she stared hard at her cards. 'Is she a snob, then, this
friend of yours? Our place not good enough for her?'

His mother lifted her lids, briefly betraying her irritation with
him. 'Not as much of a snob as she's entitled to be, no. It's not
that.'

'Me, then?' Oddly, it unsettled him that she was avoiding him.

He shouldn't have expected any different. Miss Hawkins, the woman who had taught him the three Rs, reading, writing and arithmetic, blanked him in the street, as did the lasses he'd played with since before he went to school. He didn't care about them. But.

His mother wouldn't answer him; she just glowered. 'We owe her a great deal.'

'I'm not saying we don't.'

'She does well for someone so young and—'

'And what?'

Enid sighed; he knew she was reluctant to finish the sentence, torn between her habitual honesty and loyalty to her friend. 'She was never given any guidance.' Enid played her first card. 'Or love, come to that,' she mumbled. Howard felt bad for probing. It wasn't what he'd expected his mother to say.

'I wasn't trying to be rude. I'm just curious.'

'Don't be.' She met his eyes. 'Don't.'

He knew he had to change the subject. He glanced over to where his mother had been painting that afternoon. Her commissions were largely of young men now, rather than children. Soldiers. She often worked from a photograph; the portraits were posthumous. Howard found her work brutally depressing but tried not to show it. She insisted her customers thought they were a comfort. 'Why are you painting over this?' She was covering something she'd painted years ago that had hung for fifteen years in the parlour.

'Canvases are expensive now. The materials are deployed elsewhere.' Of course: tents. Church bells that had once told of marriages had been melted down; garden gates where children once swung and women gossiped were gone too. Country houses that had once hosted parties now housed the limbless and dying. Everything was to be given over to the war effort. This tremendous effort. Everything except Howard. 'Things will go back to normal eventually,' Enid commented soothingly.

She couldn't comfort him. He was old enough to know that it would not be a normal either of them would recognise.

It was a warm enough day, although the sun kept leaping behind a cloud so he never got too hot: perfect working conditions. He'd obliged everyone by exiling himself to a point far from the village hub, up along the canal. The canal path was not much more than mud, criss-crossed by the footprints of women's boots, the prints of the village men long since washed away. His own trail was obvious, if anyone wanted to track him. It turned out today that someone did. A group of kids had been following him for the last three miles. They kept their distance, four or five hundred yards away, as he moved around the perimeter of the Owenses' land. The bravest of the gang occasionally called out, 'Hey, conchie,' and Howard looked up once and raised his hand. It wasn't clear if he was waving at them or shooing them away; anyway, they scattered like pheasants rising from the grass. Giggling and nervous. They were harmless. After that he ignored them. Not prepared to enter into what was after all just an elaborate game of Grandmother's Footsteps. He felt eyes bore into his back but disregarded them. A polite cough, again, a third still didn't cause him to look up.

'I say, hallo.' Vivian Owens stood right behind him. He barely recognised her at first. Thought she was a boy. She was wearing men's clothes, a fact he noticed at the same moment she seemed to remember; she flicked her eyes down over her get-up. A pair of trousers made from heavy, coarse fabric and held up by braces; a shirt that drowned her – she'd rolled up the sleeves but the shoulder seams were halfway down her arms. She looked like a child who had raided a dressing-up box. The only thing that contradicted the impression was the baby strapped to her back in a home-made papoose. She coloured, shrugged and then tried to explain. 'I was working up in the field near my house. I saw you. I saw the children.'

'Have you come to protect me?' She looked confused. 'From their taunts,' he clarified.

'No, I brought lunch. I thought you were a long way from home and you might not have anything with you. I imagined that feral lot hadn't eaten breakfast either.' She nodded her head back over her shoulder. The sunlight caught her hair.

He felt a bit ridiculous. He hadn't needed to be defensive or cutting. It wasn't his way. He didn't know why he felt a need to be curt with her, but he couldn't seem to help himself. The words just came out that way. 'I do have my lunch with me, as it happens.' He pointed to his bag, where a ham sandwich and a bottle of ale nestled.

'Oh, well, more for the children then.' She turned and beckoned over the gaggle of kids, who didn't need to be asked twice. They seemed to guess what was in store, suggesting she had fed them before. She set the basket on the ground and then stepped back; the children pounced on it urgently, like kittens at a cat's teats. They had hard, sharp eyes. Flints in their too thin faces. Vivian Owens looked a tad stunned by their zeal as they devoured the apples, cheese and buns. They lit up when they saw the bottle of lemonade.

'Can we keep the bottle, missus? Our mam will use it.'

She nodded, focusing on carefully removing her sleeping baby from her back. She laid her on the grass, still sleeping in the swaddling. A rosy, contented-looking thing. The village children ate quickly and then ran off, manners forgotten if they'd ever been taught. Vivian Owens gathered up the debris. There was not so much as a crumb of food left, but the napkins that the food had been wrapped in had to be collected. The entire picnic had been devoured in the time it had taken Howard to have just three bites of his sandwich. He was sitting on the ground but she still stood, towering above him, her hands on her waist, arching her back, no doubt needing a stretch after working in the fields with a baby strapped to her.

'Didn't they leave you any?' he asked.

She grimaced. 'They rather put me off my food.' She was a snob. He was right. 'I can't imagine being that ravenous, so eating after I've witnessed their hunger always makes me feel quite gluttonous.' Not a snob, then. Charitable. Sensitive. 'It's astounding to think they are all from one family.' She shook her head. 'I think there are two or three more. Seven children under the age of ten.'

'You disapprove?' Her own baby stirred. He leaned over to take a proper look. Instinctively he stretched out and ran his finger along her cheek; it was warm and as soft as cream. He pulled his hand back. Part of him still wasn't able to understand how both things could be on this earth: a plump, sleeping baby with apples in her cheeks, and putrid, blasted flesh hanging off corpses.

'Did you see, only the big one wore any boots at all, and they had clearly once belonged to his father. They flapped about like castanets when he ran. It is awful. Awful to think about. Awful to look at. The village has so many families with five, six, seven children. It all seems so excessive. There aren't enough boots or food to go around. Not enough water either by the look of them.'

'I don't know what to make of you.' He said it before he thought about it.

'Have you been spending time trying to understand me, Mr Henderson?'

He had, but telling her seemed improper. 'Bringing them lunch was a kind thing to do.'

'Well, their bellies won't rumble this afternoon, true, but it's all rather pointless. I can't fix the bigger problem.'

'The bigger problem?'

'There are so many of them. Why do the poor carry on so when proper families see the virtue in two or three children and abstaining from . . . well, you know.' She flushed and looked bad-tempered. It was clear she wished she hadn't made the observation that was leading down such a mortifying path.

'Abstaining from the pleasures of the flesh?' He purposely picked an archaic saying to highlight her prudery. He was teasing her to punish her for her ingrained condescension.

'Yes.' She wouldn't look at him.

'Maybe the posh people don't find it quite so pleasurable.'

'That's absurd.'

'Yes, you are right, it is. Maybe they don't find it quite so necessary, so urgent, because they have other things, don't they? Like balls, dresses, hunting. All that. And they've caused a war now; that's a good distraction.'

She didn't respond; instead, she carefully scooped up her daughter, hurriedly picked up the basket and turned on her heel. He watched her walk away at some speed, her buttocks bouncing satisfyingly in the trousers. He wondered how many siblings she had. He didn't know much about her.

That night Howard commented to his mother, 'I don't understand Vivian Owens' marriage. I remember old Aubrey.' In public he had to refer to them as Mr and Mrs Owens; in his head she was Vivian Owens, sometimes just Vivian, and he was always old Aubrey, even though he was still a young man and Howard hadn't seen him since he was thirteen or fourteen, a child.

'Not her type?' His mother was knitting. Socks for the men at the Front. Sometimes he helped, although it was not something he would ever admit to. It wasn't that he was like the conscientious objectors who refused to aid war; it was because it was *knitting*.

'Exactly. That's it. Not her type. Not from what I can see. She could have done . . .'

'Better?' Howard shrugged, not sure how to explain what he thought to his mother. 'At the time, when people in the village heard of the marriage, they gossiped that she must be with child, it was all so hurried.'

'I can't imagine that,' stated Howard.

'Why not? Do you think she's too innocent?'

He did not think that. 'Him. Old Aubrey. He doesn't seem to have it in him to seduce a woman before her wedding day.'

Enid threw out a glance that confirmed she had nothing other than gentle but disinterested respect for Aubrey Owens. 'As it turned out, that was all it was: gossip. They were married several months before she caught.'

'The marriage doesn't make sense. Vivian is too vivid and full, vivacious, like her name.' She had such unexpected vitality. More than a dozen ordinary people combined.

'I'd guess that someone thought she needed to be checked. Society does rather resent women with spirit.'

'Maybe.'

His mother paused with her knitting, nudged her glasses up her nose. 'Aubrey Owens is a decent, steady young man.' Her voice had a note of warning.

'Dull, actually. From what I remember. Not especially bright, not especially wonderful. Not especially anything.'

'True, not especially a rotter. Respectable, but not dazzlingly rich; comfortable, not poor.'

'A society mother's choice.'

'Maybe.'

'It has to be,' he insisted. He felt his mother's eyes upon him, wary.

'Fact is, whether we understand it or not, she's married, son.'

'I know.' The tips of his ears burned.

# JULY 1916

# 29

S HE SCRUTINISED HIM as he strode through the village and across the fields. The clothes Howard Henderson wore were simple, ordinary, like everyone else's. Just there to keep him warm, dry or cool. Unimportant to him. Yet he seemed particularly tasteful, poised. She was conscious of his height and dignity. She'd noticed that recently he often had a novel or a play shoved into his back pocket. He moved with lithe athleticism and confidence, broad shoulders and loose, narrow hips. He must know he wasn't welcome here in the village, but he didn't let that intimidate him. They often spat at him, called him Howard the Coward; if only Enid had named him something that didn't rhyme with such an irre-sistible condemnation. She'd seen and heard the taunting for herself and Mrs Rosebend gossiped about it often enough. Enid had never mentioned anything about his reception, so Vivian was not sure if she had any clue as to the extent of the jeers, or even if she was subject to them herself. How could she ask?

Oddly, the two of them didn't talk of Howard all that much. Vivian had naturally expected that a returning son might become the dominant subject of many of their conversations, for a while at least, but Enid remained largely tight-lipped about him. She'd made it clear she was wholly grateful for Vivian's successful inter-vention at Richmond and the position she'd offered him on the farm, but once he arrived in Blackwell, she rarely mentioned him beyond the question of what he might fancy for supper.

He did not seem bowed by the villagers' hatred. He held his head up high, continued walking in his jaunty, careless way; proving them wrong, she supposed. Not a coward. It gave her pleasure to watch him move. A guilty pleasure. He'd been pale when he arrived. Now he was tanned. Muscular. His hair had grown longer but it didn't seem to bother him when it fell in his eyes, wet with sweat. If he had thoughts that furrowed his smooth face and corroded his peace of mind, he seemed to have discarded them temporarily. He enjoyed the moment. The warm English evening, gifted after a day's graft.

He was so different from any man she had ever met before. Different from Aubrey, different from Nathaniel. Unlike Nathaniel, he did not crave the approbation of other men. Howard was self-contained, yet unlike Aubrey he somehow seemed to avoid any suggestion of isolation, loneliness. Even when he was almost entirely alone in his view, the whole world against him, he seemed substantial enough. It occurred to her that despite having a brother, being married and having had sex with two men – twice as many as most girls of her sort ought to ever imagine – she really knew very little about men. She wondered how many possible incarnations there were. Infinite? No, she saw patterns everywhere; they were all the same. Weren't they? Supercilious, controlling, powerful, smug.

But Howard was different, and how she could behave towards him was different too.

Like his mother, he was a free thinker. Indeed, he thought so much it scared her. Yet she intrinsically knew now that she'd probably only ever make friends with those who looked at the world contrarily. Since he thought there was something wrong with at least one system – the one that insisted men must kill one another – she began to hope that he might think there were other things that were off kilter too.

One time, late afternoon, as she walked home from a day in the fields, she came across him bathing in the lake that was just half a mile from her house. The sharp, cool blue afternoon was dissolving into sunset; the leafy trees poked the skies. The air was a liquid mauve and the colour surprised her. The pond flared and glittered. As she walked down the slope, she had a clear view; she spotted him several hundred yards before she was close to him. He plunged his head beneath the surface, totally immersed. She held her breath as she imagined the chilly water penetrating every pore in his skin. He emerged, the water cascading from his hair as he threw his head back and looked to the sky, his skin irides-cent. She was a married woman but she had never seen a naked man. Aubrey had finally swapped his nightgown for pyjamas, but he only ever took off the trouser part, and then in the dark and under the covers.

She had no choice but to keep walking in his direction; she had to get home. If she turned around, she'd have to spend the night in the fields. She decided to press on but keep her eyes on the path, not glance left or right, not acknowledge him at all. Not notice his broad shoulders, glistening and tanned, nor his white buttocks, lean and muscular. Hope he wouldn't turn around. She walked past unnoticed. The splash of his stroke in the water stirred a sudden soft pang, a beating in her heart. In her stomach. Below that.

Yes, he gave her pleasure to watch.

Pleasure and a sharp wrench of distress as well, because he was always at a distance. She had tried to get to know him. He mocked her, clearly determined in his view that she was fluffy nonsense. She'd made a fool of herself when she'd tried to express a view about poverty and responsible birth control. Although what had possessed her to share her opinion on such a matter? It was hardly small talk. Her mother always insisted there was a reason for small talk. It was a way of throwing a rope across a huge chasm; if enough ropes were tied together they made a bridge. Vivian was too impatient for that. She had seen so many stuck at the stage of 'Isn't the weather good for the time of year?' and that wasn't at all satisfactory. She'd hoped he'd be intolerant of small talk too.

He'd forgotten all about her. Even though it was she who had brought him here, freed him from that dark and dingy cell. One would expect gratitude.

Not that she wanted his gratitude.

She'd watched him politely nod at the old women who hung around thresholds in gossipy clusters, even though he must be aware that, as often as not, he was the vilified subject of their conversations. He smiled at the clusters of kids playing hopscotch or marbles. The men who spat at him, he looked in the eye.

He never glanced her way.

He seemed impervious to her. She was used to having an effect. Had she lost it all? Her looks? Youth? Vitality? She had just turned twenty years old; could it all have vanished, washed down the plughole as she scrubbed leeks grown in her own garden?

She'd seen him stop to talk to Timmy Durham, practically the only other young man left in the village. The one they said was dropped when he was a baby and was therefore not fit for service. Timmy smiled back and, short of pals himself, sometimes followed Howard through the village. She thought Howard would try to shake him off, but he didn't.

One day, as she fed the hens, she noticed the two of them mending the roof on the barn. She stared from a distance, secure that she was concealed behind an enormous pile of firewood and the washing that was flapping on the line. Timmy held the ladder steady; he passed up the tools and materials that were needed. She could see that Howard was explaining to him exactly what was required; Timmy was listening intently, head cocked to one side, face twisted with concentration. After five minutes or so, Howard looked up and stared right at her. It was as though he'd known she was there all along. Sensed her. She didn't know how to reconcile that with believing he had forgotten her existence. His eyes bored holes. Somehow his glance embodied everything he stood for. It was independent, peaceful, challenging.

She blushed and quickly emerged from behind the sheets, trying to give the impression that she had intended to walk towards them all along, not to skulk and spy. 'You're rather a big help, Timmy,' she commented. It was true; she was not simply trying to be charming.

'Howard taught me to do it right. How to hand the tools. This is a screw, this is a nail. You shouldn't get them mixed up. People do,' Timmy stuttered, slowly, falteringly. His expression was one of intense absorption and pride.

'He could do with a job. A man needs employment,' commented Howard. Vivian didn't think of Timmy Durham as a man, although he was.

'I can't employ every Tom, Dick and Harry,' she snapped, because somehow she resented him noticing something she should have already noticed for herself; she'd been here far longer than Howard Henderson. 'What would he do?' she asked with a little more patience.

Howard stared at her, square shoulders. He didn't answer her question. He had the sort of face that could heat up and swell with passion but then collapse and be cold, empty. It was like a kaleidoscope. Whichever way he was arranged, he was always magnificent. Every angle, every curve. His teeth, his eyes, his lashes.

She sighed. 'I suppose he could help you around the place. An extra pair of hands never goes amiss. Would you like a job, Timmy?'

'Oh yes please, Mrs Owens. My mammy would be so proud of me.'

'I can't pay you much,' she warned. He beamed as though she'd said the opposite. So did Howard Henderson. It was a loose, warm smile and it made something go slack deep in her belly. A bubble of tension seemed to grow between them. She needed to say or do something to pop it.

'Are you settling? Are you happy here?' She shouldn't have asked whether he was happy. It was too much. Too intimate. Why should she care whether a conchie was happy or not? Yet. She tried to defuse her comment and started to blather. 'When I arrived, I thought the countryside was so flat and dull. I knew nothing about it but I thought there was nothing to know. Then one day there was this deer. It burst out of nowhere right in front of my eyes. It was so delicate yet at the same time sturdy. Do you know what I mean? Graceful but out of control. It seemed almost human. It interested me. I began to look about. Then later I'd notice a hare sitting up in the grass, a pheasant taking flight. The horizon is always moving.' She stopped. She realised she was gabbling. Deep breath. Finally, 'It suddenly didn't seem as bad as I'd first thought. I like it here now. After a fashion. I expect you'll get used to it too.'

He smiled. 'You forget I was born and bred here.'

'Yes, I do forget that. But you left.'

He grinned. 'That's true enough. I did. Lure of London lights and all that.'

'It is rather wonderful. Or at least was.' She shrugged, struck by the thought that London wasn't likely to be a particularly marvellous place to be during a war. Where was?

'I used to play rugby on the green, with your husband.'

'Did you really?' Vivian couldn't decide who she thought was the less likely rugby player, her pale and proper husband or the conchie playwright.

As if reading her mind, 'Neither of us liked it much.'

'Aubrey is due some leave. We're expecting him home at the weekend if everything goes to plan.' Vivian smiled quickly. Other wives thought about the terrible things that might be happening to their men over there. She did not. She could not imagine. 'He hasn't seen Mabel yet.'

'That will be nice.'

'Won't it.' She kept telling herself so, hoping that it would make it so.

# AUGUST 1916

# 30

AUBREY WAS NOT entirely sure how he felt about going home, and he did not like feeling not entirely sure about things, although he was beginning to realise that uncertainty was all-pervasive; no one knew how to feel about anything much nowadays. Sometimes he could not think he had a home at all. From the moment he was given his leave papers, he became conscious of feeling that he ought to be looking forward to seeing his wife and child, which of course was nowhere near the same thing as actually looking forward to seeing them.

A child?

He couldn't imagine it. He was still getting used to the extraordinary concept that he had a wife. They had been married two years and had spent just two months together in that time. She was a stranger. It hadn't worked out as he'd expected between him and Vivian. Theirs was an Edwardian marriage, to all intents and purposes. Practically arranged by their parents. Of course, he hadn't been forced to ask for her hand. He'd been keen. And she'd had the option of refusal, hadn't she? They couldn't blame anyone. Why was he talking of blame? Was there a fault? No, no, of course not. A problem? Well, possibly. He didn't like admitting as much, even to himself. It was worth remembering that she hadn't taken that option to refuse; she'd accepted his proposal.

But had she ever accepted *him*?

He'd thought of her as such a pretty, bright thing. Uncomplicated. A swirl of silks and scents and what have you. He'd attended some parties; not all of them, the way some of the bachelors had, but enough to notice her. He'd been rather smitten for months before her mother started socialising with his and dropping gentle hints that his advances would not be unfavourably looked at. He hadn't thought she'd noticed him, but then they said she had. More, that she was interested. He'd believed them. He had not questioned whether it was likely or even explicable, even though generally speaking he was the sort of man who usually slipped under one's notice. The sort that was only discovered when he held open a door or offered up a seat. Young women had often looked at him in surprised gratitude when he retrieved a fan from under the opera chair or offered to hail a cab; invariably they nodded with no sense of recognition the next time they were introduced. He had been too flattered and elated to question the unexpected nature of her notice. He'd simply grabbed the opportunity.

It was only after they became engaged that he noticed what a funny creature she was, in fact. He began to realise that she seemed to lack the ability to conform, truly an unfortunate thing. Being part of it all mattered so. She wasn't openly, blatantly rebellious; it wasn't that she ever out-and-out refused his suggestions, or her mother's, or even *his* mother's come to that, but she never seemed to fully embrace them either. She seemed to carry with her an almost imperceptible air of resistance. Subtle but certain. She practised on the piano when asked but in a manner that guaranteed she would never improve; she had moved to Blackwell but then rather than joining the ladies in the church hall who organised the village fetes, she had started to garden, in trousers! Poor show: no one liked an odd-bod. She had fallen pregnant quickly and easily enough, which was a grand thing, although she'd produced a girl and insisted on being almost mawkishly devoted, wouldn't hear of hiring a nanny. It wasn't the done thing to feed one's offspring, like a suckling pig or a villager. He sighed. How could devotion be rebellion? He didn't know but felt it was so. Not that he could put his finger on it exactly. That was his point: he didn't know her. He wondered whether he ever would.

The Great War had come upon them so quickly. The months that they ought to have spent becoming better acquainted had been sacrificed to the conflict. Months that were turning into years. Truthfully, joining up had initially been a bit of a relief – simplistic, straightforward, simply correct. The whole marriage business, the actual having of a wife, was more complex and burdensome than he had imagined it would be. She had seemed so lively and competent when he'd inspected her across the dance floors. Assured. He'd thought perhaps she could bring some joy and certainty to his home; a home that operated under a shadow of never being entirely accepted or stable. His family were not considered quite established enough. Not quite blue-blooded enough. Not quite *quite*.

No matter how much money they had.

Because of how much money they had.

But when she'd arrived, she'd turned out to be almost a frail thing. Not all that confident or robust after all. She seemed to depend on him to make her happy. She'd turned to him, eyes flashing with expectancy. His mother had never demanded as much from his father. All his father had been required to do was ensure a healthy income. His mother had had her friends in bonnets and gloves to offer her succour.

He often thought his marriage was unfathomable.

Did it matter anyway? What with the war and everything. Wasn't there far more for him to fret about? Him over there, her at Blackwell. Nothing between them but letters and food parcels. Letter-writing! That in particular was fraught and tricky. It became quite uncomfortable to see his own penmanship trying to express the things he thought or wanted to explain, there in black ink, so inflexible, unalterable. Everything was open to misinterpretation or was a cause for concern. He decided it was better not to try to tell her anything at all. Better to play it safe, talk about the food and the weather. Better to wrap it all up in one bundle and send it to his parents at the same time. That way, any formality could be understood, forgiven. What was the point of sending stories back from the Front? Death, injuries and mud weren't the sorts of things women needed to hear about.

How could he explain it anyhow? The fear, the fellowship, the slaughter, the sacrifice. She hadn't even been to school. She had no sense of companionship or of the reliance that bordered on enslavement. She could not be expected to understand that his men were his family now. How could he tell her that whilst he knew this war was a bad business, of course, he found he was rather good at it?

It was extraordinary. He was constantly surrounded. It was a lot like school, all the officers said so. Since he was a boy of eight years old he'd bunked with peers, eaten with them, learnt, played and (in the very early days) cried with them too. They had tasted the same food: overcooked vegetables, stodgy puddings and custard. They'd smelt the same smells: dusty books, dinner halls and pre-pubescent boys sweating in the gym. Unified experience, the backbone of England. What was done, seen, heard and said as a boy made the man. They were taught to conform and fall in. It was the same in the trenches. Generally good sorts, staying sharp, doing their best. Of course there was the occasional feral character, it was to be expected. There were always those who would try to swizz. Medals handed out like gold stars, punishments dished out too, some men taking a beating in silence. Even the bullets whistling past one's ear put him in mind of the heavy wooden chalkboard rubbers that had done the same back in cramped classrooms. The relief when it hit another boy's head. Same with the bullets. No more or less. They drank beer now rather than milk. The parquet floors used to stretch out in front of him endlessly, corridors that led to halls and classrooms; the trenches were a similar warren. Mud, not parquet, but they went on and on in a comparable fashion. It was very familiar.

It was a grimy little secret, so messy it was never vocalised, even between those who were in on it. There were some things that were quite spectacular and singular to war, no doubt the things that had made men continue to involve themselves with carnage for thousands of years. Power, the raw and formidable displays of physical excellence, and the companionship. Of course, in no way was war a good thing, but in some respects it was better than school. No public schoolboy forgot what it was like when term ended. Parents came to pick them up for the holidays, but one or two were inevitably left behind: high commissioners' sons, that sort of thing. It was always a beast to be the one left. Maybe that was why they tried so damn hard never to do it in battle.

He was scared. No point lying about it. Didn't believe the blaggard who pretended otherwise. They all had little tricks to try to stop them feeling quite so afraid. Some might play an instrument; others read. It was a good idea to keep letters and reread them whilst smoking a pipe or drinking Bovril. They shared air, latrines, cigarettes. They sat thigh to thigh. There was little to say. Nothing original. Vivian sometimes sent him something: a pack of cards, a small book, recently a box of Turkish delight. He'd passed it on to his men. They fell on it like pigs trying to upturn a trough. It made him laugh! Made them laugh too. He wrote and told her they were a success. Welcome. She promised she'd look out for similar treats. Walnut toffee perhaps. Which she did. That was nice of her.

Drinking was an answer, if not *the* answer. The officers were allowed generous privileges when it came to such things. And women. There were French women for them if they chose, which he did from time to time. It was nothing to do with Vivian; she was not in that world. It didn't matter. Drinking permitted the feeling of separation, disinterest, aloofness and disbelief. They were unavoidable sensations. He found it helpful to pretend it was the drink rather than the war. Sex with whores suited him rather well. He preferred the blowsy, careless women, but the hard, resigned ones did the job too. In more careless moments some of the officers hinted that it was all a bit mechanical, soulless. He thought it was familiar and adequate. It was just a need. If she'd been there he wouldn't have touched another woman, but she couldn't be there. He wouldn't want that. Not in a million years. When this was all over, he'd give it up, this business of paying for women. Probably.

She wrote to say she wanted to send the car to pick him up at Dover, but he'd declined. The train would be quicker, even with a change in London and another in Derby. He could have sent a telegram and made arrangements for someone to pick him up at the local station, save him the walk on the last leg of his journey, but he didn't trust the train to pull in at the allotted time and he thought he'd want to stretch. Part of his brain insisted that he was putting off the inevitable; he recited Latin declensions in his head to silence the treacherous nagging.

She must be glad to see him. Women were glad to see their men come home; it was a given.

England seemed very strange. Hazy. It was quiet. He hadn't realised that he'd become so used to noise. Here there was no gunfire or yelling, no shelling or screaming. People whistled when they rode their bikes down the street; birds sang. It was as they had been told. It was a deep, vivid green and pleasant land. The shrubs, lawns and bushes still grew. At least that was not a lie. He liked the feel of his boots slamming down on paved roads and streets, rather than slopping into squelching mud and worse. He'd stood on limbs. Corpses. Bodies. Men. He wasn't sure how to think about it. When did his men turn to corpses? The moment they died? When they stiffened? When they were forgotten? Best not to think of it.

Instead of thinking, he breathed in the fresh air that did not sting his throat or scratch his eyes. He noticed the women and children and stared at them as though they were from another planet, and well they might be. The kids laughed, squabbled, sang, skipped, chased footballs and each other. They were so delightfully normal. The women looked clean. He popped into the corner shop. He wanted to offer Mr Walker his condolences; he'd lost his eldest at the Somme last month. A bloodbath. Miserable. Unspeakable. Aubrey had been there himself. Couldn't quite understand how he'd got through it when hundreds of thousands hadn't. No real progress had been made. Pitiful. Whilst he was in the shop, he bought some tobacco and a newspaper; he surreptitiously sniffed the air around the woman who was stacking shelves. She smelt of lavender water, and even the hint of her sweat was attractive because it was different to male sweat; not as bitter, somehow saltier. He thought of the beach.

Mr Walker was very pleased to see him; indeed he seemed embarrassingly grateful that his son's death had made Aubrey's notice. Aubrey always mixed up the two Walker boys. He had, however, crossed paths with one or the other of them briefly last May. He'd found the lad drunk and morbid in a tavern and had instructed his pals to get him back to base and do a better job of keeping him out of trouble.

'I had opportunity to form the highest opinion of him. I cannot adequately express my sympathy with you or my personal sorrow for his loss. Fine soldier. As is your other boy.'

Mr Walker coughed and turned to blow his nose. 'I'll tell the wife you said that, sir. Thank you.' Nod. 'Thank you.' Aubrey decided that he must make time in the next seventy-two hours to visit the homes of all the families who had lost a man. Mr

Walker's list of ailments seemed to have grown since he last enquired; listening to them made Aubrey feel ill himself. His head ached, he even felt feverish. Still, he listened patiently until at last the shopkeeper checked his fob watch.

'Good grief, sir, look at the time. You'd better get going. Your little wife will boycott my store if I keep you any longer. She must be counting every moment.'

Aubrey was surprised at how brittle and small she was.

Not the baby. Dear, sweet thing, gurgling, plump, robust enough, although not really his concern. Might have been different if it were a boy. He hoped for a boy next. The tubby creature with her unfamiliar scents, ribbons, tiny fingers and such, whilst undoubtedly pleasant, didn't touch him as he thought she might. She seemed so eternally unfamiliar. Not in any way a problem, but not part of him. He couldn't see himself in her, although Vivian insisted she had his nose and chin. She had a baby's nose and a baby's chin, as far as he could see. Same as any other baby's. She didn't feel particular or individual. They had been told that they were fighting for their wives and children; he'd thought that seeing the baby, holding her, might help him make sense of it a bit more, but his wife and child seemed so utterly removed from the war that being with them made him more confused, not less. Still, on the bright side, the baby seemed to make his wife happier.

It was Vivian's frailty that surprised him. He was used to being surrounded by burly soldiers. If he held her too tightly she'd snap, surely. When she got out of bed, her nightdress sometimes rose up above her knees; they were almost like elbows, so skinny. Her legs slipped over the side of the bed like spilt milk. It upset him somehow; he couldn't explain it, but he preferred to turn the lamps off when he was enjoying her. He didn't like to think of her smallness or her youth, particularly. It was odd to think she was only twenty-one. He was just twenty-five. Still young, if you thought about it. Yet he felt so much older. Ancient.

He knew that many of the men found their leaves disappointing. No one spoke of it, God forbid, but he'd observed it in their eyes when they came back to the trenches, in the set of their jaws. The reminder was uncomfortable for some, unbearable for others. They all hoped for too much from their visits. They all thought going home might mean they could turn back time; make the war disappear, at least help them to forget about it for a few days. Leave didn't do that; it couldn't, and they blamed the people they loved the most for the shortfall between expectation and reality. Their wives and sweethearts seemed silly, inconsequential, exasperating. They had no idea.

He felt grubby and different. It was hard to look at her. Her duty was to comfort him, to keep the home fires burning and all that, and in truth she gave it a shot. She had Cook make decent suppers, she dressed up, she fussed over him when his headache and fever developed into a cold, she kept placing the baby on his knee, but somehow her efforts seemed to hit a false note. True, it felt wonderful to have his uniform cleaned and aired, because whilst the officers had it better than the men over there, there was no hot water and such. He appreciated the new socks and underwear, but it was apparent she could offer him nothing more than her best Sunday manners. She treated him like an esteemed guest. No intimacy. Her efforts only highlighted the gulf between them. He'd been an idiot to imagine it could be any other way. They had not been close before the war; how could he have thought that separation might bring them together? It was illogical. He was angry with himself for being irrational and starry-eyed. He told himself that he ought to be grateful. The men who adored their wives and were worshipped back must feel worse than he did. Few of them would be able to bring themselves to actually say what it was like, even assuming the women wanted to hear. Losing tender confidence would be worse. Perhaps he was better off after all. Nothing to lose.

# 31

HE CAME BACK from the war not a hero, as she'd hoped, but distant and full of cold. She tried to be a good wife, the sort he'd think best. Attentive, considerate, dutiful. She bathed his feet. He sat, trousers rolled up, fat, swollen feet plunged into a basin that she'd fetched herself, the smell of Lysol drifting through the rooms. She encouraged him to drink honey and lemon and to inhale eucalyptus. He kept insisting he wasn't all that ill, and truthfully, before the war she might not have made as much of his symptoms, but she wanted to fuss. It was good that she could do something to ease him. She was glad his cold flourished during his leave and not over there, but somehow his masculinity seemed to leach out of him, and she'd been depending so heavily on admiring his bravery. She had hoped it would be an adequate substitute for love. She seemed to need this more than ever, but he was reduced, insubstantial.

She'd learnt, since they married, a special way of talking to her husband that was at once perfectly well-mannered and acceptable but not submissive. She rarely looked him in the eye. Instead she gazed at a vase of flowers and passed comment about that, or fixed her eyes on a particularly appetising plate of food and chatted about the ingredients. If she had to meet his gaze she had a way of making her face blank. It wasn't that he was despotic, or vile.

He was simply a disappointment. The trick was never ever to convey impatience or to acknowledge dismay.

She fruitlessly tried to engage him. She asked him about the war. 'Not talk for women. Not for women at all.' She suggested they have a night out in Stafford or Derby.

'Shall we go and see a film?'

'Is there one you'd particularly like to see?'

'There's always something. The Americans seem to make a new one every day. They are usually snappy enough. It's not a bad way to spend an evening.'

'You go if you want.'

'I wish you'd come too.' Did she? Probably not really. Waves of guilt washed over her. She must be a very bad person not to want to see a film with a soldier. Then again, the soldier didn't want to see a film with his wife. She enquired after his parents. 'They are well, thank you.'

'I invited them here for your leave.'

'Yes, they wrote to tell me.'

They had not replied to her. They'd long since stopped writing directly to her; their only correspondence was an exchange of Aubrey's letters, which arrived grubby, the cream-coloured paper marked with handling. *We're not quite in the trenches yet. But very close. Not long now. Which is exciting. What we're here for after all . . . Soon we'll be moved up the reserve ready for another push. We need to take some pressure off the French boys . . . In the thick of it now!* Sometimes – not always – she found a brief postscript asking after Mabel's health, written in a meticulous hand. However, they had sent two letters here in the last week, both addressed to Aubrey in anticipation of his leave. He hadn't read them to Vivian. She pressed for news but it was delivered in a way that did not court comment or further enquiry. 'Are they coming?'

'Of course. They'll be here tomorrow night.'

'Oh, I wish I'd known.' Vivian frantically started to plan menus.

She'd need to air both spare rooms and check the sheets were clean, in good repair. Flustered, she dared to comment, 'I think it's a bit rude that they didn't reply to me directly. After all, I invited them.'

'They naturally assumed you'd realise they'd accept.' He was obviously, inevitably, loyal to his family. Why wouldn't he be? But she felt locked out.

The baby helped. It was hardly possible to believe that darling, darling Mabel came from him. She did, of course; she even looked like her father. They had the same-shaped nose and chin. It had made Vivian love him a small amount, the fact that he'd given her this treasure, at least until he'd arrived home and seemed indifferent towards his daughter. Then Vivian rather thought she liked him less.

'Where did that bonnet come from?' It was unusual for a man to notice a baby's clothes, and she knew that Aubrey had only noticed Mabel's because they were a bit of a show. Not white, lemon or a soft pink; Enid had knitted her a bright blue bonnet and a matching matinee jacket too. 'She looks like a boy.'

'No she doesn't. She couldn't.' Vivian swept the baby into her arms; hugged her close, as though her daughter had under-stood the slight. She was offended for her rosebud-cheeked girl, glowing and pretty, and she was offended for her industrious friend.

'One of the ladies from the village knitted it for her. A gift.' She hadn't ever found the need to lie to him; they didn't talk often enough.

'Ought you to be accepting gifts from the villagers.' It wasn't a question. It was a condemnation. He shook his head and returned to cramming down the tobacco into his pipe. He drew on it, sucking noisily. Anything to do with his mouth was beginning to cause her distress. She tried to ignore the sucking sound.

'The war means everyone is in reduced circumstances now.'

Either financially or emotionally. 'One must make do. Be grateful.' She thought he'd have approved, but she had come to realise that her nouveau riche husband clung more staunchly to concepts of respectability than old money did. Old money had the confidence to patriotically embrace war-induced poverty; one didn't have to be quite so ashamed about it. Even her mother accepted that it was fine for the baby to wear mittens and hats knitted by the local ladies, who were bored of knitting for their boys on the Front. The secret was not that they couldn't afford to dress the baby as they would in London before the war; the secret was that the women were fed up of the war. Wished it was all over, although they could never say as much to anyone. There were still a lot of secrets; it was just that poverty wasn't one of them.

The way he looked at her made her feel uneasy. Uncomfortable. Nothing stupendously awful. His glance wasn't cruel or jealous, bitter or angry. He looked rather more inconvenienced. His expression was the sort one pulled when the eiderdown slipped off the bed at night and one had to crawl out to rescue it, the cold slamming through the body. Snuggling down the second time, peaceful sleep was invariably elusive. That was what his glance was like. He equated her with a lost eiderdown. He sat square and solid in the chair. She seemed slight; her fingers flapped in her lap as though she was knitting with invisible needles and wool.

'Which lady?' he asked suspiciously.

'Mrs Henderson. Enid Henderson.'

'The conchie's mother.'

'Yes.'

'I heard that she comes here quite often.'

'Yes, quite often.' The set of her shoulders insisted on defiance.

'Humph.' It was a funny sound but explicit. Disapproving. 'You mustn't get involved.'

She found it odd that men were forever telling women not to

get involved in each other's business – a neighbour's business, another mother's business – and yet at the drop of a hat they were prepared to fight a war for a faraway country.

'She is very good to me. Don't forget she delivered Mabel.'

'How can I forget it, you constantly remind me.' He picked up his newspaper. 'Dr Nicholson let us down badly over that.'

'He was out of town. I think he covers a large area now, across almost half of the county. So many of the younger doctors are in France.'

'Well, I suppose we must be grateful to her. I wouldn't want to be rude. I don't doubt she's respectable enough.' It was said in a way that implied he doubted it very much.

'She is,' asserted Vivian firmly.

'One son dead, the other disgraced. Poor woman. I bet she wishes he was dead too.'

'Of course not.'

'She must.'

Their conversations made her think of maids who were prone to tripping on the stairs and causing tea trays to clatter. Mistresses of such maids would look on despairingly, expecting the worst whenever the girl went about her duty. Their beady, disapproving eyes caused the maids to tremble more and led to additional accidents. Not that there was as much noise between Aubrey and her as there was between a clattering tray and a hard wooden floor, but it seemed as though the echoes of mistakes and trip-ups ran through their history. She had the sense that he was always waiting for her to mess up. With him she often felt stranded, obscure, snubbed. She missed Enid, but without discussing it, both women knew the friendship would be curtailed while Aubrey was at home. Could Vivian visit them at their cottage? Aubrey didn't like her 'gallivanting', as he put it. How did he think she spent her time whilst he was away? Was he even the slightest bit interested? She didn't imagine he thought for a moment that she might be bailing hay with Enid or watching Howard teach Timmy Durham how to fix a barn roof.

She knew Aubrey was a fine soldier. The most alluring definition of the era. She knew it in her head but not in her heart or between her legs. He'd fast gathered experience, certainly compared to some who were wet behind the ears. By all accounts he was courageous, fair, clear-thinking in the field. A damn good soldier. It should mean more. It should mean everything. It did to every other woman. It meant nothing to her.

She had to give it up. What was the use? They didn't and never would understand one another. Vivian picked up Mabel. She would leave him to his newspaper. She knew he must be reading the casualty list; everyone did, and she supposed soldiers must find it more compelling than most.

'Oh dear, Charles Rushmore is listed here. And Nathaniel Thorpe. Both of the Forty-Eighth Division. Battle of Pozières Ridge. Yes, I know of it. On the Albert–Bapaume road. They were acquaintances of yours, weren't they?'

Vivian's world lurched, trembled. She felt instantly cold and yet clammy too. The men, just boys, pushed into her head. Charles polite, eager, trying to engage her in the subject of the theatre; Nathaniel looking after his own interests, bullish but vibrant. At least that. For the first time since the night of the ball, she was glad she'd led him to the powder room. 'Charles Rushmore's wife was once a dear friend of mine. If you'll excuse me, I must go and write a letter.'

'Of course. You ought to write to Thorpe's wife as well.' Vivian thought of the letter she'd been instructed to write congratulating them on their engagement. She felt sick and sorry. She longed for the days when the action was thrillingly and securely restricted to the newspaper.

The arrival of his parents initially made things more tolerable, which showed just how strained things were between them. Then, infuriatingly, Sir Charles and Lady Owens announced their intention to stay on at Blackwell after Aubrey returned to the war. They didn't say how long they planned to visit, and Vivian was reminded that she was just a woman with very little say regarding her autonomy. She had become used to being mistress of the house. It was more hers than his; even if it had been built by his grandfather and his money paid for the staff, it was her domain. It was a long time since she'd felt the desire to inwardly scream at the provincial nature of the hydrangeas in tubs and the umbrella stand; she'd begun to view the shoots as quite cheerful and the stand as extremely practical. She liked being the manager of her own small community: Mrs Rosebend, Cook, the maids, the old men who helped on the farm, Timmy Durham. Howard Henderson. Not that she ever felt she was in charge of him. She asked him to do work for her, but no one controlled that man.

Sir Charles and Lady Owens found her arrangements paltry and lacking, even accepting that standards had slipped since the war. They questioned whether it was appropriate for her to eat lunch with the staff. Vivian remembered feeling surprised herself when the situation first arose; she couldn't recall when doing so softened from a matter of convenience to one of habit. Eating with the servants was not what she'd been brought up to do, but dining alone whilst they ate in the next room had struck her as ludicrous. 'It's terribly lonely otherwise.'

'Maybe, but we are here now and you'll have company. The practice must cease.' They renewed their efforts to persuade her to employ a nanny for Mabel, they were aghast to hear she'd employed a conchie, and they categorically disapproved of her wearing trousers.

'But it's practical for farm work.' They could not argue with her doing farm work. It was patriotic; it was what Aubrey had sent her here to do.

'You must be careful, Vivian. You are in danger of becoming rather eccentric. Strong-minded.'

'Am I?'

'Yes, that's what people say.'

'Do they really?'

'Don't sound so delighted. It isn't meant as a compliment.'

Yet she took it as one.

Without having to ask, Vivian felt sure Enid would not be welcome. She was alone again. She thought she might send a telegram to Ava and invite her to visit. She could do with the support. Ava would intimidate her in-laws magnificently; she over-awed everyone.

For all the visit had not been a success, or perhaps because it had not been, Vivian felt profoundly sad when Aubrey packed up his kitbag once again to head to the station. She offered to ride in the car with him, but he said it was unnecessary.

As he stooped to get in the back of the car, he paused, straightened. 'Just one thing before I go, Vivian.'

'Anything.' She beamed, able to be generous towards him now that he was leaving. Only a matter of minutes left.

'Your job is to make him go. Do you understand that?' She realised at once he meant Howard Henderson. 'We can find women to bring in the hay. He ought to be over there, with all us other men.'

'I know.'

'I'm sure you'll be able to persuade him.'

Vivian let her glance slide towards the handle of the car door; it had been polished for Aubrey's journey. What did he mean by that? Too much? Nothing at all. 'Did you talk to him while you were here?' she asked.

'No, why would I want to do such a thing?'

'He's not a bad man. Quite honourable in his own way.' She couldn't help but defend him.

'I try not to think of him as a villain, but he's certainly misguided and intractable.'

'There are many ways a man can stay out of the war. Those writers and artists in Sussex play at being gardeners and call it essential work. Mr Henderson works with extreme diligence.' Aubrey looked impatient. She'd be wise to say nothing more. Yet, 'I've heard of men who took jobs in factories and in shipyards the week before the military came to town asking for conscripts, but the objectors took a hard route. The most visible route.'

'I know that, Vivian. More shame on them. I just wonder whether it's suitable, having him here.'

'I need help with the farm.'

'Yes, but the appetite for conscription is becoming ever more voracious.' He squinted into the middle distance, no doubt weighing up how much military knowledge he should or could burden her with. His voice was low, his lips close to her ear so that the servants and his parents, who were seeing him off, couldn't hear. 'These battles we've fought recently mean it's a necessity. They're not giving us a running tally, but my friends in government suggest it's tens of thousands.' He looked grave. He waited for a moment to see if she fully understood. She did.

'Tens of thousands?' Such a number.

'Maybe hundreds of thousands.'

'That's ridiculous, it can't be so.' She gasped. He was saying the same as Howard.

'So you see why we need every last man.' The same and yet the opposite.

Every last man.

# 32

HOWARD WAS SITTING at the small wooden side table he'd dragged underneath the window and was using as a writing desk, so he saw her walk up the path. The house was so compact that it took just a stride for him to get to the door; he flung it open before she even knocked.

She looked startled by his efficiency, or maybe his appearance: open shirt, unshaven, no socks, definitely no tie. He thought of the time he'd been bathing and she'd walked right past him, pretended he was invisible. He knew he was not. His bare chest wasn't new to her. Nothing was. Hurriedly he offered, 'Come in, come in and wait. Mam's out but will be back before long.' It was a lie – she'd be out most of the day – but he wanted her to stay a while. Right now his mother was on the autobus to the market in Stafford, as she did on the first Wednesday of every month; he was surprised Vivian didn't know as much.

'Actually, it's you I've come to see.' Ah, so perhaps she had known it and she'd timed her visit particularly. Immediately he felt apprehensive about what it was that she wanted to say that couldn't be said in front of his mother.

'Oh, well.' He held the door open wide, stepped back so she could enter.

She hesitated, no doubt having second thoughts about sitting alone in a cottage with a man and no one to chaperone. She glanced left and right, indicating that it wasn't the propriety of the situation that worried her so much as the discovery. The street was empty, dusty; she stepped over the threshold. It took a moment for her eyes to adjust from the bright sunlight to the cool, dark interior. Momentarily plunged into blackness, she blinked, once, twice. Slowly. He supposed he felt the air move between them. When she opened her eyes he was staring right at her. Impossible not to. She didn't look as she usually did. She looked unwell, if he was frank. She was pale, bleached. She looked exhausted, hollow. He thought of those eggs they blew at Easter and decorated. She was fragile.

'What happened to your eye?' she asked, and he remembered he didn't look a picture either; he'd forgotten about the shiner. He brought his hand up and touched it as if he needed to confirm it was still tender. Courtesy of a couple of privates home on leave. Pissed off that they had to go back when he didn't. They'd got him in his own back yard when he went out for a scuttle of coal, night before last. One of them was vicious, seemed like he wanted to kill Howard. The other was jumpy, kept looking over his shoulder; his heart wasn't in it, he only allowed his mate three or four decent punches before he dragged him off and yelled that they had to be on their way. The yard was too tight on space for anything other than a scuffle anyway. It could have been worse.

'You should see the other fellow.' He smiled, but it wasn't convincing. He didn't care much about what they'd done to him, that wasn't it. Actually, he pitied the men who'd jumped him; he understood their fear, their resentment. He knew them; they'd been at school together. One was a few years older than Howard, the other – the vicious one – a year younger. He hoped they'd make it through the war.

Her gaze mooched around the room. It was a mess. No doubt she was noting that things had changed since Howard had moved in. The thick smell of meat cooking had replaced the drift of sugar and butter; sausages or sometimes a chicken were the focus now, not scones. Enid was forever scraping around for the scant luxuries that were still available. She wanted to be allowed to mother him, cosset him, even though he was a grown man. She liked to make hearty pies most of all, and he played his part; he was always effusive, appreciative. He thanked her and devoured the food, displaying greed even when he didn't feel it because there was nothing his mother liked more than seeing him appreciating her gifts. On the days that Enid couldn't pull together a treat and had to serve bread and eggs, he thanked her and devoured just as earnestly. It wasn't an act. He was truly grateful. Soft egg yolks running down the side of an eggcup: an immeasurable pleasure for someone who had spent a year at the Front.

His clothes and belongings were scattered about; he was a slob. He brushed his hair back out of his eyes and then grabbed a jacket from a chair and an apple core off a shelf in an inept and pointless effort to tidy up. He held both in his hands. Suspended. Uncertain where to redeposit them as the entire place was littered with books, ashtrays, socks, and newspapers.

'Bit of a mess, I'm afraid. I plan to tidy around a bit before Mam gets home.'

She looked sceptical. No doubt she knew the devoted and indulgent Enid didn't bother nagging her son about his untidiness. It was clear she blessed every moment he was in her sight.

'I don't mind,' she murmured. Her voice came out weaker than he'd expected. Sometimes she sounded imperious; today she sounded unassuming. 'Actually, it seems so cosy. It's rather enviable, this display of relaxed domesticity.'

'Disarray, you mean?' He grinned.

'It was never like this when I lived at home with my parents.' He suddenly had a vision of her straight-backed, sitting in an immaculate parlour, teacup balanced elegantly, not a thing out of place, certainly not a word. The image made him shiver. He couldn't imagine old Aubrey was the sort to tolerate untidiness either. She no doubt had to be on her best behaviour the entire time. So she must mind the mess. In a way. No one wanted to be shown what they couldn't have.

'Can I get you a cup of tea?'

'Am I disturbing you?' She looked him up and down and turned a bit pink. She probably thought he'd just got out of bed. The state of him. He wouldn't have answered the door to anyone else, but he hadn't been able to resist her.

'I'm writing.' It was explanation and excuse for his disarray.

'Oh!' Her face cracked with interest. 'A new play?'

'No.' She had no idea about the world. No one wanted him to write plays any more. How could she imagine they might? 'More of a diary, a memoir.'

'Then I *am* disturbing you.' She looked as though she was going to run away.

'I wasn't doing that well. It's nothing that can't wait.' At times it seemed his life was an enormous interval. Everyone's was. The men in the trenches, sweethearts and mothers, politicians and artists were all waiting for the carnage to end. A tea break wouldn't spoil anything, after all he was only beginning to pick up his pen again after a miserably long period where writing had simply been impossible. When he was Over There he had been paralysed. He'd felt inadequate – as a man, as a writer. The suffering, the carnage, he couldn't call it his own; how could he presume to capture it? Then, in Richmond, all writing materials were confiscated. He hadn't minded. He'd felt too helpless, thought the world too hopeless, to record or recall. It was only here in Blackwell that he'd thought perhaps . . . maybe. . . The feeling that he should at least try to document something, evolved into a belief that he could, and solidified into the fact that he must. Somehow, the clean air sluiced and slackened the tangle of depressed thoughts, although his ideas were not flowing consistently yet; he'd sat for two hours this morning and only written a paragraph. His mind jittered and jerked, spluttering ideas like an over-heating machine gun.

She stayed in the living room but didn't sit down even though he invited her to. He was relieved she hadn't followed him through to the kitchen. It would be a mistake. She must know the tiny dimensions of the room. They'd practically be on top of one another. She'd be able to smell the sleep on him. He'd be able to smell her soap again. He'd noticed it the minute he opened the door to her. She washed with a cake of Wright's coal tar soap. Whilst pungent, it wasn't a feminine, sweet smell; it was sterile, almost antiseptic, but since the war no one had bothered much about perfume in soaps. Resources, naturally, had to go elsewhere.

He took a deep breath, filled the kettle and over the sound of the splashing water on the tin called through to her, 'I heard Mr Owens got his leave.'

'Yes, but he returned yesterday.'

'So soon?'

'Oh, I don't imagine they can win this war without him.' Howard paused for a moment and tried to decipher her meaning. The words were those of a proud and loyal wife; the tone was inscrutable.

He reached for two mugs, then thought better of it and swapped one, then the other, for a cup and saucer. He set a tray as his mother might. The kettle would take a few minutes to boil. He had to go back into the living room; he couldn't very well hide in here. He used up the time opening the two windows and snatching up various items of clothing. She still hovered by the doorway, even now looking as though she might bolt. He again urged her to take a seat and finally she sank into one; her actions had a disproportional air of surrender. When they were furnished with their tea, he chose to sprawl, as usual, on the small two-seater sofa perpendicular to her chair. They both stared at the empty grate.

Abruptly, 'I don't understand the war either.' This was the thing he had least expected her to say. He thought she'd come to issue him with some new tasks, or perhaps – and this thought occurred to him because she looked so serious and forlorn – to discuss where she, or old Aubrey, thought he was not doing an adequate job. Instead she was picking up on the conversation they'd had when he was in Richmond, months back. He didn't understand why, but he knew enough to realise that the 'either' was inclusive, an invitation. A concession. 'I don't really understand how it started. I can't imagine how it will end.'

He thought she was asking for a genuine account. 'Well, the Austrian-Hungarian heir was assassinated by a Serb. The Serbs expected trouble and started to arm. Austria and Hungary partially mobilised in response. Russia partially mobilised to protect Serbia. Germany jumped in and spurred on Austria, who switched to full mobilisation. The French, bound by treaty with Russia and more importantly by sheer terror, mobilised too. Germany crashed through Belgium, who we were tied to by another ancient treaty. The rest, as they say, is history. War became horrifically unstoppable because of pride. No nation dared even to pause for breath for fear of being put at a disadvantage, and before we knew it, there were millions of men on trains travelling to the Front.'

He stopped. His account was accurate enough, he thought. Honed. She stared at him, eyes cool and sharp, suggesting she was infuriated by him, or even a little insulted. He paused, and then considered that perhaps she thought the most pertinent question was not how the war had started, but how it would end.

'I can't remember anyone trying for peace; everyone I knew was braying for war,' she commented sadly. She seemed preoccupied, not quite there with him in the moment.

'There was a rally for peace on Sunday the second of August

1914. I went along, but they couldn't smother the whiff of war hysteria. Too many of us are animals pulling at our chains.'

'That was the day before I married.'

'Awful timing.'

'Yes, wasn't it?'

'Such a warm, sultry afternoon. I remember walking to the march and watching unconcerned straw-hatted men punting on the Thames while their girls loafed under parasols. I wanted to yell at them, insist they join me, but I also had an equal impulse to just ignore the talk of war and do something more fun instead. I thought about drivers in goggles hurling their roaring cars round the track at Brooklands. I had a ticket you see. I could have been there instead.'

'Or any number of places.'

'Yes. I could have gone to Brighton, squeezed in amongst the hired bathing machines that trundle on to the crowded beaches.' He thought of the huts designed to protect people's modesty; nothing could offer protection now.

She must have been thinking along the same lines because she commented, 'Tragedy was inevitable by then; there was nothing anyone could do to stop it.'

'Yes. All the arrangements were in place.'

He wondered whether she understood he was still talking about the Great War, not her marriage. He thought not when she added, 'So many hasty marriages since.' She shook her head. He thought it was a peculiar thing for her to concern herself with. There were countless tragic consequences of this war: death, children being orphaned, women bearing babies forced upon them by their enemies, destruction of cities and ancient art; he'd never thought that hasty marriages deserved comment. But then he wasn't a woman.

'Did your brother have a sweetheart?' she asked.

'Of sorts. He'd been courting just a few months.'

'So he never married?'

'No, he didn't make that leap. He didn't think he'd die so soon, I suppose.'

'What do you mean?' His observation seemed to draw her focus.

'Those who marry in a hurry before they rush off to the Front seem to me to be leaping to fulfil the instincts of mankind. They want to have sex, ideally to breed. I don't think Michael thought he'd die. His lack of marriage is evidence of that.'

She nodded and fell silent as though she was considering his words. He could see her chest rising and falling ever so slightly; it was mesmerising.

'Aubrey wants me to persuade you to join up.'

'I see. Is he going to withdraw his sponsorship? You know, even without my position as an essential worker, I won't go to war.'

'Yes, I do know that. You'd go back to prison.'

'I would. Sorry.' He seemed quite cheerful about it all. His 'sorry' tossed out light-heartedly, as though it was all a rather marvellous game and he'd won.

She sighed heavily, closed her eyes for a moment as though desperately trying to shut something in, or out. 'Everyone is appalled by what is happening over there. It makes no sense at all that they want to send you.' She corrected herself. 'Send anyone. Everyone.'

'But they do.'

'Yes. I've noticed in the village . . .' She clearly didn't want to offend him by finishing the sentence. She pointed to his black eye.

'Well I don't spend many evenings in the local pub, chewing the fat with my old school pals, if that's what you mean. I'm not especially welcome.' He smiled. Not because he was happy with the situation but because he felt it was his duty to put her at ease. It struck him as interesting how regularly he smiled with a lack of sincerity or even emotion. How infrequently he felt authentically happy, even writing couldn't always make him so. Remembering was essential for writing and remembering was vile. He was most content after a day when he'd worked so hard he ached; he was peaceful when she was nearby. 'Strangely those who have already lost people are not always the worst. Some behave as expected: angry, resentful. "Why should you lie about here when my son has found a muddy grave?" All that. Others are a surprise. One more death is one too many for them. They don't push me to go.'

'Aubrey is unequivocal.'

'Yes. As are those with sons, husbands, lovers still alive but only just; those who are stationed out there. They are unilateral in their hatred towards me. They want me to get off my lazy bastard backside and go and help their men.' She fell into this category; he was telling her it was understandable if she thought this too, that he forgave her.

She didn't say anything directly, simply sipped her tea. And then groaned, 'Mustn't it be wonderful to be one of those terribly buoyant sorts of people? Those who believe it will all come well in the end.'

'I always thought you were that.'

'I think I was, a long time ago. I can hardly remember being so now. I'm so utterly fed up of the war.' They all thought it but he was surprised to hear it said. Expressing dissatisfaction with the war, however understandable and human, was considered unpatriotic and somewhat defeatist. 'I think it's awful that we've been born at this time. I try to keep colour in my baby's life by showing her my pretty dresses, the ones I never have opportunity to wear any more. Sweet little Mabel gurgles and reaches for the scarlet ribbons, the pink bows. I snip them from my garments and weave them through the bars of her cot.'

He appreciated her confession; many would have thought it

inconsequential chatter, yet he found it profoundly moving. Gentle intimacy soused the room. It was like stepping into a warm bath.

'When you came to Richmond, you mentioned that you tried to be a rebel once but it didn't work out for you.' He'd often thought and theorised about this.

'That's right. It ended disastrously.' Her pronouncement was so sad and final, he wondered whether he should pursue it. Manners dictated that he shouldn't, but something bigger pushed him on. He had to. He needed to know her.

'Sounds like an interesting story.'

'I fear it's very commonplace, actually.' He waited. She sighed. 'There was a man once – well, a boy. I suppose. When I was young.'

'You are young now.'

'No one is young any more.' It was true. The war had made them all mortal and ancient. 'He was rather lovely. At least, I thought so. Not everyone agreed with me. Nanny hinted that he was an incorrigible flirt, untrustworthy. A tease. I thought I knew better. Yes, I could see he was spirited, but I thought I would tame him.' She paused. 'Or join him.' She glanced apologetically at Howard, as though the idea was beyond ludicrous. 'Yes, I did think that, and it was such a delicious idea. Back then.'

'This isn't Aubrey.' He knew somehow it could not be.

'No, before,' she confirmed. 'They dressed me in white and then left me to dance in the arms of physically unruly and emotionally inept young men. I twirled to the strains of orchestras belting out songs entitled "Dreaming" and "Yours Forever". I can't see how anyone manages to end well.' He laughed but not heartily; he sensed that wouldn't be right. 'I got rather . . . carried away.' She paused so that Howard could understand the full meaning of her words, and then admitted with a brittleness designed to drown self-pity, 'But he wasn't serious about me.' Howard couldn't see how that was possible. He was not an overly romantic man, but he knew enough of the world to understand that she was the type to captivate. Unilaterally. If she turned her mind to it. 'After our . . . interlude, he proposed to another girl. Left me rather high and dry, I'm afraid. My reputation in tatters. I was very . . .' He thought she was going to say unhappy; instead she said carefully, 'Uncomfortable. Going against society is difficult. When Aubrey proposed, I was grateful. Relieved. Almost as relieved as Mother. So I married. I was saved.' It was clear she was trying incredibly hard not to sound maddened, yet she was nothing but. She plastered on one of her brittle, unconvincing smiles. She did it too, he thought: smiled for convention not emotion. They had that in common. She shook her head a fraction. 'Look at me now. I have a very comfortable life. So, rebelling never did me any good. If there is a moral in my tale, I suppose I am recommending conforming.'

Her life was undoubtedly comfortable. Two houses, plenty to eat and wear; her daughter would have a governess and a society wedding. These compensations were indisputable. He doubted they were anything more than that. Consolations. He did not believe she was happy, not truly.

But then who hoped to be happy nowadays? Maybe that was unfair. He was hoping for too much for her, asking too much of her. Although he did not believe she was content either. She was, he thought, more than a little angry.

All at once Howard understood the reason for Vivian's visit. She had after all come to do Aubrey's bidding, not just inform him of it. She would not withdraw his position as an essential worker, out of loyalty to his mother, but she would continue to try to persuade him to go to war, out of loyalty to her husband. He felt irritated that she had no loyalty towards him. He couldn't expect it but he wanted it.

'Or perhaps conforming is the real villain. Falling in line, marrying Aubrey?' Howard suggested. His tone deliberately light,

not betraying just how firmly he believed it. Yet it was an audacious comment to make, even as a joke.

'You are being rude, Mr Henderson.'

Howard didn't agree. He was being honest, although no one
ever wanted that. It wasn't a century for honesty; the war had
proved as much. He wondered whether there would ever be a
place for honesty again. Whether there ever had been. He was
not sentimental and refused to worship at the altar of mawkish
claptrap that insisted the past was innocent, the future bleak. Both
the past and the future were capable of both.

'I take it you are here to tell me to fall in. You are trying to
draw an analogy between your affair and my conscientious objection.' She exasperated him even more than before.

'Perhaps.' She blushed. He wondered about the root of her
colour. Possibly because he'd used the word 'affair', possibly because
she was abashed at her own laborious, round-the-house approach
to talking about anything that mattered. She must know he would
appreciate her being more direct with him. Not that it was her
fault, he reminded himself; women weren't brought up to be
anything other than coy. He didn't want coyness from her. She
could do more. Better.

'What if it is this war itself, not my objection to it, that most
resembles your love life?'

'What can you mean?'

'Both your marriage and the war are hurried, ill-considered
botch-ups. Motivated by pride, orchestrated by old duffers and
ultimately a sacrifice of the young. Just to save face.'

She stared at him aghast. For a moment he was astonished that
he had uttered the words aloud; he had no right to. He had never
been so brutally challenging to Beryl or any other woman. He'd
never before felt a need, but he did here; he wanted to prise open
her eyes. She put down her tea with great haste and leapt to her
feet; the cup rattled in the saucer. She ran her hands down her

dress, straightening it, and he noticed they were shaking. He almost admired her restraint; a chap would have hit him. 'Don't be absurd, there are no similarities. Haven't I just told you that my marriage is a great success?' She lifted her chin.

He stood up too. Their faces were just inches apart. He could hear her sharp, shallow breathing. Rather than making him feel repentant, it excited him; pushed him to be more extravagant. 'As everyone will say of the war, if we win. Everyone, that is, except the dead.'

He'd gone too far. She looked stricken. 'Of course there's terrible sacrifice.'

'What if the sacrifice is simply too terrible?'

'Duty.' She spat it out.

'It's just a word.'

'A fine one. An important, emotive word.'

He tossed out one of his own. 'Waste.'

She walked swiftly towards the door, put her hand on the handle but didn't pull it open. Instead she paused, her forehead resting against the wood.

He leaned close to her ear and whispered quietly, carefully, 'What if you hadn't married? What if you'd ignored the pressure of sniggers and calls to do the right thing? You might have been happier.'

'Or I might have been an old maid who died alone and child-less. Or, who is to say, I might have fallen further and ended up in a whorehouse or working on the street.'

He could not believe she had just articulated such things to him. To any man. To *him*. Whorehouse. It conjured up images of heavy red brocade curtains, white thighs, black suspender belts. What could she know of such places? Then again, she was a married woman, she must know things. He ought to understand that. She wanted him to recognise her experience, her know-ledge. She did not want to appear virginal, naïve or innocent.

Why? Women like her staked their lives on playing the naïf to perfection.

He felt his entire body quake. Shock at hearing her say the words, or because he genuinely hadn't considered those alternatives? Something different altogether? Desire?

She turned to him, tilted her head and asked, 'Why are you so concerned about my marriage, Mr Henderson?' The moment trembled. It was unclear which way it might fall.

He couldn't tell her.

For all his belief in honesty, and even after everything he'd impertinently and possibly imprudently said to her already, he couldn't say any more. He wanted to kiss her but he stopped still. He couldn't read her expression; a cacophony of emotions ran across her face. She was infuriated and pitying. Relieved and victorious. 'You see, things could have been much worse if I'd continued to rebel. Consider that when you are pursuing your silly analogy. There is a reason we conform within society. We're protected by it. Why would you want to walk so entirely alone?'

'I wish I didn't have to be alone in this. I wish millions saw it my way.'

'What if you are simply wrong? What if doing nothing is the absolute worst thing a person can do?'

With that, Vivian pulled open the front door and dashed out of the house. Clearly she believed it so fiercely, she didn't even want to savour the victory.

# 33

'HERE COMES THE cavalry!' Ava called loudly as her car pulled up outside the house at Blackwell. Vivian felt a surge of joy that was only just pinched by the thought that her in-laws would no doubt have heard and understood Ava's comment, and the concern that Ava had arrived by car, which would no doubt raise eyebrows. Petrol was to be saved for essential journeys; visiting one's pals could hardly be considered that. She tried to push the niggles away. She vaguely remembered being a careless girl and wished to be so again, at least for the duration of Ava's visit.

'Working outside suits you, Vivi,' Ava declared. She forsook the usual air kiss and pulled Vivian into an embrace, albeit a very elegant one. Ava had been not only amused but also impressed when she first heard about Vivian's work on the land. She had doubted Vivian would persist with it but was thrilled that she had; full of admiration.

'What makes you say so?'

'You have that papery fine skin and it's now brushed with the outdoors; apples sit in your cheeks, like a child's.' Ava's compliments were always the most wonderful to receive because they were scarce and sincere, like her visits and correspondence, come to that. Her life was too full for Vivian to expect multiple visits throughout the year, or indeed long letters, which were extremely time-consuming to write. However, since Vivian had married and moved to Blackwell, Ava had visited once every six months, as regularly as the chime on a cuckoo clock, and the consistency was appreciated. This particular visit was in addition to the timetabled ones; the response to an SOS, therefore still more meaningful and delightful. Ava had even visited when Mabel was just a month old, because that was their routine, although no one could imagine she had actually wanted to be around such a small baby. She'd arrived laden with gifts – a cashmere blanket, a silver rattle – and had declared she'd be delighted to be godmother before Vivian had yet asked. Although she'd twice commented how terribly dull it all was ('all' being the feeding, the bathing, the sneaking around the house so as not to disturb Baby), she hadn't cut her visit short to dash back to London and the War Office, where she was now employed. Instead she had added that Mabel was, 'utterly beautiful. I don't accept for a moment that she looks like Aubrey. Your eyes, your colouring. Thank goodness.' Her visits were a highlight in Vivian's calendar.

'Apples in my cheeks? Is that a polite way to say I'm tanning? I don't know if that's a good thing. Mother won't like it. You know she thinks freckles rather than the Germans are the enemy. She ruins entire summers worrying about them.'

'Do you like it?'

'I do rather,' Vivian admitted.

'Me too. Your eyes look more piercing and knowing shining from your tanned face.'

Vivian's hair had bleached in stripes; the bits around her forehead and ears were almost golden. She patted it self-consciously. The summer had arrived obligingly early. It had seemed to arrive at about the same time Howard did.

Ava cast her gaze about. 'I always forget how brown the countryside is. Brown. Nothing more.'

'That's not true,' laughed Vivian.

'Brown and green,' Ava conceded.

'A purplish brown, a fading green. Look, yellow and russet here, and over there . . .' Vivian pointed to a flaming shred of exceptional colour on a hill, 'I can see a distinct splash of crimson and a streak of gold.'

Ava looked bemused. 'Gosh, you've changed. I need a cocktail. You do still drink cocktails, don't you? You haven't altered that much.'

They spent the visit doing pleasant, easy things. Strolling, chatting and sipping tea and cocktails. Ava's presence somehow released Vivian from dealing with anything more arduous, either physically or emotionally. They talked about girls they knew in common. Their conversations were light, peppered with history and a touchstone to Vivian's former life.

'And Lydia Chatfield, is there a baby yet?' Vivian asked as she passed Mabel a wooden brick with the letter T on it.

''Fraid not. Wants one awfully.' Vivian could tell from Ava's tone that she didn't totally comprehend her friend's desire. Vivian pitied Lady Chatfield.

'And now her husband is away, I suppose, so it's all on hold.'

'In the Home Office, actually, not away.'

'Oh, did he fail the medical?'

'Something like that. Did I mention Margo Hopkins is married?'

'Really?'

'Yes. Rather well. Certainly better than any of us expected. He's not much to look at, but quite rich and awfully good at riding. All rather hurried, of course. He's rushed off to the Front.'

'Poor thing.' Vivian thought of what Howard had said about those most fearing death rushing into marriages. She hoped Margo and her husband had managed to squeeze in a wild and passionate honeymoon before he went to France.

'A lot of people are still so very excited about the war,' commented Ava.

'Odd, isn't it.'

'Is it? The men get to travel abroad. They're with their pals. I can imagine worse things.'

'I can't.'

'Their letters are quite cheerful.'

'They are lying.'

'How do you know?'

'They must loathe it, be shocked by it. All but the very worst of men must be. They just can't say. They daren't be the first to say.' Ava stared at Vivian. She looked surprised but respectful; still Vivian felt uncomfortable under her gaze. 'Does Margo Hopkins' young man come with a title?'

'Yes, he does. She's Lady Lutton now. Do you remember she always wore woolly lumpy bodices, even at dances?'

'Yet she's married very well. I do wonder about that.' Vivian had worn practically nothing under her dresses at dances. Just stockings, her belt, knickers and a light camisole. She'd thought she'd known what she was doing. She hadn't, not at all.

'Do you know who else I bumped into?'

'Who?'

'Miss Mildred Douglas. Wasn't she—'

'My old governess. Yes. She drank gin out of a teacup and didn't care much if her charges understood anything beyond their times tables.' Eccentricity was absorbed if it only affected girls, because really how much damage could be done to girls? They had no influence. 'Oh, I owe her so much. I know a great deal about practically nothing and practically nothing about a great deal,' said Vivian playfully, trying to mask her irritation with circumstances.

'It's a shame, Vivi. You strike me as rather bright.'

'Thank you.' She had been so silly but she thought perhaps she wasn't quite so now. She'd changed. She'd grown up, as they'd threatened she would.

'She does some secretarial work in the afternoons at the Foreign Office.'

'Does she? How extraordinary.'

'I assumed she'd still be teaching your younger sisters.'

'Mother couldn't trust her, after I turned so bad. They are keeping my sisters on very tight leashes after my escapade, unnecessarily tight. I hope Miss Douglas is a better secretary than she was governess.'

'Yes, or we'll all be talking German soon.' The women giggled. It was not possible to get through the war without sometimes making a joke. They couldn't be sad all the time. Although being happy was unmanageable too.

'You heard about Nathaniel Thorpe and Charlie Rushmore, I suppose,' murmured Vivian.

'Yes, darling, I did.' Ava squeezed her hand. 'Terribly sad.'

Ava had all the news because she was who she was, and because she lived in London. On her own! In an enormous bachelor-girl flat in Chelsea. She'd insisted on moving up to town to join the war effort in 1915. Nursing wasn't for her; the discipline would chafe. Factory work was insufferable, so she'd applied to the Foreign Office. Of course they snapped her up. Fluent in three languages, looked like a deity, why wouldn't they? Her own flat. No husband to interrupt her authority, no threat that in-laws might arrive unexpectedly. It seemed marvellous and ridiculous to Vivian. The war was chaotic and terrible but it brought freedom and opportunities, at least to women like Ava. She had asked Vivian once if she should feel bad about it, benefiting from their hardship, but as she didn't have a brother or particular lover serving, it was very hard to see who exactly she was cheating.

Vivian's in-laws were, as she'd hoped, quite intimidated by Ava. To avoid her they took long walks around the land and visited the villagers in their cottages. Vivian couldn't deny that their presence was appreciated by the locals, nor could she pretend it was anything other than a pain to her. When they announced that they would not be staying any longer, she had to suppress a cheer.

Generous in victory, Ava offered them her driver to take them back to Wales the very next day. Lady Owens protested briefly but Sir Charles was not prepared to miss the opportunity to ride in a Rolls.

'Although you will have to set off quite early, I should say. So my driver can get there and back before he loses the light.'

Once they were gone, Vivian breathed a huge sigh of relief. She stretched her arms wide as though embracing the house; reasserting her rule.

'You actually like it here, don't you?' Vivian could hear Ava's amused disbelief.

'I do rather. When it's just me, Mabel and our friends.'

'Speaking of which, will Enid be allowed to come and visit now? I do enjoy her so.' They had met on Ava's previous visits. Vivian had been relieved and not that surprised that Ava seemed to have total disregard for any class barrier; she had simply admired Enid thoroughly. They were kindred spirits: unconventional, independent and startling.

'Yes, I hope so. It's been far too long.'

'I get the sense from your letters that you don't see as much of her as you used to.'

'The presence of Aubrey and his parents was constraining.'

'And I imagine she's busier now her son is home.'

'Yes, that too.'

'I simply can't wait to meet the infamous Mr Howard R. Henderson.' Ava grinned mischievously. 'They've dropped the minimum height, you know?'

'You mean the army?'

'Yes. Five foot three. I could be in stockinged feet and still tower above the men they are sending to fight to defend my honour. It all seems rather desperate.' They moved into the drawing room, where the windows were wide open, letting the summer air drift into the house. Vivian sat on the large sofa, placing the sleeping Mabel close to her, Ava stood by the open window, looking out. 'And then there are men like your chap.'

'He's not my chap.'

'Well, you know what I mean. Look, isn't that him?'

Vivian joined her friend at the window. She could see him clearly, working in the nearby cow field, just at the end of the garden. He was shovelling manure into a wheelbarrow; it was dirty, low work. She wished Ava could have seen him in the pond. Glorious, sparkling, like an Olympian god. But then she was grateful Ava had not seen his magnificence. Selfishly she didn't want to share it.

'The age limit has been extended to fifty. Grandfathers, some of them. Now there's a way to dispatch your father-in-law permanently.'

'Ava, that's a tasteless joke. Besides, he's fifty-three.'

'Still, you see my point. Rather yellow-livered, your chap, don't you think?'

'He believes it's more manly not to fight.' Vivian did not feel comfortable repeating Howard's arguments. She didn't believe them firmly enough, but then nor could she dismiss them decisively either.

'Does he now?'

'Yes, he's very persuasive.'

Ava noted his broad back, his height, his wide thighs. 'I bet he is. You know, I think he is the most handsome man I have ever seen. Do you understand what I mean? Of course you do. Genuinely beautiful. He must stay here, on these lush green fields, for ever. It's such a charming backdrop for him. We can't let him be blown to smithereens.' She rooted in her bag and lit a cigarette.

'Do you think he might have a point?' Vivian knew the value of Ava's approval and support. She wanted it for him. If she could, she would protect him.

Ava shrugged. 'All I know is that it seems rather odd that he wants to be less of a man when women are so thrilled at the chance of being more of one.'

'That's just it. Maybe things aren't so very clear cut.' Vivian paused but felt compelled to be honest rather than discreet. 'I really don't see him as less of a man. I did at first, but not now.'

They both let their gaze linger on him as he bent and straightened, bent again, shovelling. His muscles rippled. He was always so active; he put everything he had into this essential work. No one could call him a slacker. His shirt, damp with sweat, had turned transparent and clung to the base of his back. Vivian wondered what it would be like to place her hand there. How was it that Aubrey seemed so fragile in comparison, when he was the soldier and Howard the objector?

'He makes me think of things. You know. Such as questions about whether it's right that the Church are telling us to go ahead and kill. Archdeacon Basil Wilberforce, chaplain to the Speaker of the House of Commons, declared that to kill Germans was a "divine service". The Bishop of Durham has spoken about the "holiness of patriotism". Yet both sides are praying to the same God. It's so confusing.' Ava's mouth hung open, her face a faintly mocking caricature of shock. 'I do read!' Vivian assured her, continuing despite Ava's teasing. 'I mean, did anyone think this through? I'm not sure they did. Certainly the people I know seemed to be caught off guard. The storm rolled in quite unexpectedly. We were all so very wrapped up in our love affairs, our careers, our babies. Those who did try to warn us and prepare were dismissed as crackpots or zealots.'

'Well, well, well, Vivi, I do believe you've become radical.'

'Would it be so bad?'

'No, not at all. But I can't agree with you. I'm all for the war. It's not that I'm the slightest bit interested in all that patriarchal guff, but I do like a man in a uniform.'

'Oh, Ava.' Vivian grinned; it was hard not to. It sometimes seemed that her friend refused to be serious for two minutes in a row; on the other hand, Vivian had a sense that at the root Ava was eternally serious, which was why her next comment was so disconcerting.

'I understand. He's a lover, not a fighter, your man.'

'He's not my man.'

'Isn't he?'

'You must stop calling him that.' She knew she sounded irritated.

'I wouldn't blame you. Not one little bit. I wonder what he does for sex?'

'What an extraordinary thing to wonder.' Vivian found she could no longer look at him. She turned away from the window, rested her bottom on the ledge.

'Is it? I think it is a perfectly commonplace thing to ponder. He isn't fighting, but he is still a man. Beautiful, hungry, lustful.' Vivian felt the words deep in her own body. Between her legs, in her head, under her breastplate. 'Do you think there is an obliging girl in the village who is prepared to forget he's a conchie because he's simply delicious?'

The thought was distasteful to Vivian, upsetting. 'I can't believe you think about such things, let alone talk about them.'

'I speculate on that sort of thing all the time, about everyone. At least everyone who is young and gorgeous. What are all the wives doing for sex now the men are away? What are you doing?'

'I can do very well without it, thank you.'

'Can you really? I can't at all.'

'Ava!' Vivian knew she was colouring but she didn't know if it was because she was embarrassed or vexed.

'Have I shocked you, darling? I do apologise. I am so truly modern. Things are very different now, because of the war, don't you think? No one is going to bundle me into a marriage just because I fancy a man.' Ava shrugged, not entirely unsympathetically. 'Sorry. No offence.'

'Oh, don't mind me.'

Ava leaned in very close to Vivian's ear and whispered, 'I'd bet your essential worker could change your mind about sex.'

'What a thought.'

'Come on. Don't tell me you haven't had it. The thought, I mean.'

'You can be very vulgar.'

'Well, if you don't want him, I could make him happy. A man of principles might be a delightful change.'

'Ava, please don't joke about such things.'

'About what things? His principles? His body?'

'Either.'

'I see.' Ava looked at Vivian in a way that suggested she did indeed see. She had seen it and she was prepared to bring it out into the open. Temporarily Howard had stopped shovelling. He seemed to be reflecting. He was leaning on the shovel, staring straight ahead, at them, eyes clear and unblinking. Of course he couldn't possibly see into the house. 'Will he have tea with us?'

'I don't know.'

'Invite him for tea tomorrow. You can stretch to it, can't you?' Vivian hesitated. 'Oh, don't be dull and say you'd rather it was just us two. I have nothing more to tell you. I've delivered all the gossip. Nothing interesting happens at the Foreign Office, and when it does, I can't talk of it. It would be lovely to have a man's company for a change.'

'I can't, Ava, I'm not sure it would be proper. A single man and two single women, alone.'

'Oh, but, Vivian, you're not single. You have a husband.'

Vivian turned scarlet and didn't know what to say. When had she started to think of herself as single? 'I shall invite Enid, if you are insistent on company.'

'Enid and the conchie?'

'No, just Enid.'

'Really?'

'Oh, I don't know,' flustered now. 'Don't call him a conchie.'

'Well, what should I call him? I'm not to call him conchie, I'm not to refer to him as your chap. Mr Henderson would be proper, I suppose, since we haven't been introduced.'

'I sometimes call him Howie, at least in my head,' blurted Vivian.

# 34

Enid and Howard walked to Vivian's in silence. It was not clear which of them was more apprehensive of the impending afternoon tea. Howard had said he did not want to accept. He didn't usually come home from the farm until near six; breaking at three so he could bathe and shave for tea at four seemed to him an extraordinary waste of time. Enid wasn't much keener herself. She did not approve of the growing intimacy between her friend and her son, between a married woman and a conchie; whichever way you looked at it, it spelt trouble. Not that either party had confided anything specific to her; nothing had been articulated. Still, she knew what was going on. She rarely saw them together; they spent a lot of time avoiding each other, which told her more than enough. However, it was problematical to refuse Ava; she had been insistent that they all meet for tea.

Enid found Ava fascinating, refreshing, promising. She hoped the world would one day be full of women who had as much confidence. She also thought she was a bit of a bossy boots and her habit of getting her own way was a nuisance if you wanted to go up against her. Ava had wanted to drive to the 'darling tea shop' in Stafford that Vivian occasionally wrote of. She maintained that she desperately needed a run out and that her driver liked to be kept busy. Enid was not impervious to the lure of riding in a luxury car, or a cream tea, and she did agree that a public outing was more seemly than an intimate tea in Vivian's parlour.

When Enid and Howard arrived at Vivian's house, Ava was outside. It looked as though she'd been waiting for them. Enid knew that the vibrant young woman had to be excited about meeting Howard R. Henderson; his looks and notoriety guaranteed as much. She felt a brief flutter of anxiety as she wondered whether Ava would try to seduce her son, whether he might respond. Such a flirtation would at least put paid to anything untoward that might be developing between him and Vivian, but she didn't want to see Vivian hurt or humiliated. It was complex being a mother to a man. A man such as her son. Of course she wanted him to turn heads, but she didn't want him to break hearts. She certainly didn't want him damaged.

Ava's introduction was forward enough. 'So here you are, in the flesh.' She lingered over the word; it was almost unseemly. 'I've heard so much about you.' She looked thrilled, genuinely excited, and Enid knew enough about her to be aware that this wasn't the usual state of affairs; it took a lot to impress Ava. She preferred to exist in a perpetual state of languid indifference.

Enid remembered the formalities that had to be observed. 'Howie, let me introduce Miss Ava Pondson-Callow. Ava, this is my son, Howard Henderson.' Ava held out her hand and Howard shook it.

'Pleasure. Where's Vivian?' His eyes flicked impatiently towards the house. He barely seemed to notice Ava's obvious and abundant charms. Enid had her answer. Things were worse than she'd feared. He cared. A lot. Exclusively. For years Enid had prayed he'd fall in love, utterly and thoughtlessly, but a married woman had not been part of her plan. Once again she was reminded that it was best to be extremely careful about what you wished for.

Ava's eyes narrowed slightly. She was no fool and recognised Howard's interest, devotion. However, she seemed relieved, happy to acknowledge it. She generously conceded to her friend. No doubt the beautiful, wealthy young woman only saw the romance and excitement of an impending illicit affair; Enid saw the transience, the tragedy.

'She's inside, leaving instructions with Mrs Rosebend. I've persuaded her to leave Mabel at home this afternoon. There's no room for her in the car and small children are particularly tiresome at teatime, don't you think? Very demanding.'

'She's still just a baby.'

'Even worse.'

Howard rode in the front and spoke to the driver about fuel efficiency; the women squeezed together in the back. The dust and noise impeded conversation. Enid found her bones rattled but the journey passed considerably faster than when she took the same route on the bus.

They were shown to a rectangular table in the centre of the room. The café was small and cramped, the tables wedged uncomfortably close to one another. Everyone turned to look at them as they threaded through the tightly packed chairs. Enid knew what sort of an impression her companions made. They were irresistible. The waitress appeared overawed; she chewed the end of her pencil and kept giggling. Vivian and Enid had visited the tea shop together on past occasions and both enjoyed the steamy, cosy, chatty atmosphere. Today, however, Enid noticed that Vivian was more reserved than usual. She studied the menu carefully, even though the choice was limited and extremely familiar; she left Ava to make conversation with Howard. If Howard asked her anything directly, she replied briefly and without raising her eyelids. He also appeared tense. His size and masculinity seemed to insult the pretty china and carefully embroidered tablecloths. He didn't fit in. He shouldn't be here.

'I have never met an actual conscientious objector before,' commented Ava, rather brightly and far too loudly. Enid and Vivian both glanced around the room to see if anyone was listening. Howard stared straight at Ava, but there was something about the way the muscles around his mouth tightened that suggested he'd also prefer it if she lowered her voice. Ava, to her credit, seemed genuinely unaware that she might have mentioned something controversial; she might just as well have announced that she had never tried plum preserve before.

'Haven't you?'

'No, but then there aren't many of you, are there?'

'I think over ten thousand men have registered as such thus far.'

'Really? I'm surprised.'

'I imagine there will be more before this war is over.'

'I suppose you must hope that to be the case.' Ava appeared genuinely interested in what Howard had to say, and Enid watched as her son registered as much. She wasn't simply a tactless sight-seer, feigning a fascination in his cause; she wanted to get to know him. She was making conversation the way people had before the war. It was a fact that in the process of getting to know Howard, one had to get to know his principles. 'I understand you served in prison for your beliefs.'

'Yes, I did.'

'Gosh, these cakes look marvellous,' commented Enid. No one acknowledged her interruption. They all had plates in front of them but none of them was displaying much of a hunger, despite the fact that the cakes and sandwiches were freshly made and usually tempting.

'Are there many men who have done so?'

'I understand that over five thousand have served prison sentences. Again, I imagine this number will continue to climb.'

'And where do you get these figures from?'

'I'm in touch with a group of organised pacifists.'

'Are you?' Enid and Vivian chorused. Both were alarmed at the prospect. Howard ought not to be getting involved with political groups.

'They're not troublemakers,' he assured them, glancing at Vivian and then Enid. Sometimes there was a look between them. Something real and alert. It frightened Enid. Ava was the only one interested in the group as a source of information rather than a cause for alarm. 'So do you know exactly how many fanatics there are in among that number?'

'Fanatics?'

Enid was almost certain her son must have understood Ava's meaning. Ava smiled, radiating charm and a refusal to be anything other than appealing.

'How many of those five thousand decline to compromise with the state in any shape or form? How many refuse to roll bandages, refuse to cook for the officers because they see it as contributing to the war effort?'

'Absolutists, you mean.'

Ava waved her hand dismissively. 'Absolutists, fanatics. It's semantics.'

'Over a thousand.'

Ava's enormous eyes widened a fraction. 'An entire battalion.'

Howard nodded regretfully. He was probably grudgingly impressed with Ava's knowledge of the war establishment, but it wasn't a comfortable analogy. All the women were wondering whether another battalion might make a difference to the outcome of the war. Were they talking about a thousand more dead men in the mud, or might it bring about a swifter resolution? Howard sighed; his vitality seeped out on to the cloth and sat among the cake crumbs. 'It was when I saw how stubborn and inflexible they were being that I lost hope.'

'Lost respect, you mean,' insisted Ava.

'No. It's complicated.'

'Try me,' Ava insisted wryly. It was obvious she could keep

up with any intellectual debate that he or anyone else threw at her.

'In many ways I do respect the absolutists more for sticking to what they believe in, but I lost hope that they had the answer. That level of intransigence is only ever going to lead to conflict. I'm a man who thinks compromise is the answer. Isn't that clear? Locking horns does no good. The Kaiser should have sat down with Asquith, Briand and Goremykin. All the big leaders round a table, that would have been the only way to avoid the bloodshed, but it never happened. The mentality of the absolutist COs made me think it never could. Men seem determined to mistake compromise for disgrace.' He paused to sip his tea. As he carefully placed the thin cup on the saucer he added, 'I suppose that's why I said I would come and labour.'

'Oh, I thought it was me.' Vivian spluttered her belief out among the quiet tinkle of silver spoons against china, the gentle clink of plates being placed on the table. She sounded like a child.

Howard turned to her, eyes alight. He grinned. 'It was. That too. You came along at the perfect moment. I might have been shot.'

It was too grim for Enid to think about.

'You can't live so separately from the rest of your country,' insisted Ava.

'I'd like to. Why not?'

'They won't let you. They will make you conform.'

'I'm fine now. Head down. In a reserved occupation.' He sounded bitter.

'Do you hate it here?' Ava asked.

'Not at all. I love it. Considerably more . . .' He paused and glanced at Vivian from under his lashes. 'It's more wonderful than I might have imagined, but I feel a bit of a lightweight. The men who really object to the war, the fanatics as you call them, are starving and beaten in prisons. The other poor buggers are out there taking God knows what for their country. I think this is too soft.' He stared miserably at the floral china cups and the iced cakes. 'Complacency horrifies me. I can imagine why mothers and sweethearts hate me now.'

'But *your* mother is happier.' Ava smiled at Enid. Enid felt heavy. He was blaming her for protecting him, but what else could she do? That was her duty. She was his mother. First. Always.

'Yes.'

'That's something.'

'Yes.' Enid thought he seemed surprisingly willing to explain himself to Ava. He'd given up doing so of late. People simply became frustrated, vicious. He usually just kept his thoughts to himself. She scrutinised him carefully. He kept his eyes straight forward, yes, trained on Ava, and yet she had the feeling that it was not her he was offering up explanations to. Vivian. It had to be a new sensation for him, caring what a woman might think and feel about his actions. Before the war, he had never cared.

'Tell me, what was it like in there? In prison, exactly?'

'They took away my voice. Literally. We weren't allowed to talk to one another. We were not permitted books, other than the Bible, and it goes without saying that we were not allowed writing materials. They did their best to strip me of my dignity and my liberty, but that's not surprising. It is war, after all. But my voice? The entire point of being human is that we are supposed to be able to say what we think, voice an objection. Do you see? If not that, then aren't we just animals?'

Ava looked pensive. She nodded her head a fraction. Enid had had as much as she could take. Determinedly she turned the conversation, and this time they all respected her enough to allow it.

'Are you staying long, Ava?'

'Sadly, no. I need to be back in the office the day after tomorrow. I'll leave tomorrow morning. Just long enough to scare off the in-laws.'

Enid smiled politely, ignoring the comment about Sir Charles and Lady Owens. 'Vivian will miss you.'

'Oh no, I don't think so. Certainly not as much as she used to.' Ava stared meaningfully at Howard. Her gaze had quite an effect. He was sipping tea and suddenly he started to cough. Vivian clumsily and quite uselessly handed him a napkin, which caused her cake fork to slip off her plate and on to the wooden floor with a clatter. Both she and Howard bent to reach for it simultaneously, their heads narrowly missed bumping. 'Oh, I thought you were going to bang your heads together,' laughed Ava. Enid thought that might be a good thing if it brought them to their senses.

The rest of the afternoon passed off without incident, although it never dissolved into a pleasant state of relaxed intimacy. Vivian and Howard were too aware of one another. It made it intolerable for them to either converse comfortably or ignore each other. They were stranded in a painful, pitiful place, full of impossible, inconvenient yearning.

Both Ava and Enid were aware that this was the case, but try as they might, they could not come up with enough banal social niceties to stretch across the chasm that longing had created. Enid thought it might have been better if she had sat diagonally opposite Ava; at least that way it would not have been so obvious that at least half of the table was stonily silent.

# 35

At first she hadn't been sure it was deliberate. She didn't know, utterly, if she even wanted it to be. It was too wonderful and too terrible. When she'd clumsily dropped her fork and he'd reached for it too. They'd brushed hands. Not a blundering bump; a careful caress. A charge, an actual spark of something glorious had buzzed up through her fingertips, all along her arm, and dispersed in a warm haze throughout her body. She was glad that she'd given up the custom of eating with gloves on when in company. She might have been able to ignore the spark, except he took advantage of the confusion and deliberately moved his chair closer to hers. They sat through the rest of the afternoon thigh pushed up against thigh. The warmth of him oozing into her.

The next morning Vivian waved goodbye to Ava with surprising cheerfulness. Usually Ava's departure caused her to feel gloomy and wretched, but today she felt heady; excitement fizzled in her gut. As much as she appreciated and loved her friend, she needed her to be gone.

She gave the note to Timmy Durham. In this context he was a safe pair of hands. She doubted he could read, but even if he could, his duty to her and his affection for Howard meant that he would not. Neither her maid nor the housemaid worked on Thursdays; she offered Mrs Rosebend a day off, insisting it was due recompense for the extra workload they'd recently experienced due to the influx of visitors. Mrs Rosebend politely resisted, insisting that it was a pleasure to have the master and his parents home. 'Not visitors as such, are they?'

'Well, no, I suppose not.' She always thought of them as such.

'Family. Nothing is as important as family, especially at a time like this.'

The comment helped Vivian alight on a different track. 'How is your sister managing?' Mrs Rosebend's nephew had been injured; took the impact in the neck and left cheek. Not a fatal wound, but a nasty one. He was in a sanatorium in Derby, drinking out of a straw, not yet able to eat solids. It wasn't clear how he ever would.

'Oh, you know.' A shrug, not so much acceptance as grudging tolerance. It was poor form to complain, but sometimes it was unreasonable to expect actual cheer. Mrs Rosebend was not married and never had been; 'Mrs' was a courteous, symbolic title, given out of respect for her position as housekeeper. She had no children of her own; the welfare of her sister's children was an urgent concern to her. 'She can't get to see him as much as she'd like. It's difficult to leave the younger two, and their da has trouble with his chest.'

'Why don't you take today and tomorrow off, then you could go and visit him.'

'Oh, Mrs Owens, I couldn't do that.'

'Why not? Wouldn't your sister like it?' It was a longer period of time than Vivian had anticipated releasing Mrs Rosebend for, but she'd manage. 'Or you could look after her husband and children, then she could go.' This proved too enticing to Mrs Rosebend's instinct to be useful.

'Well, if you're sure . . .'

Which only left the problem of Cook. Cook did not have a family that needed her attention, nor could Vivian recall her talking about particular friends she might wish to call on. Not that she was an especially maudlin person, but she had devoted her life to service since she was thirteen years old. Her commitment to her work hadn't allowed for making close friends. Vivian fretted about the problem all morning, but could not alight on a solution. She would have to brave it out. The best idea was not to make too much of the situation, not intimate that it was in any way out of the ordinary. She was the mistress of the house; she did not have to explain herself. If Ava was in her position, she would simply instruct Cook to produce dinner for her and Mr Henderson, hang the gossip, the summarising and ensuing scandal. But she was not Ava. Vivian did not have that level of audacity; she dreaded Cook's raised eyebrow, her knowing glance that would be quickly smothered under a dutiful expression of pretended disinterest. In the end, she decided to inform Cook that she was planning on eating simply and early that evening; she asked for cold meats, a pie, some fruit and cheese to be set out in the drawing room by seven. She was depending on Cook's habit of producing and proffering far more than Vivian could ever eat alone. She had invited him for eight; by then, with any luck, Cook might have retired to her room with a book and a sherry and the baby would be asleep.

Another reason she simply couldn't bear the idea of asking Cook to prepare something particular for them was that she wasn't sure he'd come at all. He had not replied to her note. Had he even received it? Vivian was gripped with panic that Timmy Durham might have dropped the envelope and another inhabitant of Blackwell village could have come across it. It wasn't in any way incriminating; she'd been very careful and brief − *Would you like to come for supper this evening? 8 p.m. Regards, Vivian Owens* − yet the brevity itself suggested a lack of formality at best, intimacy at worst. She had deliberated over how to sign off the note. *Mrs Owens* felt faintly ridiculous; simply signing *Vivian* was out of the question.

It was a unique afternoon, made exquisite and awful with anticipation. She resolved not to sit about watching the clock but instead would sort out all of Mabel's clothes; check what still fitted and what didn't, darn and trim if necessary. It was not bath night, and drawing a tub would fetch attention. The best she could do was strip and sponge. The problem of what to wear. At first she tried on her lilac georgette, but then decided it looked irksomely pretty and girlish. Anything in silk had to be discounted as too obviously grand. In the end she settled on a cobalt-blue cotton dress, not because it was her favourite but because it was the one she happened to be trying on when she saw him heading up her garden path. He was exactly on time. To the minute. She was pleased and grateful. She checked herself in the glass. It was funny: sometimes she was reasonably confident that she was still pleasant to look at; other times she feared she was simply a fright. This evening, luckily, her skin seemed smooth and clean, blemish free. Her hair was obliging, genuinely bright; it didn't dare be mousy. It had also curled and fallen in a pleasing way, not demure. There seemed to be something energetic about her appearance. She seemed alive, fluid. Open. To possibilities.

He banged on the door using the brass knocker. She dashed to open it wide before Cook was alerted, but then didn't know how to greet him. A broad social beam wouldn't be right; she didn't want to appear so straightforwardly polite and welcoming. She needed to offer him more than commonplace good manners but she had to be careful not to seem seductive or knowing – or worse, nervous and naïve.

He slipped off his shoes before he entered the house, then carefully placed them on the inside mat. It was practical; they were muddy, and although only low people generally took their shoes off at the door, Vivian felt he knew this and, since he knew this but still did so, was somehow making a point. The point was not that he was low; it was that he routinely squashed all convention.

It was as though he was finding them a new place to inhabit, somewhere outside the rules.

Or was it that it was simply sensible not to trail mud?

It was hard not to overthink the situation.

They were shiny, his shoes, recently polished. She felt a flush of pleasure that he had made an effort, and of embarrassment that she could see the weave of his socks. Perhaps he was wearing a pair she'd seen his mother knit. She felt very close to him. To show that she understood they were breaking small rules, she bent down and picked up the shoes. Her fingers hooked into the heel; they felt warm with his body heat. His feet had just been there. It was wonderfully, oddly intimate. The pit of her stomach slipped, as though she'd swallowed something pleasant yet ethereal. It was outside her experience. She thought of blancmange but was dissatisfied that the idea was so pedestrian and inadequate. She had no vocabulary for what she felt about him. She put the shoes in the cupboard, banging the door closed.

'I've brought wine.' He held the bottle towards her so she could read the label. A 1910 Merlot. Where had he got that from? It couldn't have been cheap. She'd chilled ale, thinking it was what he'd prefer; she was glad she hadn't set it out.

'How thoughtful. Will you come through? I'll get the glasses.'

She wondered what he must think of the place. She was still aware that it was modest in comparison to her family home or the Owenses London house, but to him it must still seem grand. Ostentatious? She looked at everything afresh, as though through his eyes. There were numerous cupboards, sideboards and tables; a man like him must be wondering how it could possibly be the case that someone owned so much stuff that needed to be put somewhere out of sight. There was plenty in view too: a large number of photographs of Mabel were strewn about, as well as numerous china bowls of potpourri and lavender. The wallpaper was busy – animals, birds, wreaths of flowers recurred in none too accurate patterns all over the walls; skirting boards, halls and passages were painted dark olive. There were signs that the place wasn't quite as prized as it had been: the leather chairs were worn, the decor was Victorian and hadn't been updated. Would he notice? Was he inwardly laughing at the fact that a taxidermist must have been kept on staff at some point, judging from the numerous foxes, rabbits, pheasants and deer that littered the room, petrified under glass or on the walls. Vivian wished she'd spent the day removing the clutter.

'It's very nice,' he commented politely.

'No, it isn't. It's ghastly,' she replied irritably. She reached for a packet of cigarettes and offered him one. She didn't smoke herself; she'd bought them especially.

He took one and admitted, 'Perhaps a bit crowded.'

'Claustrophobic,' she confirmed, cutting across the usual niceties. 'I try to be outside as much as possible.' He looked surprised. Would he take it as a compliment, her honesty, or would he think she had decided he was not worth social pleasantries? She looked around for a lighter but couldn't see one; she hadn't thought of it. How was it possible that in amongst all this stuff she didn't have the one thing he needed? He reached inside his pocket and pulled out a box of matches.

'A drink?' She didn't know the etiquette. Her mother would offer cocktails or spirits pre-dinner, but she wasn't going to serve dinner as such. There were pickled onions on Cook's tray; how could that ever be dinner? But was it too early to open the wine? It crossed her mind that this was the first time in her life that she had ever entertained without help. Even when Enid or Ava visited, Mrs Rosebend would guide the evening by having the maids set, if not serve. 'Maybe the wine?'

'You should open it, let it breathe.' She tried not to look surprised. 'Whisky, if you have it.' She was delighted to be given instruction and busied herself over the tray of dusty bottles and sticky decanters set by the piano. The maid couldn't manage every-thing as she ought. Vivian didn't know how much to pour. Aubrey drank gin and tonic; she knew all about that. Whisky, he'd said. Did that go with anything? Ginger ale, perhaps? Yes, she was sure her mother used to drink it that way, but was that a feminine tipple? Did one add water? Nervous, she filled the glasses to the top, took them over to him and handed one over.

'Very generous.' He was laughing at her. She'd done the wrong thing. She sat down and took a gulp; the liquid flared its way down her throat and into her gut. She felt a surge of welcome energy. He sat next to her on the sofa at a proper distance, leaving room for someone else to sit between them, not that there was anyone.

It was strange. She had longed to be alone with him, and now here he was in her house and she realised instantly that being alone with him was not enough. What she wanted from him was impossible, even more impossible than what she had wanted from Nathaniel, because she was married now, and despite the accepted fashion of the era in certain echelons of society, she did not see marriage as a way to facilitate love affairs. She doubted he would either. A man of principles. How could she consider it?

A peculiar and real constraint rose up between them. It was as new as it was unwelcome. All at once she wished he would go. Drink his whisky and leave. She found his presence overwhelming. He took her breath away. She regretted mentioning supper on the invitation because she would have to feed him now, and that would prolong the agony. What had she been thinking? That they could be friends? Ridiculous. That was not what she wanted. She'd thrown the offer out without properly considering it, but then she'd never have managed to ask him at all if she had thought it through.

They sat in a spiky silence. She watched his Adam's apple shift as he swallowed. He'd shaved.

She was grateful when he said, 'I've checked all the boundaries now. Most of them are sound enough. There's a section of wall, far south-east of the farm, that could do with repointing before winter.'

'Oh.'

'Yes. Should I get on with it?'

'Yes. If you think so.'

'Don't want it getting worse.'

'No.'

'It's not more than a hundred yards.'

'Good.'

'Shouldn't take long.'

'No.'

They fell silent again. He swirled his whisky around in the glass; the tawny amber liquid caught the last of the evening sunlight drifting through the open window.

'How's the writing going?' she asked suddenly.

'I want to write novels,' he blurted.

'Sorry?'

'I like plays, but I think the novel is the greatest form of art. For me. I want to write a novel.'

'Then why don't you?'

'Oh, many reasons,' he looked pained, then he shrugged, 'One of which is that I'd starve.'

'I see.' Another pause. 'How is your mother?' It was not the question she wanted to ask.

He looked amused. 'Just as well as she was yesterday.'

'I ought really to have extended the invitation to her too.' That had never been her intention. She loved Enid, but this was separate. She was being artful because she had to know. She probed. 'I hope she wasn't offended.'

'No, she can't be, as I didn't mention where I was spending the night. The evening.' He corrected himself. It was almost too awful, but now she knew: he too had been selective, secretive.

They fell silent again. The clock ticked and birds whistled to one another. The evening sun was still cascading into the room through the open window; Vivian had not pulled the shutters. The warmth seemed to block out the air. It was not pleasing; it was cloying and sticky.

He turned to her. 'Why have you asked me here tonight, Vivian?'

She glanced at the tray of food on the side table but didn't bother to pretend she'd invited him for supper. She was almost certain that he knew why. She wanted him near her. She wanted him. There wasn't a plan as such. She simply had to be with him. As often as she could. There were all sorts of women being free with their favours when young men – sometimes virtual strangers – came home in uniform. Not just the loose women, but the nice girls too. It was patriotic. It was kind. That sort of thing was happening. She was in a different place. She couldn't understand why she wanted to touch a man who wouldn't fight. Wouldn't stand up. But she did. She wanted to touch him more than anything. She ached to touch him. It was insufferable, and yet it seemed the only credible, real thing that she might achieve. She didn't know how to answer his question, so she asked one of her own. 'Why did you come?'

He looked around the room. 'I've been wondering about the man you were with before Aubrey.' Everything had shifted. Aubrey, not Mr Owens, and they were talking about her ex-lover. There was no going back. No pretending. 'What was he called?'

'Nathaniel Thorpe.'

'Do you still love him?'

'He's dead.'

'That's not what I asked.' He stared at her. The look was exposed. Pathetic. Unadorned confusion. The look was fierce. Irresistible. Bald longing. Her answer mattered.

'Looking back, being in love with him was unreal. Rather like a school lesson learnt by heart but not understood or genuinely believed in.'

'What do you mean?'

'Well, I know the names of the planets and have heard that Mercury is closest to the sun and that Jupiter is simply enormous, but what do I really know of them? Being in love with Nathaniel was rather like that.' She wondered now how she could ever have been so emphatically unaware, romantically optimistic and wholly naive, but she couldn't say that to him. Look where all that had landed her. Still, it wasn't all her fault. Young women didn't get much of a say; the vast majority of them were quite pleased with stupid and superficial men. She'd had no idea what a real man ought to be. What she might really need in a life partner. Now that she knew, it was too late. She sighed and admitted, 'I thought he was the ultimate crowning to my season.'

'What is this season you talk about? Bitches on heat are in season; vegetables have seasons, not women,' Howard snapped. He took a large slug of his whisky.

'I'm just trying to explain that I thought it was what I wanted.'

'Do you still love him? It's a simple question.' She thought she'd answered it; he clearly thought otherwise. 'Is it because of him that you cannot be happy with Aubrey?' he demanded.

She clamped her mouth closed and wondered when she had ever admitted that she was not happy with Aubrey. She was sure she hadn't, not in so many words. She tried so hard to be careful and proper. He was a soldier. She was a wife. 'No.' Her voice squeezed out despite her brain instructing her lips to stay shut.

'No what?'

'No, not because of him.'

'But you are unhappy with Aubrey.' Obviously he needed clarity. He couldn't risk making a mistake but he was demanding too much. She didn't want to be disloyal.

'I never said that.'

'Say it now, why don't you.' His impatience bubbled over; he slammed his glass on to the table and stared intently at her. Interrogating her.

'I can't.'

'But I am right.' The seriousness slipped from his face; he sensed his victory.

She nodded her head a fraction. 'I love my daughter, so much. I'm comfortable in this village now. I shouldn't ask for more. It really is enough. Should be.' Yet she'd invited him here.

His face flooded with concern, sympathy. 'You are so complicated. Far more complicated than I imagined.'

'What a wonderful relief that you think so. Most people would write me off as easy after hearing what you have.' She felt a need to make a joke about her perceived morality. She wanted to kiss him. She felt her whole being flow towards him. Gratitude, desire. But he wouldn't let her off the hook.

'It should be enough, but it's not.'

'No,' she admitted. Her fiercely frowning expression loosened into a look of bewildered, somewhat entertained, relief.

'What would be enough?'

Something slithered through the air. A charge in the atmosphere. She felt it in her being too. She needed someone strong in body and mind, someone enthusiastic and empathetic. She needed him. Not someone like him. Him.

Howard nodded at her. He knew.

# 36

HER LIPS FELT strangely familiar. Like arriving home after a very long journey. Somewhere known, welcome, decent, good.

The sex was nothing like that; the sex was like being catapulted out of this world into somewhere exotic and exciting, unimaginable and incredible.

He'd kissed her carefully at first, tentatively. Not quite believing that she was agreeing to it, imagining that at any moment she'd remember who she was, or who he was, and say, 'Enough.' She did not say enough, not when he kissed her lips, her earlobes, her eyelids, her neck. Not when he started to undo the buttons on her dress. Instead she obligingly, neatly, slipped out of the dress and sat accepting, willing, in a broderie anglaise petticoat. A bride, a fairy, a patch of wild daisies.

Then, as though a switch had been flicked, gentle wasn't adequate. Not for either of them. The kissing became cavernous and annihilating. He felt the blood roar around his body. A gushing tide in his brain. Now he could see and hear and feel everything so much more clearly, so much more deeply. All that had gone before was ethereal, indistinguishable. Remote. Other kisses with other people were in anticipation of this. All the words they had traded, and those they had not managed to speak, seemed unnecessary now that they were stripped, exposed by their craving and requiring of each other. They tore at their own and each other's clothes – belts, ribbons, braces, lace – mouths still clasped to one another's. Their hands raced over each other's bodies, pawing, grabbing, grasping all they could.

The summer sun had tanned her face and hands and left a V shape on her neck. The rest of her was milky, almost transparent. Her nipples were magenta, the colour of lips stained with red wine. She was soft yet firm. The coarse hairs under her arms and between her legs presented themselves as a surprise that interrupted her smoothness. She had a mole on her hip. He caught her staring at his freckled shoulders with equal fascination and wonder. They explored one another with a frankness that felt refreshing and pure, although it should have made them colour, the places their lips, tongues and fingers found. The things they did to one another. As he climbed on top of her and then inside her, she smiled, almost lazily; an acceptance of a magnificent inevitability. It was feverish, furious and reckless. He grunted and quivered; she moaned and shook. It felt astonishing. It felt crucial and true. They merged; she was in every fibre of his body. For the first time since France, he saw a body as something other than an ugly tool used to dam up the onslaught of war. A feeling of bliss and possibility built and built inside him, so wonderful it was almost fearful. He was bearing an intolerable weight, feeling a relentless and incredible thirst. He let it go. At once the weight was lifted, the thirst quenched. He wanted to scream out, but she put her hand over his mouth and instead he made a sound that was neither a howl nor a bark but something akin. He'd never made such a sound before. It was like a fox at night, animalistic, a relief. Real. Whole. She was beautiful, peaceful.

When he rolled off her, he thought there might be silence or awkwardness, but she giggled and asked, 'What took us so long?' He assumed she meant what had taken them so long to initiate it, rather than the actual act, because he thought his timing was spot on for that. They lay, flopped, in among her pale cotton clothes and his rough darker ones. Sticky. Alert. Luxuriating in their loving. She didn't move to cover herself up, and her lack of modesty rang with innocence, punched his heart.

'I wasn't sure how you felt about me,' he admitted.

'For someone so exquisite, you seem surprisingly unaware of the effect you have on people.' She rolled towards him and kissed his chest.

He wasn't unaware, he'd just been unsure of her. 'Are you hungry?'

'Starving.'

They devoured the slices of cold ham and cheddar cheese, eating them on thick slices of crusty bread with mustard and pickled onions. He thought that perhaps they ought to be shy about how pickled onions might make their breath smell, but considering where they'd just had their mouths, coyness and inhibition seemed puerile. They drank his wine. He was glad that he'd paid Mr Walker three times what it was worth. He'd paid double because the wine was rare and hard to come by at the moment, and its price once again over because he was who he was, a man who wouldn't go to war. It was worth every penny.

He searched her face for regret or remorse and was thrilled to see none. It would come, he was sure of it, but at least they had tonight. Children enjoying a midnight feast and refusing to think of the next day, when they would be stupid with tiredness or punished when it was discovered what had been stolen from the pantry.

'Tell me something about yourself that I don't know.' She bit into a crunchy red apple. The juice sat on her lips; he wanted to kiss it away.

'What sort of thing?'

'Oh, anything, everything.' He understood why she wanted this conscious and hurried exchange of facts; whilst they felt everything for one another, they knew next to nothing. He had spent time wondering what her home had been like before she married, what she liked to eat or whether she could ride a bike, did she prefer cats or dogs? It seemed she might have had the same level of curiosity about him.

'I used to go scrumping with my brother when I was a lad. I stole from your trees.'

'Oh, I know that.' She rolled her eyes, an imitation of boredom.

'You do?'

'Yes. Enid told me. You broke your arm falling out of one of the trees when you were seven years old. I also know that you kept tadpoles in glass jars on the kitchen windowsill and that you delighted in irritating our neighbours by playing knock-and-run.'

He glanced at her through the blue cigarette smoke, moved and flattered by her interest. She had talked of him to his mother, or at the very least listened attentively as his mother had spoken. He considered it. What might his mother have neglected to relate? What would amuse her? 'I can walk on my hands.'

'Can you really?' She chortled, delighted.

'Yes. Look.' Despite having just eaten, it was too tempting not to show off. He stubbed out his fag. Quickly he placed himself on the centre of the rug in front of the fireplace, kicked up into a handstand, steadied himself, found the point of slight overbalance and then carefully started to walk forward. There wasn't much room in the parlour, so he had to bring himself down after only two or three steps. He knew the blood was rushing to his head and that his penis was flaccid; he must look peculiar. He hoped Vivian was concentrating on his toned abdominal muscles, or his thighs. Maybe she was; she laughed and clapped her hands. 'That's wonderful! Can you teach me?'

'Not unless you put some clothes on. I'm not made of iron.'

She seemed reluctant to get dressed; she simply murmured, 'Another time.'

'Your turn.'

'I can't do it, I've just said.'

'No, I mean it's your turn to tell me something I don't know about you.'

'I'm awful at embroidery.'

'Whilst I didn't categorically know that, I might have guessed, so that doesn't count.' It was too boring, irrelevant. It didn't get to the heart of her.

'I hate practising the piano.'

He shook his head, 'That I did know, my mother told me.'

Vivian laughed. 'She knows far too many of my faults. Until I met your mother, I didn't know the ingredients of Christmas pudding; to this day I'm not absolutely certain what suet is.' She laughed again, self-deprecating, but he didn't like it.

'That's not the sort of information I meant.'

'I can't swim.'

'Something positive, something you *can* do,' he urged.

She paused, furrowed her brow and thought about it for too long. He was sure there must be a million things she was incredible at. Eventually, 'I can jump a skipping rope rather well.'

'Can you?' He grinned.

'Do you remember those boys I brought lunch to when you were working in the field?'

'Yes.' Of course he did.

'Their sisters taught me. I saw them one day in the street, a whole dirty pack of them skipping.' She bit into her apple again, chewed, swallowed. He loved it that she didn't seem to be in a rush. Their relationship before this evening had been characterised by staccato conversations, abrupt interruptions and differences of opinion; it was lovely to luxuriate in finding the right words, answering questions fully. 'They were having such fun. Hungry bellies, warring fathers, shoeless feet all forgotten as they jumped with their friends. You know the sort of thing, *January, February, March, April, when it's your birthday please join in.*' She chanted the rhyme, smiling, delighted with the memory. 'It got to June and I simply jumped. Abandoned poor Mabel's pram on the street. I have no idea why I wanted to join them, but I did. Of course I got into a tangle. The girls all laughed at me, but not meanly. They wanted me to play. They slowed the rope right down, to give me a chance. I quickly caught on to it. It isn't difficult.'

'Were you in skirts or your trousers?'

She thought about it. 'A skirt, that first day, I remember holding it up, but I've done it many times since. Sometimes in my trousers. Why?'

'I want to imagine it.' He closed his eyes and thought of her giddy, breathless, determined. Her hair slipping loose with each jump, her petticoat peeking out from under her skirt, her sturdy boots – which he'd noticed she always wore now, practicality overwhelming fashion – beating down on the cobbles.

'How many other lovers have you had?' It was not an original question. Any woman he'd ever had would, sooner or later, want to know as much. They craved to understand where they fitted into his line of conquests and interests. The surprise was that he felt compelled to answer her truthfully. He sometimes didn't provide a response at all, and few women insisted. On the occasions he did offer a number, it was rarely accurate; he usually pleaded two or three to avoid offending the woman he was with at the time.

'Sixteen or seventeen, I suppose. I'm not exactly certain.' There would have been more, except for France and prison. It seemed more important to be honest with her than to protect her.

'So many.' He met her gaze, wondering whether he'd find hurt or confusion, anger or disgust. She grinned at him. 'No wonder you're good.' She prodded him in the ribs teasingly and their lips found each other's again.

He glowed under the compliment. He wanted to ask her if he was her best. He didn't need to ask how many. He knew – she'd already trusted him with that – but he didn't know how it had been with them. Had she enjoyed Nathaniel Thorpe? Did the cold Aubrey Owens come alive at night? It seemed unlikely, but it was possible. Their union was fruitful, that meant something. Jealousy flared around his body, and then shame that he was jealous and curious swamped him too; both undignified, irrelevant emotions. He could not ask. Must not.

'I can't remember the other women now,' he muttered. He wanted to tell her she was unique, satiating in a way he could not have imagined. Variety held no challenge or lure for him any more. He just wanted her. Over and over and over again. Her. He hoped she'd answer his compliment with one of her own, that she'd reassure him that he was her best. That she'd . . . not died a small death with him – he'd never thought that was what it was to come, he didn't like that description; the opposite: that she'd lived a little more brilliantly. A little more deeply. She didn't respond. 'Tell me something else,' he murmured.

She looked pensive and then replied, 'I have an insatiable sweet tooth.'

'You don't look as though you have.' His eyes swept over her trim body appreciatively.

'I keep it in check, but if ever you examine my handbag, you'll always find a quarter of something lovely. Jellies, boiled sweets or toffee. There's nothing I like more than dipping my finger in the honey pot and sucking it clean.' He wondered whether she'd deliberately chosen that image to disturb him. 'I'll turn to fat if I'm ever content.'

He didn't comment. He'd always known she wasn't content; there was no point in pretending to be surprised by her admitting as much. He had no answer for her, now less than ever. It seemed unlikely that what they'd just done would lead to contentment or satisfaction. Delight, bliss, ecstasy he hoped for; guilt, fear, shame he didn't doubt. Satisfaction was impossible.

'I like liquorice,' he muttered.

'I can't abide liquorice,' she declared as she wiggled on top of him and started to kiss his jaw.

As they made love for a second time, he whispered previously unknown facts to her. 'My first dog was called Pepper,' he murmured as he kissed her thighs.

'Oh, really, what sort?' She spluttered the words through minute gasps of pleasure.

'A Labrador crossed with something hairy. You?' His voice was muffled because he didn't want his lips to leave her body.

'I had a white rabbit that I cared for poorly; a fox got it.' She placed her hands on the top of his head and ran her fingers through his hair, gently guiding him to where she instinctively knew she wanted him most. 'My favourite colour is green.'

He didn't know the name of his favourite colour, which at that moment was the colour of the flesh between her legs. 'I prefer sunrises to sunsets.'

'I like to sing when I bathe.' He flipped her over and trailed kisses up her buttocks, waist, shoulder blades.

'I like to run until my lungs ache.' He slipped inside her; she was ready for him and accepting.

'I grew my own tomatoes this year. Nothing in this world tastes as good,' she panted breathily.

He pressed his lips on to hers. 'Until now.'

It was necessary to close the window; the night air had turned nippy. Howard built a fire. It wasn't absolutely needed, but they both appreciated the romance of the leaping flames, the golden glow that was cast throughout the room. They sat on the floor, still naked, with their backs to the sofa, a tartan rug around their shoulders. They sat close to one another, shoulder to shoulder, thigh to thigh. He could smell her sweetness and her sweat.

'I have never read any of the Brontës or Jane Austen,' he confessed, only just stifling a yawn. He had to fight the urge to sleep. He didn't want to miss a moment, waste it in unconsciousness, yet his eyelids were heavy, his eyes stung with fatigue.

'I've never read anything other,' she mumbled.

'My mother looks in on me every night, even if she's gone to bed before I have. I hear her get up in the small hours and she carefully opens my bedroom door and puts her head round. She doesn't come in or say anything. I think she's literally just checking I'm . . .' He paused.

'There.'

'Yes.'

'Has she done that since you were a boy?'

'No, just since Richmond.' Which was the first time she'd seen him after losing Michael; the two things were inseparable.

'None of my family has visited me since I moved to Blackwell at the beginning of the war.'

'You haven't seen them in all that time?' He couldn't keep the surprise out of his voice.

'I've seen them twice. I've visited Highgate but they haven't been here. I don't mind. I like going to London, I miss it. I understand they don't find Blackwell especially amusing.'

'But you're here. Don't they want to see where you live?'

'There's always an excuse. My brother is at school, my father must work, there are too many of them to up-heave. The truth is, they don't think of me as theirs any more. I'm an Owens now.' She hesitated. 'At least, that's how they see me. Aubrey's problem.'

He wanted to ask if that was how she saw herself, but couldn't; he wasn't sure he was ready for the answer. 'Do you miss your siblings?'

'Yes, I suppose. A bit, but.' She shrugged. 'We weren't encouraged to be especially close. Our parents gave all of us the impression that we were rather an inconvenience, and somehow we each maintained that impression about one another. I have Mabel, which makes up for everything. I'd literally die for Mabel.' This confession had a dark intensity that trumped everything else she'd ever said to him. He thought she might ask him who he would die for. He wondered how he'd answer. His mother, of course. Although he had the feeling it would be a self-defeating sacrifice; his mother wouldn't want to live if he was lost. He used to readily drop into fights to defend Michael if a scuffle arose. When he found him, stinking and gangrenous, in the hospital in France, he'd had an impulse to beg a God he didn't believe in to take him rather than his little brother. But Michael was dead now. He couldn't die for him because he was already dead.

He sighed. Thinking about Michael caused a tightening in his chest. 'I miss Michael. I'm losing him. Forgetting him. His daft smirks, his particular voice. I used to dream about him all the time, but now I don't. I wish I did.' She put her hand on his arm and caressed it. She nuzzled into his shoulder, like a pet, fusing her existence into his. He pulled her a fraction closer still.

At four in the morning, he started to pull his clothes on. She didn't ask him to stay, which was fine. He didn't want to leave her but couldn't imagine sleeping in Aubrey's house. Not sleeping. He realised that there was a level of hypocrisy in his attitude, considering everything, but it was how he felt. He wondered where they could be together. How they might be. Not just for one night, but again and again. His head was too thick with the need to sleep for him to be able to see an answer.

He pulled the blanket tightly about her shoulders. The skin around her mouth had been made red with his kisses, her eyes were heavy as she fought sleep too, but he thought she was beautiful. Amazing. She walked him to the door on tiptoe. He carefully moved the latch and turned the handle; the door squeaked open and they both thought of Cook for the first time. The cool, clear early-morning air filled the hall like an enormous brush sweeping the night away. The sky was a delicate pink that had a frail hint of creamy yellow around the edges. The houses and hills were black against the soft promise of a new day. He stood for just a minute or two absorbing the beauty of the sunrise. The pink faded and the yellow light became more certain. He turned and kissed her one last time.

'When in June?'

'Sorry?'

'You jumped in the skipping game in June. When is your birthday?'

'The seventeenth.'

'That's the day you came to Richmond.' How could he forget that date?

She smiled and glanced out into the early morning light. 'That's right.'

'That wasn't much of a birthday.'

'No one here at Blackwell knows when my birthday is, and how would I tell them? I expected nothing from it, had almost forgotten myself. My birthdays used to be about wonderful dresses, sometimes jewels, certainly flowers. Last year my sister, Susan, sent a handkerchief; as my only gift, it was surprisingly welcome.'

'Now you are trying to make me feel sorry for you.'

'Not at all. Why would I do such a thing?'

'So that I get you a belated gift.'

She giggled; he thought it was because she did not take him seriously, but then she asked, 'What more could you give?'

He walked down the path away from her, considering her question.

# 37

SHE RETURNED TO the parlour and cleared the debris that would give her away to Cook: the wine bottle, the glasses. Before she folded up the tartan rug, she held it to her face and tried to breathe him in; she couldn't find the scent of him on it, although he lingered on her fingers and even in her hair. She pulled on her underwear and carried the rest of her crumpled clothes upstairs in her arms. She didn't wash at the enamel bowl but fell straight into bed. She was hungry for sleep because she was sure she'd dream of him.

She did not want to think.

She slept until after eleven. She forced her eyes open and was surprised to find the sun slamming through the curtains. Despite that, she felt a cold fear sitting on the back of her neck, like a sheen of sweat. Were men like women at all? Any of them? Last night she had been sure that Howard was so like her he *was* her. He'd felt as she did, moved with her, wanted what she wanted. Yet today? Uncertainty laced her consciousness. Would he call? Nathaniel hadn't. And Aubrey had wanted her well enough until they married. Did all men simply want to possess and then forget it? Move on as though nothing had happened?

No, she would not think that of Howard.

She moved her head tentatively, fully expecting it to ache with the effects of whisky, wine and a late night, but it wasn't sore. It was light and she felt an urge to laugh out loud. She rose, washed, dressed and went downstairs. She walked through the dim parlour and opened the doors on to the fresh day; the housemaid was in the garden with Mabel.

'We thought you were off colour, ma'am. Thought we'd let you sleep.'

Vivian nodded and smiled but didn't trust herself to speak. What would she say? At least his name. That for certain. She'd shout it out, repeat it time after time, squeeze it into every conversation. She might even tell the maid all about last night; how he'd kissed her and had her, filling her up with everything good and exciting in the world. That wouldn't do. She looked into the parlour but the tray had been cleared and the room polished; windows were thrown wide open. It was hard to believe he'd been there.

Yet he had.

She felt him all over her. She tingled. She thought it was likely that he'd kissed every inch of her body last night, as he'd touched every inch of her mind. He'd reached her. Weeks ago. She realised she should have closed off. A married woman, a woman who had fallen in lust before and acted upon it with dire results, should have known better, been more guarded. Every sane and shrewd part of her consciousness was bawling out for caution, prudence, discretion, wariness, watchfulness. But she had plunged. Dived. Fallen. Ignoring any circumspection that ought to be brought into effect.

'Cook has cleared away breakfast. Shall I fetch you something? Toast?'

Food? The idea was extraordinary. Vivian couldn't eat. She shook her head. The maid looked concerned. 'A cup of tea, then? Shall I put the kettle on the stove?' Vivian nodded. Tea would be lovely, but mostly she wanted the maid to leave her alone with her thoughts.

She settled down on the grass next to Mabel and reflected on last night. The skin around her nipples pulled a little, contracted. She felt an amplified throb between her legs. He'd had sixteen or seventeen women! He wasn't exactly sure how many. Was she number eighteen? Would there be a nineteenth? Of course there must. She couldn't expect him to end with her; they had no entitlement to that. She was married.

Married.

The thought slid through her consciousness but wouldn't stick. Everything about her felt fluid and dreamy. She felt entirely and utterly married to Aubrey if married meant kept, restricted, owned. She did not feel in the least bit married if married meant respected, adored, loved.

She could not think about the chance of a nineteenth woman, could not imagine it or even fear it. Now was all she had. Now was all that mattered. This instant, not even this afternoon, by which time he might or might not have called to visit her. Not tomorrow, or next week, certainly not next year. Generally people were out of the habit of counting on anything in the future; the war had seen to that. Vivian was relieved to be blind to what might be. Now. Now. It was all that mattered. She glanced back at the house. The cat was sitting in the sunshine on the warm paving stones. She liked the fact that irrespective of everything else that was going on – war, adultery, fornication – the cat simply sat and licked its tail. Self-absorption, a vice made into a comfort, a mainstay.

She started to trace a finger around the sole of Mabel's foot. 'Round and round the garden, like a teddy bear, one step,' she moved her finger to the soft, pudgy flesh behind the baby's knee, 'two steps,' she put her finger on Mabel's tummy, 'tickle you under there!' She joyfully tickled the squirming child. The two of them crawled and cavorted on the grass, no thought to decorum or dignity. Mabel gurgled and laughed, threw her head back and showed her newly cut front teeth and pink gums, her eyes squeezed shut with joy. Vivian repeated the exercise two or three further times. She'd never tire of hearing her child squeal with glee, and especially not today, when everything had to be about love and laughter and life.

She did not hear the gate squeak as he came into the garden, but on the words 'tickle you under there!' she felt his fingers under her armpits. She wriggled away, rolling over the grass, eyes wide with surprise, and although his touch was electric and marvellous, she cast him a look that chastised: the maid might return any moment. He didn't heed her warning glance but continued to tickle her, his fingers roaming across the swell of her breasts, his face bright and smiling, unconcerned with possible discovery.

'I've brought you something!' He swiftly kissed her warm neck. She moved further away from him but she wasn't really angry. He was here! He had returned! Her relief was astounding, her delight profound. He was not like the others. She'd thought not, but she'd been wrong before. It was so much more wonderful to be right than ruined. He held out a bunch of white wild flowers, cow's blossom, yarrow and meadowsweet. The bunch was bound with a purple velvet ribbon that Vivian recognised; it had been tied around the jam jar that Enid kept her paintbrushes in.

'You've stolen this ribbon,' Vivian teased.

'Yes, but for an important reason.'

'My flowers are an important reason, are they?'

'No, they are a good reason, but your baby girl is the important reason. To keep colour in her life. You can put the flowers in a vase and tie the ribbon to her cot.' Vivian didn't know what to say to such thoughtfulness. She watched as he swept Mabel up on to his shoulders and started to gallop like a pony; the tot screamed with laughter but didn't show a moment's fear. Vivian could imagine what the maid thought when she reappeared with a tray.

'Shall I bring another cup?' The question was directed towards Vivian, not Howard. The maid's brother was currently in Baghdad; she didn't even know where that was, but it sounded terrifying. She had no time for Howard. Just a few years back she'd almost fainted with excitement if he glanced her way; now she could barely stand to look at him.

'No, don't bother, thank you. I'm not stopping,' Howard replied, slowing to a canter and then carefully lifting Mabel from off his shoulders, setting her down, once again, on the ground. The maid went back inside, glad not to have to wait on him. Turning to Vivian, 'I've just come to give you your belated birthday gift.' Grinning, 'I feel I owe you.'

Vivian giggled. 'They are very beautiful.' She held the posy up to her nose and breathed in the pretty, wild scent.

'That's not it. We're going to London.'

'London?'

'You know you ache for it.'

She did. London still existed, she knew that as a rational fact, but she couldn't quite believe it. There was no hint of it in this country air.

'A holiday,' he urged.

'What will we do in London?'

He grinned lasciviously. Vivian felt hot as she thought of the night before. Admittedly there was all sorts they could do in London. Or anywhere, come to that.

'Anything you like. We'll go to the theatre. We'll shop. Visit the museums. Walk the streets. We'll look up friends if you want to.' That last idea was unreasonable and he must have known it. But the theatre. Shops. It was a delicious thought. He leaned in closer to her. 'We can't stay here.' He cast a look over his shoulder. It was true. They would sooner or later be discovered if they were together here, and yet they could not be anything other than together. They would not be able to stay away from each other;

they would expose themselves through a look, a word, a pilfered caress. They should go away, at least until they could work the heat out of this, whatever this was. Until they could stand in the same room without leaning towards one another, staring open-mouthed with lust.

'Mabel?'

'We'll take her with us.' Vivian looked doubtful, so he offered an alternative. 'We'll leave her with my mother.' Vivian trusted Enid completely, but could she leave the baby with her? People would talk.

'What would we tell her?'

'That you have some business with lawyers, that you need my help.'

Vivian was surprised at how easily the lie had come to his lips. Had he been thinking about it all night, or was he naturally duplicitous? 'Do you think she'll believe that?'

'No, probably not, but I don't care.' So not duplicitous with her then; brutally honest with her.

It was irresistible. Vivian was aware that she was being reckless, selfish and impulsive, but she couldn't stop herself.

Enid agreed to come to the house to care for Mabel. Vivian didn't ask her directly; Howard took care of that. She arrived at the house at 2 p.m. She kissed Vivian on the cheek as usual and commented, 'I like your hat. When should I expect your return?'

Vivian beamed, touching the hat tentatively, allowing her eyes to slide to Howard to see if he'd noticed her effort. She'd bought this hat last time she visited London and had regretted the purchase as soon as she'd returned to Blackwell when she'd remembered that she'd never have occasion to wear it. It was quite fine and frivolous. Yet with him, for him, there was purpose. Purpose to the hat, to everything. He was all smiles and bonhomie; not at all his usual serious, severe self at all.

She didn't know how to answer the question. They hadn't

discussed it. They hadn't really thought this through. Considering childcare for Mabel, deciding what to pack and checking the train times to Derby and the connection to London had been enough to contend with. She looked at Howard as she replied, 'I'm not sure. Two nights? Maybe three.' He nodded his agreement at three. Enid sighed, and Vivian felt she knew the meeting with the lawyer was a fiction.

Vivian straightened her shoulders, a counter to the shy flush of shame that threatened. She didn't care what Enid knew or thought, she could not stop this. Didn't really want to. She kissed her baby, and as she leaned into Enid, she heard the words, 'Be careful. Watch your step.' Of course, her friend was probably only talking about taking reasonable safety precautions on her travels, guarding her purse from pickpockets and watching her footing as she alighted from the trains on the underground, that sort of thing.

She couldn't have been instructing Vivian to guard her heart and watch her step in the more general sense. Could she?

# 38

IT WAS IMPERATIVE that they get away.

They had to have each other again, but not in Aubrey's house. He couldn't do that. It wasn't just that they ran the risk of getting caught. Because so what? If they got caught, well then. It would not be the worst thing. It would not be a disaster. It would just be something. Howard was almost sure he'd gone to her house – Aubrey's house – not quite knowing what might happen. Not knowing for *certain*. He had hoped, but not expected. That sliver of uncertainty made it tolerable to have had another man's wife in his house. Impulsively he'd been able to take her in the parlour. The bedroom was out of the question. Pre-planning it to happen again would be sordid and awkward. He didn't want them to sneak about like a gigolo and a married woman, or a man and his harlot. But he had to have her again. For him, going away was the only answer. Her too, apparently.

She had come away with him.

The thought made him shake his head with delighted incredulity. Just like that. A token of resistance but nothing more. It was a brave and fantastic thing, when you thought about it.

He'd telephoned ahead to a small but smart hotel near the Warrington Playhouse and made a reservation in the name of Mr and Mrs Henderson. He'd considered using a pseudonym, Smith

355

or Jones; it would have been more sensible and circumspect. He was notorious enough not to want to attract attention at the best of times, least of all when he was running around with another man's wife. A mixture of pride and mulishness made him decide against it. It was wrong that society dictated that sleaze and scandal must follow them wherever they went, since when he was with her he felt pure, unalloyed joy. He felt magnificent, munificent and alert. He would not capitulate, not entirely. Besides, he liked the idea of calling her Mrs Henderson. That impossible thing.

They sat opposite one another for the first leg of the journey. She remained straight-backed and formal, except when she caught his eye, then she beamed or put her hand to her mouth in a mock gasp. 'What?' he asked.

'I'm not at all lonely.'

He understood: they were a couple alone and yet not lonely. They had stepped outside society. People in love did. It didn't seem strange. He distracted himself from the intensity of his happiness by looking out of the window. It always seemed to Howard that everything and everyone in this brave little country was holding their breath, simply waiting for the war to end; even the small farmhouses exuded a sense of grim endurance; sagging grey hamlets begged for peace. Only the sheep were disinterested, unaware, and now – at least temporarily – he and Vivian too.

They had a forty-five-minute wait at Derby; they scoured the platform for familiar, unwanted faces, but there were none. He bought her a quarter of red boiled sweets, then he helped her on to the train, which meant he was able to hold her arm. Touching her in public was a privilege and caused a surge of gladness to carouse through his body. Just that, his fingertips on her elbow. This time she chose to sit next to him, and as the train juddered and clattered towards London, through countless increasingly dimly lit stations, she sometimes rested her head on his shoulder. He liked it best when they went through a tunnel or cut through the high sides of an embankment and were temporarily thrown into darkness. They used the cloak to steal kisses. He didn't care where they landed: her lips, her eyelids, her nose. It was all the same to him.

They arrived in London at ten and neither wanted to go out to eat. That appetite was second. They made love until they were both weak and exhausted. When they needed to sleep, they didn't; they climbed on one another again, skin slipping over skin, pink flesh pushing hard, up, over, in. Eventually they lost consciousness in the early hours and slept entwined in one another's arms.

Eggs and toast were brought to them when they requested it at nearly midday. Vivian was conscious that the room smelt of sex; before the tray arrived she threw open the window and then hid in the bathroom when there was a knock at the door. The elderly chap who served cast a sly glance at the crushed and scrunched sheets, then winked at Howard. 'I can always spot the honeymooners. You're doing the right thing, son; make the most of it before you have to get back over there.'

It was impossible to correct him, on so many levels. Howard tipped the old man generously and poured tea. Vivian emerged from the bathroom wearing a lilac-coloured silk robe that drew more attention, not less, to her sharp nipples, her slim thighs, her round buttocks.

They needed air by supper time; besides, the chambermaid had to clean their room. A pub in Piccadilly that had once been Howard's favourite seemed a good enough place to buy a whisky, wave away an hour whilst they waited for a table to come up. They talked and laughed, tried not to kiss, although all he wanted to do was hang on to her lips. Her rosy, perfect lips. Nowadays, if a girl allowed a uniformed man to kiss her in the street, it might still attract one or two tuts of censure, but largely people indulged. He would have kissed her in public too, even though he wasn't wearing a uniform, but for the fact that she was wearing a ring.

Not that anyone else would know it wasn't his ring, but he did. He'd broken so many rules and yet he seemed to construct many of his own just as quickly. It was awful. He knew she thought so too when he caught her narrowing her eyes, betraying her resentment when she saw other girls free and easy.

They dashed across Piccadilly and into the Criterion at nine and were given a good table. Sole was served with buttered asparagus and it was delicious. They shared a bottle of white wine and he joined her in eating pudding; it seemed more polite than allowing her to eat alone. He thought she had worn an aura of solitude for a long time, for ever, and he didn't want her to do anything alone again. The sweet meringue broke on his tongue, mixing sensationally with cream and raspberries, then clung to the top of his mouth. He poked at it with his tongue, which made her laugh.

Everyone was dancing. It was all they could do since 1914. He'd often had to remind himself that it wasn't indifference, it was terror. They did it at tea dances, in hotels or clubs. They pulled out gramophones and rolled up the carpets in private homes. They whirled around together, clung to one another, turned up the music to block it all out. Howard hadn't danced at all since the war broke out, but now he thought it might be fun. Love and wine had blurred the edges. He suggested a club and she quickly agreed. They could be part of that giddy throng; it seemed a tediously long time since either of them had been. Paying swiftly, they dashed outside. They seemed always to be in a hurry; it was as though they had a lifetime to cram into the three-day escape.

The air had cooled but that was pleasant. Showers threatened and the odd drop of rain pattered on pavements, but he couldn't mind. The streets were lit with lamps that threw off a crown of fuzzy light. He steered her through the drunks and minglers, an arm protectively around her shoulders, which was not the done thing at all. He crossed the road, glancing left and right for cars and carts, heading towards Glasshouse Street. He didn't see the woman with the fistful of white feathers. Didn't, for a moment, understand what it meant. She walked right into him, a shove not an accidental collision; the force caused her hat to slip over her eye. She pushed a feather into his hand and stupidly he clasped it. Swayed slightly. He shouldn't have taken grip. He should have let it fall to the floor, because once he had hold, he didn't know what to do with it next, and it mattered. Should he drop it on the pavement? No, he couldn't. It seemed disrespectful, inflammatory. Tuck it in his buttonhole and laugh at her? He couldn't be flip, not about the war. The images that were tattooed to his eyelids even when he fell asleep, the tangy smell of burning that stayed in his nostrils and the taste of death that doused his tongue re-emerged. Overpowering him again. Suppressed for just twenty-four hours after all. He pushed the feather hastily into his jacket pocket, took Vivian's arm and hurried on by.

'Why don't you do your duty?' the woman yelled after him. She was blowsy, a bit chubby; a wide, fat mouth that swallowed up her entire face with spite and fury.

Vivian and Howard didn't swap a word or a glance but carried on to the door of the club just fifty yards away. When they reached it, Howard wondered if the woman's accusation had made it this far too. Who had heard? Not that it mattered who else had picked up on her outrage. He had, and that was enough to ruin the evening.

'We don't have to go in,' Vivian whispered gently.

'No, perhaps not.'

They went back to their little hotel room. The door banged and rolled on its hinges. Locking them in. Locking the world out. They made love again. This time it was quieter but somehow more.

# 39

THINGS SPEEDED UP when she was with him; she felt very much alive. When they were awake, she had to touch him all the time. Feel him under her hands, just to be sure he was real. She traced her fingers across the tense white knuckles that blistered through the skin on his hand, along his arm, watching as his follicles pushed up his hairs in reaction to her touch, across the bulge of his bicep and then down over his collarbone. She concentrated on every warm swell, every hard bone, the indents, the rises. The frame of him. The man he was. Her finger traced past the broad chest and neat stomach, down the line of hair that blossomed, and then she kissed him there, took him in her mouth. Her stomach tugged with strict and guilty joy.

It wasn't just bed, although she wouldn't have minded if it were, but it wasn't; there was more. They walked in the parks, inhaling the sticky sweetness of late-summer grass. Women and girls sat in perfumed clusters on their lunch breaks; they fanned themselves repeatedly but languidly, therefore not especially effectively. They talked about clothes and their children. The only telltale sign that the war was not far away was that their dresses all looked a little shabby and make-do, and they wore their long hair in perfunctory, loose up-dos; still the comfort and practicality was attractive, and Vivian liked it more than the strict pretension of her girlhood.

They greeted one another with hugs and hugged again when they parted; she didn't remember doing that. Was that something new since the war? A need to touch. Birds sang in the trees, dogs whisked past their legs, chasing a ball or carrying a stick, children ran in boisterous, chaotic gangs. She and Howard ate picnics of sandwiches and drank from a flask. Vivian couldn't think why she'd worried about the spread of cold meats and pickled onions just a day or so before, because everyone was casual now.

They visited the National Gallery, relieved to be in the quiet, cool rooms, away from the dust and noise. They shared thoughts on the paintings and she recalled things her governess had told her about perspective, light, the symbolism of fruit or colours and such. He thought her ideas interesting, her opinions important. He repeatedly stopped at a picture and asked what she thought of it. If she said, 'I like it,' he wanted to know why. Was it the subject, the technique? He thought what she had to say mattered and so, of course, it did.

'What of this?' He had stopped in front of Monet's *Bathers at La Grenouillère*. A painting of a popular boating and bathing spot on the Seine near Bougival, west of Paris.

'I like it. Very much.'

'Why?'

'It's fresh and direct.'

'Isn't it,' he agreed.

'They all look as though they are having so much fun. I can feel the boats bobbing, moored in the shadows.'

'And Diego Velázquez's *Toilet of Venus*, what do you think of this?'

'I like it too.'

'Why?' He probed.

'She's beautiful.'

'Yes! Her back is just like yours.'

Vivian paused in front of Rubens's picture of Samson and

Delilah; the enormous bear of a man brought to his knees by a woman. She shuddered involuntarily, disturbed by Delilah, who looked on, her expression a curious mix of pity, contempt and a hardness that must have grown from cold shame at her own miserable part in delivering the man up to the Philistines.

'Brilliant, isn't it,' commented Howard.

'I don't like it. A tragic story. I despise Delilah for taking the bribe and discovering the source of Samson's strength.'

'His hair that had never been cut.'

'Quite so. The worst of it is that she cut it as he slept, presumably after lovemaking.'

'I think that's what Rubens must have thought. Her breasts are bare.'

'This painting makes me feel so very angry.'

Howard looked proud, exhilarated. It was important. Still feeling, in this world when anaesthetising was easier. Feeling was the ultimate bravery.

They went to Fortnum and Mason to shop. Vivian thought she had become indifferent to luxury, above it, but she found she couldn't help but be seduced by the exhilarating sight of the goodies on offer. Had she ever truly appreciated the beauty of the trays of sweets and tins of tea lined up like soldiers? Mr Walker's modest displays had become her only measure and expectation, but, of course, they paled into insignificance compared to these temptations. There were cakes that were pretty enough to be ornaments, wispy pastries and tantalising, intricate hand-made chocolates, all displayed in endless glass counters. It took them an hour to decide, but in the end he bought her nougat and marshmallows.

'Are you happy?' he asked.

It had been such a redundant question for so long that at first her response was simply that of surprise. Astonished that anyone still cared who was happy. Alive was enough. Bearing up was what was expected.

'Yes, yes, I am.'

They did at last go dancing. They avoided the traditional haunts, where iced coffee was served and one knew the evening was over when the band struck up the National Anthem. The problem with that sort of place was that all the men wore white tie and tails or uniform. It went without saying that as Howard had neither, they would not get access. They found a grubby, vibrant hall instead, the sort of place shop assistants and ladies' maids might enjoy. Vivian clung to his arm as he walked her into the centre of the room, packed and swollen with hot, excited people. He held her close, tight; she was sure he'd never let go. She didn't mind the fusty smell, the heaving, sweating bodies; she simply noticed that there were perhaps a hundred couples dancing cheek to cheek.

Everyone seemed desperately in love, or at least desperate to be in love. It was marvellous, although she was confident that none of them felt as intensely about one another as she and Howard did. She swayed, stepped and swooped in his arms. The movement brought a happy thought flooding into her mind. What if they *did* feel as she did? Every one of them might be besotted, enchanted, enthralled. Imagine the energy these clinging couples were generating. Shouldn't it have an impact, a real-life consequence? She closed her eyes and felt the love, the passion, the power and the accompanying anguish that had to escort love throughout a war. It soaked the room. Cloaked the room. Then she opened her eyes and noticed a row of young men with pegged-up trousers or folded jacket sleeves designed to disguise the loss of a limb lined up forlornly along the wall. Dancing days over. Some were still wearing their uniforms, hoping to kick-start if not actual desire or passion then at least some decency and compassion. One man rocked left to right on his chair, nodding his head, his eyes staring off peculiarly into the distance. Vivian watched as a tired-looking girl in a cheap, ill-fitting dress and scarlet lipstick took his hand and led him, falteringly, to the dance floor. From his tentative, inching movements it was clear that he was blind. It was a touching scene until the moment the woman accepted a coin for her trouble, clumsily fished out from the soldier's jacket pocket.

Howard saw the exchange too. 'Blasted generals. If they saw that, could they still give the cry?' He squeezed her hand, uncomfortably tight. His lips were almost on her ear; the heat of his body ran the length of hers. She wished she could soothe him. Save him.

'Why do you hate the generals so? Everyone else respects them.'

'People don't know any better. I'm in a unique position. I've seen what it's like out there. The generals may mean well, but their patriotism is idealistic, bordering on foolish. They are simply dangerously arrogant.'

'I'm sorry.' It wasn't enough, but it was all she had. He understood and shrugged, accepting her.

'It's just taking so long.' He sighed. 'It's unbearable knowing what is going on out there. Knowing that what I saw is still happening, night after night, week after week. Months. Years. Think what else we could have done in that time. Women could have fought for the vote. They might have had it now. Anyone could have studied for a degree. Children could have been born and half raised, crops planted, homes built. All we've done is destroy.'

They continued to sway rhythmically but were not attempting to step. People were forced to dance around them. Some did so gracefully, not breaking their step; others mumbled objections that they were not moving with the flow and rudely bumped up against them. 'I don't believe anyone can win a war like this.' Howard let out a grave, despairing sigh.

'What you mean is it will just go on and on until there are no men left at all to fight.'

'Possibly. Hate wins. Destruction wins. I need a drink.'

That night, as they lay in bed, satiated, stimulated, she asked him to tell her of his experiences at the Front. She had no idea. No one spoke of it, and the newspapers offered nothing other than lists of names of dead men or names of towns she struggled to find on a map.

He shook his head. 'You don't want to know.'

'I do,' she insisted gently. 'I want to know what it's been like for you. Everything. I want to understand.'

He told her how he had got to France with his strange journalist friend and a bag of cash for bribes. He mentioned particular towns and the length of time he spent billeted, and he admitted there was a lot of death and injury. He would not say more and she felt he had confided nothing. Not really. For the first time since they had become lovers, she got the sense that he was cutting her off, keeping her at a distance, and whilst she understood that he was no doubt protecting her, she still resented it. His views on the war were perhaps the defining thing about him as a man; they had met because of them, they had argued because of them. How could he think to keep the full and true explanation from her? She felt the slight sting of being patronised, and decided to push ahead. 'So how long were you at the Front?'

'A year, from October 1914.'

She sighed and turned to lie flat on her back, the sheet pulled up only as far as her waist. She was satisfied to note that his eyes rested on her breasts. He stubbed out his cigarette and kissed a nipple slowly.

'What did you do? Day to day? I understand that your friend was reporting, but what about you?'

'I talked to the soldiers, helped Basil gather information, and then, when it was needed, I did what I could for the wounded.'

'You're not a doctor.'

'No. I fetched them water and morphine. I carried them on

stretchers. Dug their graves.' He fell on to his back too as he delivered that last sentence.

Vivian wondered whether he still thought she judged him. Condemned him for not fighting. She remembered his face as he took the feather from that bossy bitch in the street. He was ashen, shocked, horrified. At the woman? At himself? She wanted to convince him of her loyalty. It was a straightforward, un-thought-through loyalty: she loved him and so wanted to be nice to him. She did not care too much if she agreed with him, or if it was morally ugly to be loyal to one man while married to another. None of that mattered to her.

'It seems so unfair that all the time Aubrey was in service but stationed in England, you were out there actually doing something, and yet he is seen as a hero and you are vilified and despised.'

'He's out there now, though, isn't he, and I'm here with you, which is hardly fair. I can't think badly of the man. It does you no credit to do so either.'

Vivian felt chastised. He thought so deeply about everything. 'Why must you be so honourable? I'm just saying that you might have joined up and not been sent away. Or you could have got yourself a job in a mine or shipbuilding, just before the recruiters came to town. Plenty did.' Thus circumventing a need to declare oneself a pacifist, or go on trial. 'There are ways to avoid the war that would have caused you less trouble.'

'Only a few ways, and none of them honourable. Besides, your husband wasn't trying to avoid the war, was he?'

Vivian sighed and admitted, 'No. He was not. He volunteered almost instantly. They just didn't send him to the Front for such a long time.'

'Well, then.'

'Well.'

She found it uncomfortable that her lover insisted on thinking the best of her husband. Howard saw Aubrey as a soldier and therefore was obligated to respect him. Vivian saw Aubrey as a man, a cold, clumsy, inaccessible man, and could not respect him, certainly not love him. Obligation be damned. She had tried. Failed.

She rolled on to her side again and kissed the freckles on his shoulder. 'What was it like, really?' she asked again, nudging closer to him, her breast pushing into his arm.

'I'm sure your husband's letters tell you all he wants you to know,' he muttered stonily.

'Don't do that.'

'Do what?'

'Patronise me. Use him as a barrier. Aubrey doesn't decide what I should or should not know and understand. He can't now.'

Howard looked pained, embarrassed. 'I'm not trying to do that. I just think we both need to remember that he exists.'

'How could I forget?' asked Vivian. She knew her situation. Understood it with horrifying clarity. Never forgot it for a moment.

'I do.'

'Do you?' She was surprised. She couldn't imagine him so engrossed, so absorbed and thoughtless. She was delighted that he might be riveted and enthralled to the point of forgetfulness.

'Yes, and I mustn't.'

'Tell me now,' she whispered.

# 40

So he told her. It was not because he wanted her to see him as a hero or because he wanted her pity or even understanding of his situation. It was not about him at all. It was obvious that she didn't respect her husband. It was painfully complex that he could think, or hope, or want that she might. He wouldn't have her if she did, and he had to have her. More than anything, that. He spoke in a perverse and not thoroughly thought-out attempt to help her reclaim some admiration for Aubrey – a man Howard didn't even particularly like, but a man who was up to his thighs in blood and mud and shit and hate, so a man he had to venerate. He felt guilty as hell for making the officer into a cuckold, but he was incapable of doing anything other. He loved Vivian as he'd never loved anyone before, with an intensity that bordered on obsession.

He loved how she was. Just that. The delicate exactness of her nose, her ankles. He adored the mellow swell of her hips and the strength hidden in her calves. There was something indefinable about her skin and her collarbone that clouted his being, knocked him senseless. He studied her in minute detail. Fascinated by the ridge of the blue-green veins that ran the length of her pale hands, the rise of the goose bumps on her arms and thighs when she was caught in a breeze, the soft pink of the blushes that might appear high in her cheekbones or low in the centre of her throat, depending on whether the colour was induced by embarrassment or exertion. It all made him breathless. She had reminded him that bodies were staggeringly, beautifully fragile rather than macabrely so. She smelt of soap and perfume. She smelt gentle. An incredible thing. Yet despite all this placid tenderness, he knew the improbable truth of her, he knew it. She was keen, alert, acute, eager. She was sex. The heart of it. The heat of it. He had found a staggering intimacy with her that no other woman had ever offered; she opened her legs and it unlocked things deep in his soul that he had no vocabulary for. She unlocked life itself. She made him feel unlicensed, excluded from obligation, restraint or regularity. Weariness shifted from his shoulders in her presence.

So why did he feel a need to remind her of her responsibility to her husband? Why did he feel a need to elevate the man in her eyes? He wasn't sure. Pride, perhaps? A deep, intrinsic sense of fair play?

He wondered where to start. Acting as a journalist, he had seen more than most. For most soldiers the war was confined to a few hundred yards of torture; his stretched for miles. What part of war could he serve up to her? Ypres? Could he tell her about those early days? A city was razed. Everything reduced to ruin and rubble. Homes blazing, women raped, children shot on their way to school. Or Loos, where Michael fell? His brother, screaming for death, crying for Enid. Perhaps Hooge? The devil's own hell. It didn't matter; he couldn't hope to make sense of it anyway. He found he could not explain the scale. What did the numbers mean? Ten men dead here, fifty more there. Three hundred in a skirmish, tens of thousands in a battle. He thought it best to tell her of individual acts of bravery, horror, brilliance and futility. That way she might comprehend what it meant to be at war.

'There is lots of preparation and waiting before the men go over the top. Do you understand that?'

'Yes, I suppose there must be.'

'I shall tell you of two weeks in a small village called Hooge where I spent some time in the summer of 1915. Remember, the war has been going on for more than two years now, and I am only going to describe two weeks.' She nodded, once, a small, purposeful movement. 'Hooge is not far from Ypres, just a couple of miles. For a time there was a chateau there called the White Chateau. It had excellent stables and rather comfortable accommodation for the brigade staff.'

'Sounds all right,' she mumbled tentatively. He knew she didn't want to get it wrong.

'Yes, it was. Gone now, of course. No chateau, only rubble, sandbags and deep mine craters. I initially drank wine there and ate decent beef. Then I watched men die there as it became a battlefield. At first I made friends with some of the soldiers, followed their progress. Basil liked a human interest story. So we drank with them in the French bars or in the officers' mess, ate with them as they dug trenches and trained. We waited with them night after night as the ground shook and men further up the process were already being blown to bits.' He sighed; it came deep from his soul and it was hopeless. 'However, I came to understand that it was intolerable to befriend them, then lose them, time after time. Relentless, insufferable. I remember one young Irish officer in particular who taught me that. He was a handsome chap, had the sort of charming smile that women like, but there was a profound melancholy in his eyes that I thought left more of an impression than the smile and the straight teeth. We struck up a conversation two or three times. He was fond of the theatre so we had that in common. He told me he'd written to his mother to say he'd met me; they'd seen a play of mine together in London once. He always gave me a wave, asked what I made of things. I stopped knowing how to answer. What could any of us make of it?

'One day he came down to our quarters on a brief respite from commanding the garrison at Hooge. We had arranged for him to join us for dinner. I remember he asked, "Would I delay you too much if I took a bath before I join you?" Wonderful manners, that sort of boy, even over there. He didn't sit with us while his bath was being drawn, but walked about in the open air because dirt and lice are socialists and they cling to officers and men alike. There were legions of them crawling over him and a potent stink came off him. Sweat and worse. He'd been in the dugouts for a while; he was expecting to move up, go into battle any day. He'd already seen too much. "Hooge," he muttered, in a thoughtful way. "Not what anyone would call a health resort, is it?" He was chirpier after his bath. We played cards and he even told jokes. After a short stay he finished up his whisky and went back to the trenches and his men. His head hung even though the officers are trained to stand tall. I could see that he expected to be killed. It was his quiet resignation that threw me. The war had been going on long enough by then that the clever men calculated the odds. "You know you are the only famous person I have ever met or am likely to." He shook my hand. "Goodbye." It was pitiful, his certainty that death was coming.'

'Did he die?'

'Yes.' Howard sighed again. Impatient and weary at once. Had she expected a reprieve? A happy ending? He supposed she had. 'I'll get to it. So Hooge became a full on battlefield on 15 July. The height of summer. It was so damned hot. I don't know, but somehow it seems even worse killing in the sunshine. These boys should have been in parks and at the seaside with their sweethearts eating penny ices. Instead they lay in vermin-infested trenches, skin scorched, mouths parched.

'The Germans had taken control of one of the mine craters; this was an important strategic position as it secured the tip of a triangular area across the Menin road. There were trenches running down to it on both sides and they had fortified it with sandbags and packed it chock full with superior machine guns that could clean up on all three sides. Do you follow? Their position meant that a straightforward assault by infantry would be a suicidal endeavour. Our trenches faced this throttlehold and our men, all volunteers, were shelled day and night. A huge number of them were ripped to fragments; others were buried alive or made insane with shell shock.

'My Irish officer was in the thick of it. He watched as his men ducked below the sandbags and scrabbled in the sides of the crater. Fragments of flesh, charcoaled hands, booted feet, burnt heads came falling over them when the enemy mortared our position. The craters were often filled with the fetid water that slopped over from Bellewaerde Lake; the boys suffered with soft rotting feet even before they died. Despite the itchy lice, the men had to stay still and steady. Moving had the potential for drawing the attention of the enemy; a lit cigarette, the sun glinting on a medal were all dangers. Besides, it sometimes disturbed the nerves of the next man in the row. They were all jittery, but a soldier losing it and screaming out, alerting the enemy to exact positions, could cost twenty lives. A man who says he's not afraid in battle is a liar, a fool or a psychopath. You don't want to be near him. Fear held them steady, as much as courage.

'I stood by the Irish officer as his men tried to dig to find deeper, more secure cover. Their shovels pushed into the yielding dead bodies of the men they'd fought earlier battles with. Human flesh, putrefying and stinking, was bonded to the mudbanks to remind them that it was no good. It was never any good. Whatever they did. If they got through one scrape, inevitably they'd be caught in the next.' Howard glanced at her; she was pale to the point of transparency, her eyes and mouth agog and wide. 'Do you want me to go on?' She didn't respond, but now that he had started talking about it, he found he wanted her to know. He wanted everyone to know. If they'd seen it, they'd hate war too. If they hated it enough, it would stop. Wouldn't it?

'A directive came from some absent generals that we had to clear out this deathtrap. The sappers mined under the roadway towards the redoubt, while our heavy artillery shelled the Germans. The mine was detonated on the twenty second of July. Our boys squatted down, utterly terrified after such an extended period of anxious expectation. The land was cracked by a blast of fire, and spewed up a commotion of sod, rocks and limbs. Our men stayed squatting as German boots and hats, legs and heads fell like rain about them. When the soil and smoke settled, we could see that the enemy's stronghold no longer existed. In its stead was a vast crater, a gouged and yawning gap. Our men were ordered to rush the crater. Rushing was unachievable; they staggered into it. Knowing that it was suicidal. They did so because orders have to be followed, above all else. They lay there panting like dogs in the smouldering earth. Waiting to be picked off.

'Our generals had asked for trouble and, of course, our men got it. Incensed by the annihilation of their strategic position and, no doubt, the men guarding it, the Germans began a manic assault on our trenches. Machine-gun fire blasted with such ferocity that our men were tossed about and danced long after they were dead. The smell of gunshot and blood drenched the air for days—'

'Stop, please stop.' A single tear was falling down her face. He appreciated the neatness of her reaction. He didn't want her to weep hysterically. It would have been unseemly somehow, and she knew this too. He caught the tear with his thumb and tasted its saltiness.

'But I have only told you of a week's action.' He said it gently, but he felt a hardness in his chest. No one over here could stomach it. That was the point. No one knew how vile it was until it was too late.

'Don't go, please never ever go there.' She grabbed hold of his hand and kissed it with something akin to rage, over and over again, as though she was storing him away, sucking him up. 'Just stay. Stay safe. Stay here with me,' she pleaded.

'Haven't I just been telling you that? I disagree with war. I'm simply not cut out to destroy, and I'm hoping that one day people will see that as a good thing. I'm never going back there.' She could barely bring her face up so that her eyes met his, but when she eventually did, he noticed that she looked doubtful, uncertain, as though she knew more than he did.

As he fell to sleep, it occurred to him that he had not told her about the exact fate of the Irish officer. He'd lost track, even in his storytelling. There was too much to speak of. Impossible to keep them all in mind. The thought made him sick with sorrow all over again, as though it was only yesterday that he'd dug the grave for the Irish officer with the charming smile and the straight teeth, who had been laid to rest without his head.

# 41

THE THREE DAYS and three nights vanished far too quickly. Vivian felt the moments slipping from her grasp. It was like hanging from a cliff and feeling the earth crumbling beneath her fingertips, knowing she would soon plunge, fall into nothingness. The time came when their train tickets and Enid's expectations called them back to Blackwell. They packed slowly and silently; a deadening fog of despair replaced the vapour of enthralment that had hung in the hotel room since they'd arrived.

'We could stay here in London. We don't have to go back to Blackwell. At least not except to pick up Mabel,' suggested Howard in a rush, but even as he suggested it, it was clear from his face that he knew it was unworkable. They would return to pick up the child and be swallowed up by respectability and duty. She wished they had brought Mabel with them. Maybe then they would have had a chance.

'How will it be when we get back there?' she asked.

'I don't know.' He shook his head. She wished that just once he'd lie and say, 'The same as it has been here,' or something else reassuring. It was useless; they knew it wouldn't be like this. They would not be able to touch one another or even to talk to one another without extreme care and meticulous planning. The freedom and spontaneity they had enjoyed these past few days would be wrenched away. The right to one another that they felt so acutely now would be thrown into doubt and uncertainty.

'We'll just have to be careful,' she urged him.

'Or not.' He stopped folding his shirts and held his arms out wide, an expansive, vulnerable gesture, something between a shrug and a suggestion.

'What do you mean?'

He came around to her side of the bed and took both her hands in his own. 'I don't care if they discover us. I don't care who knows. Do you?' His eyes shone with alert intensity and self-assurance; he was peering carefully at her, hoping to find the same expression reflected back. She blinked and he pulled away a fraction as though the movement in the air caused by her flickering lashes had been a blow. She was an open book to him.

She did care.

Not because she'd be chastised and condemned as a loose woman, an adulterous whore. She didn't mind if Aubrey divorced her and she had to endure a scandal, if her family disowned her and she was left penniless, if society was disgusted with her and she had to exist friendless. He was worth all that.

'They'd never let me have Mabel.' There it was, said out loud. The reason she would never allow their affair to be discovered, the reason she would never divorce Aubrey.

Howard blanched; he looked startled. Had he really not considered it? Determined, he argued, 'We could run away, take her with us and disappear.'

'No, we couldn't. Where would we go? How would we live? You are an essential worker under the protection of Aubrey Owens. I am his wife.' She felt reduced to little more than a chattel. She'd always known this was the case. She was female, born to be passed from parent to husband, no private wealth or means to earn an independent income. She did not have the right to vote, she didn't have any entitlements at all. She was just property. 'He'd have us tracked down by lawyers and the police. They'd have you banged up in prison again faster than you could say white feather. Prison at best; maybe this time they would go ahead and shoot you. They'd take Mabel from me and I'd never be allowed to see her again. Women are put in mental asylums for less. There isn't a judge in the land who would condone a woman having an affair with a conchie and award her custody of a child. Running away is an impossible idea.'

Howard fell silent. His face was stony. She was glad he didn't offer ridiculous and unrealistic platitudes but instead simply stated what was most true. 'Not seeing you is impossible too.'

'Yes. Yes.' Her lips found his and they hungrily kissed one another to console and to reassure.

'We will be careful, Vivian, that's all. We can carry on as we are. I'll work hard on the farm, better than ever. We can meet secretly. No one need know. We can be careful.'

She wanted to believe him. 'For how long?'

'Until the war is over. When Aubrey comes back, you can ask for a divorce.'

She knew it would never happen. Aubrey would never allow it. He didn't love her, she was certain of that. She didn't think he loved Mabel much either – there hadn't been time for it – but he'd never let them go. He wouldn't be able to bear the humili-ation. A nouveau riche family such as his could not allow that to happen. The Owens name would be forever ruined. He'd rather live with her, incessantly miserable, than publicly admit defeat.

There was only one way she could be free. If something . . . well . . . after all, the fact was, Aubrey was out there. The thought was disgusting. Vile. She felt sick at herself for having had it. She wanted to switch off her mind, the way one might switch off the motor of an engine. She tried to think of something else. The flowers in the vase on the dresser. Pink roses. Where had they got them from? Who still grew flowers? She had to backtrack. Just in case. Just in case there was a God who could read her every thought, even now. Even when there was a war going on and men were clawing for His attention, if God was listening to her, He could never forgive her. Not in all his magnificence, compassion or tolerance. The thing that had swept through her mind – the only solution to their problem – was insufferable, unforgivable. It would have been better that she die than think that about a soldier, an officer, who was fighting for King and country.

Turning back to her packing she whispered, 'Forgive me.' She whispered the same thing into the steady, cool hotel lobby, into the noise and bustle at the station and in the dusty, jolting carriage that took them north. 'Forgive me.' It was pathetic and ridiculous that she was talking to a God she doubted existed. Or, if He did exist, He had stopped listening to human prayers long ago. Yet she still feared punishment and retribution for her thoughts.

Everything was topsy-turvy.

# 42

E NID BEHAVED MARVELLOUSLY in front of Vivian's staff. She gave Vivian a detailed account of Mabel's activities over the past three days, including foodstuffs consumed and hours slept. She did not glance at Howard as he played peek-a-boo, causing the baby to giggle and gurgle. She simply commented that she hoped the business with the solicitors had been successful and then suggested that she and Howard leave promptly, insisting that Vivian must want Mabel to herself. 'No doubt you want to unpack immediately and get settled. It's always so nice to be home, isn't it?'

As they walked back to their cottage, she was less subtle and accommodating. Without preamble she demanded, 'How could you? How could you be so stupid and so selfish?' Enid knew her son too well to fail to see what had happened. They were both glowing, delirious; they couldn't take their eyes off one another. She loved him too well to keep her thoughts to herself.

'I'm not trying to be either stupid or selfish,' replied Howard calmly.

'She's a married woman, Howard. She's married to the man who affords you protection. He does that so that you can stand by your principles, not so you can lie with his wife.' He heard the fear in his mother's voice and felt sorry enough to attempt an explanation, even though he was a man and really didn't have to explain or justify himself to her, hadn't felt the need to do either since he was eight years old.

'You don't understand. It's not sordid or wicked. I love her.'

'It had to be her, did it?' His mother looked hot and bothered. Her hat was askew.

'Yes, apparently it did.' People said it all the time. 'You can't choose who you fall in love with.' Howard had always been quite ambiguous in his feelings towards such a sentiment, which was more often than not vocalised to excuse some chaos brought down on innocents because of the self-interested behaviour of the not-so-innocent. He felt a bit embarrassed to find himself articulating the platitude, but at the same time he thought it was true. He had not decided to pursue Vivian, nor had she tried to seduce him. It was bigger than that. Besides, they had a right, didn't they? A right to happiness. 'He doesn't treat her very well,' he added in a half-hearted attempt to convince his mother to see things his way.

'Does he beat her?'

'No.'

'Does he womanise?'

Although understandable, Howard thought his mother's line of reasoning was beneath her. A man's worth as a husband should not be quantified by the absence of abuse. 'Possibly, in France. Most of the soldiers do, it's encouraged.' His mother looked irritated.

'He feeds and clothes her. He is the father of her child.'

'He doesn't love her, Mam.'

Enid drew her mouth into a thin line; her lips disappeared beneath a hard wall of anguish. She knew it was true and she knew Vivian deserved to be loved. A young woman who always seemed to be suppressing her effervescent nature was bound to erupt, explode, sooner or later. There was a vigorous physicality to Vivian that had been expressed in her dancing, her work on the land, her devoted mothering. Sooner or later it had to find its true form in a heightened sensuality. Enid had long expected it. She wasn't being tediously sanctimonious; she would simply have preferred it to happen with some other man. Her son could not take this sort of risk. 'Is there any point in my asking you to call it off?'

'None.'

'Even if I beg you?' Howard had never seen his mother look so old and desperate. She had braved scandals of her own, walked a path of fierce independence and never been afraid for herself. Yet she looked afraid now. He shook his head.

'This isn't like you, Mam. You've always been an Amazonian warrior.' He tried to smile and make light of it, but she wouldn't crack a grin back. 'I thought you were careless of society's gossip or censure. I can't understand why you might feel so afraid for me. A man.'

'Yes, a man, but my son. Always that, and isn't every mother in Europe terrified for her son right now? Terrified or grieving.'

'I'm in love, not at war.'

'Howard, you are a conscientious objector and her husband is a serving officer. If anyone finds out, they'll lynch you as soon as look at you and not suffer a moment's hesitation.' He knew she was right. She put her hand on his arm. For the first time he noticed her fragility. Her skin was waxy like baking paper; she had age spots. 'Take care.'

They had arrived at the cottage. The gate squeaked and Enid walked up the path. She opened the door muttering something about needing to have a lie-down. She stayed in her room even at tea time; he had made mutton bone and vegetable soup but she said she wasn't hungry. He agreed it wasn't the most appetising of dishes. He hadn't really expected it to tempt her out of her room.

He ate alone and then sat in the back garden. The small area, no bigger than six foot square, had been turned over to hens. They were scrawny and messy but the eggs were invaluable. He'd be more comfortable sitting in the front garden among the vegetables, but he couldn't trust himself if he sat in the front. He knew that it would be too easy to swing open the creaky gate and walk – no, run – up the path and towards Vivian's house. That was just the sort of thing they could not do. There might be a maid working this evening; certainly Mrs Rosebend would be home. Their trip to London was bound to have caused comment. He couldn't compound it by visiting tonight. He would have to stay away for at least a day or two.

He threw back his head and looked at the perpetuity of stars and the unfeeling and gleaming moon. He wondered whether Vivian was staring at the moon too. She'd told him she often did. He imagined her in her bedroom, a room he'd never actually seen. He wondered how many soldiers were looking at the sky. Praying to God for what? For peace, for survival, for a new pair of boots? The village was silent. Somewhere a back door banged, signalling that someone was visiting the privy; a dog barked and its master yelled at it. He put his hand in his pocket to dig out his cigarettes. He had none. His fingers touched a downy softness, and he pulled out the white feather that the angry, coarse woman had pushed on him. The war seemed so very far away. Since he'd taken Vivian as his own, the whispers of battle had withdrawn; he could not hear the men's boots marching or the explosions. Of course these things were happening across the Channel and in reality he should never have been able to hear them on this shore, but he had, he always had. With her all the horror and sadness vanished into a phantom under the bed or a silhouette behind the dresser. She allowed him to forget the inexplicable dreadfulness.

Didn't she?

# SEPTEMBER 1916

# 43

VIVIAN EXAMINED THE scratches on her calves and smiled secretly to herself, her mind falling, with enthusiasm, back to the night before last when she and Howard had finally managed to be together, albeit in the less than glamorous surroundings of the barn. The smell of animals, hay and manure a backdrop to their loving. Earthy. She didn't care where it had to be; the only important thing was being with him. The breath caught in her throat when she thought of him. Urgent and hard, satiated and slumped. Since London there had been nothing else for her. Whether she was playing with her baby or scrubbing out the chicken pen, she felt him all through her body. She felt him sit in her soul.

The summer was almost at an end; the air had a hint of coolness. An edge as autumn began to nip. Vivian had noticed the chill smoke-blue mist on the horizon this morning; it was dreamy. It had been a blustery day and she was in the garden, hair whipped across her face, bringing in the newly laundered sheets that had caught the breeze and now smelt and felt like potential. Enid came speeding through the house, calling her name. The maid followed hastily with a look of concern, but somehow sensed that she shouldn't intrude and so fell back into the house, left Enid to it.

Vivian's relationship with Enid had inevitably cooled as her relationship with Howard had intensified. It wasn't that she wanted to lie or hide things from her dear friend, but she could not bring herself to talk of him in the usual way. She could not pretend things were unchanged and ask what he'd thought of the dumplings Enid had baked or whether she could pass on a message about sheep, but then nor could she tell his mother what she thought he was now: a miracle, a saviour, a lover. Speaking about what they had would inevitably lead to the trampling of the beautiful, ethereal essence of it. Other people's words would make it ordinary and vulgar. Others would define it as an infidelity, a wrong. Vivian was sure Enid had not bought the story about their having business in London, so it was beyond awkward carrying on as though she had.

Enid's face was unrecognisable. Crumpled like paper. Vivian's heart instantly began to bang fiercely inside her chest; Mabel was safely at her feet so her fearful thoughts leapt to Howard. She immediately began to imagine accidents that might have occurred. Had he fallen off a roof, or been trampled by an animal? Was it something to do with the tractor?

'He's gone. He's gone!' she cried. The sound she made was more like a wail; it didn't sound human.

'Gone where?' Vivian asked, dropping her basket of wooden pegs. She did not need to ask about whom they were talking; neither woman had another 'he' in their lives, not really.

'To the army. To war!' shouted Enid. As the words left her mouth, she clutched her lower abdomen as though she felt an actual pain there, like labour. Vivian ran to her, but once she was within a foot, she dared not reach out to touch her. A snarled mass of panic and resentment, Enid oozed shock and anguish. Vivian felt cursed by her expression.

'No. No. No.'

Enid nodded emphatically. 'I asked you to keep him safe and you've sent him out there.'

'No, I haven't. It's not what I wanted.' Vivian shook her head; she felt breathless, as though someone was clasping her around her throat, choking the life out of her, which in a way was true, because if he left, there was no life to live.

'He said he couldn't stay because of you.'

'Because of me?' She echoed the words, uncomprehending. She hadn't asked him to go to war, not since Aubrey had sent her to do the job weeks ago, and even then he must have known it was the last thing she really wanted.

'You always thought he should be fighting.'

Vivian couldn't remember feeling that. It seemed so irresponsible and misguided. 'Where is he now?' She was already unfastening her apron; she threw it on the ground and started to run towards the house. She could change his mind, she could stop him.

'It's too late.' Carefully. 'I haven't seen him since yesterday morning. I received a telegram this morning. He's already at a base.'

'Which base?'

'He didn't say. They're not allowed, are they? But as he's joined the army voluntarily this time, there's nothing to be done.'

'Why didn't you come to me last night? Raise the alarm then?'

Enid looked defeated, regretful. 'I thought he was here with you.'

Vivian felt her legs shake. 'Why would he go?'

'How could he stay?' Enid glanced around Aubrey Owens' farm. Her gaze lingered on his daughter and then rested on his wife. 'He couldn't live another man's life.' How could he stay here and work Aubrey's land, sleep with his wife, while Aubrey was over there? 'What if something happens to your husband? Howard would never forgive himself. It has to be a level playing field. At least that. For a man like my son. Didn't you know that much?'

Vivian fell to the floor. 'It's my fault. I sent him,' she whispered, because she knew he'd rather be right than be liked. He'd rather be the best man than a loved man.

Enid had no room for pity; her heart was breaking. 'Yes, you did. You sent my boy away. You sent my boy to war. You succeeded where the British army failed. You must be pleased with yourself.' She breathed out. It was a long, slow, heavy breath full of solemn mourning.

'He'll come back to us.'

Enid stared at Vivian but said nothing. She didn't have to; her eyes spat out her sentiments.

You are such a child.

Enid had once liked that about Vivian, but no longer.

# 44

THEY HAD HIM on a boat within forty-eight hours. He'd done his basic training before Richmond and they were desperate for men, haemorrhaging them. There was another push to be made. Wasn't there always: push after push after push; they were all condemned as Sisyphus had been to an eternity of rolling a boulder uphill then watching it roll back down again. He was sent out to serve under Major Aubrey Owens. It made sense: a bolshie conchie couldn't be trusted even if he had finally seen the light. Owens was a man who had been decorated; the two of them had known each other since they were boys, so the file said. Best place for this troublemaker was answering to one of their own, a good reliable man. A telegram was sent to Major Owens informing him of the situation, but no one wasted time waiting for a reply. Of course, Howard saw the irony: it was Major Owens he was going to be underneath now. Not Vivian. The crude pun almost made him smile internally. Or at least smirk. Almost. He couldn't imagine anything generating a genuine beam from him again.

He tried to concentrate on gaining sea legs, but the sway of the ship and the weight of the kit pulling at his shoulders only made him think of Vivian pulling him down on to the bed, the mattress moving beneath them, the squeak of the bedsprings, potentially treacherous. He felt nauseous and didn't know if it was the waves or guilt. He had tried to say goodbye. He'd wanted to tell her himself about his departure, explain – if he could – his decision, but he found he couldn't.

They'd finally found a way to be together. When they'd first returned from London, there had been long days of skulking around, making do with a wave and a tilt of the cap across the street or a few sentences passed in the field in the presence of Timmy Durham. After a week she'd caught the train to Derby; it was market day. He'd taken the autobus. They met under the clock tower and went for tea together; he held her fingers beneath the table, the cloth offering them a shield. They'd managed to find a little deserted alley where they kissed, almost savage with longing, in amongst cabbage leaves. The place had smelt fetid. She'd placed his hand on her breast, his fingers bungling and hopeless with frustration. The nearness but ultimate inaccessibility had made him want to roar. They'd travelled home on their separate modes of transport. Last Sunday she had come to his house when the rest of the village were at church. They didn't make it to his bed; he wasn't sure if that was because they'd both been aware of the time constraints, or from squeamishness on her part. He took her in the narrow kitchen, on the table where his mother baked. It was urgent and intense. She didn't stay to talk because Mabel was asleep in the pram; someone might spot her.

Then she'd sent him a note. It was not like her first one. She did not write his name or sign it either.

*Door will be open, come after 11 p.m.*

He'd assumed she meant the back door, and she had. He had swiftly walked to her house, forcing himself to contain his pace; a running man would draw attention. Yet he would run to her. The house was in darkness, not so much as a flickering candle in a window. The heat had gone out of the day and the night's coolness licked his skin. There was very little land left that had not been turned over to crops; even Vivian's garden grew carrots and potatoes rather than roses, but Howard noticed dense clumps of daisies and dandelions defiantly pushing up through the earth along the path and around her house. They were closed up tight against the night but they made him smile. He thought how he'd like to make a crown or a necklace from them for Mabel.

The house and garden were still except for some movement near the compost heap. A fox? A rabbit? He tried the handle and the door slowly gave way, allowing him unencumbered entrance. The kitchen was unknown to him; he passed a long, scrubbed wooden table that could seat eight. He knew that Vivian sometimes ate there because she liked the company of Mrs Rosebend, Cook and the maids. The china on the shelves gleamed. There was something under a tea towel: a pie perhaps? He carefully crept up the stairs, treading at the edges so as to avoid telltale creaking floorboards. At the top he froze, suddenly unsure which room was hers; then he saw a crack of light coming from underneath one, spilling on to the floorboards, lighting his way.

As he edged open the door, she fell on him, smothering his face with kisses, and pulled him into the room. He wrapped his arms around her – not that she'd given any sign that she wanted to escape. Her tongue was in his mouth, her hands slipped inside his shirt; quickly he gathered up her nightdress so his hands could slide across her bare thighs and backside. His body pulsed, convulsed with longing. He ran his fingers through her hair and it fell like a waterfall. He wondered at the beauty of her, how splendid she was.

She pulled him towards the bed, and God knows that was where he wanted to be, but he sat on the edge with sudden and inconvenient reluctance. He ferociously wished he could control his fits of conscience. She crawled behind him and sat squeezed up against him, her breasts pushed into his back, her legs astride, clamped to his hips and outer thighs. She pulled at his shoulders, urging him to lie down.

'Did you make love with Aubrey here?'

'Don't think about it.'

Yes, then. He hadn't been able to stay in the room. The sheets, the walls, the patchwork eiderdown all seemed cloying, restraining. 'Come outside with me,' he'd suggested.

'We might be seen.'

'In the barn.'

She had not been able to resist or refuse him. Carefully they crept down the stairs and fled to the barn, the moon flinging its light on to her pale nightdress, illuminating her like an angel. The straw scratched their backs, shoulders and buttocks, but neither of them seemed to care. He rolled them over so that she was above him and only her knees would get scratched. She seemed surprised yet elated to be on top. He wanted to cry at the glory of her: her pale skin, made still more wonderful because of the splashes of pink at her throat, cheeks, nipples, lips; desire marking her. Her breasts, swaying rhythmically, made him ease up on to his elbows so they could pound against his face; so tantalising and thrilling that he thought he might explode with delight and desire.

Then he knew what he had to do.

He wondered whether he looked different to her. He knew he *was* different in the instant that he made the decision. As he pushed into her, as her flesh parted and accepted him with such sweet willingness, he knew he was going to betray her by going away. Leaving her. It wasn't what he wanted. But he didn't have any choice. Love, not hate, had sent him to war.

After all, they were almost the same thing. So extreme. So perilous.

He couldn't sit in Blackwell waiting for her joy and pleasure in him to become stagnant and then to morph altogether into something sickening like disappointment, and he knew it must. It would. If he stayed. Going was the right thing and the most bloody. Telling her would have been the right thing too. Yet it was hopeless. He didn't give either her or his mother the chance to try to persuade him out of his decision. He knew how it would have been if he had tried to tell them he was joining up. They would have begged and berated him to change his mind. They would have told him he was breaking their hearts. Perhaps Vivian would have clung to him, her arms clasped around his neck, his knees. He'd have had to loosen her grip a finger at a time. His mother might have flung herself across the door in a feeble effort to stop him going. He'd have had to gently and firmly move her aside.

It would only have hurt them more when they failed.

The war was as he remembered it, worse if anything. At the beginning there had at least been shock at the horror of it all; now there was resignation, doubt that it would ever end, poor recollection of what life had once been. Most of the men seemed to understand that they were in hell and here for an eternity. They all looked the same to him. It was hard to mark anyone out to befriend or even mistrust. Their uniforms were filthy. Every last man stank of sweat, urine, blood and vomit. He caught their lice within days. Their faces were drawn, weary: thin, cracked lips, hollow cheeks, their eyes unreadable, depleted. Throughout the day they listened to the shelling and the silence; both caused fear and alarm. The shelling was spasmodic but persistent in Howard's part of the line, and it frayed nerves and caused incessant tension. Heads pounded, the earth was pounded; no one could tell the difference any more.

Everyone assumed a battle was imminent. The top brass wouldn't talk about it, but it was inevitable; that was why they were here after all. Walking into gunfire was a ludicrous concept, if you thought about it for even a second. Suicide, to all intents and purposes. Sitting in a trench waiting to be shelled somehow made them still more fearful, as they all knew to dread shell wounds more than a bullet. A direct hit would annihilate, abolish a man's very existence; something a bit off target tore off limbs and faces, leaving monsters behind. The silence was the worst. When the Germans stopped firing and shelling, horror truly set in, because then the only question was when would it begin again.

Rations and letters were the only boost. Tinned stew, a mug of tea, perhaps some bread and jam on a good day, although none of it tasted as it should; everything was watered down, thinned out. The letters were snatched from the hands of the men playing postie. Some seized upon them and ripped open the envelopes immediately, desperate to be transported back to cobbled streets, kitchen ranges and warm beds. Others savoured the moment: sniffed the letter, caressed it, kept it in their pocket until they could carve out some privacy, preferring to read it by the light of a stub of candle. Nine days in, Howard hadn't received a letter, so he didn't yet know what he would do with one when the time came. At night they slept on wooden planks. Few tried to lie horizontal; there was always the thought of a rat settling on you. Better to sleep sitting up, one man slumped against the next, stiff and cold, a rehearsal for death. Their bones ached; not even the fat lads who had righted all the world's wrongs with a pie and a pint before the war were cushioned enough to get comfortable in this life.

Her letter came on the tenth day. He'd feared she would not write, that she loved him too much to forgive him, but he was relieved that wasn't the case. She loved him more than that after all. The letter was a comfort; it offered solace when he thought the world was devoid of such a thing. Just her handwriting on the envelope provided that. She was angry and confused, as he'd expected.

*Why? Why now, when you have everything to live for, would you leave?*

He didn't know how to explain it to her. He started the reply ten times over in his head, three or four times in actuality. In the end, all he was able to say was, *You know I couldn't have done anything other.*

Sergeant Bowler came and found him, said he was wanted in the officers' dugout. Howard hadn't bothered to form an opinion of his own, but he'd been told that Bowler was the sort of sergeant none of the men liked or even feared; he was simply despised for being petty and unjustifiably uppity. His mouth stayed in a thin line, suggesting neither pleasure nor annoyance, but his eyes shone with malicious excitement. As they set off along the long corridors of trenches, Howard was more curious than concerned. He hadn't had anything to do with Owens since he arrived; why would he? A lowly foot soldier, beneath notice. Whilst they had once upon a time played games as boys on the same village green, there had been no familiarity between them since. Howard was not the sort to romanticise the past. Aubrey had been a miserable snob as a child. Even then it had seemed to Howard that he only played with the village boys to spoil their fun because his superior social status meant they'd had to let him win.

The sergeant knocked on the makeshift door, waited for the command to enter and then pushed back the gas curtain, trailing Howard behind like the spoils from a day's hunting. The officers certainly fared better than the men, but it wasn't a luxurious billet. The place smelt of paraffin and pipe smoke, with the constant undertone of damp earth. There were two bunks, a table and three or four chairs, all wooden. The gin bottle, tin cups, candlesticks and scattering of books did little to make the place look anything other than crude. There were two tin bowls on the floor, placed to catch leaks. Officers or not, rainwater still got in. Vermin too, by the look of the food bags that were hanging on ropes from the ceiling like bodies.

Major Owens was standing by the table, his back ramrod; he didn't offer a greeting or make any small talk.

'I have a letter here, Private, your letter. It's addressed to my wife. Sergeant Bowler brought it to my attention.' He pointed to the table. The letter had been opened. The thin paper shivered slightly; a draught was coming in despite the gas curtain.

Howard had known it would be read. Everyone had to be censored, most of all a troublesome conchie. That had been one of the many constraints he'd felt when writing it. However, he hadn't written anything that was against military law. Strictly speaking, his post ought to have been sent unhindered. However, his relationship with Vivian was inhibited. He met Aubrey's eyes.

'Yes, sir.'

'I've read it and I understand it is farm business. You worked on my farm for some months this summer, didn't you, Private.' An assertion, not a question. Perhaps for the sergeant's benefit. Owens' eyes were black and fierce. Howard might have shrugged off the threat they held, but there was the slightest quiver in his moustache; not even a tremble, just a fraction of something. It was almost possible to imagine it wasn't there.

Vulnerability.

Howard didn't know how to answer. What was the honourable thing to do? He wanted to say boldly that she was his; he was writing to Vivian because she was his now. His eyes shifted to the sergeant. He was staring ahead, trying not to seem interested in the matter, yet everything in his stance, from the way he threw back his shoulders to the way he jutted out his chin, suggested he patently was. So the men didn't like the sergeant and he didn't like his men; this exchange suggested he didn't like his senior officer either. He was a skinny, miserable sort of man who seemed to have only one pleasure in life: causing trouble for others. Howard sighed. How was it possible that such petty dislike and small-mindedness managed to thrive even out here?

Howard's head continued to operate, although he was doing his level best to close down his heart. He was beginning to reluctantly form an opinion of the sergeant, reluctant because he didn't want to get involved. He didn't want to be one of the men who pronounced Bowler unpopular. Falling in with other men's opinions had never been his strong suit, but besides that, connections caused pain. He'd buried three men this morning, or at least most of them; bits of bodies, bones, uniform, cobbled-together men. You'd think the bastard sergeant might have more to think about than this letter.

Clearly, accepting the lie would cause the least amount of trouble for Vivian, and for Howard himself; the least amount of embarrassment and hurt for Aubrey. However he remained silent, unsure if that was the answer. He'd once had principles, morals, ethics by which to live. What did he have now?

Howard was certain he would not survive the war. He had thought as much the moment he made the decision to enlist. He had seen too much to be under any illusion. No one's odds were favourable, but the conchies in particular had a limited life expectancy. They were always the ones ordered to mend the barbed wire, to accompany the miners digging underground, to crawl across no-man's-land and haul back the dead and wounded. The officers were more offhand with the lives of those who had caused trouble. Since he'd arrived, there hadn't been much time to think about anything. The constant bombardment blew apart reason and ideologies. It was hard to stay sure of anything. Was the war wrong or right? Was his involvement either? Was staking claim to this man's wife brave or insulting? Could these things be both entities at the same time? There was only one thing he was certain of. He would not return to Vivian.

'Yes, sir. Farm business, sir.'

Aubrey looked relieved. Howard noticed for the first time that his eyes were bloodshot, framed in purple shadows. He didn't look well. Who did? 'I trust that your farm business is now concluded and there will be no further reason for you to correspond with Mrs Owens.' It wasn't a request, it was an order, but it was politely given. Major Owens waved his hand, dismissing Howard; he sat down at the table and picked up his pen, returning to some other piece of paperwork. Obviously he considered the conversation concluded, the matter dealt with. His next words would be 'That will be all, Private.' Howard couldn't allow those words to be said.

'No, sir.' Owens' head snapped up. Irritated, he glared at Howard. 'There will be ongoing questions about the farm, sir.' Howard met Aubrey's gaze. He was certain his meaning was clear. He would offer the man a reasonable explanation in front of the sergeant as to why they were corresponding, but he would not give her up. He would not abandon her.

'You can't imagine you are indispensable to the comings and goings of Blackwell Farm,' Aubrey snapped.

'I do think that.' The sergeant coughed and Howard reluctantly added, 'Sir.' Aubrey glared, his fury flickering in the candlelight.

'You are here now, Private. Under my command.'

'I'm here, sir, yes.' It was a perceptible difference of opinion.

'You understand that it is an officer's duty to read the letters of his men.' Aubrey held eye contact, his anger and the sliver of vulnerability now submerged by something more ferocious. This man had lasted years of the war. He'd once been ruthless by necessity; now it was instinct.

'Yes, sir.' Howard wondered in that moment exactly how Aubrey would have him killed. It wouldn't be hard. They'd be moving up the line soon enough, and then the job would be done for him. If he was impatient, he could send Howard on a reconnaissance expedition tonight. If he was vengeful, he could order him not to write the letters, and then have him court-martialled for disobeying a direct order. He'd be executed the day after tomorrow at dawn.

It would all stop.

Howard was almost tempted. Why drag it out? The outcome was unavoidable; Aubrey's jealousy could only hasten the inevitable.

He stepped towards the officer and said in a low voice that he hoped the sergeant could not hear, 'I'll keep writing, and you can decide if you post them or not. Every man must answer to his own conscience, sir, but I won't abandon her. I can't.'

Aubrey looked thwarted, agitated. Then, as though he had stared at Medusa, he turned to stone. 'I shall return and be master of the farm again, you understand that, don't you, Private?'

'You might not make it back, sir.' It was almost a whisper, but the message was loud and clear.

Aubrey's nostrils flared a fraction, his pupils blackened. '*You* certainly won't, Private.'

'Yes, sir, I agree.' Howard was standing to attention, but somehow his bones slackened. He didn't want to die. Not at the root of him. He wished it was all different. Their generation had been cheated and used.

'Why are you here, Private? What made you come?' Major Owens seemed openly gripped. Howard knew he must be a puzzle to such a man, the sort of man who lived an unhesitant, unquestioning life. The thought of such obedience sickened him. It was that blindness that had landed them all here. His voice couldn't quite mask his contempt; he wasn't sure he wanted it to.

'To do my duty, sir.'

'At last.'

'I suppose I just had to find the thing worth fighting for.'

'Get out.'

Howard knew that any letters he wrote to Vivian would never be posted. The sergeant would take great pleasure in reading them, rolling in their tender intimacy, their fiery neediness. He'd take greater pleasure still in flattening, annihilating both things by withholding them from the post. If he was as vindictive as they said, he'd also show them to Aubrey. The letters would become vicious weapons. Owens would be humiliated, hurt; Vivian would be at risk. Howard tried to come up with a plan as to how else he could get his letters to her. He considered asking another soldier to conceal them in a note to their wife or sweetheart, but everyone's post was censored and the secreted letters would be discovered. He didn't want to get anyone else into trouble. He thought about writing in some sort of code and sending them to his mother, asking her to pass them on, but a code would arouse suspicion. Anything that could be written in a way that would pass censorship would have no meaning; anything worth saying could not be said through his mother. No one was allowed leave at the moment, as able fighting men were so thin on the ground, so he couldn't ask one of the lads to post a letter in Blighty. It wasn't clear what he could do.

He wrote anyway. Since he and Vivian had become lovers his inherent, essential craving to write had been firmly re-established. His thoughts were once again effluent and vivid. Now she, along with his writing, helped him make sense of the world, allowed him to escape it. Every night, like the other men, he wrote letters, but instead of handing them over to be edited, approved, then posted, he tied them in a bundle and kept them in a Fortnum and Mason tea tin. He'd bought the empty tin off another man; he'd paid six times what it was worth full, but it was rat proof and therefore priceless to him.

He knew he could not get letters to her but he thought she'd work out why. She must understand by now that he was under Aubrey's command; she had to be aware of censorship, didn't she? He expected that she'd write to him anyway. That she'd see the vital importance of keeping connected, that she'd offer him some succour and delight in this brutal nightmare, was an absolute belief of his. He understood her, she understood him. They were in love. She would write. The military couldn't stop her letters coming to him. They wouldn't be stifled.

Days and nights went by; the shelling and shooting and sheer hell of it continued incessantly. All around him was noise and chaos, except when the post was delivered. Then it was as though a cease-fire had been called. Silence fell, the men smiled, breathing in home and humanity for a few snatched minutes. Howard received letters from his mother, from Basil Clarke and even from Miss Hawkins, his old school teacher. His mother told him that the weather had broken at home; autumn was upon them. She mentioned what she was planting, painting, knitting; her letters seemed remote, constrained. He hoped there were enough glorious, shimmering autumn days in Blackwell – the sort where every leaf and blade of grass seemed to gleam with beauty – to make it impossible for her to believe that here, only miles off the coast of England, men were being slain ruthlessly, their poor disfigured bodies heaped together and crowded in ghastly indiscriminate common graves. She was not the sort to find any comfort in the fact that thousands of German men were lying in the same way. It just added to the senselessness. Her letters did not scold or harangue; they both knew such a thing would be worse than pointless now. It seemed as though she'd accepted his certain death as much as he had.

Miss Hawkins wrote to tell him she was glad he'd found the right path at last; that he'd *seen sense and picked up a gun*. She wrote that the village was proud of him. He doubted they were. Perhaps they hated him a little less now, but he couldn't imagine them hanging out the bunting because he'd changed his mind about whether he should kill men or not. Still, he appreciated her effort in writing to him, and he knew his mother's position in the village would be more tenable now.

Basil Clarke's letter was interesting, informative. Clarke was out in the thick of it again, but with the proper paperwork now, no longer an outlaw; something of a celebrity actually. *Not able to tell it as it is, of course*, he commented wryly. Howard couldn't imagine that their paths would ever cross again.

He heard nothing from Vivian. Not a line. Not a word. Still, he continued to write to her and stored the letters in his tea tin.

It became increasingly difficult to write into the abyss of taciturnity. It was impossible not to fear that it was simply another senseless act in an ocean of futility.

# SEPTEMBER 1918

# 45

WHEN SHE'D KISSED him, he'd smelt perfect. There was no other way to describe it, because he did not smell like anything other than him. Skin, his. Warmth, his. Which was perfect. A hint of sex and promise. The promise of kindness, a better path. His lips were always warm and pliable. Her tongue slipped between his teeth, a slight scrape. Another as she felt his bristles brush against her face. Every time she'd kissed him, she'd felt a growing lump in her chest, like a snowball or a wave, gathering momentum, threatening to overpower her. She'd sometimes wonder how she'd manage to get through the kiss. Would she explode with the joy of it? With longing and exhilaration mashed up in one unfathomable chaos?

This, she was almost sure, was what it had been like to kiss Howard Henderson, but it was becoming harder and harder to be sure.

His kisses were fading. As was his voice, his face. She didn't have a photograph. Why hadn't they thought to have one done in London? Because she thought she'd had longer. Forever. People talked about remembering the tone of their loved one's laugh, the exact hue of their eyes, their smile, the spaces between their freckles. She couldn't, not honestly. All she could remember was how he had made her feel. Safe. Better. They'd had a matter of days together, and now it was two years apart. It wasn't reasonable. Pinned to the wall there was a calendar. Basic, bought from Walker's store; no pictures, just dates, numbers. Pictures of idyllic scenes or kittens would infuriate her. Insult him. Next to it, a stub of pencil held in place with a tack and a piece of string. She crossed off another day. Women up and down the country, across Europe, throughout the world, were doing the same thing, she was sure, but her loneliness was not sated by the thought, nor aggravated. Her loneliness was too big to be affected by outside circumstances, even the knowledge that her position was a common one.

She just missed him.

She missed how she was his focus, how he was hers. How he concentrated on what she thought, felt. She grew when she was with him. She missed seeing the bulk of him out in the fields, bending and toiling, nurturing crops, mending roofs and fences, feeding and cleaning animals. The earthy vitality of him. She was so sure that was what men ought to do – grow, build, create. He'd been right: mankind could do more than spoil. Better. She missed seeing his gentle kindness towards Timmy Durham and his loving playfulness with Mabel. She longed for the joy of him.

Vivian thought back to when Nathaniel Thorpe had disappeared, abruptly and troublesomely, from her life. Then, she had been astounded to see how transitory desire could be. She'd been full of need and want for him, but almost overnight that had all vanished. With Howard, the opposite was true. The craving and wanting intensified. She had no room for small emotions such as humiliation, anger or shock. On the most clear, basic and under-standable level his leaving was all that mattered. Would he stay safe? Would he come back? Him not being with her was the biggest disaster she could comprehend. On another, more complex plain, it didn't matter at all. It didn't change anything. She still loved him just as much as if he was standing right by her side. The air was saturated with longing. It was all she breathed in.

Now he was gone, she at last understood what this war was. His words could not teach her but his absence had.

War was suffering. Agony. Death might at any moment so easily take him. The thought made her want to vomit. So that she could find air, she brought to mind every moment she had spent with him. Extraordinary. Bright. Loving mostly. Sometimes angry or unsure. Always complicated and emotional. Sometimes there had been a feeling of melancholy staining them. They knew they were stealing. He was stealing another man's wife. She was stealing happiness. They were both stealing from the war effort. That was how it seemed. He had to go. Or stop. Stop loving her. No, that was the one thing he couldn't do.

He was alive still. That was all she knew. Enid received letters and had enough charity in her to tell Vivian as much, although nothing more. Enid could not forgive Vivian; she lived in utter and perpetual horror of another letter from the War Office. She was a mother; when she looked at Howard, she didn't see a lofty, dark, strong man, at least not that alone. She was aware that he was grown, but she was also terminally aware of the boy she'd pushed, impelled into the world, the toddler whose chubby hand she held as he took his first inexact steps, the cheeky schoolboy who didn't settle to lessons, the handsome fourteen-year-old who set off alone to London and the excited, proud young man who held her arm as he led her to a box in the theatre to see the play he'd penned. She wanted to protect them all. All her Howards. Her only son. She couldn't forgive Vivian for endangering any version of him.

Vivian understood; she hated herself for her part in Howard's joining up just as fiercely as Enid did. She'd tried to explain as much but Enid had become a different woman since Howard had left. She'd hardened, bricked up her heart. Vivian wondered whether Enid felt guilt too. She had told her boys that it was all theirs if they wanted it, the world and what it had to offer, if only they were brave enough to reach for it. It wasn't true. This world had nothing to offer them except pain. Enid must feel cheated. Worse, she probably felt shame that she'd misled her sons. Misguided them. Let them down.

Vivian knew that Enid had put pressure on Howard to give her up. Stop the affair. Did she berate herself about that? She'd told him to leave Vivian alone because she'd feared for him. She had been trying to protect him, but now she must wish she'd turned a blind eye to their affair. She had to be asking herself whether, if she had done so, might he have stayed?

Vivian had only been a mother for three years, but she was sure that a mother's lot was to blame herself, to accept culpability and fault. However, the stark truth was that Howard no longer cared whether he was living up to his mother's expectations or not. Vivian was all. She knew it and felt the responsibility. Enid's small, symmetrical face seemed sunken, her sharp, intelligent eyes accusatory. Vivian missed the smile that had danced. They could not recapture their easy intimacy. She missed that too. She was very alone.

She continued to visit Enid regularly, finding various, ever more insubstantial pretexts, although there was no sign that her visits were welcome.

'Mabel has chickenpox, I can't get her to stop scratching. What would you advise?'

'Mittens to stop her scratching and warm baths with oatmeal to ease the itching.' The door barely ajar. Slammed shut.

'I'm organising a fund-raiser, a concert. I wondered whether you'd play the piano?'

Mouth tightening, eyes contracting a fraction. 'Yes. Ditty or classical?'

'Classical, I think.'

'Fine.' The word a sigh.

'I wonder could I have the recipe for your fig pudding. Mabel simply adores it.'

'I'll write it out and give it to Mrs Rosebend.' The air wet with something sour. Trust lost.

Enid's replies were always succinct, helpful, polite. The politeness bit Vivian; it was a poor substitute for friendship. Even in bad weather, Enid kept her at the door and wouldn't invite her to join her at the hearth. Over her shoulder Vivian saw the coal shift in the grate; the rocks, suffused with hot illumination, were mesmerising. The fire needed a poke, or maybe a log. Vivian missed the winters of 1914 and 1915. Back then, when it had grown dark outside, Enid would put on a light and draw the curtains and they'd sit together complete and cosy. No desire to move, sometimes no need to talk. Now, their silences were spiky. Raw. Vivian lived in tight dread that Enid would move away from Blackwell; it sat, a knot in her belly. Then she would be doomed to a lifetime of scanning the casualty lists for information. Lists that were tardy. Unreliable.

On every visit Vivian squared her shoulders and asked if there was news from him. Enid coolly, carefully might admit, 'He's seen some action,' or 'They've been sent to the reserve for a day or two, to rest.' Once she said, 'He cut his hand mending barbed wire. He said his tin hat was blown off.' Vivian had visibly paled, swayed and asked if she could sit down. Enid, forced to recognise that they shared the same desperate desire, fetched a glass of water and resisted scowling. Seeing the most minute thawing, Vivian grasped the opportunity.

'Does he ever mention me?' Gulping the water. Dribbles down her chin. Her eyes flashing, flickering almost instantaneously between hope and despair.

'Never,' Enid replied. It sounded like a groan of pain.

Vivian knew that however angry Enid was with her, she would not go against her son's wishes; if he wanted his mother to pass on a message, she would do so.

Pity and perhaps the trace of the attachment once shared caused

Enid to add, 'His letters are heavily censored. Far more than Michael's ever were.'

'Do you think that means things are getting worse?'

'I don't know what to think. Half of his news is scoured out with a heavy black pen. I'm left with little more than a list of what he's eaten, descriptions of the weather.' Vivian had wanted to ask what the weather was like, although she knew really. Dreadful. Aubrey told her that much. She wanted to ask if she could see the letters. Touch something he'd touched. She didn't dare, and Enid didn't offer. If he ever got leave, he didn't spend it in Blackwell.

His desertion was complete, but not accepted.

Vivian sat down at her writing desk and began another letter. She wondered how many she had sent now. It must be around a hundred, yet she had only ever received one from him. The one that said, *You know I couldn't have done anything other.* She'd thought about that sentence for hours; examined it for its true meaning, for nuance, for connotation, hints and explanations. Hours per word she must have spent pondering it. She believed that the sentence acknowledged their connection, even revered it. *You know.* Those words admitted that they had an unprecedented intimacy, but they also foreshadowed disaster and miscalculation. She did not want to admit to understanding if that meant she had to understand why he had gone. That she had, after all, forced him away. *I couldn't have done anything other.* Those words suggested that he had weighed up the situation, considered the alternatives and rejected them. He would not stay on Aubrey's land, with Aubrey's wife and child, while Aubrey fought the war Howard loathed. How could she have predicted such moral niceties? Why couldn't he have been content to enjoy her, feel grateful for their luck in finding one another when the whole world seemed lost? Why did he feel the need to sacrifice himself? She sighed. He was right, she did know why. Howard Henderson looked at the world in his own particular way, and he could no more change his principles than she could change the tides.

The silence screamed at her. It never shut up. Her head pounded constantly. She knew she was sending her letters to the right place; she had made enquiries with the authorities, and besides, on the one occasion when she had managed to get inside Enid's cottage, she'd spotted an envelope addressed to him on the mantelpiece. It was propped behind the clock that ticked away the minutes, trying to fool them into believing time was linear. When would it all end?

She remembered the things he had told her when he never imagined he'd go out there again. Scraps of flesh, charred hands and feet, burnt heads rained out of the sky into her dreams. When she dug in the fields, she thought of the soldiers' shovels pushing into the dead bodies of the men who had fought earlier battles. She remembered his words. They were tattooed into her consciousness. He'd talked of human flesh putrefying and stinking. He'd said it was no good, that it was never any good. Whatever they did. If they got through one scrape, inevitably they'd be caught in the next. He'd told her these horror stories at her own insistence. It was torture, knowing he was in that hell.

She also felt anguish knowing that Aubrey was in the thick of it too. Guilt sat a sack of coal on her heart, because she could only feel concern, perhaps pity, but not love. So after all, Howard had been right about that. The guilt would have destroyed them if he'd stayed.

She wrote to Aubrey regularly and frequently because it was her duty, and besides she was at the mercy of illogical superstition. She'd made a deal with God that if she continued to behave as a respectable, dutiful wife then He'd keep Howard safe. Even if she couldn't have Howard, even if he no longer wanted her, his safety was paramount to her. She valued his life above her own. Why hadn't he known that? She would have given him up rather than allowed him to go to war; how could he have doubted that? Now he was out there, suffering. And she was here, alone. They could have chosen an easier path.

If she planned to write to both men, she would write to her husband first, dashing something out, desperate to savour the moments when she could luxuriate in writing to Howard.

*Dear Aubrey,*

*I hope this letter finds you well. Congratulations on your latest promotion.*

*Mabel's birthday tea party was a tremendous success. All the village children seemed to enjoy the day; no one behaved roughly, which I know was your concern. She wore a pink dress that my mother sent from London. It's rather too fine for the country but she looked really very pretty. She's grown quite tall since your last leave. I'm sure you'd find her delightful. Everyone does.*

*The rations that the government have decreed are fully adequate, thank you for asking. Besides, as you can imagine, we do rather better than most as we can supplement our diets with anything we can grow or nurture on the farm. You do not need to worry about us. Please don't.*

*I do understand that leave is ever more constrained, of course, I am sure you are doing your best to visit when you can. I agree that it makes more sense for you to spend time in Paris; if you only have three days why would you want to spend two of them travelling?*

*I pray for peace.*

*Fond wishes,*

*Vivian*

It was safest to confine matters to Mabel and the farm. She found that she started lots of new paragraphs to stretch out the length of her letters, and they had always been in the habit of signing them off, 'Fond wishes', a precedent Aubrey had set in 1914. Now, her duty dispensed, she could write to Howard with a clear conscience.

*My darling, darling Howard,*

*Mabel has turned three! Three, can you imagine! You will adore her when you see her. I promise you. Her hair is long enough to put in ribbons now; at her birthday party she wore the purple one you gave her. Do you remember? The one you stole from your mother's paintbrush jar and wrapped around the posy you brought to me the day we went to London. I know you must. One of the other little girls at the party admired the ribbon and asked for it. Mabel tried to pull it out of her hair and hand it over; she's that sort, a very loving little girl. To my shame I jumped in and said she couldn't give it away. I couldn't have stood that. I offered the other child her choice from my basket of similar trinkets. Please don't be cross with me or think me selfish. I don't have much that belongs to us. You do understand, don't you? I won't allow Mabel to wear it again. I think I'll sew it into a cardigan or something; then she can't lose it or gift it. She would give away everything we have and walk around starkers if she had the chance! I don't doubt some would say I'm bringing her up soft, but how else should a child be brought up? She kisses me all the time, literally all the time. She hugs me, rubs her cold hands on my back and squirms with delight if I tickle her tummy. She sometimes licks me. I don't really like this, but she says I'm sweet like an ice, so how can I resist! She frequently demands, 'Mummy where are my kisses?' even when we are in a shop or in church, and she won't be quiet until I kiss her. I wish you were sharing this with me.*

*When you come home I'll cover you with kisses. Literally cover you. I'll kiss you until my lips crack. Come home.*

*The rationing is pretty gruesome, but in a perverse way I rather like it, I think most women do. We want to share some of the hardship. Madness really, because we're not easing anything for you, are we? But still, I imagine you can understand the sentiment. Besides, rationing is A GOOD THING, I do know that. Some restaurants and such had been making stacks of money because of course someone can always pay for potted salmon. Disgraceful, when you think that children in Wales and Birmingham were starving! There is constant talk of the black market. I've asked Ava about it and she promises she's had nothing to do with it, although she admitted she'd sell her soul for new stockings and that I oughtn't to try to stop her. She asked after you in her last letter. She always does. So besides sugar, meat, butter, cheese and margarine are now rationed. We have cards to help everyone keep on track. We had to register at Mr Walker's. At least what we have is now quite fairly divided. We're very lucky to be on a farm and not in a city or town. It's rather wonderful to be self-sufficient. I give what we don't need to the villagers. I do it willingly, but I confess I do get an extra lift because I imagine how proud you'd be if you saw me doing so. Not only proud of the fact that I've actually produced some-thing edible but that I've produced enough to share, that sharing it is my first thought. That should appeal to your socialist sensibilities!*

*I imagine you've gathered by now that I'm feeling quite buoyant and joyful today. I am. Remember I am worth fighting for, my love. I am worth staying alive for. Come home.*

*Ever yours,*
*Vivian*

She reread the only risky phrases, *You will adore her when you see her* and *When you come home I'll cover you with kisses.* A surge of nausea and threat sluiced over her like water thrown from a bucket over a cobbled street. She didn't want to challenge God or fate or whatever with any sort of arrogance or certainty. She didn't want them to feel the need to teach her a lesson. Yet she could not write *if*. Risk killing him with ill-wishing. It was all supersti-tion and unscientific, but she dared not dismiss anything. She clung. She lived in absolute terror, wondering how they had endured it. The women whose men had been there for years. Were there such women, or did the men all die too soon?

She never chastised him for not writing.

# 46

IT WAS RUMOURED by the top brass that even Field Marshal
Douglas Haig had reservations about carrying out the offensive
in Epehy on 18th September 1918. The British losses that year
had been beyond comprehension; how much more could they
take? The tally numbed some men and sent others into a state of
mania. Howard wondered about the word 'casualty'. It was insulting;
there was nothing casual about it. Sometimes that sort of thing
made him furious. Who had decided that was the correct term?
It made him want to rip off heads, beat people, scream, kick,
punch with anger, the pacifist in him well and truly obliterated.
Other times he could see the temptation to drop into the sanitised
word, let it catch him. It seemed calming. Almost. Something near
peaceful, he supposed. He had witnessed men blown apart – one
minute they were there, the next gone – and he'd seen men shot,
their bodies slumping into death in an instant. There was something dismissive about these fast deaths, something that might
allow those who had never set foot on a battlefield to call them
casualties. It wasn't the correct word for the injured, though. The
tortured. The men who screamed in agony, those who had lost
their faces, their legs, their hands, which in fact meant they had
lost the chance to sit with their children without scaring them, lost
the ability to dance, run or – often – work, lost their chance to

touch their women's breasts or thighs. These consequences were not casual, or swift; they were brutal, perpetual.

He began to imagine that at night, if he stayed still and quiet enough, he would surely hear the wives, mothers, sweethearts and children howling from across the Channel, contesting the casualties. Had the generals heard them too? Was that why there was for the first time a hint of caution, the suggestion that the men needed to rest? If so, it didn't last. Haig had a change of mind when news arrived of the British Third Army's victory at the Battle of Havrincourt on the 13th. It was in fact a modest breakthrough, but it was something. Haig thought it was worth exploiting the upturn in the Allies' morale, the assumed plunge in that of the enemy's. He approved General Rawlinson's plan to clear German outpost positions on the high ground. They had to go on. Forward, forward, always forward. There was no going back now.

'What will we have?' Lieutenant Colonel Owens asked his brigadier general.

'Very few tanks can be provided for the attack.' The brigadier general threw out a glance that assumed acceptance; he had no time or patience for debate. 'So artillery will have to be relied upon to prepare the way, you understand.'

'Yes, sir.' In fact Lieutenant Colonel Aubrey Owens didn't understand much nowadays. It wasn't that he was questioning the decisions of his seniors – no, not at all; that way anarchy lay – it was more that he was wondering what the decisions were based upon. He'd had a little time to reflect since his spell in the hospital. He'd been shot right through the leg in 1917 – damned lucky, clean wound, didn't catch an infection. Yes, damned lucky. You had to believe so. Whilst he lay in the narrow bed surrounded by men who hadn't been so lucky and pretty nurses who really should never have had to see the things they saw every day, he found that his mind had started to cloud. One would expect clarity once one was away from the constant bombardment, the heat of the battle, but he'd been surprised to find the opposite. Confusion set in.

He'd started to wonder why he'd been so keen to join up – he couldn't quite recall – and he couldn't help but deliberate on when it might all end. For him and for everyone. Would that be the same time? Might he survive? He rather thought he would. He'd been lucky so far, but he didn't understand why. Why was the man next to him taken but not him? Time after time. Everyone had their own beliefs out here. Aubrey had been saved. He was sure he was being saved for something. He just didn't know what.

'In the interests of surprise, we will not be able to provide a preliminary bombardment. Instead, one thousand four hundred and eighty-eight guns will fire a concentration of shots at the operation's zero hour and then support the infantry with a creeping barrage. Three hundred machine guns will also be made available. Our objective consists of a tightly fortified zone, roughly three miles deep and twenty miles long. It's supported by secondary trenches and various strong points.' The brigadier general slapped a wooden ruler on the map that lay unfurled on the desk, indicating the trenches and strongholds; the ruler left an indent in the paper. Aubrey gave a sharp nod. He accepted the plan for what it was. He'd been in the field now for years, and one foot in front of the other was the only answer.

He saluted. 'Understood, sir.'

The night before a battle was interminable. The divisions lined up in the trenches that had been dug by sappers, silent except for the hard breathing of men, the shuffle of heavy boots and the occasional clink of bayonets. Every man and boy was shoving down the dread and panic in his head and soul, trying to get a grip on horrendously strained nerves. Howard had trained himself not to think about the big things the night before a battle. He did not write letters to Vivian or his mother; he did not take communion or question God or the generals, as many of the men did. He couldn't find the energy the night before he was expected to kill or be killed; he didn't see the point. Instead, he focused on the moment he was in. He wallowed in the miserable reality of his physicality.

In the summer, he'd felt hot and heavy, his neck and cheeks often scorched by the sun. The smells were worse then. Bodies, alive and dead, reeked to high heaven, the rats got fatter, slower, more audacious, his feet swelled inside his boots, pushing painfully against the hard leather. The French sun was not so ferocious in September; it was pleasant. He'd spent a lot of the day with his eyes closed and his head turned towards the warmth, simply enjoying what he could. Now the sun had slipped below the horizon, dusk had brought a chill and fat spots of rain fell spasmodically, threatening a downpour before morning. The moon came up, loud and silver, but kept dipping behind lurking clouds. The young boys were shivering; Howard knew it was terror more than temperature. He offered to make some Bovril. As he waited for the water to boil on the stove, he tried to ignore the dark rumbling and the intermittent flashes in the sky. He wished it was a storm. He didn't wonder whether it was Allied or enemy shelling; it hardly mattered. He looked at his hands, scratched and cut, his stubby, grubby fingernails; he thought about the ache in his back and thighs – two years of crouching had taken a toll; he picked off lice from the seams of his jacket and threw them on the flame of the stove.

The lads were glad of the Bovril. Grateful to have something to do for a few minutes.

'It does you good, something hot inside you,' he commented. It was the sort of illusory remark that they made to one another. As though anything did any good.

The night eventually became pitch black and then the rain that had threatened materialised. The downpour was tough, relentless.

They slept with their kit on their back and tin hats on their heads, their feet in puddles. Howard could only see other men as shadows.

'Steady, lads,' said the young lieutenants, unsure but determined not to show it. Their tone suggesting camaraderie, unity.

'Hold it down,' hissed Sergeant Bowler in response to one man coughing and another whispering to a mate. His tone was considerably less friendly. Lieutenant Colonel Owens struck a match from time to time, to glance at his wristwatch, which was synchronised to those of the gunners.

Howard heard the signal at 5.20 a.m. It was still dark.

The dawn was shattered by the clamour and turmoil of the explosions and the now-familiar long screech of the shells rushing through the air. Hours of silence collapsed into a roar of fire and rage as the artillery erupted with an enormous violence. Howard and his regiment listened and waited. They were not up and over first. It was to be a slow onslaught, a creeping barrage. This command had been passed on in the guise of a strategy. Howard feared it was more to do with lack of resources than tactics, but he couldn't think about that now. A slow onslaught sounded perilous, but then it was no more or less exposed than all the other suicidal missions they had embarked upon. They were lucky they weren't first out, that was all that was worth thinking about. Some other poor bugger was taking the brunt. Funny world when all you had to be happy about was that someone was dead before you were.

They waited for the signal that the infantry advance was to begin. Howard's teeth jangled; his heart banged so fiercely he thought it was going to explode inside him. It was torture. They were animals: baited bears, fighting cocks, savage dogs. Then, at last – because yes, by now he wanted it – the watch hands pointed to the second that had been agreed.

'Time!' The company officer blew his whistle. An abrupt close-range racket broke out as trench spades were slung to rifle barrels and men equipped with hand grenades made their rush forward.

They scurried out of the trench, carelessly standing on the fingers and shoulders of pals as they scrambled up and over. When he could at last lift his head above the shattered parapets and claw his way out of the trench, Howard witnessed what he'd known he would – carnage. He'd seen too many dead bodies to recoil. It was his lack of response that was most repulsive now. However, the wounded still affected him. Their wailing was sickening, because each man's pain was fresh to that man, even if the generals had become used.

He clambered to his feet and opened his mouth to let out a ferocious, blood-curdling yell, an ancient primitive battle cry. His instincts and training dominated and he began to run through the mud and the rain. Fast, fast, fast. Arm extended, gun in hand, finger on trigger. Bang, bang. Through them – the dead, the dying, the killers, those he would kill – firing blindly forward as ordered.

The thing he had come to understand about battle was that when you were in the thick of it, it was impossible to know what was going on. The smoke from shell and gunfire was often impregnable, a dense black widow's veil. Sometimes, like today, weather obscured vision too, but besides that, the truth was that no man could see beyond his immediate neighbourhood because no man was omnipresent or omnipotent. Each soldier's war took place within a radius of a few yards.

Confusion ensued. The ground was churned up by shells and it was easy to slip, trip, fall, which was disastrous. Run, run, run. Howard pushed forward, losing track of time; minutes charging through gunfire and explosions had no relevance to time that might be spent doing ordinary things. His stride stretched, his muscles reached, his lungs overextended. Forward. Run. He sensed he was passing some men, that he was behind others. He knew he ought to stay in formation, but black smoke swirled all about. The uniforms were the same colour as the mud; it was hard to distinguish anything as much as ten yards about. Howard wondered

how it was possible that anyone might be left alive in this quag-
mire, but he knew they would be. His experience had shown that
people hung on and on, long past any expected level of endurance;
stamina exceeded dignity, morality and credibility.

Up ahead there was a rattle of machine guns, flashes of light
that might kill him. He wasn't sure exactly where they came from
– holes and hillocks, he supposed. He had sometimes wondered
whether his death would come via an anonymous shot, a swift
shell, or would it be drawn out, a gangrenous infection? He didn't
care at this moment. He could not indulge in speculation; he had
to stay in the minute. Men to his left and right started to drop
to the ground. This had happened to him in other battles; he'd
learnt not to waste unnecessary time. A glance one way confirmed
one dead, couldn't say who. A glance the other saw Blake injured
beyond help, his intestines spilling out on to the ground. Once,
Howard had come across a man in battle with just the same
injuries and had helped him the only way he knew how, by
putting a bullet in his head. It would be a mercy to do the same
again; no one would know in this confusion. However, Blake
didn't ask for it; he was screaming for his mammy, so Howard
passed on. There wasn't a right answer.

He dropped to his knees for another man, keeping his head
low. He recognised the young private, Gibbs. He was aged no
more than nineteen years old and was fresh to France, having just
completed his training in the summer. He'd been shot in the
femur and repeatedly cried out, 'Fuck, fuck, fuck.' He grabbed the
collar of Howard's jacket and pulled himself into a semi-sitting
position. Keeping his eyes trained on Howard, not looking at his
wound, he yelled, 'Have I lost my leg, have I lost my fucking leg?'
His voice hoarse with fear and panic; his spittle showered Howard's
face.

'Not yet.' Howard didn't stop to think whether he could have
been more comforting. He found Gibbs's field dressing and

hurriedly tied a tourniquet, then scrabbled in his bag, searching for water. 'The RMO will be along soon,' he muttered. They both knew it wasn't true. Medical assistance would be hours away. He looked about for a crater to drag Gibbs into for protection and weighed up the wisdom of doing so. Moving him would almost certainly cause the broken bones to tear and rip the muscles inside the leg; there was the possibility of hitting an artery, which might lead to wound-shock and the swift and enormous loss of blood. If he left him here, the stretcher-bearers would find him eventually, put on a splint; they might save the leg and the man. At that moment, another shot took Gibbs. A small, clean black hole between the eyes. Howard picked up his rifle and carried on.

The land was open and he ran on until he was upon another line of trenches. They were already battered and baggy, littered with fragments of wire, piles of loose stones and sections of steel. The English soldiers who had slept in these last night must be far up the advancing line by now. Or dead. He rested for just minutes and then scrambled up and over again. He had managed five or ten more yards in the rain and the blackness, mud spewing up into his face, his mouth and nostrils, when he fell down a deep crater.

He slid on his back, feet first, and landed roughly on something soft. It took him a moment to register that his fall had been broken by two bodies. He was relieved not to recognise either man, especially as his right boot had gone into the gut of one of them; innards, fleshy and wet, clung to his ankle. Disorientated, Howard shook his head. The noise was still deafening and the crater was dense with darkness; he couldn't see much at all. He considered how the men's deaths had occurred. Was he at risk? Instantly he surmised that one of them, the one he'd put his foot through, had probably caught a shell up top and the second had dragged him into the crater. Perhaps they were friends, even brothers. He thought as much because moving a man with his belly ripped wide open – stomach, colon, intestines slopping about, exposed, red and raw – was an act of devotion, not a tactic. The man who had attempted the rescue had been shot in the chest; he had his own gun in his hand. Howard felt fear lick his soul. Slowly he turned to look for the assailant. With effort, he could just about make out a dead German, slumped at the opposite side of the crater. He had been shot in the head; the blood from what was left of his face was still flowing. If Howard touched him, he imagined the body would still be warm.

'I got him,' gasped a voice out of the darkness. Howard turned again, peering this time in the direction of the voice. Sergeant Bowler was lying on the ground.

'Are you injured, sir?' he asked, moving speedily to assist.

'Shoulder,' the sergeant muttered resentfully through gritted teeth.

Howard examined the shoulder and knew the wound was bad; the sergeant was losing a lot of blood. For the second time in only a matter of minutes, he found himself searching a man's kit for the waterproof packet of field dressing and patching up as best he could. The anger that was with him most of the time surged through his body in a wild and unexpected wave, making him want to roar. He couldn't patch any fucking thing up. He bit on his tongue and held in the roar. It made no sense to lose it now. He didn't even like the sergeant.

'How's yours?' Howard didn't comprehend at first, but he followed the man's shaky glance. A pool of blood was seeping through his own uniform, covering it like ink on blotting paper, just above his hip. He had not felt the bullet nip the side of his body – adrenalin had protected him – but on noticing the wound, pain seared up his side. It was the first bullet he'd taken. His initial response was shock, then amusement at being shocked. Hadn't he always expected this? He undid his jacket to examine the damage.

'Flesh wound, sir.' He let out a deep breath, instinctively relieved.

He wondered whether he had the energy to apply gauze. Was it worth it? Realising that he had nothing better to do, he did apply the gauze to stem the blood flow. Then he drank some water, passing his flask to the sergeant, although he must have had his own.

Bowler drank too and then barked, 'Fasten your jacket, Private. We're fighting a war, not at a bloody pub.' Howard followed orders and wondered how long he might have to stay in the crater with this man; the three dead bodies caused him less offence.

The shelling and gunfire continued to roar around them. Intermittently, the earth swayed like a cradle; rocks and dirt showered into the crater. Conscious that his wound was not critical, Howard knew that he'd have to move out, carry on. He could hold a gun and shoot it, so his country needed him to kill someone. If he stayed put, there was a danger that he'd be court-martialled. Being shot at dawn was no longer the thing he considered the worst option; however, he didn't want to give Sergeant Bowler the satisfaction. The man had been after his blood for ever, ever since he intercepted his letter to Vivian.

He crawled to the edge of the crater. The way that lay between him and the objective seemed overwhelming. The ground was beleaguered with dead bodies and pockmarked by deep shell holes. It was sliced and cross-sliced by old trenches that had been originally dug by the Allies but were now held by the enemy, tangled with barbed wire and spotted with machine guns. Howard felt another overwhelming surge of fury. This one was almost welcome; it overrode the stabs of pain from his injury. To cross even fifty yards of such territory in the squall of the enemy's fire would be a catastrophic ordeal; it was a far greater task than that of rushing from one trench to another. The German guns continued to belch out huge numbers of weighty shells. They systematically raked the ground, desperately trying to make the English yield the position they had acquired. Howard saw men fall backwards and forwards, others blown to nothing, but, tenacious, the soldiers would not retreat. They would not crawl away from their dead and wounded.

He picked up his rifle again and started to crawl on his belly up and out of the crater.

'I'll send help to you,' he told the sergeant. They both knew that by now, many of the trenches that had formerly been neat and effective would be battered beyond recognition. The officers would be facing difficulty in getting up supplies; communication and the movement of medical assistance or ammunition would all be encumbered for many hours to come. The first objective was not aid; it was that the men held on and consolidated their hard-won positions.

Howard looked out and saw little other than smoky shadows, dense and dire. From his low position he could just about discern some English soldiers continuing the advance. One or two of the wounded were crawling without a focus or even recognition of where they were supposed to be heading. He saw it before they did.

'Get down, get down, take cover!' he yelled. Reflexively, he leapt out of the crater and started to run towards the English soldiers. He pulled on their arms, frantically trying to drag them back down into the crater. Confused, they struggled with him, scared of appearing to retreat, unsure of his advice.

'Unhand me, man!' Howard recognised the voice a fraction of a moment before he caught the man's face. Aubrey.

The blast shook the ground, like a cat shaking a mouse. Long arms of flame leapt from the shattered earth; savage, merciless heat battered them. Some of them were blown to bits, body parts and flesh raining down. Others were alight, their clothes blazing as they yelled and flailed in agony; men made into living torches for a second or two before they were cinders. Ashes to ashes. Howard smelt flesh burning and realised it was his own. The length of his left leg was on fire. He fell to the floor and rolled in the mud, beating the flames with his hands, hardly noting his palms scorching. If he'd been just a foot further to the left, he would have been totally incinerated. Men writhed in agony, thrashing like fish on a quayside. With smoking hair and limbs, blackened and burnt bodies, those who could walk fell back, forsaking the filthy ground where their dead lay.

Still firing potshots, flinging grenades if they could, the men ran to the trenches that Howard had scrambled through earlier, the same trenches some of them had set off from several bloody hours previously.

# 47

'YOU'VE COARSENED.'

'How lovely to see you, Mother.'

'Is it your nose? Your lips? Are you drinking?'

'No.' Yes. Yes, she drank now. Enough to make life's sharpness a little less nasty. No more than other women who waited for their loves to return, but more than her mother would deem appropriate.

Mrs Foster held out a slender arm, indicating that Vivian ought to help her from the automobile, although in fact she was perfectly sprightly and in no real need of any physical assistance; clearly she missed the services of a driver or a butler. All that that went with and all that it meant. She cast a glance up at the house, her eyes narrowing a fraction. She cast another around the neat hall and tidy drawing room. She didn't say anything; she didn't need to. The slight tightening of her lips, the almost imperceptible rise of her eyebrows, effectively conveyed disappointment.

Babe, who strutted through the house as though she had tenancy, was less tactful. 'I'd expected rather better,' she declared. Vivian noticed she had a slight lisp; she didn't enunciate her 'th' sound absolutely correctly. She could only imagine how this must irritate Mother.

'Barbara, you must remember that Aubrey also has a London

home. There's a war on; people everywhere are compromising. Even the very best sort.'

'Aubrey is a decorated officer of senior rank,' added Toby with a proud jut of his chin.

'We have a lot to be thankful for,' concluded Mrs Foster shortly.

'Tea, anyone?' asked Vivian. She already feared it would be the longest week of the war.

Toby was unrecognisable, inches taller than any of the women, and in uniform. It had been his call-up that had finally precipitated a Foster family visit to Blackwell. He, quite surprisingly, had insisted that he'd like to see his sister before he went to France. Mrs Foster couldn't bear an extra unnecessary moment away from her boy – who was her firm favourite by a furlong now that he'd grown so tall and splendid and since Vivian had proved to be such a nuisance – and so had insisted that she and Babe come along too. She did not covet Babe's company in the same way she did her son's, but she could not leave her in London with Mr Foster, he was not a reliable chaperone; far too preoccupied with war business to give a young girl of a certain age the proper amount of attention. As Vivian had predicted, Susan and Barbara had been brought up on a strict, short leash following her own indiscretion, which snapped taut at the first hint of opportunity for misdemeanour. Perhaps Babe knew that Vivian was the reason for her restricted youth and that was why she behaved so rudely. Or perhaps she was simply a beast by nature.

They settled in the parlour. A huge fire was burning in the hearth and the tea was brewing in the sterling silver hand-chased teapot, which usually only came out at Christmas. Vivian busied herself. She made work of lifting the lid off, squinting in, swirling the hot water and leaves before she poured.

'The house Susan is to live in is very much more lovely than this,' pronounced Babe deliberately. Susan was to marry a fifty-one-year-old viscount. Vivian had missed the announcement in

*The Times*, so the first she'd heard of the upcoming nuptials was via Ava, who'd sent a telegram. It read: *Everyone is thrilled for her stop No one is talking about his gonorrhoea stop*. Mrs Foster's letter arrived a week later; it was true, she didn't mention his gonorrhoea, or the thirty-one-year age gap, come to that. To think Vivian had once been naïve enough to believe her sister had smaller dreams than her own, or no dreams at all. She had thought Susan was simply content, which now seemed a wonderful and enviable thing to be. The engagement showed she had not been content but she did understand compromise. It was easy to mistake the two.

Vivian imagined the courtship. No doubt Susan always stayed up late in the viscount's company but was never the last to leave the party. She probably played cards and dominoes but never won at either; she'd take her defeat gracefully, praising his superior skills. Likely as not, she confined her conversation with him to hunting, fishing, dancing and music halls; she would not talk about the war. Unless things had changed drastically, she didn't have opinions on books or politics that she needed to suppress. However, whatever the viscount chose to discuss she would endeavour to give a good impression of being absorbed. Mrs Foster must be feeling triumphant.

Babe sighed quietly, barely hiding the fact that she was already bored and could not imagine anything more tortuous than a week in Blackwell. Then, when she realised that all eyes were on her, she tilted her head in a way that suggested a practised feminine patience and resignation. It was a shame. Mrs Rosebend had done her best to prepare the house. They had aired the spare bedrooms, checked the sheets for moth holes and patched where necessary. They'd been saving food coupons for weeks so that they could offer decent teas and suppers. Vivian was wearing a linen frock that she hadn't worn since she left London.

'Susan has two sweet little puppies,' Babe commented. 'The lord gave them to her.'

'The actual Lord?' Vivian asked, showing incredulity and flicking her eyes skyward.

'Don't be silly. You know who I mean. Viscount Lindup insists we use the less formal title of lord. After all, we're almost family.' Vivian didn't bother to ask what breed had been gifted. She feared some sort of silly, small dog, Pekinese rather than spaniels. Instead she stared at her baby sister and tried to find a trace of the dear child she remembered. 'Have they set a date?' she asked politely.

'Spring 1919.' Mrs Foster looked distracted and concerned. Setting dates for anything, looking too far ahead, seemed impertinent and unwise. Now that Toby was going to war, Mrs Foster had joined the ranks of women who could not quite envisage a spring next year. Springtime seemed the season most at odds with war. It was about birth, buds and beginnings. Men dying in the spring seemed more brutal than men dying in any other season.

'I am to be a bridesmaid,' added Babe. 'His niece is going to be the matron of honour.' She looked at Vivian to see if her arrow had hit the mark.

Vivian didn't expect a role in the wedding party for herself – she knew her family kept her as inconspicuous as possible, even now – but she was determined Mabel wouldn't be snubbed. 'Mabel will be a flower girl.' Her voice rose at the end of the sentence, which was a nuisance; she didn't want to ask a question. Her mother looked blank, as though the thought had never occurred to her. 'Aubrey will expect it,' added Vivian. She hated herself for collapsing back into the role of powerless daughter, whose only weight was to lever her husband's authority. Despite running the farm, managing the indoor and outdoor staff and being a mother, in Mrs Foster's company Vivian felt that she was without clout.

Dinner was not an unqualified success. A lot of the time Mrs Foster seemed unsure as to what she was eating.

'The bread is a rather funny colour.'

'It's made from cornflour, Mother.'

'It's terribly patriotic to eat corn,' commented Toby. He reached for another piece to demonstrate his enthusiasm, and Vivian thought that not every penny of his education had been wasted after all; he was a polite boy.

'And the soup is?'

'Lentil.'

Eyebrows brushing the hairline. 'No meat?'

'Trout. A local boy caught it this morning,' Vivian explained.

'Isn't it marvellous the things they come up with? What will they think of next?' commented Mrs Foster, her words considerably more enthusiastic than her expression. Vivian was entirely certain Timmy Durham had not invented fishing for trout, but she bit her tongue.

It was a relief when the clock finally chimed ten, late enough to retire without causing offence. In the privacy of her bedroom, Vivian took off her creased frock. Linen was dreadful. Why anyone bothered with it she did not know. She poured cool water from the jug into the bowl and plunged her wrists into it, wondering how she'd get through the week.

Mrs Foster and Babe had no interest in the farm.

'None of the animals are babies,' sighed Babe. 'They are barely worth looking at.' Vivian remembered thinking something similar herself so managed to suppress her irritation. The women sat inside, burning coal and making demands on Mrs Rosebend and the housemaid. Toby took more pleasure from the land and the village. The combination of his uniform and his youth meant that when he took a stroll, numerous admiring and approving glances were thrown his way. Several older men offered to buy him a drink if he had time to visit the tavern. Mabel, habitually deprived of male company, was fascinated by him. She trailed around after her uncle, too shy to throw herself into the spotlight of his attention, delighted when she found she had stumbled there. They collected the hens' eggs together and played chase. Mabel squealed with delight when Toby feigned an inability to catch her and then, when she was least expecting it, did just that.

Vivian shuddered, trying to throw off a strange ache of despondency as she observed her brother play. When they were children, the age gap had been yawning, their relationship punctuated with squabbles and spats. He teased and irritated her, she bossed or ignored him. Then he'd gone to school and soon she'd married. She hadn't had a chance to get to know him. Now he seemed like someone she might enjoy, but there wasn't time. He would be handsome, given a chance, although he wasn't yet absolutely so. He still had a splatter of spots in his hairline, his feet and hands seemed too big for his body, and he didn't stand tall; it was as though his height surprised him and so he hunched in disbelief. He looked like a boy.

He *was* a boy. Dressed in a uniform.

He was someone else that might be lost. For the first time in her life, Vivian felt a softening towards her mother. She didn't know how to convey as much. Voicing her empathy was out of the question, and the making of cups of tea could be interpreted as common courtesy rather than a heartfelt expression of compassion, so Mrs Foster remained unaware of the change in feeling and therefore naturally continued with her usual mode of behaviour – cool indifference.

It was not clear exactly what the Fosters hoped to achieve from the visit until the very last day. They were sitting together in the parlour, reading papers and books, whiling away half an hour before it was time for the car to take them back to London.

'Damn,' yelled Toby abruptly, flinging *The Times* aside.

'Who is it?' asked Vivian anxiously. Her first thought: whose name had he stumbled upon on the casualty list?

'It's going to be over soon. Before I even get there!'

'I hope you are right,' she replied emphatically. He scowled, reminding everyone of the petulant boy who'd sulked if he lost at snakes and ladders.

433

Mrs Foster looked over her reading glasses. 'I do think you are a very brave boy, of course, but I can't help hoping that you'll be given duties here in England.'

'No, not that. Can you imagine? What a tragedy.' He shook his head, irritated by the suggestion, as though her merely saying it might condemn him to such a fate. If only. How many mothers would have loved to have that power? 'I'll be all right, Mother. Look at Aubrey. He's done the duration. A hero.' Toby looked childishly buoyant. Zealous. He licked his lips and turned to Vivian. 'In fact, Vivian, I was wondering whether you could ask Aubrey to have a word with the powers that be. Someone in his position could surely have me out there lickety-split. Don't you think? Well, you must.'

'I—' Vivian wasn't given a chance to say what she did think.

'I mean, it would be so bloody to be this close and miss out. Utter humiliation.'

Vivian felt cool and saddened. Had her brother wanted to see her at all, or was his visit motivated by a belief that she could sway Aubrey? The confirmation of Aubrey's power and position and the esteem her family felt for his standing was horrible to her.

Toby sighed with exasperation, 'I hate gloom,' he said firmly, as others might state they hated cheats or drunks. As she might state she hated parsnips. He left the room to go and see about the car.

Mrs Foster exhaled heavily. 'He's still desperate to do his bit. It makes no sense. It's not like in the beginning when we thought . . . well, we all thought differently.' Then they had been proud and keen. Ignorant. She looked over her reading glasses and held Vivian's stare. 'It's so awful that all these young men have to go to war. An entire generation. I curse the Hun. Every last one.' There were butchers, traitors and sick psychos, honest men, brave men and heroes on both sides, her mother must know that. Just couldn't say it, perhaps. Vivian said nothing either. 'I understand that boys like Toby think it's rather grand to have a purpose and such, but losing them . . . it's against the natural order. I think they all ought to be here at home being self-centred and self-indulgent like normal young people. Like we were.'

Vivian had never heard her mother speak so frankly. The war had after all shaken every tree. The thought of such undeniable impact left her feeling airless, sick.

'I've never asked much from you, Vivian, you've always suited yourself.' It wasn't how Vivian saw their history, but she balled a handkerchief in her fist and kept her mouth firmly shut. 'But I do ask this. If Aubrey has any influence at all, ask him to use it to delay Toby's crossing. If Toby is right and this Hindenburg Line is collapsing, if the end is nigh . . . well . . .'

'It can't come soon enough.'

'Exactly.' Mother and daughter stared at one another, not sure what to do with their rare moment of agreement.

# 48

THE PAIN WAS excruciating. Howard passed in and out of consciousness two or three times. When he was awake, he tried to scan the confusion for Aubrey Owens, but he soon guessed he hadn't made it. The trench was populated with privates by the sound of it; no one was taking charge, although they were managing in a rough-shod, well-meant way. Someone gave him water. Someone else tried to cut away his trouser leg but a third man stopped him. 'Leave it alone. You don't touch burns. Something to do with taking off the skin. Besides, he'll catch an infection if it's left uncovered and he's already used his gauze for the bullet wound, look here. Poor bugger.'

The man's accent was Cockney. A little bit of London in the trench was welcome. Howard closed his eyes. They dashed across Piccadilly and pushed through the big wooden door of the Criterion into the warmth and opulence. Gold-panelled walls, neat table-cloths, the smell of lilies. Her slim hand clasped in his. Red lips laughing. Sleep was welcome. He hadn't slept properly for days, weeks. He knew now that he could. They were in the little hotel; he could smell the toast and see the crumpled sheets. She was in the bathroom; he could hear her brushing her teeth. She talked to him all the time, non-stop chatter. When she was washing, drawing a flannel over her thighs and between her legs; he spied her through the door she'd left ajar, intentionally he thought. She chattered when she was brushing her hair, even when she had her toothbrush in her mouth. She had so much to tell him. They had so little time. It was coming to him. Death. He felt sure of it.

When he awoke properly, the sky was getting dusky; the ceaseless downpour had eased to a defiant drizzle. His wristwatch was broken but he guessed it might be about four o'clock in the afternoon. His mouth was sandpaper. He felt about and located his flask. There wasn't much water left in it. He wanted to ask one of the men for a slug of theirs. The trench was still, silent except for the sound of rats scratching; no number of explosions could wipe them out, it seemed. He could hear the occasional round of firing, but it sounded at least half a mile off; he'd become expert at measuring such things.

'Hello,' he whispered. It was habit to keep it down in a trench; you had to assume the enemy were always alert to sound. No one replied. Howard felt about again and this time his fingers touched a nose, a mouth. The cold, lifeless face of a soldier. Someone's son. Nothing to do for him but close his eyes. He winched himself into a sitting position, then, inch by sorrowful inch, manoeuvred into a crawl. Every movement sent a searing pain up his leg, through his hip, his blistered skin screaming in outrage. The bullet wound in his side throbbed, and he paused to vomit, the acidic taste in his mouth adding to his discomfort. He crawled around the trench. Before, he'd had the impression that ten or a dozen men had taken refuge here, but now he was alone with about half a dozen dead bodies; men who had fared worse than he had in the flaming tongues of the bomb's burning debris. As he inched through the dirt, trying to find the flasks belonging to the dead men, one of them reached out and grabbed his arm. For a moment he couldn't comprehend how this could possibly be, and then he understood: the man was still alive.

'Where have they all gone?' he asked.

'Onwards,' rasped the man. He was badly burnt and difficult to look at. The hair on his head had been blazed away. His face was a primitive patchwork of black and red. One side had melted off altogether; his ear had slipped and become just a nub on his neck. Shiny and tight, his skin was unrecognisable as such, a mass of blisters and peeling. His lips were violet, like forget-me-nots. Howard couldn't understand why he wasn't shrieking and struggling. He assumed he must feel numb, perhaps shock; certainly his breathing was heavy, his pulse rapid.

He searched around and found a half-full flask tucked in a discarded kitbag. He trickled water into the man's mouth, whose eyes flashed with immense gratitude. Howard – who had long been expecting death, who had never felt truly alive from the moment he left Vivian and had even wished himself dead after he killed his first man – was now glad to be alive, if only to give this man a drink.

'Have they gone towards the Germans?' he asked.

'Orders are orders,' muttered the soldier. He didn't have eyelids. Howard nodded; he understood. Hadn't he made the same decision himself when he was safe in the crater with Sergeant Bowler? None of them dared to be called deserters. He poured the last trickles of water between the man's blistered lips.

He didn't have a clue how the battle was going; he couldn't guess how long it might take for help to come. Time was a luxury they didn't have. 'We'll need more water and some food. I'll go and get some.' The man lacked the energy to thank him. Howard wasn't even sure he had heard as he stared into the middle distance; without eyelids, it was hard to know if he was awake or asleep.

A snake, crawling on his belly, Howard inched around the land that belonged to no one. Every movement ripped at the skin on his leg. He had not bothered to look at the injury; it seemed pointless as he couldn't treat the burns. The bleeding from the bullet wound had slowed, almost stopped, that was something. He pulled the weight of his torso on to his elbows and progressed inch by agonising inch through the dead and the dying. Dehydrated, injured, exhausted, he clawed his way through hell. His goal was to collect as many flasks as he could, and perhaps some food too. In his own pack he'd had two days' supply, but he wasn't sure if his pack was still intact; he'd forgotten to check before he set off. It was perfectly possible that the men in the trench had raided it, assuming he would never regain consciousness. He didn't even resent the thought. It was understandable. Even so, he took care only to gather supplies from those who'd definitely never need anything again – men who had finally found peace. When he came across an injured man, he did what he could. He tied bandages around limbs, found them water, held their hands as they died.

Time ticked on, the loose dusk hardened into a sheet of blackness and he lost count of how many men he helped, perhaps nine or ten. Some thanked him. Others were past that. It reminded him of his time with Basil Clarke, when he'd attended the wounded at Dunkirk, Nieuwpoort and Yser and had sworn he would never be part of the destruction. The thought made him stony and forlorn. He didn't have the energy to be disgusted. How many men had he killed? Some men took pride in keeping count. They bragged about it, brought back souvenirs when they could: a lighter, a button. He didn't know the number, not for sure. He'd lobbed hand grenades on several occasions and he'd fired relentlessly in two other battles besides this one. For sure it was five, including the man he'd shot through mercy, but he couldn't imagine that all his grenades had missed their targets. It might be as many as fifty, it might be one hundred. He didn't know, and that caused him to feel both relief and repugnance.

Once he had collected several canisters of water, he set off back towards the trench. After twenty yards or so, he thought he might be moving in a circle, or certainly an oblong. The lack of light rendered things not only gloomy but obscure. It was unfeasible to know what ground he had covered. It was all the same: mud, blood, bits of uniforms and limbs, empty shells. He pushed on. For hours he crawled between the wounded, still helping if he could, although by now he was dizzy with the pain of his own wounds, all the time thinking of the burnt man in the trench who was waiting for water, who would need him to return. It was odd that he cared about one man when there were so many in need of attention. The truth was, he cared about them all; he had fixated on the burnt man because he couldn't help them all. Helping one particular soldier gave him a much-needed sense of focus; without focus he might despair. From time to time he heard voices, someone calling, 'Over here!' or 'Bring morphine, for the love of God.' It was possible that the stretcher-bearers had started their work. He hoped so.

He continued to crawl, aimlessly and with increasing difficulty, the mud soft beneath his knees and palms. As the sky began to breathe its first hint of dawn, he accepted that he had no idea where the burnt man and the trench were. He cursed himself for failing him, as he recognised that even if he could find the trench, the chance was he'd be dead by now. He'd have died alone, shivering in shock. Howard didn't even know his name. Why hadn't he thought to ask his name? Had this war brutalised him beyond even that most common of courtesies? He had sweat in his eyes, mud in his mouth, despair in his soul. He searched the sky for changes in the degree of darkness and light; if a victory hadn't been secured by either side, then the battle would no doubt recommence before daylight. The sensible thing would be to head towards the voices that seemed to be increasingly distant. He was going the wrong way. What was the right way? If the voices belonged to stretcher-bearers, they would take him to a medical unit. They would save his life. At the very least, he should creep into a trench or crater and wait until they found him.

He stopped crawling and rolled on to his back.

The action felt like a sigh. It wasn't that he was giving up, not as such; he just wasn't going on. He closed his eyes and thought of the Blackwell May Day fair. He thought of pretty girls and women in wide-brimmed hats trimmed with ribbons, lace and such. Did those trivial, attractive things even exist any more? He thought of how there would be laughter and a brass band and the jingle of the carousel. The grass always smelt sweet, cut especially for the day. He thought of being a boy; remembered his thighs stretched across the warm back of a donkey, plodding round and round the green, proud and a bit nervous too. He wondered whether he'd go on the helter-skelter next, or buy candy floss. Too much choice. His sixpence clasped so tightly it left an imprint on his palm. There was a tent displaying fresh cut flowers, cleverly arranged by elegant, clean fingers; another one for light sponge cakes. He'd use all his energy to hurl a ball at the coconut shy, wanting to make a hit more than anything. They used to do such ordinary things. Used to. It seemed inconceivable now. Here where heads fell off bodies like coconuts off the shy. The image shattered his pleasant memories and he wanted to cry, to howl. He needed the horror to leave him alone.

His leg ached tremendously. He felt light-headed. How much blood had he lost? He started to shiver as he tried to dive into another memory, something that would ease his way, not cause him to shudder and panic. There might only be minutes left. Didn't he deserve peaceful last minutes? Since the war had begun four years ago, he'd been in the thick of it for three. Could he trust his mind to give him a reprieve? He thought of Warrington's Playhouse and how he loved to be among the snug, golden backstage light, listening to the silky hum of actors doing their voice exercises as he waited with a sense of delightful anticipation for the call of curtain up. He would never feel the heat of the lamps again; never enjoy the swish of the red velvet curtain. Red. It used to be such an exciting colour; now all he thought of was blood and innards.

He was letting go. There had been enough. He had seen enough. Too much.

Now he allowed himself to think of Vivian. He had never consciously brought her on to a battle field before today; it was not the place for her. For them. Even in the trenches he was careful about when he fetched her to mind. He didn't want her sullied, ruined. The intense pain in his leg and side sapped his energy, and he couldn't keep her away. She wanted to come to him. Perhaps it was right that she visited him here; after all, he was here for her. For the scarlet curtain and the audience applause, for May Day rosettes, candy floss and donkey rides. He was here because those things had to be. Ordinary things. And extraordinary things. Vivian Owens.

Her ear lobes were slim, flat pearls; her eyelids were delicate, with fine blue veins running through them, tiny, almost insignificant, and yet when she was asleep he would stare at them for hours. He thought of her neck, brushed by the sun, her neat, smooth body. Her perfect breasts. He tried to recall the exact colour of her lips and sear that shade into his memory; he did not want to think of the pink of Blake's innards or the burnt man's face. She had a mole on her hip. He thought of her on the station platform in Derby, wearing a powder-blue dress and sucking on bright boiled sweets. She laughed at all his jokes and he told so many more when he was with her. He thought of the way she bit down on a fork; somehow it was as though enjoying her food made her flirtatious. He remembered her lilac silk bedroom robe and how it showcased her curves. She'd been messy. Missed the services of her maid, no doubt. Her clothes had spilt around the room. Silk underwear, fine stockings, delicate petticoats that she selected and then discarded but never rehung, just left scattered. He hadn't cared about the mess she made; in fact he'd revelled in it. He liked to see her most intimate garments showered about, as though she had nothing to hide from him, as though she shared her whole self. Their sex was robust, resounding and extravagant.

He had thought that she would understand that his letters were being impeded, that she would write to him regardless. It hurt him to think she must believe he had given up on her. He imagined her coming to that revelation, assuming he was no different from the other men who had let her down. He wished she had trusted him more. He wondered whether it was anger at him or private shame and guilt that had made her finally forsake him. He had thought she was more vigorous and vital than that. He'd thought that she'd withstand, that their love would endure. But he'd been wrong. After all, she had chosen Aubrey Owens. Old Aubrey. Did she think that was safer? Nothing was safe any more. More conventional? Perhaps.

Aubrey Owens was lying here somewhere in this abyss of humanity. Howard felt nothing other than pity for the man. Not jealousy or scorn, not anger or derision. He assumed that many men had let such emotions finally dissolve here on the earth between the trenches. Those who clung to such things in their last moments had lost. Aubrey Owens, wretched. A shy man. He'd lived and died alone. His marriage could not have been as he had hoped. His childhood, shot through with a toxic blend of rigid shame and astronomical expectation – both a result of society's view on the newness of the family money – had choked any genuine chance that he could become a confident husband and loving father.

Mabel. When Howard had left Blackwell, she'd been little more than a baby, just a year old. Podgy knees, gummy smiles. Naturally, not able to do anything for herself; totally dependent and trusting.

Now she must be confident on her feet, running about everywhere. Her hair might curl around her neck. She'd be talking. He imagined her asking about her daddy, as one day she surely would. She'd want to know what he'd looked like, and Vivian would show her a photograph of Aubrey; his serious face under the peak of his khaki cap. She'd want to know whether he was brave and how he had died. Aubrey Owens had been a fine soldier. No one had expected that, least of all himself, but he'd showed courage and aptitude. He was a gentleman, and the men liked that. They wanted to be led but he'd also known disappointment and they could sense it. He wasn't as bullish as some of the other officers. Not soft. They didn't want that. They didn't even want understanding, because who the hell could understand any of this? But he had common sense and that they respected. Common sense was often born from compromise. It was a shame that Vivian would not be able to show Mabel Aubrey's medals. He imagined a girl might like to see proof of her daddy's success.

Suddenly Howard felt a flicker in his belly and head. Focus. He would find the charred remains of Lieutenant Colonel Aubrey Owens and he would carry the body back to base to be buried. The medals, if they had survived, would be returned. At least he could give Mabel a grave to visit, and Vivian too. It wasn't much, but it was all they had.

It took every ounce of energy he possessed to sit up. He drank some more water, forced down some bully beef, clamping his mouth shut when his gag reaction wanted him to vomit it up again. He looked around. Daylight was nudging through the gloom, giving him some degree of orientation. Staggering to his feet, he set off in what he hoped was the direction of where that particular German shell had whistled through the air and landed. He almost forgot about his burns and bullet wound; the pain simply became a part of him.

It took him about an hour to find the spot. It was a huge

scorched area, after all quite distinctive. Black mounds that were once men were dotted about. Several of them had been blown as far as ten yards by the force of the explosion and buried in the scatter of earth. Howard limped towards those half-buried men and swept the earth off their faces until he found the one he was looking for.

Exhausted, he collapsed next to the officer, accidentally bumping up against his hip. Aubrey Owens stirred. Howard moved back, surprised, disturbed. He'd thought the man was dead. He'd been sure he must be. The not deadness of Aubrey was as disquieting as it was miraculous. He carefully rolled the officer on to his back. He looked similar to the other cooked man, the one he had left in the trench. His entire face was an outlandish mass of blisters, taut, raw skin and abrupt areas that were burnt to black holes. His uniform had been scorched away and most of his chest showed similar damage. His skin appeared to be weeping, and well it might. His left hand had petrified into a claw; the fingers on the right hand were still clasped around his gun. Howard marvelled that he had got through the night and not used the gun to shoot himself. He was sweating and shivering at once. Infection had no doubt already set in.

Dribbling water into Aubrey's mouth, Howard looked about him and considered what to do. He did not trust himself to leave and return with help. What if he got confused again and couldn't find his way back? He was almost sure of the path back to the division, now that the sky was lightening and the smoke from the gun and shelling bombardment was dissipating. He calculated that it couldn't be more than a mile or so to the Allied front, maybe less if they had made any progress. He had to believe they had. He crouched down and carefully, as tenderly as a mother picking up a newborn, gathered up Aubrey. The position of his burns meant he couldn't carry him slung on his back but had to cradle him as a man might carry a bride over the threshold. The exertion required to get to his feet felt inhuman. His back, thighs, shoulders all cried out in furious protest. He staggered like a drunk, found balance and set off.

Aubrey opened his eyes and stared at him. His eyes, so human amidst the monstrous ruin of a face, leaked resentment and curiosity. His voice was not much more than a whisper. 'Why did you come back for me?'

'I would try to save any man.'

'Any of the others I understand, but me?'

Howard couldn't tell Aubrey he'd come back to bury him; for one thing that didn't really answer the question Aubrey was asking. Why was he expending all this effort on this man in particular? His lover's husband.

Because he couldn't do anything other.

Again, the choices his generation faced were not really choices; they were reductive apologies, a faint imitation of choice. Become a soldier or be imprisoned. Kill or be killed. Go to war or never look your lover in her face again. Try to get her husband back to safety or go to hell.

After just twenty yards or so, Howard thought he might drop Aubrey. He wondered about taking off the man's boots to lessen the load but didn't dare; the value of boots had been drilled into them from day one. Aubrey's hip was banging into Howard's wound, making it unimaginable for him to think of anything other than the pain that he had to forget in order to progress. He worried that it would reopen. He couldn't afford to lose more blood; he was already weak and nauseous. One foot in front of the other, he stumbled on. Twice he thought he'd let him slip, plummet to the ground. His arms and chest stung with a weariness he'd never before known. He collapsed to his knees, but rather than lay Aubrey flat and have the effort of picking him up again, an effort he wasn't sure he was up to, he rested with the officer splayed across his thighs, like a sacrifice. He reached behind him into his pack and fished out another one of the water bottles he'd collected, dribbling some into Aubrey's mouth and then drinking too.

Aubrey muttered something but Howard couldn't hear it. He cursed the man for making the effort, because it meant he had to respond. He bent his body to lower his ear closer to Aubrey's lips, every quarter of an inch of movement new agony. 'We are alike,' Aubrey whispered. Howard doubted it, and his cynicism must have shown on his face. 'She sent me too. I couldn't get away fast enough. I'm in this nightmare because of her.'

Each time Howard hoisted Aubrey up, the muscles in his back and thighs stung viciously with the effort until he thought they would snap. Aubrey only called out twice, but he must have been in constant agony. It was merciful that he slipped out of consciousness. Sweat fell into Howard's eyes, almost blinding him, but he had no way of rubbing it away. Exhausted, he tried another position. Grabbing Aubrey under the arms and clasping his hands across the man's chest, he bent and walked backwards, dragging him, slow and rugged progress for a length of time that would never be quantified by either man.

Howard could only see his war. He did not know that just a few miles away, the Allied soldiers had cut through. They had found the German gunners and silenced them for ever. German soldiers emerged from the trenches and lurched about in a bemused, drunken fashion, stupefied by the bombardment they had endured. Then frenzied, terrified, vengeful and virtuous men fought hand to hand until the enemy were spitted on bayonets. Dying men screeched like pigs meeting their end in a slaughterhouse. The barrage progressed in short rushes. The Allies surrounded craters, shouting roughly and flinging grenades at the enemy, who were trapped like fish in a barrel. Those who tried to stagger or scuttle up the steep sides were fired upon. They rolled down again, squashing any living comrades until there were none of those left, only bodies, dead at the bottom of this pit of hell. The Allied soldiers knew that this was winning. And it was better than losing.

# 49

Dear Mrs Owens,

It is my sad duty to write to you to inform you that yesterday your husband died of wounds he sustained in battle on the 18th of September. I cannot effectively convey my absolute sympathy for you or my own grief at his loss. I can assure you that he suffered very little. I visited him on the 20th. I had hoped that the same valour and fortitude that Lieutenant Colonel Owens always demonstrated in battle would serve to pull him through. I am frightfully sorry that this was not the case.

He was an entirely impressive officer. I held him in the highest esteem. A born leader for whom his men would do anything. Indeed he was brought back from the battlefield by a plucky private who clearly worshipped him. Lieutenant Colonel Owens was leading most gallantly against the Hindenburg Line when he was hit. As you can imagine, he bravely persevered in advancing until he could go no further. In every way he was a marvellous fellow and you have the very sincere sympathy of the whole battalion in your great loss.

I return to you his personal effects that were found in his quarters and on or about his person on arriving at hospital.

*Yours sincerely*
*C. H. Horn, Field Marshal*

Vivian thought of the silver sporting trophies on the mantelpiece in the Owenses' London home. Now packed up in a trunk somewhere, she presumed. His boyhood and youth finished. All finished.

'I must send a telegram to Lady Owens.' Mrs Rosebend nodded. There was nothing to say.

Vivian turned to the boxes of belongings. They had returned his clothes; jumpers and socks that she recognised as she'd knitted them herself. She thought it would have been better if they'd given them to some other poor man to wear to keep warm. Another winter was coming. They had returned his books; no poetry or novels, but weighty tomes on military history and impressive global engineering feats, bridges, canals, tunnels and such. The books smelt damp; there was green mould on one or two. She opened his Bible. There was an inscription declaring that it had been awarded to Aubrey Albert George Owens in the Year of Our Lord 1900, on the occasion of his ninth birthday, by his Dear Mother and Father. She felt a surge of anguish; she hoped they'd bought him a train set too. There were receipts, bills and letters. If he had once kept these artefacts carefully, the soldier who had packed them had been less fastidious. They were thrown together in a jumble and as a consequence were torn and creased. She also found his shaving kit, wristwatch and wedding ring, a photograph of his parents and one of Mabel that she had sent shortly after their daughter's birth. She had sent out a more recent image; she wondered where that might be. His possessions seemed small but familiar and she felt huge relief that they were so. She needed to believe she had known him after all, as much as he had wished to be known.

The only item that was not familiar was the Fortnum and

Mason tea caddy. She pulled off the lid, which required some force, and found it was full of letters. Letters addressed to her. She recognised the handwriting in an instant.

# 50

THE ALLIES HAD taken all their objectives and advanced to a distance of about three miles, on a four-mile front. They had also been able to take 11,750 prisoners and a hundred guns. The generals were heralding this victory as the beginning of the end for Germany; the soldiers hoped to God they were right this time.

A Sergeant Farrell came to visit him in hospital. This young sergeant had a no-nonsense way about him that Howard appreciated. He'd no doubt come up through the ranks, liked the men, understood them. Didn't expect too much or too little from them. He sat down heavily on a chair by the side of Howard's bed, lit a cigarette. He pulled the smoke to the back of his throat and then let it spill.

'I saw in your report that you had contact with Sergeant Bowler in a crater.'

'Yes, sir. Did he make it?'

'No.'

'I was trying to go back.'

The sergeant shrugged, not dismissively, not even regretfully. It was as it was. 'You can't save everyone,' he commented. Not even weary, not philosophical. Practical. The best of them had been reduced to that.

Howard had already been made to account for his whereabouts

throughout the duration of the battle. It appeared he'd run when the order had been to advance slowly, a creeping barrage. He liked running. Fact. He remembered a time when he'd run in London parks. It was one of the ways he used to demonstrate to himself – and others, if they cared to take notice – that he would not agree to the accepted boundaries, that he would travel and over-come at his pace. Space was all. Limitless. Except this was not true in the army. In the army he was supposed to agree and accept. He could only conquer on command, which was a different sort of conquering altogether.

He had done his best to answer the questions in the report, but he'd been injured and disorientated; it was hard to measure whether one crater or trench was a different torment to another. Luckily, he'd run forward, towards the enemy; no one could accuse him of cowardice, although strictly speaking he had disobeyed orders, broken rank. It was unsteadying, could have led to chaos, but then what else was there out there on the battlefield? The muddle and madness couldn't be intensified by a sprint, could it? If they'd wanted to be picky, he could have been court-martialled. Sergeant Farrell had come to tell him that this time, it seemed no one really wanted to put him on trial or shoot him at dawn. For once, common sense prevailed. Concern about whether he was where he ought to have been during the show had been mitigated by his efforts to attend to the wounded in the field. They talked about him being heroic. Howard was relieved. He didn't need them to think he was a hero, but he was weary of people wanting to shoot him. He wasn't sure why he had run or if his actions in tending to the wounded had made any difference; it was simply his story. He said as much.

'Of course it made a difference,' insisted Sergeant Farrell. His tone was forced and hearty. Howard had noticed that the nurses used the same tone when talking to the patients. It was as though a wound made a man infantile. Surely the opposite was true. 'Two or three men might live to fight another day because of your actions. Possibly more. Reports are being collated, but these things take time.'

'Fight another day, eh?' So it hadn't made any difference.

As if reading his mind, Farrell added, 'Kiss their sweethearts.'

Yes, Howard supposed it made a difference if a man got to have a woman again.

He guessed that bringing an injured lieutenant colonel back to base had helped his case. By trying to save Aubrey's life, he had saved his own. He was once again in a position of owing Aubrey, which was perverse.

The nurse, a middle-aged, matronly type who reminded Howard of other people's mothers – not his own – walked past and asked the sergeant to extinguish his cigarette. At least he wasn't chewing tobacco, which was the very devil to clean up, but she held the view that smoking was unhealthy, and besides, she didn't like these men coming into the hospital and grilling the soldiers about their actions. She didn't care if the boy had run or walked; he could have flown for all it mattered. Her job was to get him well, and she was better able to do that if he wasn't being constantly bothered and asked about all the horrors.

Sergeant Farrell smiled obligingly and put out the fag. He glanced about him. Sheets the colour of pigeons, not doves; scrubbed floors. Howard wondered whether he too was appreciating the relative calm and peace of the ward. Quite a holiday from the trenches. Its neatness was what Howard prized the most; that and the morphine. There was no blood bursting here; it smelt of disinfectant and polish.

'I'm also here to tell you that unfortunately Lieutenant Colonel Owens didn't make it, I'm afraid.'

'Right.'

'He was in a bad way.'

'Yes.' Howard thought he should have felt Owens slip off the planet. After all they'd been through. After all.

'You did your best.' The sergeant searched Howard carefully. Howard didn't know how to respond and so simply nodded stiffly. He was moved. Not grief exactly. Not guilt or relief. A vicious cocktail of all three. A thought slipped through his head, nonsensical. The drugs, surely. But how would he exist now, without Aubrey Owens? How could he be, if there wasn't the other? The sergeant's dark eyes sought for something in Howard's expression, and perhaps he found what he was looking for, because he added, 'I have something for you. Found with Sergeant Bowler. They're addressed to you, though. I imagine he was looking after them for you.' The comment was phrased in such a way that Howard realised that the sergeant was making a request for collusion. A credible deceit that wasn't quite honourable, but not a scandal.

Farrell bent to reach into his case, and in an instant, Howard knew – perhaps he'd always known, just not believed. She had written. The world seemed to slant and then right itself as the sergeant drew out a two-inch-thick bundle of letters, tied with string. Bowler had intercepted them, kept them.

The letters Howard had written to her were lost out on the field somewhere, perhaps in that very crater where Bowler met his end, perhaps in the trench where he'd left the burnt soldier. Most likely he had dropped his pack as he dragged Aubrey back to base. He couldn't remember when he'd last had the Fortnum and Mason tin; he'd been barely conscious of his actions, instead on some sort of automatic survival mode. He did remember considering dumping Aubrey's boots, such was his desire to lighten his load. Was it possible that he'd been so desperate that he'd simply forgotten her? Just for an instant. Well, at least if not her, then the letters he'd written to her. Which had sometimes been the same thing these last two years. He knew the tin wasn't in amongst the few bits the nurse had handed him as personal effects: his broken watch, a photo of his mother that he kept tucked in his breast pocket. When he'd first realised that his letters had gone, he'd wanted to howl. He'd cursed himself for not keeping them on his person, but the package was too bulky to allow that. Now it did not matter that they were lost. The battlefield had swallowed them but spewed up her far more valuable ones instead. He fingered the bundle with barely containable excitement. The sergeant noticed, perhaps even understood. He stood up, suddenly self-conscious and superfluous.

'Right, I'll leave you to it, then.' Howard nodded impatiently. It wasn't that he wanted to be rude to the man, but her hand-writing was there. Just there. Tantalisingly close on the envelope. 'I've other men to buck up.'

'Of course.' The two men nodded in a way that soldiers had developed. A look that conveyed respect, that wished providence, bid goodbye, hoped for but didn't expect further acquaintance.

They were not in order. Some of them weren't even dated. He didn't care. He wanted to dive in; he'd make chronological sense of them later, using the postmarks. Now, he just had to consume. He had to have them.

They had been read before. Each of the envelopes had been carefully sliced open with a knife. He imagined Sergeant Bowler's fat fingers, fast breath pouring over her words. He knew the man was in hell. Carefully he slid a letter out of its envelope.

He saw her hand across the paper and felt it as though she had swept his hair from his eyes. He glanced and caught the first words.

*April showers have come in the form of storms this year.*

He saw it in his mind's eye as it surely had been, as it was. Vivian raising her eyes, expecting a pale blue innocent sky, finding instead a dark, brooding colour. Thick raindrops falling in heavy, fat blobs, the sort that were always a precursor to an almighty downpour. Vivian dashing to bring in the washing, locking the gate to stop it swinging and banging on its hinge.

His eyes leapt about the page. Excitement made it impossible for him to read left to right, top to bottom. Another paragraph leapt out and he nearly laughed out loud, celebrating the very ordinariness of it. She was writing to him about the weather!

*Last night the winds whipped around the village and the farms. The maids are saying that some houses lost chimney stacks and fences. The trees are naked. The scene is wan. At least the wind has blown on, bothering some other village now, or town, although the rain is still coming, not finished with us yet.*

It was remarkable, wonderful.

Like a child aching to gobble up an entire box of chocolates but needing to eat slowly to make the deliciousness last, to avoid being sick, he dragged his eyes to the top of the page, determined to start at the beginning. *10th April 1917*. Seven months after he had left her. He wondered how long the letters might go on for. When had she last written? Last year? Last week? Might she be writing to him this very minute? He allowed his eyes to rest on how she addressed him. *My darling, darling Howard*. The words were so incredible, so perfect and pure, that he coughed. Snorted. Emotion spluttered from his nose. Restraint was impossible. His eyes dashed to the final sentence. *I am worth staying alive for. Come home*. Her sense of entitlement to him was the first heartening sentiment that he'd encountered since he came over here. It exploded within him. She understood. He had gone to war for her. Now *he* had to understand. It was more important still that he returned to her.

He read another letter, and then a third.

*2nd January 1918*

*So a new year has come now. No one knows how to greet it. A friend or another slog? To be enjoyed or to be endured? Will you be delivered back to me this year? I have to believe it, my darling. Mrs Rosebend, Cook and I went to the village hall. We women danced together and with old men. At midnight a shiver* ran through the crowd. Some of the children cheered, of course, because they don't know any better. The crowd, such as it was, melted away pretty fast. Come home.

14th May 1917

I used to care so much about being wealthy. No one seems wealthy any more. Might they ever be again, do you think? Or has it all gone? Did I mistake wealth for innocence or naïveté? I have given this a lot of thought and I think perhaps I'm just being greedy. We grew up in an unparalleled age, I suppose. It's hard to accept it's over. No one wants to see their youth close, finish. But that luxuriant materialism and the serene, unperturbed comfort will never be seen again, never be felt again. That's the biggest loss. Even if in the future, when they make everyone comfortable again and manufacturing finally turns away from producing bullets and back to producing sewing machines, autocars and other things that make our lives more cosy, not vile, what has gone forever is the tranquillity, the placidity. The human race can't trust itself. Not any more. Not ever again. I ought to be content with what I've got. Ought to be.

Come home.

He would read them all and then read them through again. Over and over until he was fit and turfed out of the hospital bed, over and over until they put down their guns. Until the damn war stopped. A tide swelled through his body, in his fingers, chest, groin. Life battered its way along every nerve and artery. It slammed into his head and down his throat. He was parched, breathless. It was all too much to take in. Besides the weather, she wrote about Mabel, the farm, her thoughts, her fears, her knitting! She wrote him just the sort of letters that any woman might write to her lover.

She wrote letters like no one else ever could.

*24th December 1916*

*Do you know, sometimes I would watch you sleeping. Your face naturally collapsed into something that wasn't as determined or resilient. Most people find that a peaceful time. For me, sleeping Howard was almost difficult to look at because he didn't seem alive enough then. I worried for him. Come home.*

*12th February 1918*

*You'll think I'm quite mad but I enjoy being in the brown fields that you used to work. I remember watching you, then talking to you. Earning your smile, that was always a surprise, remembering your embrace, as shocking as an assault. I breathe deeply and try to get some of that oxygen you used to feed me, because it was so, wasn't it, my love? The atmosphere was energetic, full, from the moment we met. Timmy Durham's brother is home. His nerves are ruined. He's as you described. I met his mother in the street. She is grateful to have him back. Even as he is. She said to me that he barely speaks; she joked that she never thought she'd consider Timmy her bright lad. She took her hand out of her pocket to clasp mine, and said, 'It will pass, my dear, everything does. In the end we go jogging along side by side to one another. Pushing on.' I wish I could agree. I fear some things are such a piercing shock that nothing can ever be the same. It's probably best we all acknowledge that. I understand her acceptance, though. I wouldn't mind, my darling. The same or changed beyond recognition. Just come home. I look for signs. I suppose humankind has that in common now. If the sun breaks through the cloud when I'm working, I think good times are ahead. It might be all right. But then if it starts to pour I tell myself that everything is being cleaned and refreshed. It might be all right. Because it has to be. I'll only think that way. I can be stubborn too. Oh God knows, I miss you, though. Come home.*

*11th August 1917*

*It's different now that you are both out there. My child's father and the man I love. I now long for safe returns, for the end of the conflict, with an intensity that makes it hard to walk, to put one foot in front of the other. I know I won't be given you unless Aubrey is spared too. I pray ferociously for a husband and a lover. Greedy, frenzied praying. If there is a God, He must be laughing. I am asking for twice as much and I deserve half. Come home.*

*3rd September 1918*

*I used to be so nervous about writing things down, being known. As a child I kept a diary and I hid it under my mattress or carried it about with me, living under the constant fear that my mother or siblings would find it and punish or tease me. When I wrote in my diary, I used to adopt this (frankly!) rather annoyingly pious, supercilious voice. Far from my true self, a guarantee against snoopers. I kept my true self buried practically all of the time. Until you uncovered me. I want to be known by you, my love. Let them all read what I send to you. The postmistress, your senior officer, the man you bunk down with every night. I want to sing it from the rooftops. Be safe. Be safe. I'm waiting for you. Come home.*

He read all afternoon and into the evening. The tea trolley rattled by; he couldn't stop to eat. The young, smiley nurse left him a cuppa on the side, but it went undrunk and cold. He learnt many things. He learnt that in the beginning she had listened to the rattle of the letter box, excited; now she just dreaded the knock on the door. No news was good news. She had to believe that. He learnt that they'd been asked to use less sugar in their tea, and to make do with cheap streaky bacon instead of leaner cuts. Stale loaves could be dampened and popped into the oven to make them fresh enough to eat. He learnt that the summer of 1918 didn't obligingly arrive when everyone hoped. May and June were wet, muddy. That she'd never master more than knit one, purl one. That there was a tree in the south-east corner of the bottom field that was just crying out for a swing to be attached to its bough.

He learnt that she loved him.

He was in hospital, but not dead. No, a long way off it.

Aubrey hadn't made it.

She loved him. Still.

He couldn't think it was a decent end, not for any of them. He doubted anything could be decent again, but he could have her. That was enough. That was his everything. Aubrey was dead; he'd tried to save him but couldn't. He'd almost died himself; wanted to do so but hadn't.

He would do as she asked. He would go home.

It was at that moment – when the popular young up-through-the-ranks Sergeant Farrell was telling another private to count his lucky stars, when the stout, mature nurse was stooping to fill a basin for a bed bath, when the smiley young one was spooning tea into a slit between bandages, when Howard knew for certain that she loved him – that the Gotha GV plane, the heavy bomber used by the Luftstreitkräfte, dropped its bomb on the military hospital. The ceiling collapsed, falling timber became arrows of fire and walls crumbled to rubble. The letters flew into the air like doves, caught fire and descended as crows.

And for so many, the war was finally over.

# 51

Vivian had always known he would come home to her, and in a way he did. The letters were dated from the third week after he had left her; he had written approximately one a week for the duration. Knowing that they would never be read, he had not self-censored. They were gloriously free, honest, forthright. They were Howard. He had taken some form of solace or perhaps strength in recording his war. Or possibly he'd just wanted to write it down to prove to himself that it had all happened and he wasn't going mad imagining it.

> *19th November 1916*
>
> *I've been over the top now. Would you believe me, Vivian, if I told you it wasn't as bad as I thought it would be? Isn't that the strangest thing? I can hardly remember it although it was only yesterday. I was dazed and drunk on all sorts of things: fear, horror, fatalism. Amazement that mankind had come to this. I can't imagine any deeper depths to sink to. The worst is done. I have shot a man. I am a killer. No doubt I'll get a medal soon.*

> *17th September 1917*
>
> *I am seeing more action than most. Aubrey takes me with him wherever he goes. Friends close, enemies closer, isn't that the*

*saying? He puts us both at risk. It's funny, he thinks he is invincible and will come home to you victorious. He thinks I'll die out here. I think he is right. I'm surprised it's taking so long. They say that those who know death is coming always see it. I have seen it all, Vivian. French women rearing babies brought on them by violence. Roofless farms and houses, fallen churches. My soul has shivered, then frozen. Will anyone ever remember that once this country was one of beauty, the cornfields bronze, the poppies scarlet and bonny, the little white churches framed by orchards, trees heavy with fruit? It was once that way. Will it be again, do you think? I hope you do. I hope it will.*

*17th January 1918*

*My boots leak.*

*8th June 1917*

*I still see no difference between them and us. The boys in grey look startlingly similar to those in khaki. We all hate each other now. That's new. I do hate now. I just want it over, and if I have to kill and kill and kill and kill to end it, then I shall. I wonder, would you admire me more or less now, if you knew, if I could get these letters to you? You always thought war was the answer. When my finger is on the trigger and I'm waiting for the command, steady, steady, I have the time to marvel that that same finger has ever touched you. Been inside you. It's a queer thing if you think about it.*

*15th December 1917*

*I killed a Yorkshire lad today. He begged me to. He was very badly injured. I was doing him a favour.*

*8th March 1918*

*We had sausages for tea. They tasted wonderful.*

*13th April 1917*

*I think everyone knows that in our defence of liberty we've all lost our freedom. I'd have done anything to be wrong, but there can be no winners. I wonder how we bear it. It's the fact that it's been years now. Will it ever stop? You'll know the Americans have joined in. Most people are relieved; they believe if we have more men we can finish the job faster. I hope to hell they're right. I fear that this means we now simply have millions more men to plough through. That it will take longer. It wears one down. Do you know they still call me conchie. Of course they do. Former conchie doesn't have the same ring to it. I can't bear the name. I don't deserve it.*

*9th May 1918*

*I dreamt of you last night. You had me in your mouth. I could feel the palm of my hand on the warm, soft crown of your head, hair silky beneath my touch. When I woke up, I wanted to blow my head off.*

*15th July 1917*

*My mother sent some blackberry jam. Have you tasted it too? I wonder, was she angry with you when I left? Did she blame you? I hope she didn't. I bet she did. I hope you are friends still. I hope you have tasted this jam. It's not as sweet as I remember it. I suppose that's the sugar rations, isn't it?*

*5th September 1918*

*Mabel must be three now, or thereabouts. I don't know when her birthday is. Not exactly. I remember it being September but I have no idea of the actual date. If only you had continued to write to me, I could ask you this sort of thing. This and a million other questions that come to mind. There is so much I don't know about you. So many gaps. You could still write. It's not too late. January, February, March, April, when it's your birthday please join in . . .*

*28th August 1918*

*Some men try and say they are not scared. They are easy to spot. They are the ones who laugh too loud and too long at their own jokes, their faces flushed and furious. I think you should know how it is with your husband and his men. He is respected. Admired. Does that surprise you? It surprised me, but it is so. I have studied him. Every nerve in his body and brain is stretched to full tension, and yet he does not betray the slightest hint of irritation. Unlike many of the other officers he will not be flurried or depressed by the prevalent pessimism or even elated by false optimism. He was born for this war, and that about him which left you cold and desolate comforts thousands of men here. He does not flinch. If he returns to you, rather than me, try to remember as much, Vivian. It may help.*

*17th September 1918*

*I long for you. Simply that. Still.*

Enid had never had Vivian's faith and confidence. She had not trusted that he would come back, because why should he? Any more than Michael, than Aubrey, than the hundreds of thousands of other men? She fell to her knees and hammered the earth with her small screwed-up fists. Vivian ran to her, but once she was within a foot, she dared not touch. Enid's face was a snarled mass of panic and resentment, shock and regret. Vivian felt cursed by the look.

'No. No. No.'

Enid looked up and nodded manically. She held the War Office B104-82 form crushed in her fist. Devastation. Vivian had never understood the word in its entirety, but there it was on this mother's face. 'They've bombed his hospital. Bombed the wounded. There isn't even a body. Nothing left of him. Nothing. My boy. My poor boy.'

JUNE 1923

# 52

THE MORNING SEEMED frail; a pale yellow veiled the would-be blue sky. Delicate but possible. Verging on the promising. It would be better if it stayed dry. Bearable. The air was damp with dew and tears but smelt of fertility; grass, not death.

Epehy Wood Farm Cemetery was the final resting place of the men who had died wrenching the small village from the enemy's clutches in April 1917; of those who fell as the Germans regained it on 22nd March 1918; and of those who died as the Allies fought once again for control on 18th September 1918. Of the 997 burials, 235 remained unidentified, and there were twenty-nine additional special memorials to men believed to be buried there, although no one could say for sure. It was hard to be exact. There were names that couldn't find bodies, bodies that couldn't find names. Carnage could not, it seemed, be definitively counted. This was something Howard Henderson had known at the beginning of the war.

Lieutenant Colonel Aubrey Owens' grave lay in the east of the cemetery. Five rows from the perimeter, sixth grave to the left. The uniformity and enormity of the number of plots left some fazed and distraught. Vivian thought there was something peaceful and fair about the egalitarian nature of the stones. One man's sacrifice was the same as the next. As the next.

She didn't need gloves. She wasn't sure why she'd worn them in June. It had seemed fittingly austere and formal. Now her palms sweated. She peeled them off and pushed them into her pocket. A bee buzzed past her ear; she didn't bother to swipe it away. Whilst the clean white stones of identical shape and size looked like hard pillows, she thought they were made soft by the verdant grass and purple flowers that stretched as far as the eye could see. The bee settled on the flowers in front of Aubrey's grave. The flower trembled.

This pilgrimage to France was expensive, and Mabel certainly did not seem to be appreciating the gravity of the visit. Instead she appeared to find the experience an exciting adventure, as children did. Then again, Vivian had to acknowledge that that irrepressible energy, the ability to look forward not backwards, was what made children encouraging and wonderful. Mabel had insisted on carrying the map of the cemetery and counting out the rows in a loud voice, stretching out her strides to try to match the width of the graves, bouncing as though it was a game. Her plaits were working loose. One was often soggy, as she had a habit of sucking the end of it, no matter how often Vivian threatened that she'd get tangles of hair in her stomach.

'Perhaps we could have our picnic here? It seems very nice,' she pronounced in a clear, cut-glass voice.

'Mabel!' Vivian's response was a hissed whisper, powdered with embarrassment that anyone else might have overheard, rather than genuine distress or discomfort at the suggestion. Mabel was right. The cemetery had been consecrated almost as soon as the armistice was announced, and was well kept. Pretty. Peaceful. A perfect place for a picnic except for the other mourners milling around. Vivian didn't want to be disrespectful. She bent down to place the wreath on Aubrey's grave, her blooming belly in the way.

'It's not an awful suggestion,' said Howard. He had tight hold of Freddie's hand; at three years old, the boy was able to vanish within a moment. The headstones would prove an irresistible place to play hide and seek. Personally Howard would have liked to see his son run amok through the graves. He thought the dead lads might like to know that children played and laughed. Still. That life had gone on after all. Even though there had been a point when they'd doubted it would. Doubted it could.

Vivian bit her lip, unsure. She glanced around and noted that other visitors had unfolded deckchairs; they sat above their husbands, sons and brothers and talked to them as though they were around the kitchen table, in the parlour or on the back step. The earth that had once been rank, wet and glistening was now dried hard, unchangeable. She looked to Enid for guidance, who settled the matter. 'I think Mabel should be able to share a sarnie with her father if she fancies it.' She pointed to a patch of grass not actually on the dead, but close by.

Vivian was carrying the tartan rug – Howard wouldn't let her carry anything more; she shook it out and he jumped into action, smoothing out the corners. Enid reached inside the wicker hamper. It was a simple basket, with napkins rather than plates; she started to carefully, quietly unpack. The children bundled down, legs and arms joyously splayed. Mabel bossed her little brother and then pulled him into a clumsy hug; he accepted both things from her with an equanimity that could have been mistaken for indifference if you failed to notice his chubby hand resting on her leg. The siblings adored one another.

Howard had thought the timing of the whole trip was somewhat inadvisable. The new baby was due in four weeks, but Vivian had laughingly pointed out that once they had three children, she'd probably never find the energy to leave the house again, let alone travel to France. This was something they had to do. Not lay it to rest exactly. He didn't think that could ever happen. Nor should it. He thought of the war when he tied a knot in his tie, when he drank a glass of beer, when he put groceries in the pantry. It was always there and always would be now. Man had passed a point of no return. All he could do was pound on his typewriter and tell it as it was. As it had been. For him. For them all. He could not make sense of it, defend it or condemn it. Too late for any of that. Too late. Sometimes that thought made him wake in the night shrieking, shivering, pissing. They'd sacrificed peaceful sleeps for evermore, the war-hungry land-grabbers.

Vivian had swung it by suggesting Enid join them; she had after all delivered Mabel, so if anything was to occur Vivian would be in good hands. 'We can visit Michael too. We should.'

'Yes, I'd like to.'

He needn't have worried about her. It turned out she had sailor's legs, and the crossing had been straightforward. He'd proudly watched her as she kept the excitable Mabel and Freddie in order on the boat, instructing them to breathe deep lungfuls of sea air, laughing as audacious seagulls swept over her head and landed on the railings close by. She'd quietly, firmly squeezed his hand when he'd flinched from their hungry, angry squawking, a sound that would forever remind him of his two journeys to war. She had an air of confidence that enhanced her beauty. She was still turning heads even when she was beyond blooming and was now simply spreading. The journey was important to them both. To them all, even though Mabel might not understand as much yet. This was what he'd promised he'd give Aubrey's daughter. This at the very least. He hadn't been able to save the man, but he could acknowledge him. Honour him. They all deserved that.

'So we're going to picnic with your daddy,' he said as he eased himself down next to the children, putting his cane to one side. He was excited to see what the children would make of the French food: baguettes, soft, ripe cheeses, almond pastries.

'You're my daddy.' Mabel's eyes shadowed, concerned for a moment. Howard wriggled closer to her side, kissed her head. Her silky hair, so like her mother's, smelt of lavender.

'True. You know you are a lucky girl to have two daddies. Me and Aubrey. But he came first.' Howard found it easy to be generous; he had to be, always. He was lucky. More than that. He was jammy, fluky, beyond blessed.

'Tell me how you became my daddy.' Mabel stared up, wide-eyed, old enough to know that he found it impossible to resist her pouts and entreaties. Vivian passed around the sweet, sticky lemonade and the hard stick of bread. Freddie grabbed it and swung it like a sword.

'I've told you this story.'

'Again, again. Tell me again.' She didn't yell, but calmly insisted.

'Well, I was lying in the hospital bed . . .'

'Getting better from your wounds.' Mabel pronounced the word with incredible care and an endearing sense of solemnity. She knew this story as well as any bedtime fairy tale, but its familiarity seemed to cause ever-increasing wonder.

'Getting better from my wounds and reading your mother's letters, when a huge bomb was dropped on the hospital.'

Both Freddie and Mabel gasped. Even infants understood. Bombing the sick. Indefensible. One of the hundreds of indefensible things that had occurred. Vivian blinked slowly. Enid blanched. Neither woman would ever forget the nightmare that had scorched their lives, threatening to burn the reason for their existences. Vivian knew how things had gone, and that they *had* gone; these events were in the past. Yet every time he told the story, she was immobilised with the fear that it could have turned out some other way, as though retelling the story might play with the fabric of time and the outcome, so impossibly fortuitous, might be altered into something impossibly bleak.

Howard stretched out and took hold of his wife's hand, the cuff of his tweed jacket rising to reveal a smart white shirt and cufflinks; he'd dressed with care this morning. 'I'd dropped a letter.'

'One you hadn't finished reading,' prompted Mabel.

'It fluttered under the bed and I scrambled after it.' Not thinking about his injuries, anaesthetised to the pain because of Vivian's words. Her command. *Come home.*

'You lost your balance,' giggled Mabel.

Howard nodded, his eyes wide and foolish, as if to say, silly me. Gawky me with my bullet wound and my burns, fancy losing my balance! 'I rolled under the bed.'

He'd been under the bed when the bomb dropped, the roof collapsed. He'd been rendered unconscious, but he was alive. When they fished him out and moved him to another hospital, he was still unconscious and unidentifiable. For some reason — and it happened more often than anyone wanted to consider — in the ensuing chaos Howard Henderson had been reported missing, presumed dead. Enid had received the shattering B104-82.

'But you weren't dead, Daddy,' declared Mabel seriously.

'No, Mabel. I most certainly was not. I didn't dare be.'

Mabel cocked her head to the left, her shell-like ear anticipating her favourite part of the story. 'You had to do as you were told.'

'Yes. I had to come home.'

Vivian let out a small mew of relief. After all, Enid had been wrong. Aubrey had been wrong. Howard had been wrong. Vivian had been right. He had returned. She squeezed his fingers, needing to feel the reality of him. The beauty of him. For so long bodies had been abused, exposed as fragile and helpless. She needed to recall, on a daily basis, that they were beautiful and whole. She felt the throb of him. The pulse of him.

Home.

# ACKNOWLEDGEMENTS

Dear Jane Morpeth, what a treat you are. I'm so lucky that you are my editor and friend. Thank you for letting me take risks and letting me follow my heart (and my crazily busy head too). You are a joy.

Thank you, Kate Byrne, for your sensitive, insightful and careful editing. It's such a pleasure working with you.

Thank you, Georgina Moore and Vicky Palmer, the fabulous PR and Marketing dynamic duo. I adore it that you both combine astonishing fun and enthusiasm with incredible professionalism and results.

Thank you, Barbara Ronan, Frances Doyle and the entire sales team, who work so ferociously on my behalf. I'm very grateful.

Thank you, Yeti Lambregts, for your beautiful cover designs, they are so important. You make my books look breathtaking.

Thank you to the marvellous Jamie Hodder-Williams, who is simply an all-round lovely chap.

Thank you, Jonny Geller. Can you believe it, fifteen novels? What an exciting journey; I'm glad you're with me every step of the way. Thanks to Kate Cooper, Eva Papastratis, Kirsten Foster and all the team at Curtis Brown for your wonderful support of my work, home and abroad.

Thank you, as ever, to my marvellous family and friends who

are lovely and supportive. Thanks for facing my books frontwards in bookshops (even though we're not supposed to!), thanks for turning up to my events, listening to me when I'm terrified, listening to me when I'm elated. Thanks to my fellow authors, booksellers, book festival organisers, reviewers, magazine editors and librarians who continue to generously champion my work.

Of course, I'd like to thank my readers; without you it wouldn't make any sense, would it?

Finally, thank you, Jimmy and Conrad. You are my inspiration. You provide meaning and douse me with encouragement and love. It's all about the two of you and it always will be.

# BIBLIOGRAPHY

Whilst *If You Go Away* is a work of fiction, naturally I drew upon the recorded experiences of soldiers, conscientious objectors, actors, nurses and journalists of the time. When I was writing I found these books enormously helpful and interesting.

Biddings, Lois S., *Telling Tales About Men,* Manchester University Press, Manchester, 2009

Brittain, Vera, *Testament of Youth,* Virago, London, 1978

Ellsworth-Jones, Will, *We Will Not Fight,* Aurum Press Limited, London, 2008

Evans, Richard, *From the Frontline: The Extraordinary Life of Sir Basil Clarke*, The History Press, Gloucestershire, 2013

Gibbs, Philip, *Now It Can Be Told*, Forgotten Books, London, (originally published 1920, subsequently published 2012)

Goodall, Felicity, *We Will Not Go To War* (first published as *A Question of Conscience* in 1997), London, 2010

Holledge, Julie, *Innocent Flowers: Women in the Edwardian Theatre*, Virago, London, 1981

# SPARE
# BRIDES

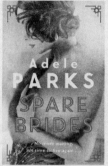

The 1920s: a time of hope, promise – and parties.
But not all the men came home, after The War.

Meet the spare brides.

Young, gorgeous – and unexpectedly alone.

Ava relished the freedom of being single.
Sarah fears no one can replace her hero husband.
Beatrice finds it hard to shine, next to her dazzling friends.
And Lydia is married, rich, privileged: so isn't she one of the lucky ones?

Then a chance encounter changes everything.

Angry, damaged, and dangerously attractive, Edgar Trent is an irresistible temptation.

And the old rules no longer apply…

★★★

Available now in paperback and ebook

Have you read all of Adele's fabulously addictive novels?

# THE STATE WE'RE IN

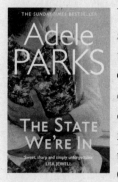

What are the odds that the stranger sitting next to you on a plane is destined to change your life? She's a life-long optimist, looking for her soulmate in every man she meets; he's a resolute cynic – cruel experience has taught him never to put his faith in anyone. But in the time it takes to fly from London to Chicago, each finds something in the other that they didn't even realise they needed . . .

# WHATEVER IT TAKES

How far would you go for the people you love? For Londoner Eloise Hamilton, there can be no greater sacrifice than uprooting to Dartmouth, leaving *her* perfect world so that her husband Mark can live *his*. Good marriages need compromises, don't they? But when a life-changing family secret emerges, Eloise suddenly finds her world imploding as she struggles to hold everything together for the people she loves. Someone is bound to be overlooked, and the damage might be irreparable . . . What if love's not enough?

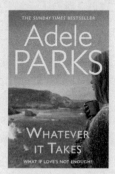

# About Last Night

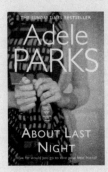

There is nothing best friends Steph and Pip wouldn't do for one another. That is, until Steph begs Pip to lie to the police as she's desperately trying to conceal not one but two scandalous secrets to protect her family. Her perfect life will be torn apart unless Pip agrees to this lie. But lying will jeopardise everything Pip's recently achieved after years of struggle. It's a big ask. How far would you go to save your best friend?

# Men I've Loved Before

Nat doesn't want babies; she accepts this is unusual but not unnatural. She has her reasons; deeply private and personal which she doesn't feel able to share. Luckily her husband Neil has always been in complete agreement, but when he begins to show signs of changing his mind, Nat is faced with a terrible dilemma. She begins to question if the man she has married is really the man she's meant to be with . . .

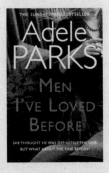

# LOVE LIES

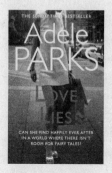

It's a girl's ultimate fantasy – being swept away by Prince Charming and living a life of luxury, wealth and celebrity. But after a whirlwind romance with pop star Scottie Taylor, modern-day-Cinderella Fern must ask herself if love is telling the truth. Can she find her Happily Ever After in a world where there isn't much room for fairy tales?

## TELL ME SOMETHING

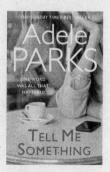

When Elizabeth and her Italian husband Roberto decide to leave London for romantic Italy, Elizabeth hopes the change in lifestyle might help her boost her chances of conceiving their longed-for child. Except it's impossible to relax with a mother-in-law bent on destroying her marriage, and Roberto's beautiful, significant ex living next door. Is Elizabeth's ferocious hunger for a baby enough to hold a marriage together or is it ripping it apart? And what about the gorgeous American stranger who's suddenly walked into her life?

# YOUNG WIVES' TALES

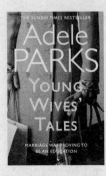

Lucy stole her friend Rose's 'happily ever after' because she wanted Rose's husband – and Lucy always gets what she wants. Big mistake. Rose was the ideal wife and is the ideal mother; Lucy was the perfect mistress. Now neither can find domestic bliss playing each other's roles. They need more than blind belief to negotiate their way through modern life. And there are more twists in the tale to come . . .

# HUSBANDS

Love triangles are always complex but in Bella's case things are particularly so as she is *married* to both men in her triangle. She plans never to reveal her first marriage to husband number two Phillip – after all, Stevie is no longer part of her life. That is until, inconveniently, her best friend introduces her new man to Bella and it's none other than husband number one. Could things get more complicated? Well, only if Bella and Stevie fall for one another again . . .

# STILL THINKING OF YOU

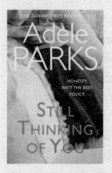

Tash and Rich are wild about each other; their relationship is honest, fresh and magical, so they dash towards a romantic elopement in the French Alps. However, five of Rich's old university friends crash the wedding holiday and they bring with them a whole load of ancient baggage. Can Tash hold on to Rich when she's challenged by years of complicated yet binding history and a dense web of dark secrets and intrigues? Does she even want to?

# THE OTHER WOMAN'S SHOES

The Evergreen sisters have always been opposites with little in common. Until one day, Eliza walks out on her boyfriend the very same day Martha's husband leaves her. Now the Evergreen sisters are united by separation, suddenly free to pursue the lifestyles they think they always wanted. So, when both find exactly what they're looking for, everybody's happy . . . aren't they? Or does chasing love only get more complicated when you're wearing another woman's shoes?

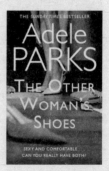

# Larger Than Life

Georgina fell in love with Hugh the moment she first saw him and she's never loved another man. Unfortunately, for all that time he's been someone else's husband and father. After years of waiting on the sidelines, Georgina finally gets him when his marriage breaks down. But her dream come true turns into a nightmare when she falls pregnant and Hugh makes it clear he's been there, done that and doesn't want to do it all again. Georgina has to ask herself, is this baby bigger than the biggest love of her life?

# Game Over

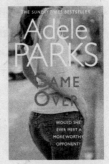

Cas Perry doesn't want a relationship. When her father walked out on her and her mother she decided love and marriage simply weren't worth the heartache. Cas, immoral most of the time and amoral when it comes to business, ruthlessly manipulates everyone she comes into contact with. Until she meets Darren. He believes in love, marriage, fidelity and constancy, so can he believe in Cas? Is it possible the world is a better place than she imagined? And if it is, after a lifetime of playing games, is this discovery too late?

# PLAYING AWAY

Connie has been happily married for a year. But she's just met John Harding. Imagine the sexiest man you can think of. He's a walking stag weekend. He's a funny, disrespectful, fast, confident, irreverent pub crawl. He is also completely unscrupulous. He is about to destroy Connie's peace of mind and her grand plan for living happily ever after with her loving husband Luke. Written through the eyes of the adulteress, *Playing Away* is the closest thing you'll get to an affair without actually having one.

© Jim Parks

Adele Parks worked in advertising until she published the first of her fifteen novels in 2000. Since then, her *Sunday Times* bestsellers have been translated into twenty-six different languages. Adele spent her adult life in Italy, Botswana and London until 2005 when she moved to Guildford, where she now lives with her husband and son. Adele believes reading is a basic human right, so she works closely with The Reading Agency as an Ambassador for Reading Ahead, a programme designed to encourage adult literacy.

Meet Adele! Visit her website for the latest
news on her upcoming events
**www.adeleparks.com**

Head to Facebook
for exclusive extras
**facebook.com/
OfficialAdeleParks**

Chat with Adele
on Twitter
**@adeleparks**